"**What a fine morning we've had,
watching our *gut* friends get married
and riding in your new buggy!
It doesn't get any better than this, Michael.**"

Entranced, he watched Jo slip the bite of pie between her lips, closing her eyes over the lusciousness of it. Did she wear such an ecstatic expression when he kissed her? Would she remain in such a fine mood as the years went by and their life together unfolded, for better or for worse?

"Oh, but it *will* get better," Michael whispered. "I figure to spend many, many years with you, Josie-girl, so I don't want to believe that we've already hit the high point. What about when we have our own wedding day, and move into our first home—and welcome our first child?"

Jo's soft brown eyes widened. Such love glowed on her flawless face, Michael could hardly stand to remain here in this noisy room with so many other people. He wanted to marry her *now* . . .

Love Blooms in Morning Star

Charlotte Hubbard

ZEBRA BOOKS
KENSINGTON PUBLISHING CORP.
www.kensingtonbooks.com

ZEBRA BOOKS are published by

Kensington Publishing Corp.
119 West 40th Street
New York, NY 10018

All Kensington titles, imprints, and distributed lines are available at special quantity discounts for bulk purchases for sales promotion, premiums, fund-raising, and educational or institutional use.

Special book excerpts or customized printings can also be created to fit specific needs. For details, write or phone the office of the Kensington Sales Manager: Kensington Publishing Corp., 119 West 40th Street, New York, NY 10018. Attn. Sales Department. Phone: 1-800-221-2647.

Zebra and the Z logo Reg US Pat. & TM Off.
BOUQUET Reg. U.S. Pat. & TM Off.

First Printing: August 2022
ISBN-13: 978-1-4201-5184-8
ISBN-13: 978-1-4201-5187-9 (ebook)

10 9 8 7 6 5 4 3 2 1

Printed in the United States of America

Scripture

I John 4:16, 18

And we have known and believed the love that God hath to us. God is love; and he that dwelleth in love dwelleth in God, and God in him.

There is no fear in love; but perfect love casteth out fear.

For Neal, for more than forty-five years.
And they said it wouldn't last!

Acknowledgments

God is good all the time—even during a pandemic. To Him be all the glory.

Deepest thanks to my editor, Alicia Condon, and my agent, Evan Marshall, for your ongoing enthusiasm and faith in my work. It's a joy to work with both of you!

Thank you, Vicki Harding, for your continuing research support from Jamesport, Missouri!

Chapter 1

Jo Fussner gripped the pew bench in her excitement, thrumming with joy as she gazed across the center of the room at Michael Wengerd. As *newehockers*, they had front-row seats at Molly and Marietta Helfing's double wedding, which was about to begin now that the church service had concluded. In his black pants and vest, with a white shirt that glowed in the March sunshine streaming through the window, Michael looked so handsome that Jo still wondered what he saw in a bulky, big-boned woman like her. But the love shining in his gray-blue eyes as he returned her gaze had the power to make her feel beautiful beyond belief.

Michael might've stayed in Queen City over the winter to make things easier for me, but his face still reflects his deep feelings for me—his belief that we should be together. It's a miracle even more special than springtime, Lord, and for that I thank You!

When Bishop Jeremiah Shetler smiled at Marietta and Molly, the brides rose from the pew bench. In their dresses of deep teal, adorned with aprons made of crisp white organdy, they looked fresh and lovely as they centered themselves before the bishop with their grooms on either side of them. Pete Shetler appeared as nervous as Jo had ever seen him—until Molly's reassuring smile brought the dimples back into his playful grin. Widowed nearly a year ago, Glenn Detweiler offered his elbow to slender Marietta, who took it with a dreamlike sigh as he placed his hand over hers.

Lydianne Christner, another of the twins' side-sitters, leaned closer to Jo. "It's the moment we've all been waiting for!" she whispered happily. As the bishop's fiancée, the pretty blond teacher was anticipating her own wedding in May, after school let out.

On Lydianne's other side, redheaded Regina leaned forward to share her excitement, as well. "And your turns are coming!" she put in. "Last year at this time, who could've believed that every one of us confirmed *maidels* would find the man of her dreams?"

Jo's heart thumped like a happy dog's tail. She and Michael hadn't yet set a date, but she considered Regina—who'd married Gabe Flaud last fall—Lydianne, and the Helfing twins the finest inspiration she could ever have. Together, the five of them had organized The Marketplace, a thriving mall where Plain crafters sold their wares. What had been a dilapidated barn last spring now stood as solid, profitable testimony to the power of friendship and the ability to make a dream come true.

"We've surprised a lot of people—and ourselves," Jo agreed.

When Bishop Jeremiah glanced their way—probably to share another smile with his beloved Lydianne before beginning the ceremony—the three women sat back again with their hands clasped demurely in their laps. Over the years they'd shared many a whispered remark during lengthy church services, but it was time to focus on the brides and grooms with proper solemnity.

"Beloved family of God, flock of the *Gut* Shepherd, Our Lord Jesus Christ," the bishop intoned in his resonant voice, "as we gather to celebrate the union of these two fine couples, we should rejoice in all that's happened in their lives over the past several months. We give thanks that Glenn Detweiler has passed through the valley of the shadow and into the light again, following the loss of his wife, his *mamm*, and his home last year. And we rejoice with his new bride, Marietta, who stands before us completely recovered from her cancer and her chemo treatments."

Folks in the congregation nodded. As Glenn stood confidently beside his bride, he looked like a man who'd been reclaimed and rescued by the love he'd found because Marietta had accepted his proposal last Christmas.

"We're also delighted to see Pete Shetler standing before us without a crutch or a cane, recovered after his fall from the Detweilers' roof in December," Bishop Jeremiah continued with a special smile for his blond nephew. "And we're grateful to his helpmate, Molly, for inspiring Pete during his physical therapy and encouraging his return to work—"

"Slave driver," Pete whispered loudly.

"Slacker," Molly teased back, just loudly enough to make the congregation chuckle.

"—and for providing support for Marietta and the Detweilers during their times of trial, as well," the bishop added. "It's my greatest pleasure to unite these twin sisters and the men with whom God has blessed them in holy matrimony today. If any amongst you can give a reason why either of these two couples should not be married, speak now or forever hold your peace."

The Helfings' newly renovated front room rang with silence. Glossy refinished hardwood floors, new built-in cabinets along the back wall, and fresh blue paint attested to the carpentry skills of both Pete and Glenn, who'd worked together to ensure that the twins' longtime residence would be ready for today's special event.

Jo was delighted that Molly would remain in her lifelong home with her new husband while Marietta would be moving into the Detweilers' house, which had risen like a phoenix from the ashes after the previous structure had burned to the ground shortly before Christmas. Signs of new life—the renewal that bloomed with the dogwoods and redbud trees in the spring—were evident everywhere she looked, and Jo felt a special surge of hope as the bishop led the twins in their vows.

She was soon pulled out of the ceremonial spell the bishop wove with his words, however, as she met Michael's gaze again. It had been such a blessing when she'd spotted him earlier this morning, striding toward her. As he'd done in her fondest dreams over the winter, he'd held out his hands and she'd grabbed them as though she'd never let them go.

"I have a surprise for you, Josie-girl," he'd whispered. "Right after the wedding, you'll see it."

Josie-girl. The sound of Michael's unique endearment had made her eager heart turn somersaults. How was she supposed to pay attention to the wedding ceremony while she wondered about the surprise he'd promised?

But one thing Jo knew, as surely as she could bake

cinnamon rolls: Michael had returned to Morning Star loving her even more than when Mamm had sent him and his *dat* away at Christmas. Michael and Nelson weren't renting the Fussners' *dawdi haus* anymore, but the Wengerds were back in her life, and they intended to move forward with the plans they'd made during her visit to their home in Queen City last December.

Life simply didn't get any more exciting than that. Jo's confidence in their future together bloomed even more spectacularly than the thousands of red poinsettias she'd beheld in the Wengerd greenhouses when she'd defied her mother's wishes to visit them.

"We joked with Marietta and Molly about how *old* they were at their birthday in December," Bishop Jeremiah was saying lightheartedly. "At thirty-five, they stand before us as a reminder that it's never too late to believe love will lead us to the altar—and that we never outgrow our need for love and companionship. God is love, after all, and He created us in His image."

As folks in the crowded room nodded their assent, Jo smiled at the twin brides. Only months ago Marietta had believed her bilateral mastectomy had rendered her too undesirable to ever marry—and Molly had stood steadfastly by her sister as they'd planned to live out their lives as *maidels* who supported themselves with their homemade noodle business. But Glenn Detweiler had believed Marietta was the perfect woman to give him a new life and raise his two young sons. Pete Shetler had recognized Molly's sense of humor and inner strength as the foundation on which to build a responsible adulthood within the Old Order community—a lifestyle he'd avoided for years.

Jo sighed gratefully. *It wasn't so long ago that I believed*

*no man would ever marry a woman of thirty-one who
looked exactly like her big, bulky* dat. *Yet Michael's eyes look
beyond my appearance and into my soul, and he shares
so many of my hopes and dreams.*

"The same thing can be said for folks who've lost the
mates they married as young people," the bishop continued, gazing around the room. "If we sincerely believe
God wants us to be happy, and that He'll provide a partner
to share our later-life journey, that person will appear. I'm
not talking about fairy-tale magic, folks," he added
earnestly. "I'm talking about the everyday, down-to-earth,
wondrous love our Heavenly Father blesses us with as
surely as He makes the flowers bloom each spring."

Across the room, seated among the men, Nelson
Wengerd raised his eyebrows in a hopeful expression. Despite Mamm's negativity and the way she'd informed him
that marriage was a trap, he seemed ready to face Drusilla
Fussner again. Jo believed it would be a blessing for her
mother to realize the Wengerds' true natures rather than
assuming they'd cause the same disappointment she'd apparently suffered during her life with Jo's deceased *dat*.

This was no time to ponder her parents' marriage,
however. As Jo refocused on Bishop Jeremiah's sermon,
she dreamed of the day she would exchange vows with
Michael. What was the surprise he'd brought her? Could
they slip out together after they'd fulfilled their duties as
side-sitters?

"It gives me great pleasure to introduce Mr. and Mrs.
Glenn Detweiler," Bishop Jeremiah said happily.

The congregation applauded as Marietta and Glenn
turned to face everyone, appearing relieved and extremely
happy. Jo thought both of them seemed younger than they

had in months, now that they'd left behind their trials to become a couple.

"And I'll also be the first to congratulate Mr. and Mrs. Peter Shetler!" the bishop said with a lilt in his voice. "*Gut*ness knows we all wondered if we'd ever see the day my nephew gave up English ways to settle into the Amish faith with a wife by his side!"

As Pete and Molly laughed along with their friends and families, Jo continued clapping. Pete had once worked at the nearby pet food factory, spending his leisure time at the pool hall with his English coworkers and running the roads in his old pickup truck with his dog, Riley. These days, he was putting his design and carpentry skills to good use: He'd completely renovated his uncle Jeremiah's home before updating the Helfing house with many special kitchen features Jo envied.

"We'll be enjoying the wedding meal in the commons area of The Marketplace," the bishop reminded everyone as they began rising from the benches. "You'll want to head in that direction as soon as you've greeted the brides and grooms."

Jo was pleased the church leaders had agreed that Molly and Marietta could host their meal in the large red barn's open area rather than squeezing the guests around tables in their small home, eating in shifts, as was the tradition. Because the twins had lost their *mamm* years ago, other local ladies had stepped in to oversee the big meal—and because Jo's bakery at The Marketplace had three ovens, commercial-size refrigerators, and other features required by the health department, it was a very convenient place to feed a large crowd.

Jo followed Lydianne and Regina through a gap in

the wedding guests, toward the small table where the *newehockers* would sign the marriage certificate as witnesses. Gabe joined his wife, Regina, as they stepped up to sign first. When Jo felt someone stopping close behind her, she instinctively knew it was Michael.

"It's a happy day," he murmured near her ear. "A time to observe the ceremony's details more closely, *jah*?"

Jo was taller than most women, so she never tired of looking up into Michael's dear face rather than over the top of his head. "And in a couple of months we'll watch the bishop and Lydianne tie the knot," she remarked. "The vows and service might stay the same, but every ceremony reflects the couple standing up front."

Michael gestured for Jo to take the pen and sign before he did. "Today's surprise will, um, drive us a little closer to our day," he whispered.

Jo's smile widened as she carefully penned her full name, Josephine Louise Fussner, on the line beneath Regina's signature. Michael was obviously so tickled about his surprise that she could hardly wait to see it. When she offered him the pen, delighting in the way his fingers lingered over hers, she wanted this day to go on and on. After being apart for more than two months, they had a lot of catching up to do.

"Right this way, sweet Josie," he murmured. He took her hand to start toward the room where they'd stashed their coats. "We won't be late for the meal, but we don't have to be the first to arrive either, ain't so?"

Intrigued by his hint, Jo chuckled as they made their way through the crowd. A downstairs bedroom near the kitchen had been designated as the place for folks to stack their coats and cloaks, and because the newehockers had arrived earlier than most of the guests, Jo and Michael dug toward the bottom of the piles. One black Amish coat looked exactly like the next, so they spent a few moments reading the name labels sewn inside the collars.

"Here's mine," Jo said, recognizing the cloak with her turquoise label and embroidered name.

"And mine. We're out of here as soon as I find my hat!"

Moments later they were stepping out the mudroom door, heading for the line of rigs parked along the Helfings' gravel lane and pasture fence. For the twelfth of March, the day was warm, so Jo was glad she'd left her heavy winter coat at home. With her hand in Michael's, she raised her face to the sunlight and said a quick prayer of thanks for this glorious moment in time, when everything except the two of them faded away.

"Jo and Michael, may I have a word before you hit the road?"

Nelson's familiar voice made her turn toward the man who'd also left ahead of the crowd. His salt-and-pepper hair and beard were neatly trimmed and—as always—Michael's *dat* exuded a sense of quiet confidence. "Your *mamm*'s not here today. I hope she's not ill?"

Jo's smile fell a notch. "She said she wasn't in the mood for a wedding. I tried to talk her into coming, figuring it would raise her spirits to eat amongst her friends, but she was having none of it. Sorry."

"No need to apologize for her," Nelson remarked with a sigh. "You kids have a *gut* time celebrating with the twins and their new husbands. I'll catch up to you later."

When he spotted other folks coming outside, Michael guided Jo toward the parked rigs again, placing his hand at the small of her back. He focused on the many buggies for a moment before his eyes lit up.

"Here we are! What do you think of my new courting buggy, Jo?" he asked eagerly. "I ordered it from Saul Hartzler's factory before we left Morning Star in December and picked it up last night when we drove into town for the wedding."

Jo's jaw dropped. A courting buggy! As they approached the open rig with a seat only big enough for two, her heart skipped like a happy schoolgirl's. "It's beautiful, Michael! Look at the way the wood shines. And what a wonderful shade of magenta you chose for your seat fabric."

Michael smiled proudly as they stopped beside his rig. "I splurged on real leather, too," he confided. "I figured this was the only time I'd be buying such a buggy, so I wanted it to be first-class for *you*, Jo. Wait here while I fetch my mare."

Off he sprinted toward the pasture, where folks had left their horses during the morning's services. Jo ran her finger along the buggy's black wood, polished to such a shine that she could see her reflection in it. Deacon Saul was known for producing a quality product—and he hadn't gotten wealthy by undercharging for his work, either. It wasn't her place to ask Michael how many thousands of dollars he'd invested in his new rig. She and Mamm had considered ordering a new enclosed buggy a couple of years ago—the most basic model the Hartzler Carriage Company made—but when they'd heard what it would cost, they decided to make do with their old one.

"*Gut* girl—you're doing fine," Michael assured his

horse as he approached Jo. "This is our Josie, and you'll be seeing a lot of her. And Josie, this is Starla, my new buggy mare. I've been working with her for the past month, but she's still a little skittish around strangers."

"Oh, aren't you a pretty girl?" Jo said as she extended her hand. The mare looked young and angular, not yet in her prime. Her coat was a deep gray, and the irregular white star centered above her eyes would make her easy to recognize in a corral full of horses. "Did you have her tethered to the back of your *dat*'s rig when you drove here yesterday?"

"*Jah*, and she did fine. She wasn't quite sure how to handle being hitched up behind the motel last night, but—"

"You can keep her—and your new buggy—at our place!" Jo blurted out. "It's one thing for Mamm to say you fellows can't stay in our *dawdi haus* anymore, but I see no reason for your horses to be stuck in that tiny patch of grass at the motel! Those English owners weren't figuring on Plain folks parking there, after all."

"Are you sure?" Michael handed Starla's lead rope to Jo so he could push his courting buggy backward to hitch up. "I wouldn't want your *mamm* to think we were overstepping her authority—"

"Starla—and your *dat*'s horse—can stay with us on *my* authority," Jo interrupted. "If Mamm makes a fuss, I'll take the blame. No arguing with me now, when you've bought a special buggy for us to go riding in. This is *quite* a surprise, Michael!" she added as she admired the way his black buggy and charcoal-colored mare looked together. Wasn't it just like Michael to get all the details right?

He took her hand to help her up the black metal steps and into his new rig. "I'm glad you see it that way, Josie-girl. I don't intend to upset your mother, but I don't plan on tiptoeing around her bad moods, either. We have a whole new life ahead of us—together. Shall we get on with it?"

Chapter 2

As Nelson drove toward the Fussner place, he admired the deep pink blooms of the redbud trees and the ivory blossoms on the dogwoods that were sprinkled among the hardwoods and cedars along the roadside. This region of Missouri was hillier and rockier than Queen City, and many wooded areas were tucked among the plowed farmsteads he passed. Spring had always been his favorite time of year—its bright green renewal in the countryside filled him with the sense of hope that came with each new planting season. Although his nursery plots and greenhouses were thriving, Nelson felt that God's own landscaping handiwork was far more magnificent than anything he could plant himself.

When he turned in at the Fussners' gravel lane, however, he immediately noticed that the cold, snowy winter hadn't done their house and outbuildings any favors. Most of the Plain homes around Morning Star took on a shine in the afternoon sun, but the Fussner farmhouse needed fresh white paint and a new roof. The red barn was showing its age, as well—and Nelson saw these potential repairs as a way he and Michael could make amends with Jo's mother to prove their intentions were honorable.

Drusilla Fussner had become the most negative, disagreeable woman he'd ever met. Over the past several weeks since she'd kicked him and Michael out of her rental *dawdi haus*, Nelson had seriously considered leaving her to stew in her own juice—but his son was head over heels in love with Jo. He wanted the young couple's courtship to continue without the dark cloud of Drusilla's objections hanging over them, so he was willing to try once again to earn her favor and friendship.

In his heart, Nelson knew Jo's *mamm* was desperately afraid of losing her only child—fearful of being left to grow old alone if Jo married. He didn't relish such a future, either. As he pulled up alongside the house, Nelson sent up a prayer.

Give me the right words, Lord—the right ideas to convince Drusilla that we'll not trap her or Jo in relationships that make them feel we've taken advantage of them. Help me understand why she doesn't trust us.

When he stepped away from his rig, he saw her—a figure in a dark, hooded sweatshirt, hunched over the row she was planting in her large garden plot. What a shame that she could've been wearing a nice dress, sitting among her friends at a wedding and a meal she wouldn't eat alone. Yet she'd chosen to work at home. Drusilla sold her vegetables at a roadside stand in front of the house, but she could've easily waited another week to plant her cool-weather crops. Nelson frowned, wondering if her emotional state had declined since he'd last been here—

Or did she skip the wedding so she wouldn't see me?

The thought warned him to approach Drusilla carefully,

and to keep the conversation light. If he was to have any chance at a long-term relationship—or even just a cordial friendship—with Michael's future mother-in-law, he had to sow seeds of kindness and trust today.

When she straightened to her full height to lean against her hoe, Drusilla still appeared somewhat stooped—older than when he'd last seen her. His heart went out to her even as he braced himself for her negative response to his visit.

"Hello there, Drusilla!" he called out so his approach wouldn't startle her. "You're getting an early start on your planting—making hay while the sun shines, *jah*?"

She looked at him warily, not moving a muscle.

Nelson removed his hat so she could fully see his facial expressions and tried again. "It's *gut* to see you. We missed you at the wedding today, so I'm glad you're not ill."

Drusilla looked as though she might brandish her hoe as a weapon if he came any closer. "What are *you* doing here? Returning like a bad penny?" she demanded. "If you're looking to rent my *dawdi haus* again, the answer is still *no*."

Nelson sighed, sorry her attitude hadn't improved over the past two and a half months. His poor son had refrained from calling Jo or writing to her all that time, hoping not to strain her relationship with her mother, but it seemed Michael's effort hadn't helped Drusilla's mood. "No, we've honored your wishes and we'll be staying at the roadside motel down the way."

"That'll cost you a pretty penny!" she said with a humorless laugh. "Is it worth your long trip from Queen City to sell your plants and produce each weekend?"

Did Drusilla feel his nursery shop at The Marketplace competed with her vegetable sales? She was making conversation rather than walking away, so Nelson didn't raise that issue—partly because he didn't intend to change his lucrative business arrangements to humor her.

"Our motel fees are the price of doing business—just as paying rent for your *dawdi haus* used to be," he pointed out carefully. "We've invested in new greenhouses to increase our production for the crowds at our Marketplace shop and for the summer produce auctions, so we're committed to the long haul. Our profits here in Morning Star have made our expansion well worth the expense."

Shrugging, Drusilla lowered the corner of her hoe to the ground again and cut the rest of the garden row she'd been planting.

Nelson remained quiet, giving her a chance to reply in her own good time. As he looked around the Fussner farm, beyond a couple more outbuildings that could use some paint, he spotted a fellow on a horse-drawn plow, tilling a nearby field. During his weekend stays last summer and fall, he hadn't gotten a clear idea about the size of the Fussner property, so he tried another topic of conversation.

"How much ground does your farm cover, Drusilla?" he asked, hoping he sounded interested rather than nosy. "Looks like you've got several acres of woods and rough terrain on your place rather than cropland—"

"Why's that your concern?" she shot back. "You sound like a man looking to finagle a poor widow woman out of her land."

Nelson closed his eyes, reminding himself to remain

polite. He was an uninvited guest, after all, and he'd apparently worn out his welcome. "That's not my intention at all," he assured her as she worked without looking at him. "Got another hoe? I could make your rows while you plant your seeds. Many hands make light work, *jah*?"

Drusilla's eyes widened in disbelief. She continued cutting her next furrow as though her life depended on it—and as though he'd become invisible.

Nelson knew better than to push too hard, but he couldn't clear up the issues that had come between them if he didn't keep trying, could he? After dropping his hat on the nearest fence post, he approached Drusilla slowly. Again he noticed how she'd aged—although it was hard to see much of her face because of her sweatshirt's hood.

"Please let me help you," he murmured as he gently took hold of her hoe. "We became *gut* friends last fall when Michael and I first started coming here—remember those fine Friday-night suppers you shared with us? I'm very sorry that's changed because our kids fell in love, Drusilla. Tell me true now—did you skip the wedding today because you didn't want to see me?"

Drusilla released the hoe as though it had become too hot to handle. "Why do you think this is about *you*, Nelson?" she demanded. "What with Jo being in the twins' wedding party today, she's back to thinking she has a chance to marry—"

"Oh, she has much more than a chance," Nelson put in with a smile. "Is it such a bad thing that Michael believes Jo hung the moon? They'll be very happy together—if you'll *let* them be happy, Drusilla."

He paused, holding on to a last ounce of hope as he

pursued this conversation—for the kids' sake, and for his own. Deep down, Nelson believed Drusilla needed the love and companionship Bishop Jeremiah had preached about today as much as he did. He was lonely, just as she was. And the good meals and conversations they'd shared last fall, before their kids fell in love, had convinced him that Drusilla Fussner could be a very pleasant woman when she put her mind to it.

"I'm hoping you and I can spend some time together this spring, Drusilla," Nelson murmured, "because I'm ready to be happy again, too. Aren't you?"

Drusilla sucked in her breath—and then she burst into tears.

As Jo's *mamm* raced toward the house, Nelson stood in the garden, stunned by her reaction. He hadn't intended to come on so boldly—and yet, after spending so many autumn weekends in one of the *dawdi hauses* Drusilla rented to tourists, after being invited to the table with her and Jo, his intentions had been no secret. He'd enjoyed her company then, and Michael's growing fondness for Jo had convinced him to share his feelings with Drusilla— until the evening she'd revealed how trapped she'd felt in her marriage. She'd hinted that her husband, Joe Fussner, had enticed her into hitching up with him only to slap down her opinions and feelings once she'd become his wife. Drusilla was certain Jo was destined to share the same sour fate.

Bless her, Jo had come to visit the Wengerd Nursery and had spent a lovely couple of days with them in December, despite her *mamm*'s misgivings. The two young adults had discovered a kindred spirit—a deep respect and love for each other—and during the ride back to Morning Star, they'd agreed to court.

Nelson had been overjoyed. Jo had brought shy Michael out of his shell, and they were so well suited—so happy together.

But when he and Michael had brought Jo home, Drusilla had stepped outside wearing an expression that would've given God Himself pause.

You Wengerds can go right back where you came from. Don't come back, and don't think you'll be staying in my dawdi haus *anymore. You're not welcome here.*

Drusilla's words—and the vehemence with which she'd spoken them—still stung him after all this time. Nelson sighed. He might as well make good on his offer to help her, because he was in no frame of mind to return to the wedding dinner.

Gripping the hoe firmly, he cut shallow trenches in the tilled soil.

I should be drawing lines like this where Drusilla's concerned, too. She's made it clear she wants nothing to do with me. How many times do I need to subject myself to her attacks before I take the hint?

Drusilla stood at the kitchen window mopping her face with a dish towel, absolutely mortified. What had come over her that she'd burst into tears when Nelson had insisted on helping her?

Why can't I control my emotions? These days, the least little thing upsets me, and it takes a long time to get over it.

Her thoughts were troubling enough that she began

crying again—even though such a reaction made no sense. Now that she'd come inside, surely Nelson would leave rather than checking on her again—

Why doesn't he just forget about me? Can't he understand that I want no part of him or the relationship he seems to be pursuing?

As Drusilla let out a long sigh, she realized that Nelson had treated her much more patiently than most men— including her Joe—would have. Instead of berating her for skipping the Helfing twins' wedding, he'd come to see if she was all right . . . and that touched Drusilla more than she cared to admit. Not many fellows would've stepped into the garden and offered to help her, either. Even though Nelson was wearing his Sunday church clothes, he was sprinkling the rest of the radish and lettuce seeds along the rows he'd cut.

By the time Nelson had covered the rows he'd planted with loose soil and placed the hoe against the fence, Drusilla was feeling better—not that she'd go outside to thank him for his help. She was far too embarrassed to do that. As he placed his broad-brimmed, black hat back on his thick mop of silvery hair, she had to admit that Nelson cut a fine figure, lean and muscular, and that the lines etched into his handsome face from years of laughter made him extremely appealing.

But when Drusilla remembered his prediction about Michael and Jo being headed toward the altar soon, she tensed up again.

If only I could convince Jo what a trap marriage can be. But she's too starry-eyed to listen to my warnings . . . just as I was at her age.

Drusilla wished her own mother had warned her about the pitfalls of men's pretty words, and about how husbands changed their tune after they had wives under their control. Her marriage to Joe Fussner had been nothing like she'd dreamed it would be: after the first week, when he'd accused her of betraying him, the relationship had spiraled downward, and she'd never escaped his insinuations—or the way he'd taken out his anger in their bedroom.

No one else had ever realized the private hell she'd endured, because it was only proper to keep such personal problems behind closed doors. As isolated as she'd felt most days, Drusilla might as well have locked herself into a closet for all those years.

That's all behind me now. Best to leave things as they are—nice and private. If I open myself to a relationship with Nelson, I'll be vulnerable again. And miserable. Bad enough that Jo and Michael wear such lovestruck, moony-eyed smiles that I can't help but see how happy they are.

As Nelson drove his rig toward the road, Drusilla inhaled deeply to settle herself. Michael's well-meaning *dat* might be leaving for now, but—unfortunately—she knew she hadn't seen the last of the Wengerds.

Chapter 3

Never had Michael felt more conspicuous. Seated at the *eck* table with the rest of the wedding party, raised on a dais in the corner of the crowded commons area of The Marketplace, he felt as though everyone in attendance could see each move he made. Did they notice his feet sticking out from below the long white tablecloth because his legs were so long? Were they whispering because he'd gone back for a second plateful of the wonderful food—and he had three pieces of pie in front of him?

After the long morning in church, he'd been ravenous—and so excited about surprising Jo with his courting buggy—that he wasn't entirely sure what he was doing at any given moment. All Michael knew was that he felt deliriously happy now that he was with her again. As they'd approached The Marketplace in his new rig, he'd felt excited about seeing the Wengerd Nursery shop and the other Plain stores after several weeks away, but that sense of anticipation was nothing compared with the way his heart soared because Jo was seated beside him.

"I don't suppose you could spare a bite of that dark chocolate pie?" Jo leaned closer to cut off the tip of it with her fork. "It'll give me the strength to stand up and get myself a piece. They just haven't given us a *thing* to eat today, ain't so?"

Something about Jo's tone struck Michael as the funniest thing he'd ever heard. He laughed out loud, playfully swatting her hand—and then realized that he'd given everyone another reason to gawk at him. "You can share *my* pie, dear Josie," he said near her ear. "I have no idea why I took three pieces—"

"You're happy, that's why." Jo paused with her forkful of pie in front of her mouth. "What a fine morning we've had, watching our *gut* friends get married and riding in your new buggy! It doesn't get any better than this, Michael."

Entranced, he watched Jo slip the bite of pie between her lips, closing her eyes over the lusciousness of it. Did she wear such an ecstatic expression when he kissed her? Would she remain in such a fine mood as the years went by and their life together unfolded, for better or for worse?

"Oh, but it *will* get better," Michael whispered. "I figure to spend many, many years with you, Josie-girl, so I don't want to believe that we've already hit the high point. What about when we have our own wedding day, and move into our first home—and welcome our first child?"

Jo's soft brown eyes widened. Such love glowed on her flawless face, Michael could hardly stand to remain here in this noisy room with so many other people. He wanted to marry her *now* and begin the life he'd only dreamed of during those long, lonely weeks in Queen City when they'd been out of contact.

"I can't wait, Michael," she replied. "I love you so much."

For a few blissful moments the crowd and the noise disappeared, and it was only him with Jo, in the sweet, private cocoon he longed to share with her when they became one. "Glad to hear it, because I love *you* so much that—"

"Careful, Wengerd, or we'll be getting you two a room!" Pete teased from the center of the table.

Glenn laughed good-naturedly. "I smell smoke! Have you two set the tablecloth on fire?"

Michael backed away self-consciously. He'd been a mere inch—and a moment—away from kissing Jo right here in front of God and everyone else.

"Don't listen to these guys," Molly put in with a chuckle. "It's *gut* to see you two looking so happy. And besides, Jo's *mamm*'s not watching, so enjoy yourselves."

"Have you set a date yet?" Marietta inquired. "Lydianne and Bishop Jeremiah plan to tie the knot on May nineteenth—"

"Not that you need to wait that long!" Lydianne insisted playfully. "I have to finish out the school year and allow time for wedding preparations—"

"And as far as I'm concerned, you could begin your pre-wedding instruction this afternoon, and we could conduct the ceremony any time after we complete those sessions." Bishop Jeremiah, who was serving as an honorary side-sitter so Lydianne would have a partner at the *eck* table, flashed them an encouraging smile.

"All in *gut* time," Jo declared, reaching for the plate with the chocolate pie on it. "After all, Michael picked up his new courting buggy last night, so we should enjoy it for a while before we take up the responsibilities of being married. Right, Michael?"

"Whatever you say, Jo," he replied without missing a beat.

The rest of the wedding party laughed out loud, yet Michael was fine with their merriment at his expense— because hadn't his woman given the best answer while making him feel like a million bucks? He *did* want to enjoy this phase of their romance, to make up for the time they'd lost over the winter. And he didn't want folks to think they had to get married because he'd jumped the gun . . . even if he'd often thought about it.

"So you'll be selling garden stuff again come Saturday morning?" Glenn asked. "It'll be *gut* to have you and your *dat* back amongst us."

"We'll miss seeing you, though, because we four will be out collecting wedding gifts this weekend," Molly remarked. "Lydianne and the bishop will be manning our noodle store and Glenn's wood shop in our absence."

Michael nodded. "Dat and I brought along several flats of vegetable seedlings to sell on Saturday, as well as bags of topsoil, fertilizer, and other stuff folks need to get their gardens going. I'm glad to be back in Morning Star," he added, with a smile for Jo. "We've built new greenhouses at home and we've planted a lot more vegetable and flower seedlings, thinking our sales will be even better this spring than they were last year."

Pete nodded. "You fellows will have lots of repeat business," he agreed. "So where'll you be staying? I'm sorry you and Drusilla got crossways in December—"

"You know what?" Molly put in eagerly. "You could

rent one of the *dawdi hauses* at our place! We'd be pleased to have you and your *dat* there on the weekends, Michael."

"Great idea!" Pete grinned at Michael, his face alight as he thought of something else. "If you'd feed and water Riley while we're visiting relatives to collect our wedding presents these next several weekends, I'd be willing to lower your rent—"

"Phooey on the rent!" Molly insisted. "Keeping Riley out of trouble—and out of the flower beds—would be worth way more than what Marietta and I charge our tourist guests. Riley's going to crave some company, because he's used to going everywhere with us."

Michael's eyes widened as he considered the newly-weds' offer. Pete's big, playful golden retriever would be a lot easier to deal with than Jo's cranky *mamm* had been—and the Shetlers' accommodations would feel much homier than the roadside motel where he and Dat were currently staying.

"That's a very generous offer," he said, scanning the crowded tables in the commons area. "I'd like to run it past Dat. I'll find him right now—"

Jo, too, looked at all the people who were finishing their meal. "There he is, coming in the back shop owners' entry," she remarked with a nod in that direction. "I wonder where he's been?"

"And why he's got such an odd look on his face," Michael added as he scooted his chair away from the table. "I'll be back in a few. Meanwhile, feel free to sample my pie, Josie. I can bring back more, if you like."

"Only if you spot a piece that's calling your name, Michael. I've got three pieces here to choose from, after all," she teased.

After he stepped down the dais steps, Michael strode toward his father, keeping to the outer edge of the room. Dat stopped at the end of the buffet line and picked up a plate.

"Are you all right?" Michael asked him in a low voice. "I—I admit I've been so caught up in Josie's company that I didn't realize you weren't here eating dinner."

"And that's as it should be." Dat looked down the length of the steam table at all the food. "Thought I'd pay a call on Drusilla, and—well, it was a puzzling encounter."

Michael's eyebrows went up, along with his emotional antennae. "How so? Jo said she wasn't sick—"

"She burst into tears when I offered to help her plant her garden. Ran for the house as though she needed to hide from me." Dat shook his head, still bewildered. "When Jo said her *mamm* wasn't in the mood to attend the wedding, I was already wondering if part of Drusilla's problem might be depression. But I'm no better than the next man when it comes to consoling a crying woman."

Michael nodded. "*Jah*, nothing you said would've helped, most likely. Sorry to hear that, Dat. But I do have an interesting offer for a different place to stay on our weekends in Morning Star," he added.

"Oh?" His father chose a slice of turkey breast and spooned gravy over it.

"Pete and Molly want us to stay in one of their *dawdi hauses*, rent-free, because we'd be feeding Riley and keeping him out of trouble while they're out collecting their wedding presents," he said in a rush. "What do you think?"

His father laughed, which relaxed the tension in his

face and shoulders. "Do you really believe anyone can keep Pete's dog out of trouble, son?" he teased. "We'll be working at The Marketplace all day each Saturday, after all."

Dat spooned a large mound of mashed potatoes onto his plate. "But it's a generous offer," he continued. "And it would be better than staying so close to the main highway, where we catch all the traffic noise—and the horses don't do so well. We can give it a try, I suppose."

"And if it doesn't work out, we'll go somewhere else," Michael agreed. "Jo has offered to let me leave Starla and the new buggy in her stable during the week, so we'll need to take over some feed—"

"Do you think that's wise, Michael?"

Michael blinked at his *dat's* point-blank question.

"I know Jo meant well when she made her offer," his father continued as he spooned creamed celery onto his plate. "Even before Drusilla's outburst today, however, I would've tread very carefully when it came to parking a rig and your mare on her property.

"But I'll let you work that out with Jo," he added quickly. "I don't intend to become a buttinsky parent. I'm concerned about how much static Jo might catch because her *mamm* perceives your arrangement as an intrusion—or she thinks you should be paying her for space in their stable."

"Ah. I hadn't thought about that. Jo and I can chat about it when we leave, after we finish our pie." He glanced at his father's loaded plate, and then around the crowded room. "Want to join us up on the *eck*? There's room for another chair—"

"Nelson, it's *gut* to see you back in town!" a familiar voice called out nearby.

Michael and his father turned to see Reuben Detweiler, Glenn's *dat*, approaching the buffet line. The elderly gentleman had fared well over the winter, judging from his new suit and fresh haircut.

"Can I bend your ear?" Reuben asked as he picked up a clean plate. "Now that the snow's gone, I'd like your advice about planting some new bushes and trees at our place—as a wedding present for the kids. Come and sit with me!"

"I'll be happy to." Dat turned to Michael, appearing pleased that Reuben wanted his company. "Enjoy your day with Jo. We'll make our decisions when you get back to the motel tonight—and mostly, we'll feel blessed that so many folks in Morning Star are glad we've come back, *jah*?"

"We will. See you later, Dat—and don't wait up," Michael added with a grin.

For fun, he passed by the dessert table and plucked up the last piece of dark chocolate pie. A fourth plate of dessert was over the top, but he was really taking it to Jo.

And why shouldn't he, if a simple dessert made her happy? After all, his Josie delighted him in more ways than he could count.

The stars were twinkling high in the canopy of the late-night sky as Michael drove the courting buggy onto the lane leading to the house, yet Jo felt anything but tired. "What a wonderful-*gut* day it's been," she said with a happy sigh.

"Whoa, Starla," Michael murmured, halting the mare near the road. "One more kiss before we say *gut*-night?"

Jo lifted her face to his and immediately got lost in the heavenly, gentle pressure of his warm lips on hers. She'd lost count of all the times they'd pulled off the road to kiss after they'd left the wedding festivities. They'd spent the late afternoon and evening riding around the countryside, enjoying the spring blooms and each other's company—making up for lost time. It still amazed Jo that she and Michael were finding so many things they had in common as they talked and dreamed aloud.

"It was nice of Pete and Molly to offer you and your *dat* a *dawdi haus*—if you think you can handle Riley," Jo added with a chuckle. "He's a fine dog, but he's young and rambunctious. And what'll you do with him while you're working on Saturdays?"

"That'll be my main question when I see Pete and Molly again," Michael replied softly. "I'll have to find out about feeding him, too."

"Well, no matter what you decide about that offer, I'm still fine with you leaving Starla and your new rig with us during the week."

Michael gently clapped the lines on the mare's back. "We'll bring some oats and hay for Starla next week, and I'll leave you some money tonight so your *mamm* won't think I'm freeloading."

"You'll do no such thing!"

"I think it's best," Michael insisted as they drove up the long lane. "Dat came over to see how she was doing this afternoon. I guess your *mamm* burst into tears, and Dat had no idea why."

Jo's eyes widened. The squares of pale yellow light shining on the lawn told her Mamm had left a lamp burning, but she had no idea if her mother would still be up.

"I tried my best to talk her into going to the wedding," she said with a sigh. "Mamm doesn't want to go *anywhere* these days—says she's too busy to attend quilting frolics or other fun activities. She uses my baking as her excuse—tells our friends she can't cook our meals or do the cleaning until I've made my breads and goodies for the shop. Even though that's not true."

"Do you think she's depressed? Should she see a doctor?" Michael asked with a worried frown.

His questions struck a bothersome chord. She'd been wondering if Mamm should schedule a checkup; she'd have to suggest that soon. It was a touchy subject. Drusilla Fussner tended to treat herself—whether it was achy joints or depression or poison ivy—or to say it was God's reminder that she was getting old. Mamm despised doctors; thought they charged an outrageous amount for office calls.

When Michael had stopped the mare a few yards from the house, he handed Jo some folded money. "Take this," he said as he pressed it into her palm. "And please let me know if my buggy's going to cause trouble between you and your *mamm*. That's not what I want."

With a sigh, Jo tucked the money into her apron pocket. "I suppose I see your point—but I didn't intend to make your arrangements in Morning Star more expensive, Michael."

He lifted her chin. "You're worth it, Josie-girl," he said softly. "It's been the best day ever, and I'm looking forward to spending more time with you tomorrow and then on Saturday at our Marketplace shops."

After he kissed her gently, Michael hopped down to

help her from the rig. "I'll walk you to the door so I can say hello to your *mamm* if she's still up."

"We've been out so long this evening, I have no idea what time it is," she admitted with a soft laugh. "She's probably already gone to bed, so—"

As the front door opened, they saw Mamm silhouetted against the pale lamplight. Jo steeled herself for whatever her mother might say. If she'd burst into tears when Nelson had been here earlier, there was no telling what state she might've worked herself into by now.

"Michael Wengerd, keeping my daughter out into the wee hours is inexcusable. Nothing *gut* happens between young people at this time of night," Mamm said tersely. "What was I to think as the hours ticked by? For all I knew, you'd been hit by a car—"

"But that didn't happen! You're always thinking the worst," Jo protested. "I told you Michael and I would probably stay out after the wedding dinner—"

"I'm sorry we caused you such concern," Michael put in patiently. "I'll get Jo back earlier tomorrow night. *Denki* for waiting up to see that we're all right." He lowered his voice to whisper near Jo's ear. "*Gut*night, Josie-girl. I'll see you tomorrow afternoon, as we planned."

Nodding, she watched him get back into his beautiful new rig. Michael had barely driven past the outbuildings when Mamm started in on her.

"So, is that a new courting buggy I see? Does this mean you're going through with your plans to marry him, after you didn't hear a peep from him all winter?" Her mother stood in front of the door with her arms crossed tightly across her chest, as though she might not allow Jo inside until she'd given satisfactory answers.

Jo was suddenly too tired to tolerate her mother's inquisition. "*Jah*, we're getting married, sometime in early summer, most likely," she replied firmly. "The time we spent apart didn't change our feelings, Mamm. I love Michael with all my heart, and he loves me, too."

"I hope you won't come to regret your foolish notions, daughter. You have no idea what you're getting yourself into, letting a man take control of your life."

Something inside Jo snapped. Between her mother's muttered lines, she heard the same insinuations Mamm had expressed about Dat last December before she'd told the Wengerds never to come back.

"I'm thirty-one, Mamm. Old enough to make my own decisions—and to stay out late—and mature enough to hear about why you don't trust men," she challenged. "So tell me what Dat did to you that was so awful."

Her words and her tone sounded disrespectful, but Jo was tired of trying to guess what had made her mother so resentful about her marriage.

"Even if that were any of your business, young lady, I wouldn't discuss such things with you in the dead of night. We're both going to bed."

With that, her mother turned and stalked through the house. The tattoo of her heels on the hardwood floors reminded Jo of carpenters driving nails with their pneumatic nail guns. And wasn't Mamm nailing her with accusations? Implying that she and Michael had behaved improperly by staying out so late?

As Jo entered the front room, the clock on the mantel began to strike the hour. *Ping . . . ping . . . ping,* until she'd counted twelve of them. Midnight.

Jo scowled as she turned off the lamp and headed

upstairs. Tomorrow morning it would be futile to mention Mamm's exaggeration of her late arrival home, or to ask why she'd gotten so upset during Nelson's visit.

If not then, when? How long will she avoid discussing Dat's behavior? And how long will I tolerate being treated like a child?

Chapter 4

As Michael drove his courting buggy down the lane toward the home of the newlywed Shetlers early Friday afternoon, it was all he could do to keep poor Starla moving forward. Pete's golden retriever, Riley, was circling them as he barked raucously—apparently unconcerned about the mare's wide-eyed fear and skittish gait.

"Easy, girl—keep going now," he murmured, holding the harness lines tightly. He was already rethinking Molly's offer to let him and Dat stay in the *dawdi haus*, because he wasn't sure Starla would do well with such a boisterous dog causing so much commotion every time he came or went in his buggy.

"Riley! Be quiet!" Molly called out as she stepped from the kitchen onto the stoop.

If anything, the dog barked louder, gleefully continuing to circle Michael's rig and mare as they approached the house.

When Bishop Jeremiah came around from behind the house, however, the scene changed. "Riley, *sit*," he said in a quiet, no-nonsense voice.

The dog's backside immediately hit the ground. When

Riley turned to gaze at the bishop with his tongue lolling out, absolute adoration brightened his face—such a change in his demeanor that Michael laughed out loud.

"I don't know what sort of magic you worked on that dog, but can you teach it to me?" he asked as he halted Starla beside the house. "Dat and I want to take the newly-weds up on their offer to stay in their *dawdi haus*—but I'm not sure we can handle Riley."

"He can be a handful," Molly admitted with a shake of her head.

"Not to worry!" Bishop Jeremiah said as he strolled toward the rig. "I've been discussing that very matter with Pete, and we think Riley will feel more at home with Mamm and me whenever the lovebirds fly the coop. We've already got bowls and chow for him there, from when Pete was renovating the house, so it would be no trouble. And we'd know that the flower beds here—and Riley himself—were safe and intact."

Michael's relief must've been written all over his face, because Molly chuckled. "So you and Nelson want to stay here? That would be awesome—and so much homier for you than the motel."

Michael nodded. "We won't be watching Riley, so we'll be happy to pay some rent," he offered. "And if it doesn't work out for me to leave my new buggy and mare at Jo's, could I possibly pay you for some stable space, too? After the way Drusilla acted when I took Jo home last night, I suspect she won't welcome any reminders of me while I'm in Queen City during the week."

The bishop's brow furrowed. "Jo's *mamm* was still in a mood last night? After I chatted with your *dat* at the wedding meal, I decided to visit Drusilla today to see what's going on," he said. "When someone skips wedding festivities to work in her garden, it's a cause for concern—not to mention how rude it was."

Michael nodded. "I'm picking Jo up around three today—or do you want her there when you chat with her *mamm*? We don't have anything specific planned—"

"You're not fooling *me*, son," the bishop teased as he approached the rig. He gently stroked Starla's neck while he studied the buggy's detailing. "Any fellow who's acquired a fine ride like this one has a *plan*—and I'm happy to see it. I was hoping your absence over the winter hadn't changed things between you and Jo."

"We're still *gut*," Michael assured him. "But we'd *really* appreciate it if you could help us get to the bottom of Drusilla's crabbiness. I suspect she's still telling Jo not to marry me, and I'm not sure how much longer Jo can handle her resentment."

"She shouldn't *have* to handle it," Molly put in quickly. "What mother could possibly object when a fine fellow like you wants to marry her daughter? It makes no sense to me."

"I'll see what I can find out—after you and Jo have left." Bishop Jeremiah flashed Michael another smile. "If you'll excuse me, I'll get back to helping Pete with the new engines we're installing on the twins' noodle-making equipment. *Gut* to see you, Michael. Riley, you come with me, boy."

The golden bounded after the bishop as though he'd been invited to share a steak dinner, leaving the yard quiet.

Michael glanced at the neat white house and outbuildings, which were all freshly painted and in good repair.

It would indeed be an improvement for him and Dat to stay here, away from the traffic in town. Several mature trees gave the place an air of springtime serenity that reminded him of his home back in Queen City, and they would provide welcome shade in the summer.

"I'll talk to Pete about how much rent to charge," Molly said. "You'll have to provide your own meals while we're gone, so it'll be different from when we cook breakfast for tourists who come to visit Morning Star."

"Maybe we can work something out in a trade—maybe Dat and I could tend your flower beds, and even bring you some new plants in exchange for the rent," Michael suggested as he glanced at what was growing around the house's foundation. "We've got some great-looking seedlings with us this weekend, if you want some for your vegetable garden."

"What a fine idea!" Her smile accentuated her deep green eyes and rosy complexion. "What with increasing our noodle production to keep up with customer demand—not to mention taking care of our new husbands and collecting our gifts on weekends—Marietta and I won't have as much time as usual to tend our gardens."

"Fair enough. That way we'll all benefit if Dat and I stay here." Noting the happiness blooming on Molly's face, Michael couldn't help smiling back at her. "Well—you folks are busy. I'll go help Dat set up our displays at The Marketplace so we're ready for a rush of customers tomorrow. I'm eager to be back in our shop there."

"Your customers will be glad to see you, too. Lots of folks have been asking when you'd return." The loud whirring of an engine made Molly look toward the white-frame building where she and her sister made their noodles.

"After the guys finish their mechanical work, the bishop's loading up our boxes of bagged noodles so Lydianne can mind our shop tomorrow. Jeremiah's going to run Glenn's wood shop—you'll likely see him during lulls in the traffic."

"Always *gut* to spend time in Bishop Jeremiah's company." Michael started toward the buggy. After he was seated, he took up the harness lines. "Let's hope he can smooth Drusilla's ruffled feathers—and get a sense of what's causing them—when he visits her today. It'll be hard for Jo to be fully happy as my wife if she can't settle things with her *mamm*."

"I'll keep you all in my prayers, Michael," Molly said, returning his wave.

"*Denki* for working out a rental arrangement with Dat and me," he called out as he turned the rig toward the road. "We'll plan on being here next Friday afternoon."

On Friday, Jo stood at the kitchen counter wrapping a big tray of cookies to sell from her bakery case the next day. Preparing for Saturdays at The Marketplace usually excited her, but her spirits were sinking lower with each word her mother spoke.

"I'm telling you, Josephine, if you allow that boy to park his buggy in our stable, you'll be planting the hook for heartache," Mamm insisted as she swept cookie crumbs from the floor. "If he spent so much money on that fancy rig, it's a sure sign that he's got no financial sense. Money will slip through his fingers like water, and you'll be scraping by for the rest of your life."

In her frustration, Jo banged her metal pan against

the edge of the countertop. "If you'd gone to Wengerd Nurseries with me in December—if you'd seen the *scale* of their operation, and the way Nelson and Michael have carefully increased their production to meet the demand of their customers here in Morning Star—you'd have an *inkling* of their financial savvy," she blurted out. "But no! You'd rather squawk at me without knowing any of the facts—and without answering my questions about why you feel marriage is such a rotten deal. If you'd just tell me that, straight out, we could stop having this same painful conversation day in and day out!"

Her mother's eyes widened as her knuckles turned white on the broom handle. "I wish the bishop could hear your *tone*, young lady," she muttered. "You'd be on your knees confessing your uncharitable attitude at church, sure as I'm standing here."

Jo glanced out the window, wishing Michael would show up early. She needed a handsome prince to swoop in and rescue her before she said something that Bishop Jeremiah *would* expect her to confess. "All right, I'll rephrase that."

She took a deep breath, praying for patience again. Always these days, she seemed to be praying she wouldn't grab Mamm's shoulders to shake some sense into her.

"*Please*, Mamm," she began again in a contrite voice. "If you'll tell me why being married wasn't your cup of tea, I'll try to understand why you get so upset when you talk to me about it . . . without really talking about it."

"What went on between your *dat* and me was private," her mother snapped. "If you can't trust me when I warn you not to tread the same path, we have no reason to continue this conversation."

"*Gut!* Case closed, and you'll stop preaching at me," Jo said triumphantly. "Promise?"

Mamm's jaw dropped even as her eyes narrowed. "Fine. In the end, we all have to deal with the decisions we make."

"*Jah*, we do." Jo tucked the ends of the final piece of plastic wrap around her metal pan, wishing she felt that they'd actually settled the matter. "I have no idea how late Michael and I might be tonight, so please trust us to behave ourselves and to stay safe on the roads, all right? You really don't need to meet us on the porch again."

Her words, spoken with an undercurrent of rancor, appalled her. Before she'd fallen in love with Michael, Jo would never have dreamed of saying such things to her mother.

And isn't that the saddest part? If I'd never found a man to marry—if I still figured on living at home with Mamm for the rest of her life—she and I would be on the best of terms.

The sight of a charcoal-gray mare coming down the lane lifted Jo's spirits. "I'll see you later, Mamm. Enjoy your afternoon, all right?"

Jo carried her pan of goodies to the worktable in the mudroom, where her other supplies for Saturday were waiting to be loaded into her wagon. Without a backward glance she made her escape, feeling freer with each step she took toward Michael.

When he stopped the mare a few feet in front of her, Jo didn't wait for him to help her into the rig. His courting buggy glimmered in the afternoon sunlight—but its shine was nothing compared to the love she saw sparkling in his beautiful gray-blue eyes.

"Happy to see me, eh?" he said lightly.

"You have no idea." Jo scooted next to him, longing to pull him close for a kiss—but her mother was probably watching them from the window.

"Ah. Having a tough time with your *mamm* today?"

"You have no idea," she repeated softly. "But I'm with you now, Michael, and that's where I always intend to be—and *that* makes me happy."

"Glad to hear it." When he clucked to Starla, the buggy lurched forward, circling back toward the road. "Seems like a nice afternoon for a ride to Willow Ridge. I've heard they have a great café—and before we enjoy our supper there, I'd like to visit the gift shop Glenn's mentioned, where he consigns some of his chairs and toys."

"Fabulous! We're on our way!"

Michael glanced at her as though she was boiling like a cauldron of hot, sticky apple butter rather than bubbling over with joy. Rather than getting scalded, he wisely saved his questions for later.

And that was another reason Jo loved him so much.

Chapter 5

When she heard wagon wheels rolling up the gravel lane, Drusilla straightened to her full height, stretching her tired back muscles. Her oldest gray dress and faded brown kerchief weren't fit clothing for entertaining company—but then, if Nelson insisted on bothering her every time he came to Morning Star, he deserved to see exactly how raggedy she looked when she was working in her garden or cleaning house. Maybe he'd realize he didn't want to take up with her, and he'd leave her alone.

The sight of Jeremiah Shetler made her throat go dry. Drusilla had suspected he might come calling after she'd skipped the Helfing twins' wedding—and who knew what Nelson might've told the bishop after his visit on Thursday? Wasn't it just like men to put their heads together and inform a woman that she'd broken their rules?

"How goes the gardening, Drusilla?" he called out as he halted his horse. "We've had some fine weather lately for planting, ain't so?"

Jeremiah's cordial tone didn't fool her one bit. She didn't respond right away—and she didn't leave the spot in the middle of the long, mounded row where she'd been planting potatoes. When he'd crossed the grass and stopped at the nearest edge of her plowed plot, Drusilla put on the best smile she could manage.

"How are you today, Bishop?" she asked, looking toward the large boxes he was hauling. "That's quite a load you've got in your wagon."

"I'm taking the twins' noodles to The Marketplace so Lydianne can run their shop tomorrow while the newly-weds are out visiting." Without any warning, Jeremiah started toward her, stepping carefully between the rows of lettuce, radishes, and peas she'd already planted. "All work and no play makes us cranky, Drusilla, so I was troubled when you spent Thursday here in your garden rather than joining us for the wedding festivities."

He hadn't left her a graceful way to explain—and Drusilla didn't dare sass the bishop when he took the shovel from her hand. After glancing at the hole where she'd placed her last chunk of seed potato, he dug one about four inches deep a foot away from it and then continued down the row.

"You might as well talk to me while we work, Drusilla," Jeremiah said gently. "I suspect you're not happy that the Wengerds have returned, and that Jo and Michael still plan to marry. But I also sense there's a deeper reason for your unhappiness these days. Care to tell me about it?"

As she stuck the cut side of a seed potato chunk into the hole Jeremiah had dug, she felt as though she, too, was in a pit—and there was no jumping out of it.

"If you know so much about it, Bishop, you tell *me*," she shot back. "Selling vegetables at my roadside stand is how I support myself, you know. Maybe I just wanted a little time to myself on Thursday! And maybe it *irritates* me that you and Nelson and Michael—and even my own daughter—seem to think my feelings don't matter anyway! So why do you ask?"

Drusilla hated it that she was on the verge of tears again. Why was she suddenly so angry? And why on earth had she spouted off to a man who could actually hold her accountable for what she said and did? Unlike Nelson, Bishop Jeremiah wouldn't be going back home to a different city. He'd be keeping track of her now, for sure. And he wouldn't let her alone until she'd answered his questions and shown a marked improvement in her behavior.

And God love me, I don't know what to say or how to get back to normal.

The bishop stuck the shovel in the mounded row, leaving it to stand by itself. When he gazed at her with his warm brown eyes and extended his hand to her, palm up, Drusilla swallowed hard. Surely he didn't intend to hold hands with her! This visit was getting stranger by the minute.

She clasped her hands at her waist, hoping he'd take the hint. "I—my hands are all dirty, and—"

"I'd never let a little topsoil come between us, Drusilla," he said, still offering her his large, strong hand. "God created His children in a garden, after all. And even after they displeased Him—frustrated Him terribly, no doubt— He stuck by them."

"But He drove Adam and Eve *out* of the garden!" she protested. Where was the bishop going with such an odd conversation?

"God did not, however, allow them to die from eating the forbidden fruit," Bishop Jeremiah pointed out. "When they knew they were naked and tried to hide from Him, He made them clothes and gave them another chance. He never gave up on them—and He never forsakes us, either."

Jeremiah's expression softened. "Will you pray with me, dear? When we have no idea what else to do, we can be grateful that God still hears our cries for help."

He wasn't going to let her out of this, so Drusilla gingerly placed her hand in his. When his long fingers closed around hers, enveloping them with his strong yet tender warmth, she bowed her head and clenched her eyes shut—mostly so she wouldn't burst into tears.

"Heavenly Father, we come before You to ask for Your guidance and Your unfailing grace," Jeremiah said in his resonant voice. "Just like Adam and Eve, we continue to mess things up and misunderstand each other. We thrash about in our pain, inflicting our misery on others, and most of the time we feel powerless even when we're absolutely sure we're on the right path. In our confusion and our frustration, hear us, Lord, and grant us Your peace and Your abiding love. Help us recognize Your still, small voice and move toward Your light, for we ask these things in Your Son's holy name. Amen."

For several moments they remained quiet, still holding hands. Drusilla felt some of the pain and frustration he'd mentioned in prayer draining out of her—but she still didn't know what to do about them. When Bishop Jeremiah released her hand, she let out the breath she didn't realize she'd been holding.

"*Denki*, Bishop," Drusilla whispered.

"You're welcome. I'll see you in church on Sunday, if not before," he murmured. "Take care of yourself."

She watched him cross the garden and the yard before he sprang back onto the seat of his wagon. What had just happened? Drusilla still had no answers about her unpredictable moods, but she felt enormous respect for the man who'd just held her up in prayer as though she was precious. As though she—and her troublesome emotions—*mattered*.

Drusilla returned Bishop Jeremiah's wave, gazing after his wagon until he'd driven out of sight. Suddenly drained, she covered the last of the seed potatoes she'd planted and started toward the house, leaving the spade to mark where she would take up planting—on another day.

For now, she just wanted to rest in the Lord. She couldn't figure Him out any more than she could understand Nelson—or Joe—or any other man who asked impossible, irritating questions. But at least He didn't expect her to fix His dinner.

When Jo stepped into Simple Gifts, a barn that had been converted into a consignment store where Plain artisans sold a wide variety of handcrafted items, her mouth dropped open. "Oh my," she whispered as she gazed around the main level and up toward the open mezzanine. "Oh *my*."

"Wow, this is really something," Michael agreed as he reached for her hand. "The same concept as The Marketplace, yet it has a completely different feel to it. Take your time looking around, Josie-girl. If something catches your eye, it's yours."

Jo exhaled in amazement. "What *doesn't* catch your

eye in here? Look at these beautiful pottery dishes, and the quilted table runners, and—well, it seems they also have furniture makers here in Willow Ridge," she remarked as she stepped forward to run her fingers over a glossy walnut sideboard. "But if I were ever to choose fine pieces like these, I'd rather give the Flauds my business."

"Duly noted. I figured you'd see it that way."

Jo glanced quickly at the man beside her and saw a secret sparkling in his beautiful eyes. Was her mother right about Michael having a tendency to spend more than he should? "You *cannot* mean to buy such pricey furniture when we first start out, Michael," she whispered earnestly. "A basic table and chairs—simple, sturdy bedroom pieces—are all we'll need—"

"But a very special occasion calls for something beyond simple and sturdy, *jah*?" he interrupted gently. His blue-gray eyes widened as he held her gaze. "I only get to marry you once, Jo. I want to provide you with a home that makes you happy—as happy as you looked when you first stepped into this wonderful shop."

She swallowed hard. "But—but if we start out living with Mamm, we won't have the space for new furniture. And if we have our own home, we'll have so many other expenses—"

With a gentle finger across her lips, Michael silenced her objections. He stepped closer, slipping an arm around her. "Josie, will you please be my wife?" he murmured urgently. "We've talked around this subject for a long while. Now it's time to make it official. Marry me, *please*?"

"Oh, Michael!" She gasped as she hugged him close.

"*Jah*! *Jah*, I'll marry you. It's all I've been able to think about—"

"Me too. You make me so happy, Jo," he put in as he embraced her. "I'll give you a simple, solid life—but we're going to have nice things, designed to last our lifetime together."

Savoring the strength in his slender arms, Jo blinked rapidly. It wouldn't do to burst into tears—especially because they were standing in the middle of a store, and a red-haired woman in a dress of bright purple plaid had paused in the next aisle to give them a moment's privacy.

"Do I have it right? Have I just witnessed the most exciting moment of your lives?" she asked eagerly. "Let me be the first to congratulate you two. I'm Nora Hooley, and I'm honored that you made such a promise in my store this afternoon!"

From up in the mezzanine, a couple of English shoppers began clapping. "Congratulations!" they called out.

"*Gut* for you!" a Plain lady at the back of the main level chimed in. "I wish you a long and happy life together."

As she and Michael eased apart, Jo's cheeks burned with embarrassment. She'd been so caught up in the moment of Michael's proposal, she'd lost all track of where they were standing. "*Jah*, I guess we look pretty obvious—"

"You look radiant and joyful—both of you," Nora remarked happily. "I don't know that anyone's ever proposed in my store, so this calls for a special gift to celebrate! Whatever you find today, it's yours at fifty percent off."

Michael's breath left him in a rush. "Be careful,

Nora. You've got some big-ticket items and I'd hate to shortchange the folks who've made them."

"We understand about such things, because we run shops at The Marketplace in Morning Star," Jo said. "So please don't feel you have to—"

"I *want* to," Nora insisted. She came forward and placed her hands on their shoulders, beaming at them. "Rest assured that my crafters will receive their full amount, no matter what you choose. It's *gut* to meet you Marketplace folks! Glenn Detweiler has told me how well your businesses have been doing—and we love his birch chairs and wooden toys here. I think it's wonderful that we can operate our shops in towns so close together without anyone suffering the downside of that competition."

Jo smiled. She'd only been in Nora's presence a few minutes, but she already liked her immensely. "That's how we see it, too."

"I think we each have items we specialize in—like Jo's bakery and my family's landscaping business—while you're offering pottery and other items we don't carry," Michael remarked as he looked around. "*Denki* for your generous offer, Nora. It'll be an honor to find something special to commemorate the moment we got engaged."

"Let me know if you have questions. I'll leave you to your browsing now."

As Nora headed back to the checkout counter to help a customer, Jo shook her head in wonderment. "It's not every day a storekeeper offers such a generous discount," she remarked. "I can't imagine Martin Flaud giving us fifty percent off if you'd popped the question in his furniture shop back home."

Michael chuckled. "I suspect you're right about that.

But we can't forget that when folks around Morning Star chipped in to replace all the furnishings and supplies the Detweilers lost in their house fire, Martin and Gabe didn't bat an eye about donating three new bedroom sets and an oak kitchen table and chairs."

Jo picked up a blue pottery plate to study its design of painted daisies. As she also admired the set of golden-yellow plates that were painted to resemble sunflowers, she couldn't help thinking what fun it would be to eat from such colorful dishes every day—until she read the price list posted on the display cabinet.

"I have expensive taste," she said with a sigh. "As much as there is to look at here, we should probably keep moving or we'll never see it all."

Did Michael think she was a cheapskate? Jo noticed a glimmer of resignation in his eyes, but as they walked past ornamental metal garden gates, fancy hand-tooled saddles, as well as colorful braided rugs and woven baskets in many shapes and sizes, they chatted quietly about the high quality of all the items they saw.

Upstairs, Jo gazed at three-dimensional banners that featured Amish children in swings or pony carts. It amazed her that the little girls' *kapps* and the boys' straw hats were actual garments that had been cut in half and carefully sewn to the hanging. They paused to look at several quilts before heading back down to the main level.

"Here again, if I wanted a really nice quilt, I'd rather get it from Martha Maude or the other ladies in her shop," Jo remarked.

"I agree," Michael said. "I'd rather support our local shopkeepers—but there are plenty of items here that are totally unlike what our crafters from Morning Star make.

Did you see *anything* you'd like, Josie-girl? I hadn't intended to leave empty-handed."

His boyish smile teased her as they started down the stairs. Michael was such a handsome man, and he had an eye for more colorful items than a lot of Amish folks Jo knew. If anything, her walk around the Simple Gifts shop was a reminder of how faded the linens at home were, and how plain and practical her *mamm's* choices had been when she'd selected household items as a bride.

Jo shrugged shyly. "Oh, I liked it all! But if I raved about every item that caught my eye, you'd think you should buy them all for me. And look at these little carved wagons and horses," she added as she carefully descended to the main floor. "It's a sure bet Glenn made them."

Michael stopped at the bottom of the stairway. When the clock near the checkout counter chimed five, he looked up at her.

"We might want to head on over to the Grill N Skillet," he suggested. "From what I hear, folks often wait in line to be seated on Friday and Saturday nights."

When they had almost reached the door, Jo turned to wave at Nora, who was checking out another customer. "*Denki* for chatting with us!" she called out.

"*Jah*, you have a wonderful store," Michael put in. He held the door for Jo, shielding his eyes from the late afternoon sunshine as they strolled down the driveway toward the county road. "If the aroma from those smokers behind the café is any indication, we're in for quite a treat."

Jo nodded, inhaling deeply. The Grill N Skillet was only a block away, and she immediately noticed a quilt shop sign on the far side of the building. "I don't see a line of folks waiting to eat, so would it be all right to take a quick look in the quilt shop first?"

"Why don't you go on ahead and I'll catch up to you?" he suggested. "I meant to get a business card from Nora."

Before Jo could respond, Michael jogged back toward the big barn that housed Simple Gifts. She suspected he wasn't all that excited about looking at fabric anyway.

When we're married, we'll have to remember that we each have our own interests. And now we have to set a date and talk about where we'll live and make so many other important decisions! And we have to tell Nelson . . . and Mamm.

Jo walked resolutely toward the quilt shop, determined to enjoy every moment of her dinner with Michael and whatever else they shared before she got home. After that, she would have plenty of time to endure her mother's reaction to the news of her engagement.

Chapter 6

All the way back to Morning Star, Michael fought a smile. If Jo suspected his real reason for returning to Simple Gifts—and why it had taken him several minutes to catch up to her at the quilt shop—she wasn't letting on. As she chatted about the wide variety of grilled meats and delectable side dishes on the buffet at the Grill N Skillet, his mind circled back to the items he'd selected for her at Nora's shop.

The redheaded shopkeeper had been pleased to see him again. "I was a little surprised that you hadn't picked out a single thing while you were here," she'd remarked. "But I sense your fiancée comes from a frugal household and hasn't had a lot of practice at receiving gifts that aren't practical and plain."

"You've pegged her right," he'd assured Nora. He'd ordered eight place settings of the dishes that resembled sunflowers and eight settings of the blue dinnerware with the daisies, along with a few serving pieces for each set. He'd also spotted a pale yellow tablecloth with wildflowers embroidered around its border. "If you'll hold these, I'll pick them up when I return to Morning Star next week. I haven't figured out when to surprise Jo with her gift, but the right time will come."

Jo's tight sigh brought Michael out of his musings. "Should I tell Mamm about our engagement when we arrive home or wait until tomorrow morning?"

Michael felt sorry that she was even asking such a question. Didn't most young women blurt out their happy news the moment they saw their mother, no matter how late it was? In the darkness, Jo's dear face was shadowed, but he didn't need to read her expression to sense her mounting tension.

"Dat will be delighted to hear we're officially engaged," he said softly. "He and I have talked about the subject many times over the past months—but I understand why you're planning your strategy for telling your *mamm*. I suspect it'll be a lot easier to tell our friends tomorrow while we work at The Marketplace."

Jo chuckled. "They've been expecting this news for a while. But I need to tell Mamm first, so she hears the news from me rather than through the grapevine. Guess I'll gauge her mood when we get home and go from there."

The companionable silence they shared for the next several minutes was punctuated by the steady *clip-clop, clip-clop* of Starla's hooves on the blacktop. The night air was chilly, but with Jo sitting so close to him, neither of them felt cold. The traffic between Willow Ridge and Morning Star was light, so Michael estimated that he'd have her home by eight forty-five.

As he drove onto the lane leading to her house, Jo sat up straighter. "Do you want to come in for coffee and cookies?" she asked softly.

"Do you want me to? I could be there so we could announce our news together—or not, depending on how you want to handle it."

Her rueful smile touched him. Michael longed for the day when Jo could be wholeheartedly happy with her life—and her marriage—without having to think so much about how her mother would react to everything they said and did. He pulled the courting buggy up alongside the house where they wouldn't easily be seen from a window, and gently lifted Jo's chin with his finger.

"No matter what happens, I love you, Josie-girl," he whispered.

A tremulous smile softened her face. "*Denki* for that, Michael. If Dat were alive, he'd be so happy for us, but— well, everything changed in a big way when he passed."

Michael nodded, recalling that Big Joe Fussner had succumbed to pneumonia, which he'd caught while hospitalized for a bad case of the flu about five years ago. Rumor had it Joe had waited too long to seek treatment, but his death had made a lot of Amish folks in Morning Star—including Drusilla—even more reluctant to visit a doctor than folks of their faith already tended to be.

The love light on Jo's face made him forget all about such unfortunate situations, however. She closed her eyes and tilted her head, inviting him closer. Michael poured every ounce of his affection into kissing her, anticipating the day when they could share so much more. When they eased apart, Jo glanced toward the front door.

"I'll take it as a *gut* sign that Mamm hasn't stormed out onto the porch again," she murmured. "Come in, Michael. Sharing refreshments is the normal thing for a courting couple to do—and I'm tired of second-guessing her moods. What will be will be."

"I agree completely."

He helped Jo down from the buggy and hitched Starla to the porch rail, mentally preparing himself for whatever acidic remarks Drusilla might make. When they entered the front room, however, the downstairs was quiet. A lamp on the end table provided the only light.

After Jo peered around, she motioned him into the kitchen. "She must've gone to bed already," she said in a low, relieved voice. She lit the lamp on the kitchen counter and turned to smile at him. "Shall I put on some coffee to go with our cookies?"

"Milk sounds better," he replied as he sat down at the table. "We'll have an early morning, getting ready for our day at The Marketplace, so I'll skip the caffeine. Being with you has gotten me so charged up, I'll have trouble sleeping as it is."

With a girlish giggle, Jo rushed into his embrace. "You say the nicest things, Michael. And it *has* been a fabulous day, ain't so?"

He savored the sweetness of her lips again, sensing her eagerness to be with him for the rest of their lives. It was a dessert far more delicious than Jo's delectable cookies—not that he turned any of those away.

As Nelson arranged flats of broccoli, cauliflower, and cabbage seedlings outside The Marketplace on Saturday morning, he studied them carefully. His heart was light with the news of his son's engagement, so he felt especially generous—or perhaps he knew, deep down, that Drusilla felt more threatened than pleased by their children's announcement. He was setting aside the best two flats of each of those early vegetables for Jo's *mamm* when a familiar voice hailed him.

"Why am I not surprised to see you out here at sunrise, Nelson? You're the early bird catching that proverbial worm, ain't so?"

Nelson turned to chuckle at Bishop Jeremiah. "And what would *you* be trying to catch out here so early?" he teased.

Jeremiah shrugged. "Now that the weather's warmer, I wake up rarin' to go. For the next few Saturdays, you Wengerds and I will be neighbors. It'll give us a chance to compare notes on Drusilla," he added as his dark eyebrows rose. "After visiting with her yesterday, I believe we menfolk don't stand a chance at curing what ails her. This situation calls for wisdom—and empathy—only another woman can give her."

Nelson considered the bishop's observation. "You might have something there," he said with a nod. "I recall my sister, Nadine, going through an emotional bramble patch a few years ago—"

"So did Mamm, and it drove my brother, Jude, Pete—and me—to distraction," Jeremiah put in. "Will it be all right if I enlist my mother's help—maybe encourage her to spend some time with Jo's *mamm*? I'm concerned about Drusilla's health, but I'd also like to smooth the path for *you*, Nelson. If you want me to."

Nelson pondered his answer as he placed Drusilla's six flats of plants under his wagon seat. "Sometimes I wonder if I'm asking for more trouble than I really want over the long haul," he admitted. "But last summer when Michael and I started staying in her *dawdi haus*, I truly enjoyed her company. As fall became winter, though, Drusilla's moods seemed to deteriorate from one week to the next. I don't mind telling you that it hurt when she ordered us to find someplace else to stay."

Bishop Jeremiah nodded. "I'll understand if you back away from a relationship with her—any man would be wary. But I feel I should give Drusilla whatever help I can, for her own sake—and because Jo and Michael will be in for a rough start if *someone* doesn't intervene."

"Speaking of the kids," Nelson put in happily, "they'll soon be coming to you for their premarital counseling, Bishop. Michael popped the question yesterday, and he's ecstatic that they're officially engaged."

"So am I! I'll be sure to congratulate them today." Jeremiah removed his hat to smooth back his dark hair. "Do I dare hope they'll set up housekeeping in Morning Star? Or will your son be staying close to your nursery operation in Queen City?"

"That decision's still in the works. It'll depend some-what on whether I can convince Drusilla she wants an-other husband." Nelson cleared his throat. "Just between us, Bishop, I've been asking myself what the attraction is. I sometimes catch myself considering a relationship with her more to help Michael and Jo than because I love her for my own reasons. And that's not such a *gut* idea."

"You're wise to recognize that distinction, Nelson. It's one of those situations God can probably clarify better than I can, so I'll keep you in my prayers."

"I appreciate that. And *denki* for whatever help you can get Drusilla to accept, too," he added with a shake of his head. "She looked so befuddled when she burst into tears the other day. I—I'm hoping these seedlings will convince her that I care about her, even if we never get to the courting stage."

"We'll all do our best." Bishop Jeremiah looked closely at the black plastic trays of vegetable seedlings. "What're you charging for these? Mamm would be delighted if I took some home to her today. She's been gnashing at the bit to get her cool-weather plants in the ground."

"Take whatever you want—and don't even think about paying me," Nelson insisted. "If you and your *mamm* are willing to work with Drusilla, I'll give you all the vegetables and flowers you want and still come up owing you. Take her one of those pansy pots, too, with my sincerest thanks," he added, pointing to the back of his wagon. "I suspect those will disappear fast once our customers arrive."

When the bishop had made his choices, Nelson set out the remaining flats. After he'd arranged the pansy pots closer to the front of the building, where folks would spot their bright yellow and purple blooms from the road, he went inside to be sure everything in the shop was ready. After two and a half months of being absent from their busy Marketplace store, it would be easy to overlook some of the details he'd once seen to without having to think about them.

The aromas of sweet dough and cinnamon made his stomach growl. It wasn't yet seven o'clock as Nelson headed toward the Fussner Bakery to greet his future daughter-in-law before she got busy with customers. He admired the way she showed up week after week before the sun rose so she'd have oven-fresh pastries and other treats to entice folks as they entered The Marketplace.

Jo was a congenial, steadfast, dependable young woman—the best mate God could possibly have created for his introverted son.

He wasn't surprised to see Michael in the kitchen, too, helping Jo remove huge pans of cinnamon rolls from one of her ovens.

"*Gut* morning, Miss Jo!" Nelson called out as he approached the serving counter. "I hope you know I was *delighted* with Michael's news last night."

As she set down her big metal pan, Jo's face bloomed in a becoming shade of pink. "I'm delighted, too, you know. I've spent most of my life believing I'd never find a man to marry, so your Michael is a bigger blessing than you can imagine."

Nelson pondered her remark. Although Jo was taller than most women, with a solid build—not fat by any means, but not a head-turner, either—he wondered why such a likable young woman would ever believe that about herself.

Ah, but remember what her mother's been saying about marriage. Poor girl probably didn't dare entertain any thoughts of romance as she was growing up.

It wasn't the time to burst her bubble with curious questions, so he glanced at the large, puffy, raisin-filled coils of pastry she'd baked. "You're a blessing to us, as well, Jo. Can I give you a hug to welcome you to our family? And maybe be a taste tester when those rolls cool?"

Jo lit up like the lights on a carnival boardwalk. When Nelson opened his arms, she embraced him exuberantly. He wasn't surprised when Michael came up behind Jo and hugged her, too, completing their cozy family circle.

"*Denki, denki, denki*," she murmured gratefully. "I'll get you a plate as soon as I frost them, Nelson. You've done so much for us."

As the three of them eased apart, he had to ask the question her remarks had brought to mind. "How did Drusilla take your news? Michael said she was already in bed when you two got back last night, even though it wasn't very late."

An odd expression made her smile falter. "Hard to say," Jo hedged. "When I made my announcement this morning, Mamm wasn't surprised, of course. But she wasn't jumping up and down for joy or bursting with wedding suggestions, either."

Nelson smiled sadly at her. "Let's take the happiness we three share and hope we'll eventually wrap your *mamm* in it, as well. Meanwhile, I've set aside some flats of seedlings for her garden," he said as Jo began spreading a liberal layer of frosting over a pan of the warm rolls. "Shall I take them to her? Or would it be best if we all dropped them off this afternoon?"

Jo's eyes brightened. "Oh, she'll appreciate your seedlings. She didn't buy any yesterday because the ones at the farm supply store looked picked over."

Sensing she might be in for a difficult evening with her *mamm*, Nelson said, "What if you kids pick up a couple of pizzas after you leave here this afternoon? I'll head over a little earlier with Drusilla's plants and tell her we've got supper covered," he suggested. "Hopefully, she'll realize we've been thinking of her—and you won't have to scurry around fixing a meal after you've been working all day."

"Well, *I* like that idea, no matter what Mamm might think!" Jo quickly cut two large, frosted rolls from the pan, laughing because Michael had already fetched a plate for them. "You Wengerds win the prize when it comes to being kind and thoughtful!"

Nelson hoped Drusilla would see things the same way. All he could do was keep trying.

Chapter 7

Before she'd opened The Marketplace's front doors for Saturday's business, Jo checked her baking cases one last time. She'd set out her usual brownies, sweet rolls, and a selection of cookies, but she was also hoping her new lemon coffee cakes would be a big hit. Now that she and Michael would be planning their wedding and their life together, she was already thinking of ways to spend less time in the kitchen each week. Pans of coffee cake—some cut to serve out in the commons area and some wrapped to go—seemed like a feasible alternative to some of her more labor-intensive, cut-out cookies.

"I just heard the most fabulous news, Josephine Fussner! Congratulations!"

As Jo turned to greet Lydianne, who'd come to run the noodle shop next door, she felt as bubbly as a shaken can of soda pop. The blond schoolteacher hugged her hard, laughing in her exuberance.

"*Jah*, it's pretty exciting now that Michael and I are officially engaged," Jo agreed as she shared her friend's embrace. "We haven't set a date yet, but I doubt it'll be more than a few weeks after you and the bishop get hitched. When *is* your big day, by the way?"

"School lets out on Friday, May fifteenth, and we'll see you in church the following Tuesday, the nineteenth," she replied. "I'm hoping you and Michael will serve as side-sitters?"

"Wouldn't miss it for the world. *Denki* for asking us, Lydianne," Jo replied. "We're getting a lot of practice at that these days, with all of us original Marketplace *maidels* tying the knot." Jo glanced out toward the commons area, where her red-haired assistants, Alice and Adeline Shetler were removing the basket of grounds from a big coffee maker. "I suspect, as the bishop's wife, you'll no longer be working here on Saturdays—"

"*Jah*, that's how it'll have to be."

"—but I haven't heard whether Molly and Marietta plan to keep running their noodle shop . . . if the church leaders would even go along with them working, now that they're married," Jo remarked in a faraway voice. "Has Bishop Jeremiah said anything about that? I have to wonder about the future of our businesses, if none of us original founders can keep them running."

Lydianne's expression sobered. "Jeremiah hasn't mentioned it, and I haven't asked," she admitted softly. "I didn't want to stir up a hornet's nest by reminding him or the preachers or Deacon Saul about our situation."

"That's been my tactic, too. It's a topic Michael and I will have to discuss soon—although I know he and Nelson intend to keep their nursery store going. They've invested a lot in new greenhouses, so they won't quit coming anytime soon." Jo gestured toward the main entrance, inviting Lydianne to walk with her. "Let's see if the girls are ready to serve, and we'll open the doors. It's almost nine."

"Time to start another whirlwind sales day," Lydianne said with a chuckle. "I'm still amazed at how much business we do each Saturday. And because the church district still collects a commission from all of our sales, I hope our leaders will figure out a way to keep us going. I'm also hoping Jeremiah will at least let me continue to do The Marketplace accounting at home."

Jo nodded. She and her *maidel* friends had agreed from the beginning that their Old Order congregation would reap the benefits of the new shopping mall—mostly because their church had bought the property it stood on. Since last June, when they'd opened the doors, The Marketplace had repaid the renovations made to the old stable that housed it, the construction and furnishing of the new schoolhouse, and the district's initial investment in the property. Now the shops' commissions donated a hefty weekly sum to the church's aid fund, which had paid for the rebuilding of the Detweiler family's home and stood ready to cover large medical expenses or whatever else its members might need.

When Alice and Adeline flashed Jo their simultaneous thumbs-up, Jo returned their signal. The Shetler twins were quite efficient at managing sales and keeping the tables in the large commons area wiped clean as they offered customers coffee and trays of goodies—

But I'm not sure they'd be able to keep the bakery's shelves stocked each week, the way I have. It's a big commitment of time for whoever might take it over . . . and I have to keep in mind that another shop manager might not do things the way I do. Michael and his dat *understand that, but even if the church leaders allow married women to work here, the Wengerds might not believe I should be so focused on my business once I have a household to run. And maybe babies to tend.*

Putting on a smile, Jo set aside her concerns. After she removed the padlock and chain that held the big, barn-style doors shut, she called out her usual Saturday morning greeting.

"All right, shopkeepers, we're open for business! Let's make it a *gut* day!"

As usual, when Jo carefully swung the door out, several customers were waiting to come in—and a few had already picked out pansy baskets from the Wengerds' outdoor display.

"*Gut* morning!" Jo called out. "We're glad to see you all on this fine spring day."

As customers came eagerly through the doors, Jo recognized many of them as folks who shopped at The Marketplace fairly often. "I'm glad the Wengerds are back," one of them remarked.

"I'm going to pick up my special-order quilt today!" another lady chimed in.

"And I'm heading straight to *your* shop, Miss Jo, because nobody else makes breads and brownies like yours!" a tall, slender man said. Elliott Remington came every week, so he knew what to expect—and his compliments made Jo feel wonderful. Over the past several months, the two of them had struck up a gratifying friendship.

"You might want to try my new lemon coffee cake," she suggested as she walked alongside him. "I've just taken a big pan of cinnamon rolls out of the oven, too—

and of course those walnut brownies you like are waiting for you in the front case."

"Mmm!" Elliott said as his face creased with his grin. "Your goodies are the highlight of my week, Jo. I don't miss my wife nearly so much when I'm here among all these friendly shopkeepers, getting my Saturday sugar fix."

Was it prideful to feel special because of his compliment? Jo felt so honored to be a bright spot in this lonely man's life, she cut him a sample of the lemon coffee cake as she put his usual order of other treats in a to-go box. "Tell me what you think of this. I've considered offering more coffee cakes—for spring brunches and such—if this one goes over well."

As Mr. Remington closed his eyes over his first bite, she had her answer. He moved to the side to allow a couple of ladies to place their order, but as soon as they'd paid, he came to the counter again.

"You've got a winner, Miss Jo! I'll take that small lemon coffee cake along with my other stuff, please," he said, pointing to a disposable pan in the front of the case. "I'll go out and chat with your girls now, while I enjoy my coffee. Thanks for the special service—and your special smiles."

A steady stream of customers kept Jo busy all day. In the brief lulls, she realized how empty her life would feel if she was no longer allowed to operate her Marketplace shop. The hours of her week would be much freer, and she wouldn't be nearly as tired on Saturday evenings, but she would really miss her interaction with customers—especially the ones she'd gotten to know over the past several months.

Jo was wondering how to approach Michael about her working after the wedding, when a happy voice interrupted her woolgathering.

"So, it's official between you and Michael! Congratulations!" Regina blurted out as she rushed forward to embrace Jo. "I *told* you he'd ask!"

After she'd savored her friend's hug, Jo eased away to look at Regina. Her freckled face radiated newlywed happiness that lit up the entire bakery. "It's so *gut* to see you. Did you bring in more of your embroidered linens to sell in the furniture shop?"

"I did—along with this table runner that's a custom order," Regina replied as she unfolded it.

Jo ran her finger over a lifelike brown rabbit that held a yellow and orange butterfly on its raised paw. "Oh, but this is cute! And look at all these different colors and designs you stitched on the Easter eggs."

Regina had a real talent for embroidering the nature scenes she'd once painted and sold as watercolor artwork—before she'd been shunned for creating pieces that were decorative rather than useful. When Gabe had defended her God-given talent by confessing his own advanced musicianship, the time they'd spent together during their month of being shunned had eventually led them to the altar—as well as the decision that Regina would no longer work at The Marketplace.

Jo was pretty sure that Gabe's *dat*, Martin—an influential member of the church—had overridden Regina's request to work in the Flauds' Marketplace shop after she'd married his son. A wife's place was in the home—that was a mandate of Old Order marriage, even if the *maidels* who'd organized The Marketplace wished it wasn't.

"So . . . how're you doing as a stay-at-home wife?" Jo asked quietly. "Has it been a big adjustment? Do you miss being here?"

Glancing toward the furniture shop next door, where they could see Gabe and a customer between the open slats that separated the two stores, Regina lowered her voice. "It gets awfully quiet when I'm there by myself all day," she admitted. "If I couldn't embroider my linens, I'd go crazy—but we've just found out that I'll have a whole new craziness to occupy my life in about six months."

Jo sucked in her breath. "Oh, that's wonderful! Congratulations, Regina!" she exclaimed as she hugged the slender redhead again.

"It's also scary, because I've not been around many wee ones," her friend admitted. "But both of our families are excited about the news, and setting up the nursery will help keep me busy until the baby—oh, there's the lady that ordered this table runner," Regina put in. "See you later, Jo."

By midafternoon, Jo's bakery cases were empty. Her lemon coffee cakes had been a big success, and as she and the Shetler twins cleaned up the kitchen, they talked about other flavors to make. Adeline and Alice were delighted with the news of her engagement—and when Michael showed up in the bakery's doorway, they greeted him with extra enthusiasm as they went out to check the tables in the commons area.

"Busy day?" Jo asked as he approached the kitchen.

"All I have left is the little plate of goodies I put back for you, Michael."

"If Dat hadn't set aside those seedlings for your *mamm* first thing, he'd be going to your place empty-handed this evening," her fiancé remarked. "We thought we'd been optimistic, loading so many flats of garden seedlings and pansy bowls, but we've spent the last hour taking orders for folks who came a little too late. It's been crazy today!"

The blissful expression on Michael's face as he sampled Jo's lemon coffee cake paid her the ultimate compliment. She decided to let him enjoy his treat without asking whether he'd expect her to stay home after they were married.

Moments later, he'd eaten every crumb and his gray-blue eyes sparkled. "Dat has given me the rest of the day off—because he knows I'd like to spend it with you before we head back to Queen City tomorrow morning," Michael added in a soft voice that teased at Jo's emotions. "Can your two assistants close up for you? Or do you need to do some accounting before you can leave?"

Her thoughts raced ahead to the pleasure of riding through the countryside, taking in the beautiful spring day. "Alice and Adeline can clean up, *jah*—and I'll ask Lydianne to collect the day's receipts from the shopkeepers. I can go in about ten minutes."

Michael leaned so close that Jo thought he might kiss her in plain sight of the bakery doorway. Instead, he brushed her cheek with a gentle fingertip. "I've been waiting all day to be with you," he whispered. "I'll go hitch Starla to the rig and meet you around back."

Jo nodded, thrumming with her intense need to be

with Michael. His quiet affection was the perfect cure for her tired feet, and a ride would lift her spirits before they spent time with Mamm this evening.

Who could tell what sort of mood Mamm might be in when the Wengerds appeared unannounced—even if they were bringing her gifts and supper?

Chapter 8

Nelson took his time driving to the Fussner farm, figuring it would be best if he didn't arrive too much before the kids came with the pizza. He was ecstatic about their successful day of sales—and the many customers telling him how happy they were that he and Michael had returned to The Marketplace.

As he mentally recounted the day, it soothed his soul to drive along the back roads looking at the farmsteads around Morning Star. He wasn't surprised that he saw no land up for sale, because when a family wanted to move, their relatives or neighbors—or other Plain folks they knew—were quick to snap up the acreage before it was advertised. Nelson sensed that Michael and Jo would be happier in Morning Star than in Queen City, but that they wouldn't want to live under Drusilla's roof.

As he approached the Fussner home from a different direction than he'd come before, he paid special attention to the rocky, wooded areas on either side of a meandering creek. Was this rugged land part of Drusilla's farm? It was easy to see why no one had ever cleared these acres to put them into crops—and although they took away from a farm's overall productivity, Nelson felt that the forested areas around central Missouri had a special beauty. Wildlife flourished in such a habitat, and in the summertime nothing soothed him like a walk in the dense shade alongside a gurgling stream.

What are the chances that you'd ever convince Drusilla to join you on a walk here?

Nelson filed that idea in the back of his mind. He clucked to his horse, realizing he had a long way to go before she'd agree to such a stroll—yet the vivid green of the new leaves and the sprinkling of pink redbud blooms and ivory dogwood blossoms gave him the incentive to *try*. Drusilla reminded him of a jigsaw puzzle: in order to fully understand her, he'd have to consider her personality piece by piece until the entire picture came together—including the pieces that didn't seem to fit anywhere until he'd studied them from different angles.

As he drove his wagon up the Fussners' lane, Nelson prayed for patience and compassion. He was pleased that Drusilla seemed to be putting away her gardening tools for the day, because it gave them a common topic to talk about.

"Hey there, Drusilla!" he called out, halting the horse. "How's your garden coming along? I've brought you a little something."

As Nelson stepped down from his wagon seat, he heard the crunch of gravel behind him. It seemed a stroke of wonderful luck—or the hand of God at work—that Michael was driving his courting buggy toward the house with Jo close beside him in her own rig.

"We brought pizza, Mamm!" she exclaimed out the

buggy window. "Your two favorite kinds—with extra cheese!"

Drusilla paused at the edge of her garden plot, holding her rake and hoe. "Why do I get the feeling this is a plot you three have cooked up?"

Nelson set aside her suspicions as he pulled a flat of broccoli seedlings from beneath the wagon seat. At least Jo's *mamm* appeared curious rather than cantankerous as she watched him.

"Of course there's a plot," he quipped. "These little plants come from our plot of land in Queen City to yours— broccoli, cauliflower, and cabbage, for now. Where shall we put them so they'll be sheltered from the cold snap we're to get tonight?"

When her eyes widened, he caught a spark of something resembling pleasure. "These seedlings look really healthy. My cold frames are right over here."

"Perfect." Nelson smiled at his son and Jo. "I bet our helpers can carry the rest of the flats over for us."

He followed Drusilla to the side of an old shed that hadn't seen paint for several years. As she lifted the glass tops of the rectangular wooden frames that flanked its foundation, she gazed again at the green seedlings that had popped up from the black soil in the flat he was holding.

"This is a very thoughtful surprise," she murmured as Nelson leaned down to place the flat inside the cold frame. "But what chance will my little roadside stand have this summer with you Wengerds selling so much produce at The Marketplace? Why would anyone want to come down our dirt road to buy my vegetables when yours are right there in town, on the main highway?"

Nelson blinked. He'd never considered his nursery's shop, which was open only on Saturdays, as her competition—especially because produce auctions were scheduled throughout the summer, and Drusilla didn't seem concerned about them.

"I've been thinking about that," his son remarked as he placed two more flats in the frame alongside the first one. "And I don't see why you couldn't sell your vegetables in our shop on Saturdays. We could keep your profits separate. You'd still be able to run your roadside stand during the week if you wanted to."

"I could even take your produce when I go to open the bakery, if you didn't want to venture into town so early," Jo offered as she handed two more flats of seedlings to Michael. "Matter of fact, we could sell some of your jellies there, too, if you'd like."

"And if we project this idea into the future," Michael continued, "we could *expand* your stand and help you run it after Jo and I are married. Growing things is what Dat and I do—and nobody else around Morning Star has a nursery and greenhouses. So why not us?"

Nelson had been observing Drusilla's expression, and he saw the exact moment when his son's optimistic plans had crossed the line.

"So that's the way of it?" she demanded tersely. "You Wengerds figure on taking over my business rather than competing with it? Meanwhile, what am I supposed to do with myself and my time—work for *you*?"

"It was only an idea," Nelson put in, hoping to smooth her ruffled feathers. "We've got plenty of time to figure out the details—and lots of options, Drusilla. It was never our intention to take over your business—"

"This is my livelihood you're talking about! Growing things is what *I* do, too."

With a sigh, Nelson wished he could turn back the conversational clock. "Maybe we'd like to *provide* your livelihood, dear," he pointed out softly. "It's what men do for their women, after all."

"I'm not your woman!"

"And I'm not saying you have to be!" Nelson shot back before he could catch himself. It wasn't in his best interest to get sucked into the rising tide of Drusilla's emotions, so he quickly diverted the conversation. "On the subject of income, if that four- or five-acre parcel of wooded land just down the road—where the creek cuts through—is your property, you might be sitting on a gold mine."

Her eyebrow rose in disbelief. Drusilla planted a fist on her hip, challenging him to fulfill the expectation he'd just set.

"Say, by the time Michael's put the last flat of seedlings in the cold frame, we can have our pizza on the table while it's still nice and hot," Jo suggested quickly. "It's best to continue our discussion on a full stomach, *jah*? I was on my feet all day and I'm starved!"

Grateful for Jo's diversionary tactic, Nelson gestured for Drusilla to precede him to the house. Once again, he reminded himself of the Bible's words about love being patient and kind—and he told himself it was time to seek his sister's help with the difficult woman who was muttering to her daughter as they entered the kitchen.

"Who had this supper idea anyway?" Drusilla groused. "I was all set for a nice quiet evening, figuring you and Michael would stay out—"

"But now you won't spend any more of the day alone,

Mamm," Jo put in valiantly. "And I've never known you to turn down sausage and mushroom pizza, or the kind with Canadian bacon and pineapple."

After they'd washed their hands and Jo had set plates and utensils around, they took their places at the table. Nelson bowed his head. *Be with us as we coax Drusilla out of her bad mood, Lord. For just a moment, she was pleased with the seedlings—*

"What sort of gold mine did you find in my woods? Does this mean you've been snooping around on my land, Nelson?"

He blinked, not yet finished saying his silent grace. Although he'd taken the seat at the head of the table—as Drusilla had invited him to do last fall when they'd been on friendlier terms—it didn't escape him that she'd chosen to sit at the opposite end, facing him, rather than at his left. In her faded kerchief and shapeless gray dress, she appeared older and more worn down than the last time he'd spoken with her. Or perhaps it was her deep frown that made her seem so shriveled and thin.

"As I drove here this afternoon I noticed the huge old walnut trees on your land, Drusilla," Nelson replied carefully. "You might be amazed at what a timber cruiser would offer you to harvest those trees. I could ask the fellow I know to look at them and give you an estimate. I was certainly glad I did that with the walnut trees on my place."

"We got paid thousands of dollars apiece, as I recall," Michael put in as he passed one of the pizza boxes to Jo's *mamm*. "Easiest money we've ever made."

"Easy come, easy go," Drusilla blurted out. She helped herself to two slices of the sausage pizza and passed it on to Jo. "*If* I went along with this idea, what would *I* have to do?"

Nelson bit back a smile. She seemed to be taking his conversational bait. "Once he counts the walnut trees and you accept his bid, he'll bring in the heavy equipment to cut them down and haul them off. Then you get a check."

"And he won't tear up any of your crop land, either," Michael assured her. "They'll find the shortest path through the woods to the road and drag them out that way."

"But I won't have any more black walnuts to use for my baking," Drusilla protested. "A few of those old trees are still putting on nuts."

"Mamm, if each tree will bring you thousands of dollars, you'll be sitting pretty for years—and you could afford to buy bagged walnuts at the bulk store," Jo gently pointed out. "What do you have to lose?"

"So you're in on this scheme, too, Josephine?" Drusilla's tone rang with accusation. Nelson wondered if they'd all be sorry he'd brought up the subject.

Jo took some pizza and passed the boxes to him, blessing him with a grateful smile. "No, Mamm, this is the first I've ever heard about timber cruisers, but it sounds like an idea worth pursuing. Maybe we wouldn't have to sell off part of the farm, like you were thinking earlier, if we could sell those trees."

Drusilla took her time chewing a bite of pizza before she answered. "I'll think about it."

It was the best Nelson could hope for. He ate more quickly than he'd intended, and he didn't suggest a walk in the woods with Drusilla for fear he'd wear out his welcome. After he'd wished the ladies a good evening, he waited in the wagon while Michael spoke with Jo. As his son approached him a few minutes later, the eager anticipation on his face took Nelson back to the time when he'd been crazy in love with the boy's mother—partly because Michael had his *mamm*'s gray-blue eyes and pale complexion.

"I'm taking Jo out for a bit and then she'll drop me off at the motel," he said. "Don't wait up—I have a room key, you know."

Nelson smiled indulgently. "You're all right with Jo driving back home alone? And you're sure it's a *gut* idea to leave your courting buggy and mare in the Fussners' barn all week?" he asked softly. "It could become a source of contention between her and her *mamm*."

"Jo wants me to. She made the original offer, and she's sticking by it."

Nodding, Nelson picked up the harness lines. "See you later, then. I was glad I saved those seedlings—and thought of harvesting those walnut trees—but I'm still walking on eggshells where Drusilla's concerned."

"We'll all three work on it, Dat."

He wished he felt as confident as his son sounded. "With God's help, it'll all turn out the way it's supposed to—even if you get married and I don't," he added softly.

Chapter 9

Drusilla pushed the sleeves of her dress above her elbows and fanned herself with a piece of paper, but it wasn't doing much good. Why was she feeling so over-heated all of a sudden? Where were those old cardboard fans from the funeral home? And why did church seem like it was lasting forever this morning? If Preacher Clarence Miller's sermon droned on for another minute, she might just stand up and tell him she'd had enough of it.

That man can babble all day and not say a thing. Lord, You could've let the lot fall differently when You chose Clarence as our preacher.

She let out a sigh so loud that Bishop Jeremiah's mother, seated beside her on the pew bench, began to chuckle—and then couldn't get control of herself. Margaret Shetler's mirth was contagious, and the more she cleared her throat and pressed her hand against her mouth, the funnier her predicament became. Drusilla was soon stifling her own laughter, until the monotonous preacher scowled at the two of them. But he finally brought his meandering message to a close.

After the final hymn—which, at fifteen verses, also seemed impossibly long—Bishop Jeremiah pronounced the benediction to end the church service.

"My friends, before we break for our common meal, I'd like you to know that I'll be attending a short retreat for the area's Old Order bishops at the end of next week, March twenty-sixth and twenty-seventh," he announced in his resonant voice. "We'll discuss a number of topics and issues common to our congregations. While I'm away, you can count on Preacher Clarence and Preacher Ammon for any assistance you might need. Are there any other joys or concerns we need to share before we eat?"

Folks looked expectantly at one another, but the room remained silent. Drusilla felt the urge to head for the bathroom, located near the back door, and then slip out to walk home—even though she realized some of the ladies would probably spot her and then quiz her mercilessly.

"Shall we say a word of thanks for our food?"

Drusilla dutifully bowed her head as Bishop Jeremiah blessed their meal. The *amen* was still lingering in the stuffy air of the Nissleys' crowded front room when she popped up off the pew bench in hopes of escaping for a few moments of fresh air out on the back stoop.

Margaret, however, blocked her path. "Forgive me for distracting you during the sermon," she began, "but when Clarence—"

"Oh, there's *nobody* more distracted than Clarence Miller when he's preaching," Drusilla whispered quickly. Realizing how inappropriate her remark sounded, she amended it by adding, "I'm always glad when your Jeremiah is speaking to us, Margaret. His sermons have a *purpose*. Everything he says feeds into the message he wants you to take away. Your son's truly been touched by the Master's hand when it comes to speaking on Sunday mornings."

Margaret straightened her shoulders, pleased. "He has the gift of gab, *jah*, and he knows how to focus it on our Lord's intentions," she said with a nod. She reached into her apron pocket and pulled out a small brown paper sack that had been folded over its contents a couple of times.

"You haven't seemed like yourself lately, so I thought I'd share some supplements I tried when my mood needed lifting," Margaret whispered near Drusilla's ear. "For most of us, this phase eventually passes, but it can be bothersome—and it's not easy to talk about, even amongst us women. But call me, if you want."

Drusilla blinked, stuffing the packet into her pocket before the folks around them saw it. "Um, *denki*, Margaret," she stammered. "*Jah*, I—I'll do that."

Surely every woman in the kitchen would notice how red her cheeks had turned, either from embarrassment or a flash of heat. Drusilla busied herself filling water pitchers, hoping no one asked her if she was feeling all right. She was tired of that question—not that she had a polite answer for it.

"Such *gut* news I heard yesterday, about Jo and Michael!" Cora Miller piped up as she took hold of two pitchers. "You must be excited, Drusilla."

"And she couldn't be hitching up with a nicer fellow, either," Martha Maude Hartzler chimed in. "Have they set a date?"

Drusilla drew a blank. "I—I haven't heard," she admitted. "Now that Michael's got a courting buggy, they don't spend a lot of time with *me*, you know."

The women around her laughed good-naturedly. Drusilla remained at the sink until she'd filled all of the plastic pitchers, relieved when the other ladies carried on their own conversations or took food to the tables the men were setting up in the front room. She was glad most folks chose to chat with Jo about her engagement—and it helped that the Wengerds had already left for Queen City. Nelson would surely be checking on her if he were here, and the last thing she wanted was for her friends to speculate about his interest in her.

Curiosity made Drusilla hang back in the kitchen after the other women went into the front room. She took Margaret's packet from her pocket and unwrapped it with trembling fingers, hoping no one came looking for her. The box was familiar—she'd seen this product in the drugstore, where women's remedies were sold, but she'd never dared to try it.

Drusilla skimmed the information on the side of the box. It contained a number of herbal ingredients like black cohosh, red clover, and flaxseed—but how was she to know if these concoctions worked? She couldn't think of a single one of her friends who'd ever acted as angry or volatile as she often felt these days. And even though Margaret had offered to chat with her, how would she work up the nerve to start such a conversation?

Frustrated, Drusilla rewrapped the box and stuck it back in her pocket. If the bishop's *mamm* had given her this remedy, it must mean that her moods and her behavior were more obvious and erratic than she'd realized—

And they are! I don't mean to snap at folks as though I might bite their heads off, but I can't help it.

*Maybe I should try this stuff before the bishop himself—
or even Nelson—confronts me. That would be the ultimate
humiliation. . . .*

"Mamm? Are you all right?"

Drusilla turned, flushing with guilt. She was immediately struck by the sincerely concerned expression on her daughter's face—a face that was the spitting image of her *dat*'s. Jo paused in the doorway, as though she anticipated a tongue-lashing.

A pang of remorse zinged Drusilla's heart. Jo was the last person who deserved the impatient words her mother shot at her like arrows. After a lifetime of gently discouraging her tall, bulky daughter from daydreaming about a fairy-tale romance, Drusilla owed Jo encouragement and kindness now that she'd fallen in love with a very likable young man.

Yet such kind, motherly words seemed impossible to come by when mood swings got in her way—and that happened every day, it seemed.

Drusilla put on the best smile she could muster. "I was just checking on something, dear," she murmured as she headed for the front room full of chatting friends. "*Denki* for looking after me."

As Nelson approached the small, neatly kept yellow house across the road from Wengerd Nurseries, he composed his thoughts carefully. He was happy to spot his twin sister, Nadine, enjoying her Sabbath afternoon in her front porch swing. Her dress of deep coral—a color most Old Order women considered too flashy—set off her flawless complexion and the steely-gray hair tucked under her white *kapp* as she waved to him.

After Nelson married Verna years ago, his *maidel* sister had built a small house down the road to give his new family more privacy at the Wengerd homeplace—but he suspected she'd also wanted to escape changing dirty diapers and being awakened in the night by his crying babies. Nelson cherished Nadine because she was his only sister, and also because as his twin, she could read his thoughts and understand him better than anyone else on the face of the earth.

Nadine was also his counselor and sounding board in business matters: her role as Wengerd Nursery's book-keeper had freed Nelson to focus on their recent expansion with new greenhouses to accommodate the brisk sales at their Marketplace store.

Nadine also knew how to have fun. And as a woman who'd never married, she tended to express her thoughts more freely than those who had husbands.

"So you made it back alive from Morning Star?" she called out. "Your throng of Saturday customers—and that um, *woman* you've told me about—didn't do you in?"

Over his months of staying in the Fussners' *dawdi haus*—and being booted out at Christmastime—Nelson had shared many of his impressions of that household, so Nadine was aware of Drusilla's unpredictable moods. Because his sister had endured many of the same symptoms he'd witnessed during his devolving relationship with Jo's *mamm*, he chose his words carefully.

"I lived to tell about it," he agreed, stopping at the bottom of the porch steps. "And the folks coming to our Market-place store would've snapped up twice as many pansy bowls and flats of seedlings if we'd taken them. Drusilla, however, remains a pickle of a different color—"

"And just as full of vinegar, I take it."

There it was—Nadine's uncanny ability to discern his unspoken thoughts. Nelson paused. If he criticized Drusilla's erratic behavior—or made light of it—Nadine would feel he didn't take the other woman seriously.

"I've come for your advice, sis, because I don't want to make that situation any trickier than it already is."

Nadine's eyes widened. She patted the empty side of her swing. "All right, let's talk about it. I've got tea in the fridge, if you want some."

Nelson waved off her offer. As he took a seat beside her, Nadine's concerned expression told him she was preparing for a more serious conversation.

"You know, I can recall how excited you were when you and Michael started going to Morning Star last summer," Nadine began softly. "You seemed so taken with Drusilla, I figured it was only a matter of time before you married her—and maybe even moved there to start up another nursery.

"And I was really happy for you," she continued earnestly. "I couldn't miss the deep disappointment you were trying to hide at Christmastime, when you said you weren't going back to your Marketplace shop for a while. I figured your decision was about something besides nursery business, but I didn't want to pry."

When she placed her hand on his wrist, Nelson covered it with his own. "*Jah*, and of course you asked what I'd done to irritate her," he recounted with a pensive chuckle.

"And I was wrong—insensitive—to imply you'd worn out your welcome, Nelson. I'm sorry."

Nadine's apology touched him deeply. When he'd come home in December, smarting from Drusilla's rejection, he hadn't gone into a lot of detail about why he wasn't returning, so it wasn't his sister's fault that she'd misread the situation.

"I should've trusted you with more of what happened at Christmas, but I was licking my wounds," Nelson explained. "When Drusilla ordered us to find someplace else to stay, I saw any chance for a long-term relationship evaporating—even though I'd done everything in my power to make it work."

"But you visited her this past week. You didn't go to Morning Star only because Michael was in that wedding, or to open your Marketplace shop again," Nadine observed. She focused on the woven porch rug in front of them as they swung forward and back. "How did it go?"

Nelson hoped his words would sound sincere. Nadine appeared to be in fine fettle of late—he didn't want to bring back her mood swings by talking about them in the wrong tone.

"Remember a few years ago, when you got so out of kilter?" he asked gently. "You told me once that you'd feel like a grouchy old man one minute and then suddenly a whiny, impossible drama queen would possess you and jump off the deep end, as though your mind was no longer your own. That's what's going on with Drusilla. And I have no idea how to handle it."

"*Jah*, because bless your heart, you're a man—"

"Bishop Jeremiah agrees that we need the wisdom of other women to guide us—and Drusilla," Nelson put in quickly. "He's concerned enough about her that he's asking his *mamm* to chat with her, and I said I'd consult with you, as well. From what I've seen, Drusilla's the victim of her runaway emotions, but she's also forgotten how to have fun. And you're the best person I know for cooking up a *gut* time, Nadine."

His sister's laughter rang out, reverberating against the roof of her porch. "Are you asking me to win her back for you, Nelson? Because if you are—"

"No. I'm asking you to show Drusilla who she really is, for her own sake. I'm asking you to be her *friend*." Nelson sighed, shaking his head. "When I went to see her on Thursday, our visit was cut short because she burst into tears and retreated into the house. I could tell she was every bit as bewildered about it as I was, too."

His sister closed her eyes. "I'm so glad I've gotten beyond all that," she whispered.

"How'd you do it? What helped you? Would you consider going to Morning Star with Michael and me and spending time with Drusilla—just you women?"

Nadine focused on him again, chuckling. "So many questions! And the answer to that change-of-life situation is different for every woman going through it."

His sister thought for a moment before continuing. "I wish I could tell you there was a magic potion we could give her, Nelson, but none of the drugstore remedies I tried did much *gut*," she admitted softly. "I had to hang on to my *kapp* and wait for that phase to pass—and pray that you and everyone else I dealt with still had their head attached after they'd been around me."

Nelson nodded, grateful that his sister was willing to discuss such a difficult time of her life.

"Some women are pretty sensitive about this topic—embarrassed—so we can't come on like a house afire," Nadine continued in a faraway voice. "If I suddenly show up with you and Michael, talking about mood swings and runaway emotions, Drusilla won't like it. We've got to come up with another reason for me to be there—connected to something you're doing in Morning Star rather than Drusilla's emotional state."

"So you're willing to meet her? To create some sort of diversionary tactic that will help her?" he asked gratefully. "I appreciate your jumping in with me this way, sis."

Nadine let out a short chuckle. "Well, it gives me a chance to meet this woman," she pointed out. "And I'm pleased that you're maintaining your interest in Drusilla during a difficult time of her life. Most men would write her off with rude remarks about her turning into a bossy old battle-ax—or that other word that begins with a *B*. I hope she realizes what a special man you are, Nelson."

Her compliment caught him by surprise. Although he and Nadine had always supported each other's separate interests, his sister's teasing often overshadowed her more serious side. "*Denki* for saying that," he murmured. "It means a lot."

Nelson stood up, walking the length of the front porch as he considered his options. "Michael and I have agreed that sometime this spring, we want to paint Drusilla's house and outbuildings as a favor to her and Jo. If you'd come along—"

"Why limit that project to just the two of you? Why not ask the other men around town to pitch in, and at the same time the women can bring over the noon meal and organize some sort of frolic . . . maybe something to make household linens or a quilt for Michael and Jo?" Nadine mused aloud. "That way, if Drusilla spins off on an emotional tangent, she can't aim it at *you*. And your painting project will get done in a day or two rather than over the course of weeks."

Nelson's jaw dropped. "You're a genius."

"Of course I am. But I'm a self-serving genius," Nadine pointed out with a laugh. "This way, the kids will receive something useful for their new home—because I'm not as *gut* at that sewing stuff as other ladies are. I can be the organizer. The instigator."

"Hah! You were always instigating mischief when we were kids," he remembered fondly. "I'm grateful that you'll put your talent to work on a project like this one, for Drusilla. *Denki* from the bottom of my heart, sis."

"Anything for you, Nelson," she said with a warm smile. "If you'll give me the bishop's phone number, I'll contact his *mamm*. Between the two of us, we'll make this a project that brings the Fussner and Wengerd families closer while we help Drusilla get through her rough patch."

After he and his twin discussed a few more ideas for the work frolic, Nelson headed home. His spirits had been lifted to the point that he whistled as he walked. The sky looked bluer, the springtime foliage shone a livelier shade of green, and all around him the birds were singing as though they, too, believed Nelson's chances of making Drusilla happy had just improved beyond his wildest dreams.

He stopped at the road, gazing up at the sun's radiance

until he saw bright stars pulsing all around him. It felt like a good omen.

Help these dreams move forward, Lord. I'm ready for a wife again—and I hope that's Your plan for my life now, as well.

Chapter 10

Jo inhaled deeply as she pulled four pans of sour cream and apple coffee cake from the oven and set them on racks to cool. She congratulated herself on baking more items that required less attention to detail than cookies and bars, because if Michael came to Morning Star early to spend extra time with her, she'd still be ready to do business at The Marketplace. It was Wednesday, and she was well on her way to having enough baked goods to fill and refill her bakery case on Saturday.

"Whatever you're making today smells especially *gut*, Jo," Mamm remarked from the mudroom. She was folding laundry on the worktable after bringing it in from the clothesline, and she sounded sincerely complimentary.

"I'll set one of these pans aside for tomorrow's breakfast," Jo said. "I've decided to include more coffee cakes and single-layer dessert cakes at the shop, for some variety."

Mamm entered the kitchen with an armload of clean underwear, pausing to look at the pans of cinnamon- and sugar-topped coffee cakes. "Who says I'm going to wait until tomorrow to try some?" she teased. "Sometimes it's torture when you've been baking all morning—"

A loud knock at the front door made them look up.

Mamm let out a short laugh. "You'll have to see who that is, Jo. I can't go to the door with our underthings!"

"*Gut* point." As Jo wiped her hands on a towel and headed for the front room, she hoped it might be Michael at the door, surprising her—

But the short, stocky fellow on the front porch bore no resemblance to her fiancé. He appeared to be in his forties, wearing English work pants and a plaid shirt with the sleeves rolled to his elbows. The clipboard in his hand suggested that he might be with a utility company or doing work for the county.

"Have I found the Fussner place?" he asked.

"*Jah*, you have. How can I help you?"

His smile carved lines on either side of his mouth. "I'm Connor Yorke, here to give you an estimate on what the walnut trees in your woods might be worth if I harvest them. Nelson Wengerd gave me your name."

Jo's eyes widened. "You came sooner than we were expecting you—and that's fine," she added quickly. "Mamm and I had never heard of timber cruisers until Nelson told us about you. Do I need to show you where the trees are, or—"

"According to this aerial photo of your property, your walnut trees are in these two areas." He flipped his clipboard to show her an overhead view of the farm, with a couple of highlighted spots close to the creek. "The estimate won't cost you anything, and if you'd like me to proceed after you see it, I'll get your signature and set a time to come back with my equipment. Shouldn't take more than an hour for me to look things over and write up your offer."

"That—that'll be fine," Jo stammered. "We'll be here when you finish."

As the timber cruiser jogged to his pickup, Jo's pulse quickened. If Nelson's guess was correct, this fellow might have some lucrative news for them—something to assure them that Mamm would have money to live on if Michael wanted Jo to relocate to Queen City. She needed to talk with him about this, to clarify their plans so her mother would know what to expect in her future. Jo was hoping to remain in Morning Star so Mamm wouldn't be by herself—and so she could keep running her Marketplace shop. But she could understand why Michael and his *dat* might not want to be around a woman who found fault with every little thing.

When Jo turned, Mamm stood watching her from the kitchen doorway. "Don't count any chicks before they've hatched, Jo," she warned softly. "Nelson thought he was doing us a favor, suggesting that this man look at our walnut trees, but that doesn't mean we'll be banking a big check like he did. Frankly, I thought his story sounded too *gut* to be true."

Shrugging, Jo walked back to the kitchen. "Doesn't cost us anything to find out—and if we don't like what Mr. Yorke has to say, we don't have to accept his offer. I recall Dat talking about how he was clearing out some of the saplings and damaged trees in our woods to allow the walnuts and oaks a better chance to grow. Maybe he was thinking about selling those trees years ago."

As she mixed ingredients for a batch of honey corn bread, Jo thought of several improvements they could make around the farm if the timber cruiser's offer was a good one—although she sensed Mamm would bank the money to cover future expenses she felt were more important than farm maintenance.

The two of them had been living very frugally since Dat passed. They'd sold off the last of the Belgian draft horses he'd bred for a living—which made her thankful that her Marketplace shop was providing them with some income now. Jo was well aware that if they didn't paint the house, the barn, and the other buildings—and replace some missing roof shingles—their negligence would come back to haunt them. Her father had talked about doing this maintenance, but when he'd developed breathing problems, all projects that demanded physical exertion had gone by the wayside.

Jo sighed. As she put the honey corn bread muffins in the oven, she wished—for the hundredth time—that her father had seen the doctor sooner when he'd developed such a deep cough. His death had been a sudden, rude awakening because Dat hadn't talked to either her or Mamm about the farm finances, even though Jo had often offered to help with the family's bookkeeping.

She was pulled out of her woolgathering when Mamm returned to the kitchen with an odd expression on her face.

"I just checked the phone messages. Margaret Shetler called," her mother said with a shake of her head. "Seems she wants to hold a sewing frolic to make some linens for your new home. In the same breath, she said something about a bunch of men coming over to paint that day, as well. I couldn't make head nor tail of it."

Jo's eyes widened. What were the chances that the

subject of painting had come up during a call from the bishop's *mamm* just when she'd been thinking about that very topic? Was it coincidence, or was God working along the same lines she was?

"Why not call Margaret and see what she has in mind?" Jo suggested as she went to the oven. The muffins looked perfect—nicely rounded and golden on top—so she pulled out the trays and set them on racks.

"It's *you* who should be discussing household linens," Mamm insisted. "And why would I want men working here on the same day? Think of fixing food for a crowd like that! Not to mention the fact that *we'd* be expected to pay for those groceries *and* the paint *and*—well, what was Margaret thinking?"

Jo refrained from pointing out that every building on the farm needed attention. Her mother's good mood had obviously spun into a downward spiral as she'd listened to Margaret's message.

"How about if I call her?" she suggested gently. "I'll do it after we have some lunch—including this apple walnut coffee cake, while it's still warm."

Mamm waved her off with an impatient sigh. "How can I think about lunch when the bishop's mother has taken it upon herself to invite half of Morning Star over here—without even consulting me first? Just *sell* that pan of coffee cake. It's what you'd intended to do with it anyway."

As her mother stalked out through the mudroom, slamming the door behind her, Jo was once again reminded that her life with Michael would be anything but pleasant if they started out their marriage in this house.

Seems like a fine afternoon to pay Margaret a visit—

*get out and about for a while. If she's willing to host a
frolic for me, the least I can do is take along a pan of fresh
coffee cake.*

Jo was pressing foil over the top of Margaret's gift
when she heard a knock at the door. As she spotted the
timber cruiser through the front room window, she wondered if her moody mother had already met up with
Mr. Yorke—but his smile suggested otherwise.

"You've got quite a nice stand of valuable timber along
your creek," he remarked as Jo stepped out onto the
porch with him. "Not only black walnut trees but some red
and white oaks have grown to a nice height and diameter—
without a lot of other trees to compete for soil nutrients
and sunlight."

"*Jah*, in years past my *dat* cleared out the excess under-
growth there," Jo put in. "Maybe he'd thought about having
somebody like you look them over someday."

Mr. Yorke held his clipboard so she could see his descriptions on the bid sheet. "Trees are most valuable for
plank lumber when their trunks are at least nine or ten
feet high before the lowest branches, and when they
haven't sustained damage from, say, livestock eating their
bark or being hit by brush hogs and other equipment," he
explained. "The best trees also tend to grow in wooded
areas rather than out in pastureland or yards, because
they grow straighter, without sending branches in all
directions."

Jo nodded, noting his compact handwriting and the
figures he'd written beside his descriptions.

"I identified four very tall, old walnut trees that are
more than forty inches around—a rare find—as well as
at least a dozen other trees suitable for harvesting in the

woods near the road," he continued. "And in the second area I showed you on the map, you have a nice stand of oaks. I do indeed think your father did some prudent timber management in years past in order for these trees to grow the way they have."

Mr. Yorke pointed to a figure at the bottom of the bid sheet. "I'm offering you sixty-two thousand dollars for what I've seen, with the contract stating that you'll receive more if we harvest additional trees after we've made a more accurate count."

Jo was struck dumb. She glanced through the open door, but she suspected Mamm was holed up in her gardening shed—and in her present frame of mind, her mother wasn't likely to believe what Mr. Yorke was saying anyway.

"I—oh my, I had no idea," she finally stammered. "I'll need to discuss this with my mother—"

"I'll leave your copy of the estimate, Miss Fussner, so you can contact me whenever it's convenient," he said as he tore off the self-carbon copy of the agreement. "My number's at the top of the page. We can schedule your harvest once we've gotten your approval."

After he'd wished her a good day, the cruiser strode toward his pickup and drove off. Jo stared at the estimate again, almost afraid to breathe for fear the numbers might diminish before her eyes.

It would take *years* for Mamm to earn $62,000 from her produce. The money they would receive from harvesting their trees was quite a windfall, and they wouldn't have to lift a finger—except to sign the contract.

Jo ate a quick lunch and tucked the cruiser's estimate into her apron pocket. She picked up her pan of coffee cake and headed for Bishop Jeremiah's house. As a man who owned a farm with several acres of woods, perhaps he could shed some light—or at least give his opinion—about the transaction Mr. Yorke was proposing.

And if the bishop's mother had offered to organize a sewing frolic on her behalf, Jo had surely been blessed beyond her wildest expectations. Some days were clearly better than others. No matter what sort of mood Mamm was in, Jo decided to make the most of this remarkable afternoon.

When she went to the pasture to choose a horse, Jo thought it was a fine sign that Starla came trotting to the fence without being called. Michael's young mare was filling out more each day and becoming more responsive each time Jo approached her.

"Are you telling me you'd like to go for a spin, Starla?" she asked as the deep gray horse munched the sugar cube she'd offered. "Let's do it!"

What a joy it was to hitch Michael's courting buggy to his mare rather than driving Mamm's old, enclosed buggy. The bright sunshine made Jo smile as she drove to the road—and when she found a small envelope from "M. W." with a Queen City return address in the mailbox, her mood improved even more.

My dearest Josie,
It was so wonderful to spend time with you last
weekend! I love you so much, and I'm looking
forward to sharing your love and laughter for
years to come.
　　　　　Your Michael

Such a simple message, yet Michael's words made Jo shine inside.

Somehow, it'll all work out. Someday, all the pieces will fall into place.

Chapter 11

On Friday afternoon Michael felt so elated, he thought he'd pop. He and his *dat* and Aunt Nadine had just picked up Jo's pottery from the Simple Gifts shop and they were on their way to Morning Star for an extended weekend. His engagement had been a turning point in his life, and now that he'd found the perfect gift for Jo, his love burned even brighter.

"Those are the prettiest dishes I've ever seen, Michael," his aunt remarked as their large wagon rolled down the county highway. "So bold and colorful! We might have to stop through Willow Ridge on the way home so *I* can pick out a set—something different from yours, so Jo won't think I'm a copycat."

Michael laughed. "Jo wouldn't mind if you chose the same design. It's not as though you'll be living next door to us, after all."

"And where will your home be?" his aunt asked. "From your conversations, I sense you'll live in Morning Star, but will you be on the Fussner place or finding land of your own?"

"This would be a *gut* weekend to figure that out," his *dat* remarked, steering the horse into a turn at an intersection. "I think you'll be happier in your own house, but it's a matter of where you can build one. It makes the most sense for you to live somewhere on the Fussner place, but Drusilla's feathers might get ruffled at the thought of you *taking over* part of her property."

"*Jah*, no matter what we suggest, she seems to feel we're plotting against her," Michael said with a sigh. "But we haven't seen any other land up for sale, either."

"Maybe I can help win her over," Nadine remarked. "Drusilla's lost her husband, so I suspect any sort of change to their farm feels like a betrayal of his memory. Margaret Shetler says nearly all the district's women plan to attend our sewing frolic while you men paint the buildings, so surely Jo's *mamm* will realize that her friends— and you two fellows—want the best for her.

"Here again," she added with a shrug, "I've never lost a husband, so I might have Drusilla figured all wrong."

"No matter how things go these next several days, we appreciate your help, sis," Dat said. "This whole idea was designed to fill a need we saw—a job we figured Drusilla and Jo couldn't tackle on their own. Sometimes, though, folks misinterpret the projects you do as a favor to them."

As the three of them chatted, the rest of the drive to Morning Star went quickly. They passed between several towering walls of stratified rock that had been blasted away when the road was built—typical scenery for this part of Missouri and particularly pretty, with spring wildflowers growing in the rock crevices. Michael had always liked the hilly, wooded stretches of countryside because they would remain untamed by housing developments or farm machinery.

When they pulled in at Pete and Molly's place, Riley raced around the big wagon, barking to greet them. Michael was glad to see Bishop Jeremiah on the front porch—and relieved that he'd agreed to take the rowdy golden retriever to his farm whenever the newlywed Shetlers were out of town.

"*Gut* to see you folks!" the bishop called out before pointing his finger at the dog. "Riley, *sit*. That's enough of your noise."

The dog immediately obeyed—which made Nadine laugh out loud. "What a well-behaved dog! Surely you two fellows could handle him."

"Oh, the bishop has a special way with Riley," Dat said as he drove up alongside the house. "And Riley will have a better time over at Jeremiah's place anyway. Right, Bishop?"

"Mamm and I have a soft spot for him, *jah*—partly because he's a much quieter dog when Pete's not around."

Jeremiah shielded his eyes from the sun as Michael clambered down and helped his aunt to the ground. "Nadine, we're all looking forward to getting acquainted with you," the bishop said. "Mamm sent you folks a casserole and some other food so you wouldn't have to cook this weekend. She's really excited about the hen party on Monday.

"And Nelson," he continued, "I've ordered the paint for the project we men are taking on. Pete's letting us use his commercial paint sprayers. He'll be back Sunday

night, so he can help us tackle all those buildings at the
Fussner place come Monday."

"Wow, that'll be great!" Michael said. "Our paint will
go on a lot faster—and thicker—that way."

Bishop Jeremiah nodded. "We invested in those sprayers
when he was remodeling the old stable that became The
Marketplace. It was money well spent, because he and a
few other fellows got that building painted in one day and
recoated the next."

"I really appreciate your organizing the local men to
help with this," Michael's *dat* said with a nod. "Let me
know how much that paint bill comes to—"

"It's already been covered. You Wengerds—and Jo—
have brought in so much church commission money from
your shops that Deacon Saul and I have agreed we should
pay for the paint."

Michael's jaw dropped. He and Dat had calculated that
their improvements at the Fussner place would cost at
least a couple of thousand dollars—depending on how
many coats of paint they applied and how much roofing
material they needed. "That's very generous," he said.
"We'd still be happy to chip in—"

"Because I was figuring it as a wedding investment for
the kids," Dat chimed in. "If all goes well, there'll be a
Wengerd greenhouse or two in Morning Star before
long—maybe on the Fussner place and maybe else-
where, depending on whether Drusilla goes along with
that idea."

The bishop's face lit up. "See there? How can we lose?
It's a blessing that you'll be opening a branch of your nursery here in Morning Star—and an even bigger blessing

to have Michael and Jo settling here instead of going to Queen City."

Jeremiah's expression suggested that he knew a juicy piece of news. "You'll find this out as soon as you see Jo and her *mamm*, but I'll share it because I believe it'll help make your case with Drusilla," he said in a lower voice. "Jo came over a couple of hours ago to talk to Mamm about Monday's hen party—and to show me their estimate from the timber cruiser you recommended. I was so amazed, I took down the fellow's number so he can look at the walnut and oak trees growing on *my* farm."

Michael smiled at his *dat*. "We were hoping Yorke would find enough *gut* trees to override Drusilla's doubts about our suggestion—"

"Well, if sixty-two thousand dollars doesn't convince her, nothing will," Bishop Jeremiah put in quickly. "A windfall like that is money dropping from heaven."

"Or growing alongside her creek," Dat remarked.

"Jo and Mr. Yorke established that the trees were in such great shape for lumbering because her *dat* had done a lot of prudent clearing years ago," Jeremiah continued, "so it's almost like Big Joe Fussner prepared this gift, and you've found a way for Drusilla to claim it."

Michael went warm inside. He sensed Jo would feel her *dat*'s hand in this transaction, as well. "That's even better," he murmured.

"Glad to hear this," Dat said with a nod. "Jo mentioned once in passing that Drusilla had considered selling off part of the farm to provide a cash cushion for her later years, so now she won't have to do that. You don't happen to know which part of the property she was thinking about, do you?"

"First I've heard of that," Jeremiah replied with a shrug. "But I can tell you that a lot of pastureland's been lying fallow since Big Joe passed. He didn't raise much except hay and alfalfa, because a lot of the land is too hilly or the soil's not suitable for corn or soybeans. But it was a great place for him to raise Belgian draft horses."

Aunt Nadine, who'd been following the conversation closely, brightened. "Seems to me such a farm would have room for Michael and Jo's new home, as well as a greenhouse or two—especially when there's a creek to provide water for some irrigation," she pointed out.

She slipped her arm around Michael's waist. "Maybe your favorite aunt can plant the seeds of that idea while she gets to know Jo's *mamm* over this long weekend. It could be an opportunity for you kids, and it wouldn't take any of Drusilla's land out of production, either."

Michael returned her hug. "With all of us Wengerds convincing Drusilla we're on her side, how can we lose?"

"Oh, don't go tempting fate with *that* question!" Bishop Jeremiah put in. "Lately it seems that Jo's *mamm* can sour on something in the blink of an eye. We'll do our best on all these endeavors, but let's leave it up to the Lord to work out His will. Life always turns out better when we live it God's way rather than going in our own direction."

"Amen to that," Dat agreed. He looked at the two white *dawdi hauses* behind the newlywed Shetlers' home and then glanced at the large wagon they'd loaded with flats of seedlings. "Michael, let's drop off the luggage and your pottery and then take our plants over to The Marketplace. If they're unloaded and watered today, that's a lot less we have to do before customers arrive tomorrow. Would you rather stay here, Nadine, or go into town with us?"

Aunt Nadine, whose features closely resembled her twin brother's, gazed around the property. "I'll get us settled in and see that supper's ready when you fellows come back—and many thanks to your mother for thinking of us, Bishop," she added cordially.

"And thanks for taking the dog with you, too," she added as she focused on Riley. "He's been sitting there very politely while we've chatted, but something tells me he'd be off like a shot—or up to his yellow ears in trouble—the minute you take off without him."

As though he'd understood every word, Riley let out a loud, raucous bark. He remained seated but began wiggling in anticipation, his big tongue lolling out of his mouth as he grinned at Jeremiah.

"*Jah*, get yourself into the rig, you pesky pup," the bishop teased, gesturing toward his buggy. "I'll fetch your chow from the mudroom and off we go. These folks have things they want to do."

Dat nodded. "Pick the *dawdi haus* that suits you, sis. We'll see you in a bit."

As Michael strode to the wagon alongside his *dat*, his thoughts spun like kaleidoscopes. "That was an interesting discussion," he said. "A lot has happened since we were here last weekend."

"And it's just the first wave of events, I suspect." Agile as a monkey, Dat clambered up onto the wagon's seat and took up the lines. His eyes shone and he looked like a man on a mission. "The next few days will determine a lot about our future, son—especially my future with Drusilla.

Let's pray she'll believe we have her best interests at heart.

"And if she doesn't see it that way," he added as he drove the wagon toward the road, "let's pray I have the sense to retreat gracefully and to thank God for watching out for *my* best interests."

"Imagine meeting up with you Wengerds!" Jo teased as she drove her wagon toward the large red barn that housed The Marketplace. "I had *no idea* you fellows would be unloading your flats this afternoon just as I was bringing in a load of my bakery stock."

Michael's laughter rang out as he straightened to his full height. "It's *gut* to see you, Josie-girl! What a nice surprise."

"*Jah*, you're just the sunshine our little seedlings need to look their best for tomorrow," Nelson added.

Jo pulled her mare to a halt and climbed down from the rig. Once again she was amazed at the number of flats Michael and his *dat* had transported from Queen City, but she had no doubt that all of their nursery stock would be gone by the time the shops closed tomorrow afternoon.

"And you fellows certainly sent a ray of sunshine when you directed Mr. Yorke to our place," she put in gratefully. "Mamm left the house in a hissy fit before he brought his estimate to the door, so she hasn't seen it yet, but here— take a look. Bishop Jeremiah seems convinced our trees will bring this much, but I confess I was struck dumb when I saw the bottom line."

Michael smiled like the cat that ate the canary. "Truth

be told, we just heard your news from the bishop," he said as he and his *dat* stepped close enough to read the offer.

Nelson skimmed the page, nodding, before he focused on Jo. "Handle this as you see fit, dear, but in your place, I'd be emphasizing how your *dat* laid the groundwork for this timber estimate," he suggested gently. "I'm glad I noticed those walnut trees and suggested Yorke pay you a visit, but I'm not the reason all this money's coming your way. Don't make me out to be the hero when you show this to your *mamm*."

Wasn't it just like Nelson to shine the light on someone else rather than take credit for a nice surprise?

"You're a hero in *my* book, Nelson," Jo murmured. "The way Margaret tells it, lots of folks will be at our place Monday for a sewing bee, as well as your painting project—and they're bringing all the food! What a gift you folks are giving Mamm and me—and Michael and me."

Michael's face shone as he gazed at her. "We've also brought along *dat*'s sister, Nadine, this weekend—"

"And it was *her* idea to have the hen party," Nelson put in quickly. "She's a free spirit, of sorts. And she believes your *mamm* will benefit from spending more time with friends who've probably been through the same, uh—life changes she's experiencing. Drusilla seems intent on isolating herself, and that's probably not *gut* for her."

"Truth be told, Aunt Nadine just enjoys a *gut* party," Michael explained. "And she's interested in seeing where you and I might be taking up residence after we marry."

A little bolt of electricity raced up Jo's spine. Her fiancé had just given her curiosity the perfect opening, hadn't he? "Where do you think that will be?" she asked softly. "You seem to be leaning toward Morning Star, but *not* toward living with Mamm—which I fully understand."

The two men exchanged a glance that told Jo they'd discussed this matter.

"Ideally, we could find—or build—a home in Morning Star and open a new branch of the nursery business," Michael replied in a hopeful tone.

"A while back you mentioned that your *mamm* had considered selling some of your property—which probably won't happen once she sees how much your walnut harvest is worth," Nelson added. "Do you have any idea which part of the farm she was thinking about? Or whether she'd let you kids have it instead?"

Jo's eyes widened. In her mind she could picture a pretty little house down the road from Mamm's place, as well as a sign for Wengerd Nurseries and a few glass greenhouses.

"I'm not sure," she mused aloud. "Maybe you fellows should figure out the best place to put your nursery buildings and go from there. This is Mamm's future you'd be improving as well as Michael's and mine, after all."

Nelson's eyebrows rose. "You're assuming she'll want *me* to be in this picture," he murmured. "Although I *could* remain at the Queen City store while you kids started up a new one."

"Oh, please don't give up on Mamm yet." Sensing the heartache Nelson was trying to hide, Jo gently grasped his arm. "Let's hope this weekend's activities will help her see you for the wonderful-*gut* man you are. But even if my mother doesn't come around, *I* appreciate all you've done for us, Nelson," she declared. "It's such a relief to know our house and outbuildings will be restored before they sustain any serious damage from lack of maintenance that Mamm and I can't do ourselves."

Michael's *dat* gazed at her with a grateful shine in his eyes. "You're welcome, Jo. I'll do everything possible to get you kids off to a solid start."

"If we build a house, you can live at *our* place, Dat," Michael pointed out. "You've told me you'd welcome a fresh start, and you can have one in Morning Star even if Drusilla's not part of that picture, ain't so?"

"We'll cross that bridge when we come to it," Nelson said. "We'll see what comes of our work frolic on Monday and go from there."

All this talk of a potential home with Michael made Jo feel bubbly inside—and it gave her an idea, as well. "Why don't you fellows bring Nadine for supper this evening?" she blurted out. "Although I don't have a *thing* planned for a meal—"

"Just so happens Bishop Jeremiah left us a casserole today—and we brought some other food along—so we can make it a potluck, *jah*?" Michael put in, raising his eyebrows at his father.

Nelson nodded. "I was hoping to introduce my sister to your *mamm* this evening, Jo, figuring you kids might be out in the courting buggy. You could still drive out after we eat—"

"Or we can stay put," Jo suggested as she slipped the timber estimate into her apron pocket. "Who knows where the conversation might lead once Mamm sees Mr. Yorke's bottom line? Maybe with all of us there, she'll be more inclined to talk about a homesite for Michael and me."

"And maybe another surprise might appear, too,

Josie-girl," Michael said with a mysterious note in his voice. "Sometimes the least-planned get-togethers turn out to be the most memorable, ain't so?"

What could he possibly mean by *that*? Jo was learning that her fiancé was a pleasantly unpredictable man, so she didn't pester him. Best to let him play out his surprise in his own good time.

"Well, then! I'll take my goodies into the bakery and get home, so Mamm will have time to prepare herself for company," she said happily. "This'll be a *gut* evening for her to wear something besides an old work dress and a kerchief."

Chapter 12

"The Wengerds are coming for supper *again*? This is getting to be a habit." Drusilla raised her eyebrow at Jo. "And Nelson's bringing his sister? With all your baking, we haven't cleaned the house or—"

"Nadine will be the last person to care about clutter or dust," Jo put in. "When I met her in December, her projects-in-progress were stacked on tables or stuffed into canvas tote bags. She confessed that she only cleaned before church was to be held at her place—and she didn't apologize for it! Relax, Mamm. You'll love her."

Drusilla shook her head doubtfully. "If they're bringing a casserole, what are *we* putting on the table? I was figuring on a bowl of cereal—"

"We've got an apple coffee cake, remember?" Jo went to the cupboard and took down the oatmeal and brown sugar. "If I open a couple of jars of peaches and put a crisp in the oven, it'll be a nice, warm dessert—and you'll get your cereal in the topping," she teased.

There seemed to be no escaping her daughter's plans, so Drusilla went upstairs to change out of her work clothes. It wouldn't do to give Nelson the idea she was fixing herself up for *him*, so she chose an older dress of deep green polyester. As she stood at the dresser to pin a clean *kapp* on her head, Drusilla was caught short by her reflection in the mirror.

Who was that haggard old woman? For a moment, it seemed her mother had slipped in unannounced—a thought that made Drusilla press her lips into a tight line.

I swore I'd never do and say the things my mother did, yet here I am. Just as cross and cranky as she got in her later years.

With a sigh, she went into the bathroom and took another one of the supplement tablets from the package Margaret had given her. According to the directions, it was too soon to know if they were helping, yet it made her feel better to do *something* about her moods. If Nelson's sister was coming, Drusilla certainly didn't want to burst into tears over any little thing—or nothing at all.

When she entered the kitchen, Jo was humming—and wearing a secretive smile. Drusilla felt unnerved by all the happiness her daughter was exuding now that she and Michael were engaged, but she'd have to make the best of it. Any advice about avoiding the pitfalls of marriage was useless at this point.

"Mr. Yorke came back with his estimate earlier today, Mamm. You'll be pleased, I think."

Drusilla took the piece of paper from Jo's hand, fully prepared to scoff at the offer. To her way of thinking, the only value in those old trees was the walnuts she gathered. Certainly Joe had never let on about a *gold mine*, the way Nelson had. She skimmed the list of descriptions and locations, but when she spotted the figure at the bottom of the page, she sucked in her breath.

After a few moments, Jo grasped her shoulder. "Mamm? Are you all right?"

"I—I—" Drusilla frowned at Jo. "How can this be? These are just old *trees*. There should be a law against leading widow ladies astray about the value of—"

"Mamm, this is legitimate." Jo gazed at Drusilla, her brown eyes wide and sincere. "I couldn't believe the amount, either, so I showed the estimate to Bishop Jeremiah. He and I can both recall how Dat used to clear away the underbrush and stray saplings to give those walnuts and oaks an opportunity to grow tall and straight.

"Mr. Yorke told me that's why our trees are worth so much," Jo continued in a whisper. "Dat must have planned all along to harvest those trees someday. But you and I would never have known that unless Nelson had pointed them out."

Drusilla swallowed hard. As she looked at the estimate again, the figures started to swim on the page. "Sixty-two thousand dollars," she murmured. "That's more than it cost Joe to build this house."

Her husband's image floated into her mind, the way he'd looked when they were newlyweds—tall and burly and broad-shouldered, with a full head of dark brown hair. Big Joe Fussner was a man to be reckoned with in those days, when he'd raised Belgian draft horses that stood eighteen hands high and weighed more than two thousand pounds. He'd provided his family a steady income—a comfortable living—but had he also been looking ahead? Planning for a day when he wasn't physically able to handle his horses?

"It's your decision about harvesting those trees, Mamm," Jo said softly. "This is your farm now, and no one intends to deprive you of any of its potential income. It makes sense to sock away whatever money you can, because one of these days you won't be able to plant and sell so much produce. Just saying."

Drusilla sighed slowly. Truth be told, her back and hips were bothering her a lot more this spring. Jo's earnings from her bakery had been a bigger blessing than she wanted to admit, but once her daughter married, she'd have to put her shopkeeping days behind her. And what if Michael decided the two of them would move to Queen City?

The oven timer dinged, bringing Drusilla out of her thoughts. "I'll think about it," she said as she returned the timber cruiser's estimate to her daughter. "Right now, we'd better get ready for our company, ain't so?"

By the time Jo had taken her peach crisp from the oven and finished setting the table, a rig was rolling up the lane. Although Nelson had mentioned his sister during his weekend visits last fall, Drusilla felt nervous about passing muster once Nadine saw how run-down the house looked. Would she think her brother could do better, as far as spending his time with a woman who'd let her property—and her appearance—slip over the past few years?

Too late to worry about that—not that Nadine's opinion should influence Nelson's feelings for me . . . if he still has any, after the way I've treated him lately.

"You go out and welcome them, Jo. I—I'll wait here," she said, suddenly shy.

Jo nodded, leaving Drusilla a few more moments to mentally prepare herself. Why was her heart pounding so hard? Why was she making such a big deal of meeting a woman Michael and Nelson had always described as laid-back and fun-loving?

Through the window, she watched the three Wengerds step down from the buggy as their enthusiastic greetings rose around Jo. Nelson was carrying a casserole pan and a paper grocery sack—and Michael had taken a big box from the back of the rig, winking at Jo. As they all entered the front room, talking and laughing, Drusilla convinced herself to stop hiding in the kitchen and join them.

"Drusilla, it's *gut* to see you, dear. This is my sister, Nadine," Nelson said when he saw her in the doorway. "Nadine, this is Jo's *mamm*, Drusilla Fussner."

Drusilla stepped toward them and then stopped, trying not to stare. "Nadine, it's a—a pleasure to—my word, except for the beard you look exactly like Nelson!"

As Nadine grabbed Drusilla's hand, she burst out laughing. "*Jah*, poor man. I always say he was doomed in the womb, being born my twin. If we put him in a dress and *kapp*, folks would be fooled until he opened his mouth, right? But listen to me going on," she continued without stopping to draw breath. "It's so *gut* to meet you at long last, Drusilla. *Denki* for having us over on such short notice. You're a saint."

Nadine's torrent of words had made Drusilla's head spin. But she was suddenly *laughing*. "We can spare poor Nelson the dress and *kapp*, all right?" she asked as she grasped Nadine's hands. "Whatever's in that casserole smells wonderful, so let's dig into it while it's nice and hot."

"While you ladies are setting out the food, I'll rearrange the table a bit." Michael led them toward the kitchen and set his box on the countertop. When he unpacked five royal blue plates, Jo's mouth dropped open and her hands framed her blushing face.

"You—Michael, you got me those dishes with the daisies!" she cried out as she rushed over to hug him. "What a fine surprise!"

"I got you a set of the sunflower dishes, too," he said. "But I figured you'd only want one pattern on the table at a time."

Drusilla thought her daughter was going to burst into tears from more happiness than she could handle. She couldn't recall ever seeing Jo display so much excitement, yet Michael had figured out the key to unlocking the young woman's hidden emotions. As he took up their off-white plates, Jo set her new dishes on the table, shifting each one so the daisy design was arranged the same at each place setting. Her dark eyes glimmered as she stood back to admire the plates.

"These are even prettier than I remembered," Jo whispered. She gazed at Michael in amazed adoration. "You're the best, you know it?"

"Anything for you, Josie-girl."

Drusilla's heart swelled at this exchange of affection. She went to the table to admire one of the plates, running her finger along its painted design. "I've never seen plates like these. Did someone you know paint them, Michael?"

"We found them at the gift shop in Willow Ridge," he replied. "The owner told me an Amish lady from Clearwater makes them."

"I've informed the boys we'll be stopping at that store on the way home so *I* can buy a set in a different pattern,"

Nadine put in as she, too, studied the plates. "It's not as though I often have company, but these dishes are so cheerful, they'll make every day feel like a special occasion."

It struck Drusilla that even though Nadine was a middle-aged *maidel*, she enjoyed life in a way most folks never considered—or even bothered to imagine.

After all, if a set of colorful plates could transform this drab old kitchen, what might they do for my outlook on life?

"I hope you'll use your pretty dishes every day, Jo, instead of tucking them away for special occasions," Nadine went on as she removed the foil from the casserole. "Life's shorter than you think. And too many folks settle for less than they deserve."

Jo smiled as she put a serving spoon in the casserole and set it on the table. "Michael's not one of those people," she said with another adoring glance at her fiancé. "I'm a blessed woman."

When they sat down and bowed to return thanks, Drusilla had a lot on her mind. Within the few minutes she'd known Nadine, she'd been jolted awake—made aware that she often settled for things rather than going after something better, even if it only involved an adjustment of her attitude. As they passed the food, Nelson held the hot casserole pan so Drusilla could spoon a portion onto her plate. The aromas of hamburger, seasoned tomato sauce, rigatoni, and cheese made her realize how hungry she was.

"How was your day, and your week?" he asked gently. "If I know you, those seedlings we put in your cold frames last week are already shooting up in your garden plot."

Drusilla's eyes widened. Was he flirting with her, right

here in front of everyone else? "Those were some of the healthiest little plants I've ever seen, so *jah*, they're off to a *gut* start," she remarked. "But I—I was *not* ready for what the timber cruiser told us. When Jo showed me his estimate, I nearly keeled over."

The laugh lines around Nelson's mouth deepened when he smiled at her. He didn't say anything. Just waited for her to finish sharing her thoughts without expressing his own.

After a few moments, the curious expressions around the table prompted Drusilla to express an opinion that rushed out before she'd really thought about it. "What a gift, to learn that Joe had probably planned to harvest those trees someday. I'm going to do it! It's like walking in the woods and finding a fortune—money growing on trees, even if our parents told us that never happens."

The way Nelson held her gaze did funny things to her stomach. "Would you like me to walk down there with you, to see exactly what Yorke's talking about?" he asked softly.

Now he was crossing a line, moving faster than she could handle. "I—maybe—we'll see," Drusilla gasped. "I just wanted you to know that I appreciate your help with this. I—I had no idea."

"You're welcome."

Drusilla focused on passing the hot casserole dish to Nadine, hoping she didn't appear as flushed and flustered as she felt. Was this emotional upheaval a side effect of the supplement she'd taken earlier? She hadn't spent any time at all comparing the pros and cons of accepting Mr. Yorke's offer, yet she sensed her decision was exactly the right one.

Was this how it felt to step into the future instead of clinging to the past? Was change for the better every bit as stressful as struggling to keep things the same?

When Drusilla noticed Nadine, Michael, and Jo smiling at her, she sensed they were on her side, willing to help her as time went by. And wasn't that better than digging herself an emotional pit and hiding in it, all alone?

Chapter 13

Monday dawned clear and bright, and as Nelson and Michael arrived at the Fussner farm, the promise of blue skies and sunshine was the best blessing anyone could hope for on the twenty-third of March. Pete Shetler had already unloaded his two big paint sprayers near the barn, along with several five-gallon buckets of paint. Even better, Pete was already scraping the loose paint from the old red structure's upper walls while Glenn was replacing some rotten boards. Glenn's *dat*, Reuben Detweiler, was pressing blue tape along the frames of the lower-level windows.

"You men got up earlier than the chickens this morning!" Nelson called out as he parked the rig. "I'm delighted to see you younger monkeys on the scaffolding and high ladders, because heights aren't my best friend anymore."

Pete stopped his scraping to wave at them. "My uncle tells the same story—"

"And we're used to climbing around up here, so it's best for you, um, more *mature* fellows to work on the lower walls," Glenn teased.

Reuben laughed out loud. "I didn't reach the ripe old age of eighty by being stupid!" he teased. "You'll not catch me on anything higher than a six-foot stepladder."

Nelson chuckled as he and Michael clambered down from the rig. "In my case, I'm not so sure *older* means *wiser*, but it's my ticket out of a lot of jobs I don't want to do anymore. Got any more scrapers?"

By the time he and his son were removing loose paint from a side barn wall, Bishop Jeremiah arrived with his *mamm*. His brother, Jude, was following close behind with his wife, Leah. The women exchanged greetings with the men before carrying large boxes of food and Leah's two little girls into the house. As Leah and Margaret returned to their rigs for bins of fabric, Gabe Flaud and Regina pulled in.

"Have we found the painting party?" Bishop Jeremiah asked in a loud, jovial voice. "Matthias Wagler's working at the carriage factory today, but even so, we've got eight men—and thirteen women with a handful of kids—coming for the day, so it's already a hugely successful event."

"With numbers like that," Jude Shetler teased, "I'm real glad to be on the outdoor team rather than in the house with all those hens!"

Seeing that the painting crew had all arrived, Pete climbed down from his scaffolding to speak with everyone. "We're getting an early start, so I hope we can scrape the barn and the stable this morning, and replace all the rotten wood," he suggested to the fellows who'd gathered around him. "After lunch, we should be able to spray the first coat of paint on those two buildings, and maybe prep the house. Tomorrow, whoever can come will apply the second coat to the barn and stable, and then paint the house—and meanwhile, anybody who feels able can replace some shingles on the roofs. Does that sound like a feasible plan?"

"We've got an experienced crew here," Gabe remarked as he assessed the gathering. "We worked well together getting The Marketplace ready—almost a year ago now—and most of us helped build Glenn's new house in December."

"We've got the Wengerds joining us this time, too," Glenn pointed out. "Awfully nice of you fellows to help us—"

"Let's not forget that this project was their idea in the first place," Jeremiah pointed out. "In the best-case scenario, we'll be welcoming Michael and Jo to our congregation this summer, after they've married—and we're hoping Nelson will also move to Morning Star and establish his nursery business here."

"We'd be glad to have you, too!" Reuben chimed in.

"*Jah*, you've been a fabulous addition to our Marketplace shops," Gabe said, flashing a thumbs-up to Nelson and Michael. "You've become great friends and neighbors during your weekends amongst us."

Friends and neighbors. Nelson nodded happily at the compliments these fellows paid him and Michael as everyone chose tools to start the day's work. He'd always been active in his Queen City congregation—an avid supporter of community events there, too—yet the prospect of moving to Morning Star to open another Wengerd Nursery facility excited him. Most men his age were content to settle into whatever businesses they'd already established, but Nelson knew that Michael intended to remain in Jo's hometown.

And that would alter Nelson's life a *lot*. If he stayed in his current home, even with Nadine across the road, at the end of every day he'd be alone.

"So, Michael, where will you and your bride set up housekeeping?" Jude Shetler, the local auctioneer, asked as he joined them with a scraper. He seemed pleased to be getting better acquainted with Nelson and his son rather than calling a sale today.

Michael energetically sent loose paint chips flying with his scraper. "*Gut* Lord willing, we'll build a house here on the Fussner farm," he replied. "You know how it is, though. Sometimes the women have other ideas."

Jude laughed. "It's all about the women at my place. With Leah, the teenaged twins, toddler Betsy, and now baby Adah, my boy Stevie and I don't stand a chance."

Nelson sensed this might be an opportunity to open a few more local doors. "Do you know of any land that's for sale around here, Jude? In case it doesn't work for us to live on this place?"

He'd avoided mentioning Drusilla, so it wouldn't sound as though their future depended entirely upon her—and so Jude wouldn't get any ideas about a relationship that might not go anywhere. "We'd want property accessible to a main road, so our nursery would see the most possible traffic."

As the muscular auctioneer gave his scraper a powerful shove down the side of the barn, faded red paint chips flew. "Nothing comes to mind," he said as he paused to think about it. "Maybe the Detweilers or the Flauds would sell you a parcel, because they're not farming much of their land anymore—but the back side of this place would be your best bet for business traffic. The road on that side's a main thoroughfare through Morning Star, so it's paved.

"But *jah*," Jude added with a knowing smile, "you'd have to convince Drusilla to turn loose a chunk of Big Joe's land."

Nelson pushed his scraper from above his head to the ground in one smooth movement. "You got that right, Jude. Her husband has passed on, but in her mind, Joe still runs the place."

Jude raised his eyebrows playfully. "All of us guys agree that if anybody can move Drusilla forward, it's you, Nelson."

Nelson blinked. Despite his efforts to keep their relationship under the radar, were he and Drusilla the subject of local gossip? "*Denki* for your support, Jude. Just yesterday she decided to sell her walnut trees, so maybe the wheels of change are turning. Only God knows at this point."

"And He's not saying!" Michael chimed in.

"It'll be fine, however it works out," Nelson insisted— because no matter what Drusilla decided about him, the rest of these folks considered him one of their community now. He already belonged here.

And that counted for a lot.

Chapter 14

Jo stood quietly to observe the minor miracle that had transformed the front room into a quilting workshop. Margaret Shetler and Martha Maude and Anne Hartzler had generously provided bins of colorful fabrics, and they'd brought along tables to accommodate all the ladies who wanted to make her and Michael a quilt.

As lunchtime approached, they'd finished cutting fabric wedges for a large Dresden plate quilt. Nadine, Regina, and Leah were stacking the pieces for each square on tables. The Hartzlers were setting up two portable sewing machines from their Marketplace shop, as well as the car batteries to operate them, so they could stitch the pieces into the squares that would form the quilt top. Molly and Marietta were helping Rose Wagler put away the fabric scraps, templates, and scissors—and Mamm, Cora Miller, and Delores Flaud were in the kitchen preparing to set out the noon meal for everyone who'd come today.

Our place is buzzing like a well-ordered beehive today. These ladies love us enough to make Michael and me a special gift, and their men want to help us maintain our farm. What an amazing gift . . . all because Aunt Nadine

*believed a party would help my mother—before she'd
even met her.*

As though Michael's vibrant aunt had overheard Jo's
thoughts, she looked up—and winked! Jo laughed, because Nadine's bubbly personality brightened the entire
room. She approached the table where the quilt pieces
were stacked, amazed at the wide range of colors and
prints that would decorate the bedroom she would share
with Michael for years to come.

"Look at these purples and greens and dark pinks and
blues," Jo murmured. "So many colors, in paisleys,
plaids, and polka dots! Who would've thought to put so
many prints side by side on a quilt top?"

"Martha Maude and Anne have wonderful eyes for
color," Nadine remarked with a nod. "When I visited
their Marketplace quilt shop Saturday morning, I was
delighted by the bright combinations and patterns on
display there. Every customer who buys one of their
quilts feels an immediate jolt of joy every time they look
at their purchase."

Jolt of joy. Didn't that describe Nadine Wengerd to
perfection?

Glancing toward the kitchen, Michael's aunt lowered
her voice. "I think I'll ask the Hartzlers to make a quilt
for your *mamm*—totally different from yours, of course,"
she added quickly. "What colors do you think she'd like?"

Jo's eyes widened. "Oh my," she murmured. "Mamm
will fuss a blue streak. She knows how much the Hartzlers
charge for their work—"

"So what? This isn't about the money, Jo. It's about
making Drusilla feel she deserves nice things," Nadine
explained. She playfully raised her eyebrows. "And who

knows? It might actually be a gift for *Nelson* to give her. Do you see where I'm going with this?"

Across the table, Regina laughed as she stacked fabric wedges. "I like the way you think, Nadine!"

"*Jah*, who wouldn't be impressed if a fellow gave you a Hartzler quilt?" Leah put in with a nod. "Nelson would appreciate your idea, too. Sometimes men want to give their women a beautiful gift, but they can't think of one on their own."

"You're a *gut* sister and a wonderful aunt," Jo agreed. "You've probably noticed how, um, *faded* our home looks, so any colors you might choose would cheer the place up, ain't so?"

Nadine smiled kindly, smoothing another completed stack of fabric pieces with her agile fingers. "When you've lived in a home for so many years, you stop really *seeing* your furniture and linens. It's time we gave Drusilla an infusion of color energy. Even if she doesn't marry Nelson, we can brighten her life with a special gift," she mused aloud. "No harm in showing her some love. It's what Jesus taught us to do, after all."

Jo felt blessed as she made her way toward the kitchen to help set up for lunch. It was a welcome sight to see her mother at the counter between Delores Flaud and Cora Miller—and Mamm was *smiling*! Setting out a meal was such an ordinary chore, yet her mother seemed happier than Jo had seen her in years—especially considering the way she'd originally balked at having so many folks at the house for the day's activities.

Her mother looked up, seeming pleased to see Jo in the doorway. "If you'll tell the men it's time to wash up, we'll have the food ready by the time they get here," she suggested. "What a feast our friends have brought!"

"I'm on it!" Jo said.

As she stepped outside, the sunshine warmed her—and so did the sight of so many men gathering around the pump by the barn to wash their hands. Blue tape outlined every window of the outbuildings, and several new, primed boards stood out against the dark red walls. Pete was showing Michael how to operate a paint sprayer, and Nelson was nodding over something Bishop Jeremiah was saying. It was yet another example of teamwork, where every man had found a job he could do—everyone could be a part of the improvements to the Fussner farm.

"You're the only one missing, Dat," she whispered. And yet she didn't feel sad, knowing he'd be so grateful to the friends who were maintaining his homeplace.

Setting aside her moment of nostalgia, Jo strode forward. "I hope you fellows are hungry!" she called out. "We've got a wonderful lunch waiting for you— "

"And a place to sit down, I hope!" Reuben put in.

"Not if the rest of us get to the tables first!" Bishop Jeremiah teased as he clapped Glenn's *dat* on the back.

"Puh! If I can keep up with an eight-year-old grandson, I can beat the likes of *you* to the table, Bishop!"

To prove his point, Reuben jogged toward the house. When he reached Jo, he stopped to catch his breath—but his eyes were shining with mirth as he glanced at the men behind him.

"Come and start the food line, Reuben," Jo said as she slipped her arm through his. "First one to arrive this morning deserves special privileges, the way I see it."

"Now you're talking!"

"And you're looking mighty spry these days," Jo continued as they stepped onto the porch. Not long ago, folks had been concerned that Glenn's *dat* was slipping mentally. "Life with Marietta must agree with you."

Reuben paused as he opened the front door for her. "Best thing to happen to our family in a long while, that woman is," he said gratefully. "She and Glenn have only been married a week and a half, but it seems as though she's been with us for years. We still miss my Elva and Glenn's Dorcas, of course, but Marietta has filled in the potholes of that bumpy, dead-end road we were on after we lost them. Life's *gut* again."

"And I'm very happy for you," Jo murmured, suddenly overwhelmed by the emotion of his words. "It's amazing how one person can make all the difference between happiness and heartache."

"Amen to that," Reuben agreed. "I'm off to fill my plate now. *Denki* for your kindness, Jo."

Within minutes the rest of the men were filing into the house. As they formed a line to spoon up the fragrant casseroles and colorful salads on the kitchen counter and table, Bishop Jeremiah spoke up. "Let's pause a moment to give thanks, shall we?"

At once the kitchen grew still. All heads bowed.

"Gracious Lord, we give You all praise and thanks for the opportunity to gather here on this glorious day of Your making," the bishop began. "Bless the hands that have held scrapers and brushes, and bless the hands that have prepared this food, and bless us every one into Your service. We ask this in the name of Jesus, the son of a carpenter, who fed folks in body and soul during his time on earth—and who nourishes us throughout our lifetime, as well. Amen."

The room became animated again as the men dished up chili mac casserole, chicken spaghetti, coleslaw, and other filling foods. Bishop Jeremiah was the last man to take a plate, behind Michael and Nelson, when he recalled something else he wanted to share.

"Just thought I'd remind everyone that tomorrow afternoon, I'll head for that gathering of the area's bishops," he said as he snatched a warm roll from a basket. "We'll be meeting near Carrollton, so Mamm's going along to visit with an elderly cousin who took a bad fall last week. Your prayers for both concerns will be appreciated."

Folks nodded as the women urged Jo's *mamm* and Nadine to step into the serving line.

"We'll see you for church on Sunday, though, *jah*?" Gabe asked above the chatter.

"That's the plan," Bishop Jeremiah replied.

The line moved quickly, and soon Jo was seated beside Michael with a full plate and a fuller heart. The tables in the front room were now lined with longtime friends in folding chairs who filled the room with their conversations.

"You won't believe the quilt these ladies are making for us!" Jo said to Nelson, Nadine, and Mamm, who also sat within earshot. "As efficiently as Martha Maude and Anne work, I won't be surprised if the entire top is sewn together today. And they've chosen such bright colors, too!"

"I can't wait to see it," Michael said as he forked up a

big bite of chicken spaghetti. "We've made wonderful-*gut* progress on the painting, as well. Things are really falling into place, with a little help from our friends—and our families," he added with a nod toward their parents and his aunt.

His gray-blue eyes sparkled at he focused on Jo again. "I've also had an interesting chat with Bishop Jeremiah. What would you think of setting our wedding date for Thursday, June fourth, Josie-girl? That would give him and Lydianne a couple of weekends to collect their gifts after they get hitched on May nineteenth—"

"Let's do it!" Jo blurted out, grabbing his hand under the table. "It'll give us a date to aim for and—and we'll have more than two months to get ready."

Michael's face lit up like a summer day. "We'll also be ahead of the big produce auctions at The Marketplace—though the nursery business will be booming," he added with a glance at his *dat*.

Nelson's face creased with mirth. "When *aren't* we busy, son? You and Jo should set your date when you want it, and we'll plan accordingly. Congratulations!"

"Oh, that's exciting!" Nadine chimed in. "Weddings—and the preparations—are always more pleasant before the summer heat and humidity set in. Don't you think so, Drusilla?"

Mamm's eyes had widened. She set her fork carefully on her plate. "I was under the impression you'd planned for a longer engagement," she said beneath the conversations around them. "Is there a reason for this rush, Josephine? Something you're not telling me?"

Jo's jaw dropped. Her mother might as well have pitched a rock at her. "Absolutely not!" she rasped. "How could you think—we'll talk about this later, Mamm. This is not the time or the place."

Her mother sighed but didn't drop her gaze. "I was just recalling that two and a half months ago you went to Queen City against my wishes—"

"And I thought we'd laid any doubts about our behavior to rest," Michael countered, leaning forward to speak quietly to Mamm. "If *that's* the kind of math you're doing—if Jo and I had something to hide—we'd be pushing for a wedding much sooner than June, ain't so?"

An uncomfortable silence settled over their table. Jo was relieved to hear that Gabe, Glenn, and Pete, seated on her other side, were discussing their strategy for spraying paint on the barn—unaware of Mamm's remarks. Nelson glanced at his twin sister, who graciously kept any show of emotion from her face as the two of them remained silent.

"Have it your way, then." Mamm glanced at her half-eaten meal as though she was no longer interested in it. "Wouldn't be the first time a baby took control of a courting couple's calendar."

When her mother rose to carry her plate to the kitchen, Jo didn't have the heart to follow her. Why on earth would her mother think she was in the family way? Did she still not trust Jo and Michael to behave appropriately?

"I'm sorry," Jo murmured to Michael and his family. "Until now, Mamm has seemed happier than she's been in a long while, but her moods swing without any warning. No telling what's going to come out of her mouth next."

"No need to apologize, Jo," Nelson assured her.

Nadine's expression became pensive. "I'll chat with

her after the other ladies have gone. I had the same trouble a while back. My emotions ran hot and cold, and I had no control over the faucet whatsoever."

After she took a forkful of her slaw, Nadine smiled kindly at Jo. "I'm delighted you kids have set your date. It's best to enjoy this happy time of your life, and to make your plans. Drusilla will surely come around."

As the meal ended and the men went back to work, Jo hoped Nadine was right.

While Cora and Delores helped Mamm clean up the kitchen, Molly and Marietta handed wedges of fabric to Martha Maude and Anne, who machine stitched them into plate shapes before adding the fabric circle in the center. Regina and Margaret were handing them the fabric pieces that formed the squares' backgrounds.

Leah Shetler and Rose Wagler took their little girls outside to play in the sunshine. When they left with Jude so they'd be home when the Shetlers' son, Stevie, and Gracie Wagler got out of school, the other folks began calling it a day, as well.

After a long stint at her machine, Martha Maude stood up to stretch. "What a great day, Jo!" she remarked. "I'll take these squares home, and it won't be long before the top of your quilt's completed."

"Then we'll gather with whoever wants to hand stitch the layers together," Anne said as she collected her scissors and other equipment. "You might see us working on it in front of the shop this Saturday, depending on customer traffic. When we have the quilting frame set up out there, it gives us something to do—and gives folks something to watch."

"I can't thank you enough for organizing this frolic—

and for the fabric and your time, too," Jo said. "What a wonderful, thoughtful gift."

As she helped the Hartzlers carry bins and equipment to their rig, Jo stopped to gape. The red barn glimmered in the afternoon sunlight, looking fresh and new. The stable was also painted, and it looked better than it had in years. What a difference a day made, when friends came over to work!

"See you at The Marketplace on Saturday, Jo," Molly said as she and Pete were preparing to leave.

"Wouldn't miss it for anything!" Jo replied. "*Denki* for all your hard work today—and yours, too, Glenn and Marietta! And yours, Reuben!"

The Detweilers, Shetlers, and Flauds departed, and soon Bishop Jeremiah and Margaret were stepping up into their rig, as well.

"Have a *gut* trip to Carrollton," Jo called out to them. "I hope your cousin's health improves—and I hope the bishops' gathering goes well."

A few moments later, Nelson and Michael walked over from the barn. Their clothes were spattered with deep red paint, but they wore pleased expressions. "We'll go back to the Shetlers' *dawdi haus* for the evening, so we can rest and be ready to paint the house tomorrow," said Michael's *dat*. "This will give your *mamm* a break after having a houseful of company all day."

"That might be best," Jo agreed. "She's not used to having so many people here, or having her routine interrupted. Now that folks have gone, I'm going to call Mr. Yorke, to see when he can schedule us—before Mamm changes her mind."

"We'll count that as definite progress," Nelson said

with a tired smile. "Tomorrow's another day, and we'll see you then, dear. Soon as we fetch Nadine, we'll be off."

Jo nodded. Rather than interrupt whatever Nelson's sister might be saying to Mamm, she walked over for a closer look at the barn and the stable. She'd have all evening to spend with her mother, after all.

Unfortunately, she wasn't looking forward to it.

Chapter 15

"I wish these do-gooders would mind their own business and leave us alone," Drusilla remarked as she watched the Wengerds' buggy come up the lane early Tuesday morning. The bishop's rig wasn't far behind it, and she saw that both Nadine and Margaret had chosen to return with the men today. "It's one thing to fix up the barn and stable, but Pete's already tromping around on the roof, replacing shingles. There'll be no end to the racket while the men paint the house today.

"And besides," Drusilla added after another thought occurred to her, "I thought Jeremiah and his mother were heading off for his bishops' meeting and her cousin's today."

"They're not leaving until this afternoon." At the kitchen counter, Jo was mixing ground beef, sausage, eggs, and seasonings for meat loaf. Her daughter still appeared perturbed about yesterday's difficult conversation—and it was clear Jo wasn't pleased that Drusilla wouldn't help with the lunch preparation, either.

"Really, Mamm! We're blessed that our friends have been so generous with their time and effort," her daughter continued stiffly. "It's a wonder the Wengerds are even coming back, after the bomb you dropped yesterday."

"I apologized to you for that. Can we move on now?"

"What are you figuring to do while everyone's here?" Jo shot back. "Bishop Jeremiah will be on you like a duck on a bug if you keep acting so antisocial. And ungrateful."

Drusilla sighed. Jo was right about that.

She'd taken the last of the supplements Margaret had given her in the wee hours this morning, when she'd felt too sweaty and anxious to sleep. Drusilla wanted to curl up in a ball and hide from Nadine and the bishop's *mamm*—but she wouldn't get away with that, either.

"About our little tiff yesterday," Drusilla said hesitantly. "I'm sorry I implied you might be in the family way—but I was also concerned because you let Michael and the bishop set your wedding date, as though you had nothing to say about it. You're letting the men make the important decisions, Jo. I never thought you'd fall into that pattern, considering how you've charted your own course for so many years."

Jo's hands went still. Her shoulders relaxed, but she still didn't appear very forgiving. "I could've suggested a different date, but I saw no reason to," she pointed out softly. "And you've changed the subject, Mamm. I asked what you plan to do with Nadine and Margaret today—they'll be at the door any minute now."

Drusilla sighed. "I suppose I'll put on a happy face and work outside."

She winced when Pete dropped something heavy on the roof—a bundle of shingles, most likely. "If I have to listen to these sudden noises all day, I'll go crazy. Or *more* crazy," she added after a moment. "Jo, I really am sorry about these moods. Sorry I can't control them, and sorry you have to endure them, too."

Before Jo could respond, the front door opened. "Knock, knock!" Nadine called out.

"*Jah*, we've returned like a couple of bad pennies," Margaret teased.

"Come on into the kitchen!" Jo called out. "*Denki* for coming back today."

Drusilla squared her shoulders, determined to make a good show despite her misgivings about having company again. Nadine's cape dress of bright lime green was the flashiest garment Drusilla had ever seen an Old Order woman wear, but she bit back a remark about it—because the bishop's *mamm* was placing a small brown paper sack on the counter as though it held a secret surprise.

"Oh, I haven't made meat loaf in such a long time!" Nadine said with a warm smile for Jo. "Here's some mac and cheese to go with it. And *gut* morning to you, too, Drusilla!"

"We've also got some applesauce I made with cinnamon red hots," Margaret chimed in as she lifted the quart jars from her picnic basket. "And I seem to have so many green beans on my shelves, I brought some of those, too. Time to clear out last year's veggies to make room for this summer's crop, ain't so?"

Margaret's royal-blue dress appeared crisp and new, and as Drusilla looked at her two guests, she felt like a dusty little sparrow by comparison. Why had she chosen to wear a gray dress she'd made shortly after Joe passed?

Because it was a toss-up between this dress and the brown one—I need to sew some new clothes.

"Another nice meal for today," Jo remarked as she began to shape two large loaves from the meat mixture. "*Denki* for bringing food again, ladies."

"I'm happy to help, dear," Nadine said. "Michael suggested that your usual baking routine has probably been interrupted these past couple of days—"

"And I'll have you know that the coffee cake you brought us last week was gone within an hour," Margaret said with a laugh. "Jeremiah *inhaled* it—but then, I ate my share, too. It's no wonder your bakery sells out early every Saturday, Jo."

"That's because my Josie-girl is the best cook ever!" Michael put in as he stopped in the kitchen doorway.

He greeted everyone, but Drusilla couldn't miss the special light in his eyes when he focused on Jo. For fear of sounding like a broken record—or alerting Nadine and Margaret to her foul mood—Drusilla refrained from repeating her warning about how men were all full of pretty words and promises while they were courting. She wanted to believe that Michael was as wonderful as he seemed, but she couldn't help having doubts. Or was she just hesitant to give the couple her blessing because she didn't want to lose her daughter to *any* man?

Jo beamed at him, arranging the meat loaves in a large blue roasting pan. "Flattery will get you everywhere, Michael," she quipped.

As Nadine and Margaret laughed, Drusilla felt the heat surging up from under her dress. Didn't Jo's flippant remark suggest the wayward behavior she'd been preaching against? She didn't want to think her tall, big-boned daughter—the spitting image of her *dat*—would attract a man who couldn't keep his hands off her, but Drusilla suddenly needed to leave the kitchen, before she blurted out something she'd regret.

"I'm heading out to hoe the garden," she announced brusquely.

As she strode through the mudroom, Drusilla wasn't surprised that Nadine and Margaret followed her. When the men cranked up the generator, its rumble was noisy enough to discourage her guests from talking to her—and the loud splash of the paint striking the house made her walk even faster.

When they'd reached the nearest garden plot, Margaret spoke first. "Drusilla, are you all right? You took off in such a hurry—"

"Are you having a bad day, dear?" Nadine cut in. "If you want to talk about your crazy mixed-up feelings and hot flashes and mood swings, we're here to help. Margaret and I have been there and done that, and we lived to tell about it."

Drusilla didn't stop until she'd opened the tool shed. At least the generator was noisy enough that the men couldn't have heard their remarks, but Nadine had made it sound as though she and Margaret had actually *discussed* their female troubles—and hers—and compared notes. Were they really expecting her to bare her soul about such an embarrassing topic?

Drusilla entered the unlit shed and turned toward them. Her red face surely resembled the lights at a railroad crossing—and she felt as though a train was rushing right at her. But there was no escape: she had to answer them.

"I know you mean well, but I can't talk about such private matters," she said in a quavering voice. "This is just a phase. I'll get through it."

"Did you try those supplements?" Margaret asked gently. "I brought you some more, in case you hadn't gotten to the drugstore yet."

"I'm not sure those pills worked for me," Nadine put in with a shake of her head. "But I suspect a lot of women take them because it makes them feel they've done *something* to help themselves. They feel more in control because they believe they are."

Drusilla blinked. Was that why her morning had gone so well yesterday? Was that why she'd enjoyed getting acquainted with Nadine, until her dosage—and her patience with Jo and Michael—had run out?

"You might have something there," she admitted. "And it does say on the box that it takes a few weeks to notice any improvement. *Denki* again for thinking of me, ladies."

"We didn't want you to go through this alone, Drusilla," Margaret put in softly.

"That's the ticket," Nadine agreed. "It's true that with God we're *never* alone—but I doubt He's ever experienced night sweats or mood swings that leave Him feeling powerless, either."

As the three of them laughed, Drusilla felt her tension draining away. It was hard to remain grouchy with Nadine around—and her longtime friend, Margaret, was looking after her, as well. They understood her embarrassment and her need for privacy.

"Maybe your patience and understanding will be the best medicine, ain't so?" Drusilla murmured. "The main reason I came out here was to escape all that racket the men are making. You're company, so I feel funny asking if you'd want to work in the garden—"

"I'm with you, Drusilla," Margaret said quickly. "The noise from the generator and those guys on the roof was already driving me nuts. If you've got an extra hoe—"

"Give me a hoe or a spade, too," Nadine insisted cheerfully. "Are we planting today or weeding?"

Drusilla felt a genuine smile overtaking her face. She led them to the wall where the hoes, rakes, and other long-handled tools were held upright behind a wooden slat that spanned the width of the shed.

"Take your pick!" she replied. "I've got turnip and beet seeds, as well as potato eyes and onion sets for a second planting of those—and after that sprinkle of rain the other day, the weeds have popped up in the first plots I planted."

"Let's do the worst first," Nadine suggested as she grabbed a hoe. "Once we conquer the weeds, we'll feel so inspired that planting those potatoes and onions will feel like a frolic, *jah*?"

Drusilla smiled. How could she argue with Nadine's upbeat attitude?

Chapter 16

"You fellows have gone above and beyond," Michael said as Pete and Glenn were preparing to leave after the day's painting. "We couldn't have completed these projects so efficiently without your sprayers and scaffolding."

When Pete grinned at him, the short, blond whiskers along his jawline caught the late-afternoon sunshine—nearly two weeks of new beard growth since he'd gotten married.

"Happy to help," he said. "I was glad I could finish here before I start some other carpentry and painting jobs I've bid on. Lots of folks—English and Plain—are calling me, now that they've come out of hibernation and realize how faded their houses and barns look."

"We wish you all the best getting your new business underway," Michael's *dat* put in. "And Glenn, we really appreciate your taking time away from making your furniture and toys, too."

"It's been a nice change of pace, and a chance to work outside in this fine weather," the dark-haired woodworker remarked. "And where would my family be if all our neighbors hadn't pitched in and built us a new home last winter? See you Saturday at the Marketplace!"

Michael watched Glenn load paint rollers and drop cloths onto Pete's wagon. "You newlyweds aren't collecting presents this weekend?"

Glenn shook his head. "Bishop Jeremiah told me this morning that Margaret's cousin in Carrollton isn't doing too well, so they'll be spending an extra day or so there. And that's fine! I don't want my customers to forget who I am, after all. Some of them will be ordering lawn furniture pretty soon."

Minutes later, Michael waved at the two young men as they drove down the lane. Bishop Jeremiah and Margaret had left after lunch, so he and Dat and Nadine were the only guests still at the Fussner place. As he looked at the red barn and stable, and the house with its fresh, white shine, his exhaustion and sore muscles felt worthwhile.

"We did Jo and her *mamm* a big favor," he said softly. "The place looks better than it has since before Big Joe died, I'm guessing."

Dat nodded. "You and I and Jo know that, even if it might be best not to expect Drusilla's enthusiastic appreciation."

"She's taken a shine to Aunt Nadine, though," Michael pointed out as they walked toward the house. "We can be thankful for that."

As he looked in the direction of Drusilla's garden plots, he saw that his aunt and Jo's *mamm* were planting potatoes. It was a good sign that the two women were chatting and laughing as they worked.

Halfway up the porch steps, he caught the aromas of sweet dough and vanilla drifting from the open windows.

When everyone had gone in to eat lunch, the kitchen countertops had been covered with pans of coffee cake and loaves of banana bread Jo was baking for her shop, so Michael was eager to see what she'd been making all afternoon. Once inside, he and his *dat* passed a couple of long, folding tables where dozens of shaped sugar cookies cooled—eggs, ducks, crosses, and flowers.

"Somebody's getting ready for Easter!" he said as they entered the kitchen.

Jo turned from her sink full of dishes. "Hard to believe, but Easter's only a couple of weeks from this Sunday. Holiday goodies always sell out fast."

She wasn't letting on, but Michael sensed his fiancée was tired from being on her feet all day. He grabbed the white flour sack towel hanging on the stove handle and began to dry the mixing bowls in the drainer.

"What if we all went into town for supper?" he asked, glancing at Dat. "Or, if you'd rather we Wengerds went back to the Shetler place so you can relax—"

"And miss out on the cold supper I got ready for us last night?" Jo interrupted. "If you three leave, Mamm and I are going to have potato salad and sliced ham coming out of our ears."

"Oh, *that* wouldn't be pretty!" Dat teased. "If you've already fixed our meal, I'll set the table, all right? You've saved us from scraping together the leftovers from the *dawdi haus* fridge, dear."

As the three of them chatted, Michael dreamed of the day when he and Jo would fill their own kitchen with this same love and easy cooperation. He also noticed that the appliances and her work area here were much more limited than what she had in her shop.

"I'm glad our painting project didn't take you away

from your baking again today," he remarked. "Considering how many hours you spend getting ready for Saturdays at The Marketplace, would you like our home's kitchen to have a double oven or two and a big fridge like you have in your bakery? Just thinking ahead."

Jo's hands stilled on the bowl she was washing. A sparkle lit her eyes and all signs of her fatigue vanished. "Are—are you saying it'll be all right for me to work in my bakery after we marry?" she whispered. "I've been wondering how you feel about that subject, but I didn't know how to ask."

Michael slipped his arm around her waist. "You know, the married women in lots of Old Order districts are working in local shops these days. I have no problem with that—at least not until our kids start arriving," he replied as he held her gaze. "I want you to be happy, Josie-girl. I know how much you enjoy seeing your customers and baking the treats they love."

"Oh, Michael, I—you have no idea how *very* happy you've just made me." Jo turned to look at his *dat*, who was taking silverware from the drawer. "And what about you, Nelson? What's your opinion about me working at The Marketplace after Michael and I are married?"

Dat chuckled. "You're talking to a fellow who couldn't manage his Queen City nursery without his sister's help—although, *jah*, she's a *maidel*. But you've been banking your profits to support your *mamm* into her later years, and I suspect you'd like to keep doing that."

"It's my responsibility to look after her," Jo agreed solemnly.

Michael caught a subtle shift in his father's demeanor as he carried the silverware to the table.

"If your *mamm* and I were ever to marry, she—and

you—wouldn't have to worry about her future, ain't so?" Dat mused aloud. "Meanwhile, Michael will be the man of his household. I'll go along with whatever he decides about where you spend your time and energy, Jo."

"I feel so much better now that we've talked this out," Jo said in a low, emotional voice. "Someday soon, Molly and Marietta and I will have to speak with Bishop Jeremiah about running our shops at The Marketplace—but here come Mamm and Nadine," she added with a nod toward the window. "For this evening, our goal will be to keep both of them chatting and happy, *jah*?"

"Works for me." As Michael continued drying Jo's baking bowls, he felt a closer bond with her—was glad he'd paved the way for her to keep her bakery open. Jo clearly had a God-given gift for hospitality—and for managing The Marketplace—even though he intended to support their family with the profits the nursery stores would bring in. Still, her baking money might come in handy while he and his *dat* established a new Wengerd business in Morning Star.

But where would they live?

As Drusilla and Aunt Nadine entered the house, sharing a story, Michael hoped their lighthearted talk signaled an opportune time to discuss this topic. A new home was the only piece that still needed to fall into place before his dream—his future with Jo—would be complete.

It felt good to sit down to a simple cold supper, just the five of them. Jo's *mamm* seemed downright jubilant about all the gardening she and Margaret and Aunt Nadine had accomplished. Michael nodded in the appropriate places of the conversation, planning how to word his request.

He might have only one shot at getting a *yes* from Drusilla. It felt more complicated—and nerve-racking—than asking Jo to marry him had! He and Dat had discussed various aspects of living on the Fussner farm, but everything depended upon Drusilla. Her answer would determine his and Jo's future—and it would probably set the course Dat would take, too.

Aunt Nadine glanced at Michael as she spooned a second helping of potato salad onto her plate. "You seem lost in thought, dear," she remarked. "Are you relaxing after two days of scraping and painting? Or do you have something on your mind?"

Michael's eyes widened. There was no getting around such a direct question—especially because Drusilla was also watching him, awaiting his response.

"Truth be told, I'm wondering if Jo and I could build our home on that plot of land on the other side of the creek, where the county road runs," he said to Drusilla, hoping he sounded confident and well-intentioned. "It would be a *gut* location for some Wengerd greenhouses, too, so I'm willing to buy that parcel for whatever you think would be a fair price."

Jo sucked in her breath. Michael had talked with her about having a home on her family's farm, but she'd agreed to go along with her *mamm*'s wishes. Dat sat quietly, supporting Michael with a hopeful smile.

Drusilla didn't drop her gaze, but she sagged in her seat. "I—I guess I never considered selling any of Joe's farm—"

The lift of Jo's eyebrow contradicted her mother's statement. "It's *your* farm now," she pointed out softly.

"Some parents want their kids to build a house on the homeplace to keep the family close together. I think it's commendable that Michael doesn't expect you to give us the land, and he's not suggesting you'll need to move into the *dawdi haus* so we can move into *this* house."

Michael purposely hadn't mentioned the money angle. He didn't want Drusilla to feel the Wengerds were taking over her farm—as she'd protested about earlier—and he didn't want to make Jo's *mamm* feel she was being stingy. But he couldn't erase what Jo had said.

As long moments of silence ticked by, his heart sank lower.

"Isn't it enough that I've sold off those trees as you suggested?" Drusilla finally rasped. "Why are you expecting me to change *everything*, just because you're marrying my daughter?"

Michael knew better than to rise to that bait, but he was grateful when Dat leaned in to clarify the conversation.

"You've taken some big steps, Drusilla," his father agreed gently. "I'll point out that Michael's asking to live on your land—to purchase some of it, if you prefer—because there's no property up for sale in this area. He knows you and Jo have always been close, especially since your husband passed."

Drusilla blinked. She focused on the kitchen wall as though hoping to find the answer to Michael's question written there. "I—I'll think about it," she muttered.

"Fair enough," Michael said with a sigh.

Aunt Nadine cleared her throat, placing her hand lightly on Drusilla's forearm. "What my nephew's trying *not* to say is that if he can't open a branch of Wengerd Nursery here in Morning Star, he'll remain in Queen City. That'll leave you here all by yourself to manage this farm, Drusilla," she said softly. "And that'll mean that Nelson won't have much of a reason to spend any time here either, ain't so? It's really not my business, but I hate to see either you or my brother live alone any longer."

Drusilla's forehead furrowed as she looked at Michael. "You kids could live in this house with me. There's plenty of space—"

"No, Mamm. I don't think that'll work," Jo murmured sadly.

Michael felt a welling up of regret, knowing how difficult it had been for his fiancée to express that conclusion. But at least she'd been honest with her mother.

"I'm just asking you to consider our situation, Drusilla," he said with a sigh. "As a woman who sells her garden crops for a living, you'll understand that if Dat and I are to build new greenhouses so we can earn some income from them this season, I'll need your answer sooner rather than later."

"So once again you Wengerds are telling me what to do, yet pretending you're not." After she said this, Drusilla slumped, holding her head in her hands. "Sorry," she murmured. "I'm too tired to think about it right now. I'll give you my answer by the end of the week."

"That'll be fine," Dat said. He gazed purposefully at Michael, signaling the end of the conversation. "We'll be heading home early tomorrow morning, and we'll return on Friday afternoon, as usual. We'll see you this weekend, Drusilla."

Chapter 17

By Saturday, Jo's spirits had been restored. She and Michael had spent Friday evening at the newlywed Shetlers' place with Molly, Marietta, and their husbands, playing Yahtzee and eating carryout pizza. It had been so much fun to laugh with couples their own age—and Jo had paid close attention to the updates Pete had installed in Molly's kitchen when he'd remodeled it.

As she stood with Marietta and Molly on Saturday morning as Alice Shetler opened The Marketplace's double doors, Jo couldn't help smiling.

"Do you ever tire of seeing the excitement on our customers' faces?" she asked. "I believe we offer an experience—and merchandise—they can't find anywhere else."

"We do," Molly agreed. "And that's one *gut* reason for my sister and me to remain in our Marketplace shop now that we're married. We'll lose out on a lot of income if we can't work here any longer. Pete's remodeling projects don't earn steady money for us yet, so my noodle profits really come in handy."

"*Jah*, Glenn and I are both hoping that Mrs. Helfing's

Noodles will continue operating here," Marietta remarked. "I have no idea who would run the shop if the church leaders force us to stay home—"

"And paying someone else a wage would really cut into our profits," Jo pointed out. She sighed, spotting some repeat customers heading her way. "Bishop Jeremiah would scold us for having such a materialistic mindset, but he also realizes that I've been setting aside most of my earnings to ensure Mamm's financial security."

"One of these days the subject will come up at church," Molly said with a sigh. "But for now, let's get in there and do what we do best. *Gut* morning, folks!" she called out to the people entering the open commons area. "Anybody hungry for homemade noodles?"

Jo smiled at her friends' enthusiasm and entered her shop just ahead of her first customers. Her bakery cases looked especially inviting with dozens of colorful Easter cookies on display, so she wasn't surprised to hear some immediate reactions.

"Oh my word! I have to have three of those duck cookies for my grandkids!"

"Look at the dark chocolate crosses. Those will be just beautiful for Easter dinner at my house."

"Miss Jo, you've outdone yourself! I'd like to buy that bright pink egg cookie, and four of the larger bunny faces—and yes, the dark chocolate crosses look divine, as well."

For the next hour, Jo and Adeline filled white paper sacks with cookies, breads, and coffee cakes while Alice ran the cash register. Jo was so engaged in chatting with eager customers that she didn't notice her mother and

Michael's aunt until they were looking over the top of the display case at her.

"Mamm!" Jo blurted out. "And Nadine! What a fine surprise."

"I couldn't resist the chance to visit your bakery again—and to see how the boys are doing in the nursery shop, of course," Nadine put in with a chuckle. "When your *mamm* admitted she'd never been to The Marketplace, I told her it was high time she came to see what all the fuss is about."

Mamm looked a little sheepish, but at least she was peering into the glass bakery case with great interest. "What happened to those dozens and dozens of cookies you decorated all week, Josephine? My word, I've never seen so many flat pans as you carried out to your wagon this morning."

Jo gave her mother an exaggerated shrug, delighted that she was in such a jovial mood. "They're gone, Mamm! I guess I'll be making a lot more of them over the next couple of weeks, until Easter."

Mamm's eyes widened as she did some mental calculations. "And you were charging a dollar apiece, *jah*? I guess you'd better forgive me for all the times I told you that was too much to pay for a cookie!"

Her mother gazed at the stainless-steel stoves and industrial-sized refrigerator behind Jo, appearing awed by the bakery's interior—and by how many folks were coming into it. "I had no idea how wonderful-*gut* your shop is, Jo—and the other stores, too. This Marketplace is amazing."

Jo blinked. Nadine's company had once again worked

a minor miracle on her *mamm*'s disposition. And for that, she was grateful.

Nadine beamed. "When we stopped at the quilt shop, we chatted with Martha Maude and Anne, too. They're about halfway finished with the hand stitching on the quilt for you and Michael," she added. "It's exciting to see how quickly it's coming together."

"I'll have to look at it when I get a free moment," Jo remarked. "Excuse me while I restock the shelves."

"We'll get out of the way and let your customers do their shopping," Nadine remarked, slipping her hand through Mamm's arm. "Let's go next door, Drusilla. We haven't been to the Flauds' furniture shop yet."

Jo waved as the two ladies left. She was amazed that her mother was going from one store to the next with Nadine even though Mamm always claimed she had nothing to shop for. Michael's cheerful aunt had clearly become her mother's new best friend. Margaret Shetler had provided some supplements and support, but Nadine's laughter was proving to be the best medicine for Mamm's change-of-life challenges.

By one o'clock the bakery cases were bare. Jo wasn't surprised that disappointed folks who'd spotted earlier shoppers munching her cookies in the commons area were coming in to place Easter orders.

"How about if we clean up while you take the orders, Jo?" Alice suggested. "You have a better idea what you'll be baking than we do."

"*Gut* idea. And then you girls can have the rest of the day off—with pay," she added. "I'll wipe down the tables and clean the coffee makers today."

Two identical freckled faces lit up as the twins stood at the sink. "We don't mind staying to help," Alice insisted.

"But we could also buy Leah one of those pretty planters the Wengerds are selling, the ones with hyacinths and calla lilies," Adeline pointed out to her sister. "And then we could finish sewing the new dresses we want to wear to church tomorrow."

"What a wonderful-*gut* plan!" Jo remarked. "You've got better ways to spend your afternoon than hanging around here. Is Leah's birthday coming up?"

Adeline glanced at her sister, shrugging. "Nope. But she's so busy with little Betsy and Adah—not to mention Stevie and all her livestock—that she'll never get around to putting a planter on the porch. And she's been awfully *gut* about letting us work here on Saturdays."

As Jo jotted down another customer's order for Easter morning coffee cakes and cookies, she was pleased to hear that the redheaded Shetler twins wanted to give their step*mamm* a gift. Not so long ago they'd been getting into one questionable situation after another, running around with English fellows who were nothing but trouble. What a blessing it was that Jude and Leah's teenage daughters—the bishop's nieces—were maturing into much more reliable young women these days.

After her helpers had gone, Jo headed for the coffee stand in the commons area with a plastic dish bin. Husbands often sat at the small tables chatting while their wives shopped, and selling cookies and brownies to them was a big boost to Fussner Bakery's income each week. It wasn't unusual for Amish men from Morning Star to sit and visit in this area, either—but when Jo spotted a trio of familiar beards and hats, it gave her pause.

Why would Deacon Saul, Preacher Clarence, and Preacher Ammon be here, all of them together? And where is Bishop Jeremiah?

Jo reminded herself not to let her vivid imagination run away with her. She didn't think any of the church leaders had spotted her, but rather than avoiding them, she began busing dirty dishes at the far end of the commons. Wiping the tabletops as she went, Jo worked her way toward the table where the district's leaders leaned in toward one another, speaking in low, insistent voices.

". . . better state our case while . . ."

". . . young women should know better than to . . ."

". . . has to be voted on *tomorrow*, while the congregation—ah, Jo Fussner!" Preacher Ammon blurted out as she cleared a nearby table. "You're not in your shop! Don't the twins usually clean out here?"

How would he know that? I've never seen him or Clarence out here.

Jo's mind was whirling with other questions, but she stuck to the issue Ammon Slabaugh had mentioned rather than giving him fodder for future discussion. "I've sold out for the day, so I gave my helpers the rest of the afternoon off," she explained quickly. "Sorry. I didn't mean to disrupt your conversation."

Before Deacon Saul or Preacher Clarence could say anything, Jo picked up her bin of dirty dishes and made a beeline for her bakery. As she arranged the cups and saucers in the dishwasher, she told herself not to read anything into what she'd just stumbled on to. But the three men's body language and lowered voices had delivered a message, hadn't they?

Rather than trying to fill in the gaps of what she'd barely overheard, Jo tried not to speculate about the preachers' presence at The Marketplace. The church district shared the shopping center's profits, after all—and maybe, as with her mother, the men had finally come to see the place for themselves.

Jah, right. And I'm engaged to an English millionaire.

It was possible that Michael, Nelson, and Glenn had chatted with Saul and the preachers—and maybe Bishop Jeremiah had joined in, because he often spent time with the Wengerds and Glenn when he came to The Marketplace. When Jo stepped out of her shop to visit Michael, however, she saw that Saul, Ammon, and Clarence were still deep in their conversation.

It seemed best to stay near the shops' doorways rather than passing through the commons, so Jo waved at Molly and Marietta in the noodle shop and glanced into Koenig's Krafts on her way to the quilt shop.

"Look who's here!" Martha Maude exclaimed from her seat at the quilting frame. "We're coming right along on your quilt, Jo. What do you think?"

Jo traced the looped pattern of tiny white quilting stitches with her fingertips, again amazed by all the prints and colors. "This is incredible," she whispered. "*Denki* again and again for this wonderful gift, ladies. It's too bad such a bright, colorful piece will be hidden away in the bedroom where our guests won't see it."

"Oh, I suspect plenty of folks will look your place over after you and Michael move in," Anne remarked, intently focused on her stitching. "Any idea where your home will be? I'd think your *mamm* would be eager to have you two living close by."

Jo leaned closer to study the quilt, considering her answer. Had Deacon Saul's wife and *mamm*—and everyone else—heard that her mother had balked at Michael's request? "We'll figure it out," she replied vaguely. "Sometimes when folks don't give you an immediate answer, they have something even better up their sleeve, ain't so?"

After chatting for a few more moments, Jo made her way to the stores at the end of the row. Glenn's wood shop had a handful of customers inside, browsing his shelves of wooden toys and admiring his unique birch lawn chairs. Jo's whole being brightened when Michael stepped out of the nursery store.

"You've only got two planters left," she remarked, gesturing at the floor around the shop's entry. "Having a *gut* day?"

"My day always takes a turn for the better when I see you, Josie-girl." Michael's face lit up as he approached her to speak near her ear. "But our entire future took an upturn when Aunt Nadine stopped by earlier with your *mamm*. If it's all right with you, I'll ask Pete about drawing up plans for our new home this evening—because your mother has agreed to let us build it on the land I asked her about!"

"Oh!" Jo exclaimed as her eyes widened. "*Oh!* Mamm's having her best day in a long, long time—and I believe your aunt is the reason for that."

Michael squeezed her shoulders but backed away when he remembered that they were in public. "Aunt Nadine has an undeniable talent for making folks happy," he agreed.

"And—maybe the most amazing part—we're to receive that land as our wedding gift. Which means that instead of investing a chunk of change on the property itself, we'll have more to spend on exactly the kind of house you're dreaming of, Jo. So think big!"

She longed to grab Michael in a hug—but they were within sight of the church leaders. "If Deacon Saul and his buddies weren't over there," she murmured, nodding in their direction, "I'd be shouting hallelujah and maybe even dancing between the tables. But all that jubilation can wait," she added excitedly. "Michael, this is the best news ever!"

His gaze lingered briefly on the men in the broad-brimmed hats. "*Jah*, those fellows have been here for a while," he said quietly. "When they chatted with Dat earlier, they mentioned that Margaret's cousin in Carrollton passed away unexpectedly, so Bishop Jeremiah's staying over for the weekend to conduct her funeral service. Maybe they're figuring out the scripture for tomorrow and who's going to preach on it."

Jo kept her previous suspicions to herself. Why dampen Michael's exciting news by speculating about the furtive way the two preachers and Deacon Saul were leaning so close over the small table that their black hats nearly touched? She couldn't change anything those men were planning anyway.

"Well, then!" she said brightly. "If you want to bend Pete's ear about a house, I should offer to provide supper tonight for him and Molly, ain't so? It seems the least we can—"

"Right after you and I thank your mother for giving us that land," Michael put in as he held her gaze.

Jo nodded. "*Jah*, you're right about that. We'd better thank her profusely for her offer—before she changes her mind!"

Michael laughed, making the love light dance in his beautiful gray-blue eyes. "Dat and I thought we'd drive over to your place after we close the shop, and then after you and I say our thanks, we can visit Molly and Pete. But you should check with Molly about that, *jah*? Maybe they won't want our company two nights in a row."

As Jo laughed along with her fiancé, she was floating. Less than a month ago she'd been wishing her love for Michael Wengerd would bloom into something permanent, and now they were engaged, they'd set their wedding date, and they were planning the new home they would share for years to come.

After she'd spoken to Nelson, Jo went to the noodle shop to talk to Molly—and she saw Saul and the preachers heading out the front doors.

Help me not to dwell on circumstances and sketchy information, Lord, because You have this situation in hand. Instead, let me focus forward on the wonderful life You've granted me with Michael. Let me be grateful for the many gifts his family—and You—have brought into my life lately. What a blessed woman I am!

Chapter 18

Nelson waved at Michael and Jo as the courting buggy started down the Fussners' lane Saturday evening, heading to the Shetler place. Their love took him back to when he was a young man starting out with Verna, and he thrummed with excitement for them. The parcel of land Drusilla had given them was an ideal spot to erect greenhouses and open a nursery store—and he'd assured his son that those buildings and some startup inventory would be his wedding present to them.

Michael and his bride were set up for a solid, promising future. As Nelson returned to the Fussners' front porch, where Drusilla sat in a well-worn wicker chair, he wondered what his own future would look like. Because Nadine had spent most of the day with her new Morning Star friend, she'd remained at the Shetlers' *dawdi haus* to give Nelson some time alone with Drusilla.

The next few hours could make or break his chances at a fresh start. He might determine whether he'd be living in Michael and Jo's new *dawdi haus* or taking up residence as Drusilla's husband—or deciding that he'd be better off remaining in Queen City. Nelson tried not to let his future loom over the present moment as he sat down in Drusilla's other wicker chair.

"Awfully nice of you to bring us that planter of tulips and hyacinths." Drusilla's tentative smile suggested that she, too, realized the evening might have a far-reaching effect on their relationship. "Those springtime colors really perk up the front room. That picture window's the best place to keep those flowers, *jah*?"

Nelson nodded. "Forced bulbs do best indoors, and when the blooms die back, you can keep the bulbs to plant outside in the fall.

"I'm glad you like them, Drusilla," he added as he gazed at her. "Next to Christmas, when our greenhouses are filled with poinsettias, the Easter season is my favorite time at the nursery. We grow a lot of lilies for churches—but I thought you'd rather have something more colorful."

"*Colorful.* The perfect description of your sister," she remarked. "Every time I see Nadine, she's dressed in a color I wouldn't *dream* of wearing. Yet on her, it looks perfect."

It never hurt to express a sincere sentiment, but Nelson warned himself not to sound falsely complimentary. "I suspect you'd look very pretty in dresses the colors of those pink and purple tulips we brought you," he ventured. "Matter of fact, if you were to make a dress that shade of pink and sew me a shirt from the same fabric, I'd wear it!"

When Drusilla's eyes widened in disbelief, Nelson chided himself. What had possessed him to make such a claim? Nadine had offered to make him shirts from her flashy fabrics, but he'd always declined in favor of more conservative, masculine colors.

"If I went to the effort to make you a shirt, Nelson Wengerd, you better believe you'd wear it!" she shot back.

His jaw dropped—and suddenly they were laughing together. It felt like such a lighthearted, fortuitous moment that Nelson pushed his dare a little further. If the thought of him wearing a pink shirt brought such a sparkle to Drusilla's eyes, why not go for it?

"All right, then, when we come back next weekend, I'll bring you some fabric and a shirt pattern in my size," he offered. "This implies that we'll be seen together in our matching clothes, *jah*? Or what's the use of sewing me a pink shirt?"

Drusilla's eyes narrowed playfully. "All right, you're on," she said softly. "*Gut*ness knows I could use a new dress, and you've just given me a reason to make one."

Nadine, I owe you big-time for the way Drusilla is remembering how to laugh and smile. And Lord, I hope You won't let me step in it, because there's still a chance I'll put my foot in my mouth.

Nelson relaxed. The Drusilla he saw this evening took him back to when he'd first met her, not quite a year ago, when he and Michael had taken shop space at the new Marketplace. She'd been pleasant and gracious about renting her *dawdi haus*, and eventually she'd invited them to share suppers in her kitchen when they arrived on Friday evenings.

Could he and Drusilla recapture that easy, no-pressure friendship? Could they discover that they were compatible enough to make a fulfilling second marriage?

"Do I recall that Connor Yorke was to harvest your

trees this past Thursday?" he asked. It seemed like a safe topic of conversation—something to keep her talking to him.

"He did. Took him two full days and a lot of heavy equipment."

"Would you mind if I walked over to see how that tract of land looks now?" Nelson asked gently. "Would you come with me, dear?"

Drusilla's wide eyes made her look like a timid young girl, but after a moment she stood up. "Truth be told, I haven't been over there yet. I—I watched from the loft of the barn for a while, where I'd be out of the way of all that machinery," she admitted.

"They make a lot of noise felling those trees," he remarked as he started down the stairs. When he got to the yard, with Drusilla a few steps behind him, his heart went into his throat. He reached out his hand, praying she'd take it.

She blinked. Kept her hands to herself as she walked briskly past him. "If we cut across the pasture behind the barn, it'll put us there faster than if we walk out to the road."

Swallowing a sigh, Nelson followed Drusilla, telling himself she was shy—that he'd surely have other chances to hold her hand. It wasn't the first time a lady he fancied had made him wait, after all. He'd offered to drive Verna home from singings a dozen times before she'd accepted.

Rather than fall into stride beside her, Nelson took the opportunity to lag behind—to watch her walk. From this angle he could follow the curve of her hip to where her gray cape and apron defined a waist that had remained remarkably slender over the years. Drusilla's dress fell to midcalf, showing off shapely legs in black stockings above her no-nonsense black rubber-soled shoes. She'd be an attractive woman if she wore something besides faded old dresses in dull, dark colors—but he knew better than to say that.

As they approached the creek, he also knew better than to get caught looking her over. "I imagine the skyline you saw from the barn loft had changed a lot by the time the crew left yesterday," he remarked as he caught up to her. "But you still have plenty of other trees along the creek— and it looks like Yorke preserved some of your wild-flowers, as well."

"But it'll be a long while before the grass grows back where he dragged out all those trees," she remarked, pointing to the bare dirt trail that led to the road. As though she'd caught herself complaining again, Drusilla let out a slow sigh. "I suppose that's a small price to pay, considering that his check will exceed his original esti-mate. *Denki* for suggesting that Mr. Yorke pay us a visit, Nelson. You did me quite a favor."

When she held his gaze a few moments longer than normal, Nelson's pulse thrummed more intently. "You're welcome, Drusilla."

When she looked at the creek, which whispered as it meandered over a small outcropping of rock, a few awk-ward moments of silence made Nelson feel like a clueless schoolkid. The sun was behind them, sinking lower behind the barn. As the hush of dusk approached and the shadows of the trees deepened, Nelson sensed this wasn't the time to offer her his hand again. So he nodded toward the east.

"What if we cut across this field to look at the land

you're giving the kids?" he suggested. "I've driven past it, but I haven't walked around it or seen much beyond the cleared area near the road."

Drusilla fell into step beside him. "I haven't been out this way since I don't when," she admitted. "Joe always handled the farming details such as reseeding pastures for his Belgians and planting the alfalfa and so on. This was his parents' place."

Nelson thought twice before he responded. It wasn't so much *what* Drusilla had said as the way she'd expressed it that hinted she'd never been emotionally invested in this farm . . . as though she hadn't felt truly at home here.

As they kept walking, he sized up the parcel of land, trying to locate the best places to build greenhouses. Some of the soil contained a lot of clay and rock; those areas were well suited for the buildings he and Michael would construct, while other areas would be ideal for plots where young nursery stock could be planted.

As they came within sight of the road, Nelson spotted a familiar open buggy pulled by a dark mare and followed by another buggy. His heart beat proudly as he watched his son swing Jo to the ground while Pete and Molly clambered out of the rig behind them.

Intuitively he stopped, blocking Drusilla's progress with his arm. "Shall we leave the kids to decide where their new house will sit?" he asked softly. "It's an exciting time for them. I recall lying awake nights, seeing layout sketches and construction details in my mind once Verna and I could finally afford to build our house in Queen City. It was a big dream come true, moving out of my parents' upstairs and into our own place."

Drusilla remained quiet for a long time, watching the silhouettes of their children in the deepening dusk. "For me, nothing changed much," she murmured with a shrug. "When Joe's folks passed on, the place remained the same as it had been for generations."

Disappointment and regret tinted her words, although her tone of voice remained calm. Resigned. Nelson recalled Drusilla's earlier claims that her husband had lured her into marriage mostly to suit himself, and that he'd betrayed her young trust in him. Had Big Joe Fussner truly misrepresented his intentions—changed into a domineering husband after leading his younger bride on with pie-in-the-sky promises?

Or had Drusilla's unhappiness been her *perception* of their marriage? Nelson had experienced her tendency toward a negative mindset firsthand, after all.

It's something to keep in mind if I take our relationship any further.

When she shivered slightly, Nelson realized that the temperature was dropping with the setting of the sun—and they hadn't eaten supper. "Shall we head back to the house?" he suggested. "I'd be happy to spring for a meal in town, if you're interested."

Drusilla's eyes widened as she turned to walk alongside him again. "But I'm a mess—not dressed for—"

"You look absolutely fine, dear," he hastened to assure her. "When you were at The Marketplace today I thought you stood out from the crowd because you were having such a *gut* time. They say a smile's the finest thing any of us can put on. I'll wear mine if you'll wear yours."

She let out a short laugh, cautiously picking her way over some broken branches as they neared the creek. "As we walked around those shops, I was reflecting Nadine's radiance—"

"So if I look just like her, maybe that happiness can carry over, *jah*? Maybe you can practice up for when I'm wearing that pink shirt," he added with a chuckle.

Drusilla stopped short, planting her fist on her hip. "Nelson Wengerd, are you flirting with me?"

"Are you finally noticing?" he shot back.

She stood stock-still, assessing him in the gathering shadows of the trees. It was unnerving, the way Drusilla studied him for several moments, but he didn't drop his gaze. If she was willing to look into his eyes for such a long time, maybe she was seeing him for who he truly was . . . shifting her longtime opinion about men who behaved differently after they'd gotten what they wanted.

"All right, then, let's have supper—but feeding you seems the least I can do, after all the painting and fixing up you've done around the place," she said. "It'll just be bacon and eggs—"

"I love bacon and eggs. Truth be told, I've had my fill of pizza lately."

As a smile eased over Drusilla's face, her sigh resonated more with contentment than dissatisfaction. And wasn't that a big step forward?

"You're a *gut* man, Nelson. Patient and kind."

As they started back to the house, his whole being shimmered with hope. It was wonderful indeed that she was describing him in the terms the apostle Paul had equated with *love*.

When she reached for his hand, Nelson felt ten feet tall.

Chapter 19

Jo sensed the tension in the Hartzlers' front room was ramping up as she and her friends filed into their row for the Sunday morning service. News of Bishop Jeremiah's absence had circulated quickly among the women as they'd carried their food for the common meal into Martha Maude's and Anne's kitchen earlier—not that folks seemed to feel anything was amiss. It was normal procedure for the preachers and the deacon to conduct worship in the bishop's absence, so most ladies were expressing their concern over Margaret losing her cousin sooner than she'd expected to.

Jo, however, couldn't forget the furtive air that had cloaked the table where Deacon Saul, Preacher Ammon, and Preacher Clarence had huddled on Saturday. Their black hats had almost touched, hiding their guarded expressions—which had only confirmed her uneasiness.

"Is it me, or do the Hartzlers have their furnace cranked up?" Marietta murmured. After she'd led her four friends into their usual row, she handed her new stepson, baby Levi, to her sister so she could remove her shawl.

Jo's lips curved. Marietta, still extremely thin from last

winter's chemo, was usually pulling her wrap more closely around her shoulders rather than taking it off.

Molly wore a grave expression, as well, as she bounced her little nephew on her knee. "Hang on to your *kapps*, girls," she whispered. "When the cat's away, the mice will play. Let's hope they play *nice*."

As Jo took her seat between Molly and Lydianne, she leaned close to the bishop's fiancée. "What have you heard from Jeremiah? Any clue about his bishops' meeting or our service this morning?"

The blond schoolteacher shook her head. "The last phone message I got was on Friday, saying he'd be staying in Carrollton for the funeral he was to conduct yesterday," she murmured. "I think he'll be back tomorrow."

When everyone was seated, Gabe Flaud sang out the first phrase of the opening hymn from the men's side. His wife, Regina, seated at Lydianne's right, was focused on her *Ausbund* as she joined in the hymn. Rather than radiating her usual cheerfulness, her freckled face looked pale and drawn.

Was Regina dealing with morning sickness? Or did she, too, worry that the day might bring difficult decisions for the five friends who'd worked so hard to make The Marketplace a thriving enterprise?

Near the end of the second hymn, Saul and the two preachers emerged from the deacon's office, where they'd been deciding who would preach the morning's sermons. Was it her imagination, or were the three leaders sharing a smug secret as they removed their black, broad-brimmed hats in one accord to signal the beginning of worship? Jo tried not to overthink their motives as Preacher Ammon opened the service by reading one of the prayers from his service book.

When Deacon Saul stood up with the Bible, however, his gaze lingered on Jo and her four friends before he opened the large book to one of his markers. "Our first Scripture reading today is from Paul's letter to the Ephesians, chapter five, verses twenty-two through twenty-four. Hear the word of the Lord," he began in his commanding voice. "'Wives submit yourselves unto your own husbands, as unto the Lord. For the husband is the head of the wife, even as Christ is the head of the church: and he is the saviour of the body. Therefore as the church is subject unto Christ, so let the wives be to their own husbands in every thing.'"

Jo sat up straighter, willing herself not to return Molly's elbow nudge and call attention to their fidgeting. The passage about wives submitting to their husbands was a common Scripture for wedding ceremonies, so the congregation had heard it dozens of times. More troublesome than Paul's words was the way Saul's lips curved tightly as he flipped backward to his next selection.

"Our second reading comes from First Corinthians, chapter fourteen, verses thirty-four and thirty-five—further wisdom from the apostle Paul," he added before clearing his throat ceremoniously. "'Let your women keep silence in the churches: for it is not permitted unto them to speak: but they are commanded to be under obedience, as also saith the law. And if they will learn any thing, let them ask their husbands at home: for it is a shame for women to speak in the church.'

"A reading from the Holy Scriptures," Deacon Saul

declared as he closed the Bible. "Let us write these eternal truths on all our hearts."

Jo wasn't surprised to hear the rustle of aprons against dresses as several of the women shifted, glancing at one another with questioning expressions. When she caught sight of Martha Maude's raised eyebrows, Jo sensed she might deliver her own private sermon to her deacon son after everyone went home. Even Cora Miller and Delores Flaud had stiffened at the second passage—and Jo's mother was frowning, as well.

Along the row where Jo sat among her friends, five bodies had tightened, bracing for the shorter of the morning's two sermons. Preacher Ammon stood up, taking his place a few steps in front of the preachers' bench as he glanced at the men at his left and the women seated to his right.

"This Sunday we'd planned on Bishop Jeremiah's summary of the bishops' retreat," he began. "Quite often he discusses how other bishops are reining in their congregations' tendencies toward more liberal, worldly behavior, so it seems reasonable to prepare ourselves for such restraints—especially because we'll be observing the most solemn day of our religious year, Good Friday, before we meet again for a regular church service on Easter Sunday.

"More specifically," the preacher continued sternly, "in light of the fact that all of the original *maidel* founders will be married by midsummer, we feel the need for a major change of The Marketplace's administration."

Lord, please keep me in my seat with my mouth shut during this sermon. Help me to make an appropriate plea for reconsideration when we have a Members' Meeting following the service.

Jo's friends sucked in their breath, as though they, too, were fighting the urge to blurt out their protests during Preacher Ammon's sermon. Across the room, Pete and Glenn also appeared upset at the direction the service was taking—and when she caught Michael's eye, Jo read his undeniable support for her rather than agreement with what seemed to be the theme for the day.

Her conflicting thoughts were whirling so fast that it was several minutes before Jo focused again on what Preacher Ammon was saying. Who did these church leaders think should take over management of The Marketplace? Would she and the twins have no say about how business was to continue in her bakery and their noodle shop? Were the preachers and Deacon Saul proposing that a *man* run their stores on Saturday while she and Molly and Marietta only provided the products to be sold there?

Or are these men saying I'll have to quit baking once I marry Michael? If that's the case, my store won't need a new manager because it will cease to exist!

Little Levi let out a squawk, bringing Jo out of her woolgathering. As his cries escalated and Marietta tried in vain to settle him, Jo wondered if the little boy was reacting to his *mamm*'s tension—or maybe she'd squeezed him harder than she'd realized.

Jo focused on the sermon again, trying to connect Preacher Ammon's closing remarks about women's behavior in biblical times with his original statement about changing The Marketplace's administration. As often happened, he'd wandered from the path he'd started upon during the twenty minutes he preached, so when he finally sat down, Jo and her friends shook their heads in confusion. Marietta carried her crying baby back to the kitchen, although everyone could still hear the ruckus Levi was raising.

The next several minutes were spent in a silent kneeling prayer, but Jo felt too keyed up to communicate with God. Surely the Lord was aware of what was being proposed in this worship service. Surely He would guide the church leaders—and the men on the other side of the room who would be affected, as well—to speak up and settle this matter immediately after the worship service.

But they had a wait ahead of them. When Preacher Clarence rose to deliver the second, longer sermon, Jo sighed. She missed the way Bishop Jeremiah presented his point coherently and then stopped talking.

Her thoughts wandered as far afield as Clarence Miller's did: first he seemed to be exhorting the men in the congregation to take a firmer hold on the reins at home—to pay closer attention to their families' finances, and to reestablish themselves as the irrefutable heads of their households.

Jo tuned out the preacher's reedy voice as she focused on each man's face across the Hartzlers' large front room. A few of the older, more conservative fellows sat with their arms crossed, nodding at Clarence's suggestions.

Michael and his *dat*, however, appeared deeply concerned. Glenn Detweiler and Pete Shetler, the most recent members to be baptized into the Old Order—not to mention being the husbands of two very successful shop proprietors—shifted uneasily. Even Gabe Flaud, whose wife, Regina, was already following the stay-at-home rule, seemed uncomfortable with the direction the service was taking.

"In closing," Preacher Clarence said, marking the beginning of the end of his ramble, "let me repeat the decision that Deacon Saul, Preacher Ammon, and I have made. The Bible clearly states that wives will submit to their husbands and stay at home. Therefore, in order to be in more perfect alignment with our faith and our God— and because The Marketplace is on church property—we *must* reorganize its management. We commend the Flaud family and Regina for leading the way by their example."

Regina stood up suddenly and rushed from the room, her hand over her mouth. Jo, Molly, and Lydianne glanced back at her retreating figure and instinctively scooted together on the pew bench.

When Preacher Clarence introduced the final hymn as though he'd said nothing controversial, Jo's field of vision became a red blur. Her heart was pounding so fast that the hymn's rhythm felt offbeat, plodding, and impossibly slow as she thought about all the ways she intended to object—to table this discussion until Bishop Jeremiah returned. She planned her phrasing carefully, hoping she wouldn't arouse the preachers' stubbornness—and maybe condemn herself to a kneeling confession for saying what she truly thought during the Members' Meeting that would follow the service.

But after the hymn, Preacher Ammon pronounced the benediction and then said, "All right, folks, let's set up the tables and enjoy the fellowship of our common meal."

"Nobody's touching those tables until we hold a Members' Meeting!" Martha Maude declared. "You preachers— and *you*, Saul—know full well that the changes you're proposing can't be carried out without some *discussion* and input from the members. And without the bishop being present."

"And besides that, you got it wrong, Preacher Clarence," Saul's wife, Anne, chimed in stridently. "The passage Saul read said wives are to submit to their husbands— but nothing is mentioned in the Bible about them having to stay home! We all know of wives in other Amish communities who work in their families' shops, after all."

"I fully agree with the need for a Members' Meeting," Gabe put in from his pew in the middle of the men's side. "These radical changes you're proposing affect *all* of us who own Marketplace shops, not just the women who originally organized this enterprise. With all due respect to you preachers and our deacon, you've had no involvement with our businesses. You have no idea how drastically your new rule will change the dynamic there."

"Amen to that," Nelson put in firmly. "At least three of our stores might close if the women who run them are told to stay home—especially if you don't allow them some time to train new managers. It's highly irregular— and unfair—for you three men to decide the fate of The Marketplace without consulting our shopkeepers first."

Deacon Saul's eyebrow rose. "Why do you think you have a say in this, Nelson?" he asked in a coiled voice. "You're not a member of this congregation, after all."

A stunned silence rang in the room. Jo swallowed hard, glancing desperately at Molly and Lydianne. Their pale faces told her that they, too, knew better than to speak out and invite serious repercussions from the church leaders.

"You might as well call a meeting, because—as you can see—we're holding one anyway," Martha Maude stated in a huff. "Quite frankly, the cash cow our church has milked for the past several months will dry up in a hurry if we shop owners allow you church leaders to take over. And I for one refuse to go along with *any* of this until Bishop Jeremiah's here."

"*Jah*, and don't think for a minute that we women will stay quiet in church about this, Saul, just because of that passage you read," Rose Wagler put in vehemently. "Our congregation has never shushed the women's opinions before, so why would we tolerate it now?"

Jo's head was spinning from the other shopkeepers' rapid-fire remarks. She was relieved that the Hartzler women, Gabe Flaud, Nelson, and Rose had spoken before she blurted out something that might jeopardize their chances for a discussion. The church leaders, however, appeared unmoved by the speakers' reasoning.

As though they'd planned a strategy beforehand, Deacon Saul and Preacher Ammon rose to stand on either side of Preacher Clarence, forming a line that suggested a solid, unified barrier no one was going to cross. As the man who oversaw the church's finances—and as the proprietor of the local carriage factory, Morning Star's most lucrative Amish business—Saul Hartzler was the most influential member of the church. He looked out over the gathering with the air of a man who would brook no argument.

"Let us not forget that along with Bishop Jeremiah, Ammon, Clarence, and I were ordained by this congregation after being chosen by the falling of God's lot," he stated in a voice that filled the room. "We have prayed earnestly on this matter, seeking the Lord's wisdom and direction. If we leaders believe our faith is best served by having our wives remain at home, it's because God has inspired our common thought. Our decision stands."

The bottom dropped out of Jo's stomach. Her temples throbbed, and her desperate thoughts were spurred on by poor little Levi's wails at the back of the room. Not quite a year ago, it had been *her* idea to transform a dilapidated old stable into what had become Morning Star's premium venue for Plain crafts. She'd poured hours and days and weeks of her life into organizing The Marketplace, as well as into stocking and managing her own wonderfully successful bakery there.

Jo's hopes and dreams were on the line. Everything she'd worked so hard for was about to fly out the window. Within the course of a morning's church service, her income stream and her entire life were about to flatten as though Saul and the preachers had dropped a huge boulder on her from an upstairs window.

All Saul cares about is counting the money! He doesn't know a thing about maintaining The Marketplace or scheduling local events there or—or anything about what our customers have come to love and expect from us, either. Poor Mr. Remington will be devastated.

Something inside Jo snapped. The vision of Elliott Remington's forlorn face when she told him she could no longer bake compelled her to rise from the bench without even thinking about it—because *someone* had to stand up for the five young women who'd made The Marketplace such a boon to Morning Star's economy.

"I'm still single, and *I* will continue to manage The Marketplace!" she cried out. "The Shetler twins and the Miller girls and the Flaud sisters can help me!"

Chapter 20

Michael's heart stopped.

As his pulse pounded in his ears, drowning out all rational thought, he was vaguely aware of Preacher Clarence forbidding his young daughters to work where they'd spend so much time among English customers. Martin Flaud put in that his daughters would be interviewing to fill the teaching position Lydianne would vacate when she married the bishop in May, so they wouldn't help run the shops, either.

But all he *really* heard was Jo, declaring in front of God and everybody that she would rather manage The Marketplace than marry him.

I'm still single, and I *will continue to manage The Marketplace!*

There could only be one possible way to interpret her impassioned remark. The fire in her dark eyes and her strident voice had left nothing to his imagination.

Without a word to the men who were murmuring around him, Michael quickly slipped to the end of the pew bench and out the Hartzlers' back door. He suspected the uncalled meeting would continue for a while, but what did it matter?

The woman who'd claimed his heart and soul had suddenly cast him from her life without a word of warning.

He stumbled past the line of parked buggies in the lane, his vision blurring with tears. He didn't want to leave Dat and Aunt Nadine without a rig, so when Michael reached the road, he broke into a run.

By the time he'd reached the Fussner farm, all he could think to do was hitch Starla to his courting buggy and drive off.

Chapter 21

Before her words had even died away, Jo was kicking herself. She'd just blurted out the worst possible sentiment. She'd just made the most horrible snap decision *ever*. Oh, she'd said what needed saying, but the wounded expression on Michael's face as he left the room told her she'd gone about it in the worst possible way.

Suddenly mortified—not even sure exactly what she'd said—Jo sat down. Instinct told her she should be racing out the door to apologize to Michael, but her legs felt too shaky to make the trip.

"You tried your best," Molly murmured, slipping her arm around Jo's shoulders. "But we never stood a chance."

"Jeremiah's going to be *livid*," Lydianne whispered as she linked her elbow around Jo's. "How do Saul and the preachers think they can ramrod this decision without consulting the bishop? And without the congregation's vote?"

"*Jah*, we've not heard the end of this," Molly muttered. "But we were in for some changes anyway. This pot's been on the back burner for a while, and now it's boiled over."

The older women in front of them rose from the benches, mumbling among themselves, but Jo was too numb to pick up on what they were saying. If only she hadn't gotten so carried away—if only she'd reminded herself that because she and Michael were engaged, he had a stake in everything she did and said. The last thing she wanted was to stay for the common meal and answer questions about what she'd do now that her fiancé had walked out on her—or listen to folks cluck over her stupidity.

"I'd better check on Regina," Lydianne said as she stood up. "Poor thing, her system's really upset and this contentious talk didn't help."

"*Jah*, I'm thinking Marietta could use a break from that crying baby, too," Molly remarked, gazing at her twin near the kitchen door.

"Wait, can I ask you all something?" Jo swallowed hard. If she posed her question, she'd better be prepared for her friends' straightforward answers. "Um, what exactly did I *say*? In the heat of the moment, I got so upset that the words just rushed out. And now I've humiliated Michael—"

Lydianne and Molly shrugged, appearing puzzled. "You reminded the preachers that you're still single—" Molly began.

"So you'll keep running The Marketplace," the bishop's fiancée continued. "You said nothing out of turn, Jo, because you're *not* married yet—"

"And you'll buy the rest of us some time until we can

figure out how to keep our shops afloat," Molly finished. "It won't be easy for Marietta and me to hire help or adjust our noodle factory production, but we'll feel a whole lot better if *you're* holding the purse strings, instead of Saul."

You said nothing out of turn . . . you'll buy us some time.

Jo let out the breath she'd been holding. None of her friends seemed aghast at what she'd blurted out—but they'd obviously heard her words from a different perspective than Michael had.

"Then again," Lydianne continued, "by the time we've hashed this out with Jeremiah and the other church members, the management of The Marketplace might look totally different. We probably should've planned for this issue when we first got organized."

Molly let out a humorless chuckle. "*Jah*, but we *maidels* were too excited about trying something *new*. And besides, when Martha Maude and Anne signed on to run their quilt shop, who knew that Saul would object to his wife working at *this* late date?"

Although Jo agreed with what her friends were saying, their remarks didn't address the heart of the matter: she'd betrayed Michael.

The other women were making their way toward the kitchen to set out food and prepare a meal she had no appetite for—but her mother broke away from the crowd to speak with her. As Mamm sidled between the two nearest benches, her brow furrowed, Jo braced herself for some negative criticism.

"Let's go," Mamm said in a whisper. "I see no point in listening to all this hubbub that Saul and his buddies have churned up. If people ask," she added, gazing at Lydianne and Molly, "you can say Jo took me home because I'm catching a flu bug or something. *Please*?"

Lydianne smiled. "We can do that."

"I'd leave, too, but our deacon and the preachers would think we shopkeepers can't handle their heat," Molly put in. "Folks who don't know much about our joint enterprise might have questions, and I want them to get answers from *us* rather than our church leaders."

"*Gut* point." Jo noticed that the men were setting up tables and most of the other women had entered the kitchen. She put her arm around Mamm's shoulders, as though she was helping her along. "Let's go down the hall and out the side door."

"Before Nadine realizes I'm leaving," her mother remarked as they headed in that direction. "I don't feel like answering to her—or to Nelson—right now."

When they stepped outside, Jo wasn't surprised that Michael was nowhere to be seen. She'd dealt his heart a heavy blow, after all, and she'd stayed at the meeting rather than following him. Was there a way to convince her fiancé that her remarks about running The Marketplace had nothing to do with her love for him?

I hurt him pretty bad. I've never seen him look so upset—not even back in December, when Mamm told him and his dat *they weren't welcome at our house anymore.*

As she hitched Nellie to their rig, Mamm clambered inside it. Her mother kept glancing toward the Hartzler house, as if fearing that the other two Wengerds might come looking for her. Considering the smile she'd seen on her *mamm*'s face when she'd returned home last night,

Jo was guessing Nelson had finally convinced Mamm that she could be happy with him.

Jo sighed as she stepped up into the rig. She and Michael had shared so many wonderful ideas about their new house as they'd walked around their lot with the Shetlers, dreaming out loud about their fine future.

Had she lost her chance to live in that new home? What if Michael feared he would always remain a lower priority than her bakery—even if she complied with the rule about wives staying at home?

What if he doesn't want to marry me anymore? It'll be a bitter pill to swallow if I can keep managing The Marketplace because I'm going to remain a maidel *forever.*

During the drive home, Jo's thoughts spiraled lower and lower. She was glad Mamm wasn't in a talkative mood, even though the silence gave her more chances to torture herself with mental images of a very lonely future. When they got home, it struck her immediately that Starla wasn't whickering a welcome as Jo opened the stable door.

The courting buggy was gone. Michael had already been here to whisk it away.

As she stared at the vacant stall, Mamm's earlier words rushed back to torment her. *I'm telling you, Josephine, if you allow that boy to park his buggy in our stable, you'll be planting the hook for heartache.*

In the two and a half weeks since she'd encouraged him to park his beautiful new rig at their place, Jo had become so accustomed to the sight of it—and so attached to Starla—that those parts of Michael already felt like integral pieces of her life. Their absence stabbed at her, bringing tears to her eyes.

Pressing her lips together to prevent a crying fit, Jo drove into the stable and unhitched Nellie. She spent an extra few minutes stroking her mare's soft neck, sensing that the horse already missed having a companion—and hoping Mamm would head to the house to figure out something for their lunch.

When Jo closed the stable door, however, her mother was standing in the yard, gazing at the freshly painted house and outbuildings.

"Well, at least you've been spared the fate of marrying a man who would only smash down your hopes and dreams after the wedding," Mamm remarked with a sigh. "Michael wasn't terribly committed to you if he turned tail instead of standing up for you at church today."

Jo's eyes widened. "Mamm, I broke his heart!"

Before her mother could reply, Jo hurried to the house and went upstairs to her room. It seemed all too clear that Mamm had resumed her previous negative mindset.

Congratulations, Miss Fussner. If Michael's too wounded to take you back, you get to live with your nagging, fault-finding mother for the rest of your life.

Chapter 22

First thing Monday morning, Nelson entered the nursery office to find a phone message from Jeremiah Shetler, asking him to call back as soon as possible. As he dialed the number the bishop had left, he prepared himself for whatever the leader of Morning Star's church district might say about what had transpired in his absence. He was startled when Jeremiah picked up on the second ring.

"Nelson, *denki* for getting back to me so quickly," the bishop said. "After hearing about yesterday's service and the *conversation* afterward, I'm calling a special Members' Meeting. I'm hoping you and Michael can be here for it. Will Wednesday evening work for you?"

Nelson blinked. "I—well, *jah*, I think we can do that. I appreciate your thinking of us—"

"After what I heard from various folks when I got home yesterday, I need a rational, balanced perspective on the situation our deacon and preachers have stirred up," Jeremiah explained. "Do you have a minute now, so I can ask you a few questions?"

"Sure, I can talk—if it doesn't bother you that I'm not

a member of your congregation," he added cautiously. "Saul pointed that out loud and clear."

The bishop let out an exasperated sigh. "It seems our deacon has made a number of presumptuous statements, which is one reason I'm counting on you—as a Marketplace shopkeeper and a levelheaded businessman—to help us untangle all the wires that got crossed yesterday. I'm truly sorry if he offended you, Nelson."

He relaxed in his chair, settling in for what might be a lengthy chat. "I wasn't so much offended as I was dismayed about what'll happen to The Marketplace if Hartzler takes it upon himself to become our manager."

"You and several others," Jeremiah put in quickly. "Martha Maude and Anne have threatened to close their quilt shop. Molly and Marietta—who've doubled their noodle factory's capacity—are wondering if their investment was a big mistake. And Lydianne gave me *quite* an earful after hearing some of the local women speculate about The Marketplace closing down altogether."

Nelson's eyes widened. It had taken only a matter of hours for folks to come to such drastic conclusions. "Sounds like the gossip mill must've been churning full force," he remarked softly. "Nadine and I left for home as soon as we'd finished eating, so I missed most of that talk."

"The way I hear it, Jo also . . . took some folks by surprise."

Was the bishop commiserating—or fishing? Rather than delve into his son's emotional state, Nelson replied carefully.

"As the organizational force behind The Marketplace from the beginning, Jo spoke her mind, *jah*. We shopkeepers understood where she was coming from," he continued in a low, controlled voice. "We felt we should've been consulted about the matter of married women being banned from working in the shops before the issue was raised at church—especially while you were away."

"That pretty well sums it all up," Jeremiah agreed. "Let's set our meeting for six thirty Wednesday evening, and meanwhile let's consider some constructive alternatives to correct the damage that's been done. I sincerely hope you Wengerds won't decide that Morning Star's not the right place for you to establish a branch of your nursery and—and to put down some roots."

Nelson smiled to himself. The bishop sounded very concerned about his family's future involvement in the community. Once again, however, he preferred not to talk about Michael and Jo's situation until they could work it out privately.

"Like Molly and Marietta, Michael and I have made some extensive investments to keep up with the demand for our products at The Marketplace," he said. "I don't want to give up my shop there—but I also won't submit to Saul's takeover methods, the way Clarence and Ammon preached about wives submitting to their husbands."

"Ah, the submission issue," Bishop Jeremiah said with a chuckle. "We'll talk a lot about that on Wednesday evening, too. See you then, Nelson. Give my best to Michael and Nadine."

Chapter 23

As Jo sat down on her usual pew bench Wednesday evening, she prayed for control of her emotions. Before long, Lydianne, Regina, Molly, and Marietta took their seats around Jo, their expressions expectant. Jo sensed that her friends hadn't gotten any more sleep than she had since the preachers' decree about married women at Sunday's service. This meeting would decide their fate once and for all. Only baby Levi, who shook a stuffed bunny as he kicked in his carrier basket, seemed unconcerned about the meeting that was about to begin.

Folks were talking in low voices as they took their places for this very unusual gathering. Unlike Sunday morning, they didn't begin by singing hymns. As Preachers Ammon and Clarence assumed their places on the preachers' bench, the bravado and confidence they'd exuded during their Sunday sermons was noticeably missing.

Bishop Jeremiah arrived next, visually taking attendance as Saul made his way along the side of the room to slide onto the preachers' bench. His stiff expression suggested that he'd endured some dressing down from the bishop—and probably from his *mamm* and wife, as well.

But who knew what he might say this evening? Several of the older men shared Saul's conservative views, and they might confront Bishop Jeremiah if he followed a progressive path they didn't approve of.

Jo spotted a familiar head of salt-and-pepper hair and held her breath. Nelson sidled over to an empty spot on the men's side, met her gaze from across the room, and smiled gently before he sat down.

But Michael wasn't with him.

Her heart constricted. Was Michael avoiding her? How could she apologize? Dozens of times over the past few days she'd longed to call Michael on the phone, but she hadn't wanted to bare her soul in a phone message, which Nelson—or any Wengerd Nursery employee—might listen to before Michael could hear it. She hadn't sent him an apology in the mail, either, because when the bishop had informed everyone of tonight's meeting, Jo had hoped to speak with Michael privately.

He probably figures I have nothing more to say to him—and apparently he has nothing to say to me, either. I'm not sure how long I can endure this empty silence that looms between us like an impenetrable fog.

But I guess I deserve to suffer. I brought this on myself.

As Jo let out a forlorn sigh, blinking back tears, Lydianne and Molly reached for her hands.

"It'll all work out," the blond schoolteacher whispered.

"We'll stand by you, Jo," Molly murmured. "No matter what happens tonight, we're all in this together."

"Folks, let's call this Members' Meeting to order with a prayer," Bishop Jeremiah said above the low chatter of the crowd. "Our Lord and our God, we come before You this evening to discern our congregation's way . . ."

Jo obediently bowed her head, composing herself while everyone's eyes were closed. She had to remain calm—had to conduct herself in a conscientious, faithful way if she was called upon during the meeting. Her red-rimmed eyes spoke for themselves; she asked God to bolster her soul with courage and His grace.

God's help was the only hope she had. Mamm, who'd returned to her cranky ways and condemnation of Michael's courtship, wasn't giving Jo any support. Even if the members decided she could keep working in her bakery after she married Michael, she might've condemned herself to remain a *maidel* with her careless words on Sunday morning.

"Amen." Bishop Jeremiah paused after his prayer, scanning the crowd with an unusually tense expression. "*Denki* for coming tonight, everyone. Before we delve into the divisive issues that sprang up in my absence, I want to express my gratitude to those who left phone messages and sent cards of condolence concerning the passing of Mamm's cousin. Your love and concern mean a lot to us."

He clasped his hands behind his back, standing taller as he composed his thoughts. "It's this same love and concern that should be foremost in our hearts and minds as we talk through what happened here on Sunday morning," Jeremiah continued. "Suffice it to say that I have met with Deacon Saul and Preachers Ammon and Clarence to express my disappointment and dismay over their behavior at Sunday's service. I have left their apologies or confessions up to them individually, in their own *gut* time, according to how God guides them."

Jo wasn't surprised that although the older women seated in front of her glanced at one another, they remained quiet. So did the men on the other side of the room.

"That said, tonight we'll not be discussing the decisions they made at church, because we need to move forward," the bishop stated. "Are we in agreement about that?"

A tight silence filled the room. The three men on the preachers' bench were studying the floorboards as though something intensely interesting was written there for them to read.

After a moment, the members of the congregation nodded. No one felt the need to challenge Bishop Jeremiah's handling of a very difficult situation.

"The issue raised—about whether married women should be allowed to work away from home—is one we need to deal with, however," the bishop said. "This topic was a hot potato at the bishops' retreat, and I suspect that many of my colleagues from neighboring districts will soon be grappling with the same decision we're facing.

"Truth be told," he continued with a hint of a smile, "The Marketplace has become so well known in this region that many of those other bishops asked me about our policy on working wives—hoping to model their decisions after ours."

Jo shared a quick smile with her close friends. Apparently they were leading the way toward a more progressive future for Amish businesswomen—even though this meant that the burden of responsibility for a faith-based policy now rested on their shoulders. It was a situation the five *maidels* hadn't foreseen on that sunny day last April when

Jo had declared that the old Clementi stable would make a wonderful place for shops. She wasn't one bit sorry for all the time and effort they'd poured into making The Marketplace the successful enterprise it was. She wouldn't change a thing—

Except for what I blurted out on Sunday—the pain it caused my dear Michael. But as the bishop has said, I must move on. I must accept whatever comes of my hasty declaration.

"The other bishops and I have noted that in today's economy, it's becoming much more difficult for Amish men to support their families by farming," Bishop Jeremiah said as his gaze again swept the crowd. "This congregation is a perfect example of that, because not a one of you fellows makes your living solely from the land anymore. You all have other income streams—and a lot of you women also sell items you make or raise at home. I live well on the income from my crops because I own more tillable acres than most of you—and because I've had no children to raise. *Yet.*"

Jo couldn't miss the tender glance the bishop shared with Lydianne as he allowed folks to process what he was saying. The love they shared in that one look served as yet another reminder of what Jo would miss if she and Michael couldn't talk things over. . . .

"We bishops also realize that it's more expensive for young men to invest in land these days, and for young couples to start out without incurring a lot of debt," Bishop Jeremiah said. "And it stands to reason that our younger folks are creating the future of the Plain faith—even as we older members realize that one of these days, our children will be supporting us," he put in as men and women nodded.

"So it behooves us to consider the possibility that married women—with the consent of their husbands—should be allowed to earn some income away from home," Bishop Jeremiah went on matter-of-factly. "And we're to approach this possibility *not* because we seek to become more affluent—for that flies in the face of the most basic tenets of the Amish faith—but to enable our families to put food on their tables and pay their bills. Shall we discuss this, folks? What are your thoughts?"

Preacher Clarence shot up off the bench behind the bishop. "The Bible tells us that the man is the head of the household!" he insisted. "It's the husband's job to bring home the bacon and the wife's job to stay home and cook it."

Jo caught Regina's sigh as several folks around them chuckled at her uncle's old joke. Clarence Miller was a hog farmer, so his choice of words—and his opinions about women—were well established.

Regina knew firsthand about being supported by the man in her family: after she'd been shunned for secretly painting wildlife scenes and selling them in her Marketplace shop, Gabe Flaud had rescued her from the Millers' very tiny guest room and her uncle Clarence's repressive ways when he'd married her last fall.

"On the flip side of that coin," Gabe said as he, too, stood up, "my Regina has willingly given up her God-given talent for painting—and she has also given up working at our Marketplace furniture shop on Saturdays. Although she never complains about making these sacrifices, I can tell she's not as happy as she was when I married her."

Gabe looked lovingly at Regina before he continued making his point. "She misses being around people, and she misses sharing the gifts God gave her—"

"Wait till that baby shows up!" Preacher Ammon teased. "She'll have more than enough to keep her busy then!"

Gabe remained standing as the good-natured chuckles died away. "But there's a difference between being busy and being *happy*," he continued. "I believe our women should have a say about what they would *like* to do—"

"You're way off the mark now, Flaud," Deacon Saul countered tersely. "And we all know you folks don't need the income from Regina's paintings. Your furniture factory's barely able to keep up with all the orders you get now that you have a shop at The Marketplace. I saw that for myself on Saturday."

Jo sighed. If this discussion became a contest between the old ways and a new future, they'd be here all evening and not come to a decision.

"Aside from what Gabe's saying about our women having more choice," Glenn Detweiler put in as he, too, rose to his feet, "we need to consider what happens to the long-established noodle business that my Marietta and her sister have continued from their *mamm*'s beginnings. What a waste of their investment in equipment—not to mention what a shame it would be if folks could no longer buy Mrs. Helfing's Noodles—if we declare they can no longer work."

"Glenn and I have talked about this a lot," Pete Shetler chimed in with a smile for Molly, "and we've agreed that as long as our wives can care for our families without wearing themselves too thin, we're *gut* with letting them make their noodles and sell them at their shop on Saturdays. We know of wives in other Amish communities who're doing that, after all. *Their* preachers seem to be all right with it."

"And if our wives have to hire outside help—or if folks who're not as personally invested in The Marketplace take over its management," Glenn put in with a purposeful glance at Saul, "the businesses we've built up there will go downhill in a hurry. It just won't be the same. And then we'll *all* lose out."

As the chatter got louder, Bishop Jeremiah raised his hand for silence. "These are all valid points we're making," he said with a nod, "and many of the other bishops I saw last week were saying similar things."

He turned to look at the men on the preachers' bench. "I find it ironic, Saul, that you've called out the Flaud family when your wife and *mamm* have been running a very successful quilting shop despite the fact that they don't need the income to keep a roof over your family's heads," he said lightly. "When they rented shop space, I recall you saying it was high time you saw some return on all that fabric you'd been paying for when they were quilting as a pastime."

"*Jah*, someone needs to mention that part," Molly murmured beneath the chuckles that filled the room.

"I'm surprised Martha Maude hasn't jumped in yet," Marietta added.

"What I'm saying is that we get nowhere by pointing fingers at others," Bishop Jeremiah continued in a louder voice. "I believe the solution lies in understanding everyone's needs—and in providing a way for The Marketplace to continue as a viable enterprise. Our church district owns the property and is a direct recipient of its profits, so it behooves us to ensure its future. After all, what will we do with that huge building if all the shops close?"

He turned to look at the women's side, focusing briefly on Martha Maude and Anne before smiling at Jo and her friends. "This wouldn't be a balanced conversation without input from you ladies who've made The Marketplace what it is," he said.

"We haven't had a chance to get a word in edgewise," Martha Maude pointed out with a short laugh. "I've said *plenty* at home, believe me. And I appreciate the way you're handling this, Bishop—giving us all a say instead of just making a decree about the way things will be."

"*Jah*, I agree with that," Regina put in. "God has blessed our district with a fair, levelheaded bishop—as well as with husbands who can look beyond their own interests. I couldn't ask for anything better than that."

After a moment, Molly spoke up. She remained seated, but her robust voice carried clearly around the room. "Glenn and Pete—and Gabe—have spoken to the main points Marietta and I would make," she remarked with a proud smile at her new husband and brother-in-law.

"And we get an enormous amount of help in the noodle factory from Glenn's *dat* and Billy Jay," Marietta pointed out. "The business is now a two-household project. But we're concerned about what happens as our families grow. As *maidels*, we had no idea The Marketplace would become such a success when we first opened it."

As though he totally agreed with his *mamm*, little Levi squawked joyfully as he tossed his bunny out of his basket.

Bishop Jeremiah was nodding as each of the shop-keepers commented. When he focused on Jo, the butter-flies in her stomach went wild. She did *not* want to repeat what she'd said on Sunday—or allude to how her words had affected her engagement to Michael—but it was only fitting that she, as the organizing force behind The Marketplace, should add something to this important conversation.

Her heart might be breaking, but she felt responsible for her friends' businesses—and she needed to direct the future of Fussner Bakery, as well, because who knew? She might be supporting herself and her mother for years to come.

"My concern—my fondest wish—is that we can find a way to maintain the relationships we've been building with loyal shoppers who return time and again," Jo said as images of Elliott Remington and other longtime customers came to mind. "They come to The Marketplace as much to watch the Hartzlers quilting at their frame, or to ask the Wengerds for advice about their gardens—or to chat with Glenn about how he makes his birch chairs—as they do to spend their money.

"Over time, these folks have become our *friends*," Jo added earnestly, "and I'd hate to let them down by allowing the warmth and—and the *welcome*—they receive in our shops to fall away if we women can't be there anymore."

"That's it exactly!" Martha Maude chimed in. "Folks shop at The Marketplace because they know the quality of our products—and they know *us*. They're not all

English, either. Lots of Plain folks come from all around the region so they can support Amish crafters when they shop for special furniture, toys, and gifts."

For a few moments the room rang with silence as church members digested a message that was about something much more personal than the exchange of money and goods. Bishop Jeremiah was nodding, composing his next remarks, when Saul cleared his throat ceremoniously.

"It's all well and *gut* for you women to tell us about the shoppers whose attention apparently justifies the many hours you devote to stocking your shops—hours of care that your families don't receive from you anymore," the deacon said in an ominous tone. "And from what I saw on Saturday, most of them *are* English. My concern, as a leader of this congregation, is that you've become so addicted to your customers' praise and generosity that you've forgotten all about the value of your souls—and the sacrifices your families must make so you can continue running your stores."

Angry heat surged up into Jo's cheeks. Deacon Saul's viewpoint supported the conservative old ways and the *Ordnung,* yet it was precisely that attitude that would destroy everything she, Regina, Lydianne, and the twins—and the Hartzler women—had done to establish The Marketplace. She was about to spring up and defend her friends once again—

But when Nelson rose from his place on the men's side, Jo kept her seat. She sucked in her breath to calm the frantic beating of her heart. Anything Michael's *dat* said would more effectively combat Saul's words, because the men would *listen* to Nelson.

"After I heard what the preachers and Saul said on

Sunday, I went home and did a lot of thinking," Nelson began. "I also called Glenn and Gabe—because this situation affects us men shop owners, too. And I think I've got a solution."

As always, Nelson sounded levelheaded and professional. Jo knew no one would dare remind him that he wasn't a member of this congregation tonight, either, because Bishop Jeremiah had personally invited the Wengerds to attend their meeting.

Hearing his calm, no-nonsense tone, folks sat at attention, glancing at one another in anticipation.

"I propose changing The Marketplace's management to a family cooperative where the wives who founded it will still have a voice in its operation," Nelson said as his gaze swept the large gathering. "And—as long as Bishop Jeremiah and their husbands agree—I'd like our women to continue running their shops on Saturdays for as long as we all agree it's not detrimental to our families. After giving it a lot of thought and prayer, I'd be willing to assume the role of this cooperative's main manager."

Jo's eyes widened as she and her four friends exchanged glances. Folks around them began nodding, murmuring among themselves, until Nelson spoke again.

"I'm saying this, Deacon Saul, because Jo and your wife and your *mamm* have it right," he insisted. "The Marketplace isn't just about our livelihoods—it's become a vital part of our lives. Your carriage factory is successful because you create a quality product, and you build the specialty parade carriages yourself—because you enjoy doing it. We shopkeepers insist on quality products, too," he added emphatically. "We love what we do, and we prefer to remain in control of how our products are sold and how our group business is managed."

"That's the ticket!" Glenn blurted out. "As a shop owner and the husband of a shop owner, I like Nelson's idea a lot."

"I agree one hundred percent," Gabe put in with a decisive nod. "We men can step up and become more involved in The Marketplace's management—and we can decide when it's time for our wives to stay home."

"This sounds like a workable solution to me," Martha Maude chimed in. "If Anne and I can't maintain the customer contact we've come to enjoy so much, we'll pull out—and if too many of us shopkeepers feel that way, Saul, you won't have any profits to count.

"And why would we as a church district want to lose the funding we've been receiving—money that has paid for our new schoolhouse and the property it sits on, as well as our teacher's salary?" she added, looking to the women around her for their support. "What do *you* say, Bishop?"

Jeremiah was a tall, muscular man whose presence filled whatever room he was in, but he was looking to the preachers' bench and the front rows of the men's and women's sides, where the older members sat, to gauge their reactions to Nelson's suggestion.

"As bishops go, I realize I lean toward the more liberal side of things," he replied. "This is an important decision we're making—a choice that will drastically alter our district's *Ordnung*. I need to hear opinions from you men and women who'll be living with this change we're proposing. Even the folks who don't run shops will be affected by the decision we make this evening, so we want everyone to speak up."

When Bishop Jeremiah focused on the two preachers, Clarence Miller's strained expression soured as though he'd bit into a lemon. "You already know how I feel about it," he muttered.

"*Jah*, no *gut*'s going to come of this," Ammon declared. "Such a choice shatters the very foundation our Old Order is founded upon. If we agree to this, our women will no longer put their families first—"

"You mean they'll no longer be waiting on you, doing your bidding," someone near the front of the women's side put in.

"*Jah*, maybe men'll have to learn to do laundry or even *cook*," another woman said. "What's the world coming to?"

Jo stifled a laugh. Who would've guessed that Preacher Ammon's *maidel* sisters, Naomi and Esther, would make such remarks in public?

"Duly noted," the bishop said, fighting a smile. "Anyone else?"

"I'll tell you what," Reuben Detweiler said from the front row on the men's side. "I'm one of the oldest dogs in the room, Preacher Ammon, but Glenn and I had to learn some new tricks when we lost our women last year. And it didn't hurt us one little bit.

"Now that we've got Marietta taking care of us, Billy Jay and I really enjoy helping at the noodle factory, too," he added, his weathered face lighting up. "We see it as doing our part to keep the family—*everyone* in the family—happy and productive. I have no problem at all with Marietta working in her Marketplace shop, because she's maintaining a family business, mostly from home, same as she's done all her life."

"And she and I have agreed that if her noodle business starts taking up too much of her time and energy," Glenn put in earnestly, "we'll either hire some help, or we'll cut back on the business. Frankly, I'm grateful for my wife's income. Even though I sell my outdoor furniture in two different towns now, sales are better in the summer than in the winter—"

"But people eat noodles all year 'round!" Reuben put in with a laugh.

"It's the same at our house," Pete Shetler agreed. "I'm just getting my remodeling business established, so noodles put food on our table in more ways than one."

Bishop Jeremiah was nodding, looking around the room for whoever might comment next. He smiled at Delores Flaud and Cora Miller.

"What do you ladies think about this?" he asked them. "The decision we make about allowing wives to work away from home will shape your teenaged daughters' futures in a way we didn't think about when our generation was their age."

Jo couldn't miss the way Cora glanced at her husband on the preachers' bench. Delores was also considering what her husband, Martin—a school board member and a very influential man in the congregation—would say if she expressed an opinion different from his. When Gabe had married Regina last fall, Martin had stated in no uncertain terms that she'd be doing her special embroidery at home and she would *not* be working at The Marketplace anymore.

"Seems to me the greater *gut* might be served best if we, as a church district, move forward with this change—

with the understanding that husbands will have the final say," Delores said after a few moments. "That way, the man remains the head of his household—"

"But wives—especially wives of the breadwinning generation—will have more input about how they spend their days," Cora added with a nod. "Maybe it's time we Amish didn't cling to such cookie-cutter expectations— that every rule of the *Ordnung* always applies to every member. Sometimes one size does *not* fit all. Districts most often lose their younger people because their elders are unwilling to make relevant changes."

A couple of rows ahead of Jo, Mamm raised her hand. "I agree with that. I'm very grateful for Jo's bakery income because our soup would be pretty thin without it," she stated. "But if we vote *jah*, we need to understand that such a major change in Amish policy affects the relationships within a family."

Jo's jaw dropped. Her mother had just said a mouthful— even though Mamm's unspoken reference to Michael's absence sent a shimmer of regret up Jo's spine. A few women turned to nod at her, their gazes supportive yet speculative. It wouldn't be long before they'd be asking her about the state of her engagement.

"These are *gut* and thoughtful points," Bishop Jeremiah summarized. "Are we ready to vote? We're not deciding on a member's shunning or readmission, so the decision doesn't have to be unanimous. Can we vote with a show of hands rather than going down each row?"

"I'm *gut* with that, as long as we have a clear majority," Martin said. "If it's a close vote, we'll have just as many unhappy folks as satisfied ones—and that'll make for trouble."

"*Jah*, we need a decisive *go* or *no go*," Matthias Wagler chimed in. His wife, Rose, sold her candles in the Hartzlers' quilt shop, and now that they had baby Suzanna as well as school-age Gracie, he was probably hoping the church's policy would better define Rose's future at The Marketplace.

"Fair enough," Bishop Jeremiah said. He turned to the three men on the preachers' bench. "I'll ask you fellows to help me tally the raised hands, please."

The bishop inhaled deeply as he looked out over the gathering. "Such a momentous decision calls for some time in silent prayer before we vote," he said in a solemn voice. "We should examine our hearts and ask God to guide us in the direction He would have us take as His people. We should consider how Jesus would react to our decision, and whether such a change will further His kingdom here on earth. He died for us, after all. The least we can do is live for Him."

Jo swallowed hard as she bowed her head. Bishop Jeremiah had just reminded them that they were first and foremost servants of God and Christ. It made her wonder if her desire to keep The Marketplace going was more for her own gratification than for any greater good her hard-earned dream was serving.

Did people really *need* to shop for Amish goods in a trendy, renovated stable? Did their Amish church and school—and the town of Morning Star—truly benefit from the time and effort she and the other shopkeepers poured into The Marketplace each week?

Or had their commercial success only made them more worldly—more self-centered, like the English who strove for everything to be bigger and fancier and *busier*? What if she and the other shopkeepers had become greedy because they'd discovered how profitable their products could be? Had the women forgotten their place in God's grand scheme of things?

Lord, I need some really fast guidance—so send me a sign! Help me discern what You'd have me do, because I believe that no matter what happens with my shop at The Marketplace, You'll be with me and You'll take care of us all. I'm grateful that You've led Nelson to volunteer as our new manager because it means he's committed to living in Morning Star . . . hopefully with Michael and Mamm and me?

Chapter 24

"Lord God, our Father, we ask Your wisdom to guide us now as we make this very important decision about the direction our community should take. Amen," Bishop Jeremiah said, bringing their silent prayer to a close.

As the bishop looked out over the gathering in his front room again, Nelson thrummed with the rightness of his offer to become The Marketplace's general manager. He would lean heavily on Jo's guidance and would discuss the details with her before he took up the reins, yet he felt that the folks in the crowd—especially Bishop Jeremiah and the preachers—saw his offer as an acceptable way for the shopkeepers to continue running their businesses. Nelson couldn't read all the faces around him as folks opened their eyes to focus on their church leaders again, but he sensed that no matter how the vote went, God would guide them to do His will.

"To summarize," the bishop recounted, "we're voting on whether married women will be allowed to work outside the home, and if so, we're leaving the final decision up to the man of each family. Is that the way we all understand it?"

Folks nodded as they glanced at their friends and family members. An atmosphere of solemn anticipation filled the Shetlers' front room. The next few minutes would determine what course the Old Order Amish of Morning Star would take for years to come.

"All in favor of this change, which allows married women to work at the discretion of their husbands, please raise your hands—but only one hand apiece, please," Jeremiah teased when Reuben thrust both of his arms high above his head.

Chuckling, those in favor of this important change slowly held up their hands. As Nelson's arm rose, he was pleased to see that most of the men were in favor—even Martin Flaud. He wasn't surprised that Ammon, Clarence, and Saul sat with their arms crossed as they tallied the vote.

Nelson was especially glad that Drusilla's hand was held high—as were all the other women's hands. Her remark about the benefits of Jo's income had apparently struck a chord with some of her more conservative friends. He'd sensed Drusilla's support for Jo was deepening, too, despite the way Michael had ducked out of Sunday's meeting.

And he couldn't help thinking how lovely she would look—like a deep pink zinnia—in a dress made from the fabric Nadine had helped him choose on their way to Morning Star. Nelson envisioned Drusilla's laughter when he gave it to her—

But he refocused his thoughts on the vote that was in progress.

He noticed that Jo's eyes were wide with wonder, and that her hand was the last one to go up—as though she'd had second thoughts about what God might want her to do.

When Nelson met her gaze, he again wished his son had come to Morning Star with him. Jo's pink-rimmed eyes and sorrowful air were clear signs that she'd suffered from her declaration that she would keep managing The Marketplace—and that she assumed her fiancé's absence meant Michael's feelings toward her had changed.

"And now let's see the *no* votes," Bishop Jeremiah said.

The deacon and the two preachers immediately raised their hands high, proud to stand firm in the old ways. Nelson believed they were expressing the opinion they believed God wanted, rather than merely objecting to change, and he respected that.

"By my count we have a clear majority in favor of this change," Bishop Jeremiah announced. He turned again to his colleagues. "Is that how you fellows see it?"

"What's *your* decision, Bishop?" Clarence shot back. "Seems only fair that we know how you feel about this issue."

Jeremiah squared his shoulders, accepting the underlying criticism that rang in Miller's remark. "I abstained so my opinion wouldn't influence anyone else's vote," he explained. "I'm in favor of allowing our married women to work away from home—but *only* because their husbands are to determine whether that's appropriate.

"So you'll know, Lydianne and I had a lengthy debate on this topic," he put in with a fond smile for his fiancée. "And we've agreed that once she becomes my wife, she'll no longer work at The Marketplace on Saturdays, as befits a bishop's wife. When Lydianne lobbied for doing the bookkeeping at home, however, I accepted her wish to remain involved in the business that she and her friends have established."

Nelson nodded, pleased to hear this. If Lydianne continued paying the bills and keeping track of shop rent and receipts, it would free him up to concentrate on other aspects of managing The Marketplace. It would also mean he would have more time to devote to establishing the new Wengerd Nursery in Morning Star . . . unless Drusilla was having second thoughts about her land offer because Michael had left on Sunday and hadn't come for this meeting.

So many things were affected when my shy, sensitive son left town without a word. We have a lot of fences to mend, Lord, and I need Your help to bring him around.

"That said," Bishop Jeremiah continued in an upbeat voice, "we as a district have decided, by a sizable majority, to implement a *major* change in our conservative Old Order ways. I ask you all to be patient and watchful as we move forward."

He shifted his weight, his expression growing more solemn. "As we all know," he continued, "the path to God's salvation can become a slippery slope when we allow ourselves more freedom. Take care, friends. We won't see the Lord's light if we become blinded by our worldly pursuits. With that, I adjourn this meeting."

Jeremiah nodded toward both sides of the room. "Let us prepare our hearts for next week, when we contemplate Christ's path to the cross and observe that most solemn of days, *Gut* Friday. I'll see you for worship on Easter morning. *Gut* evening, friends."

Nelson rose from the pew bench feeling bubbly with

the fresh opportunity the church district had just approved. The conservative congregation in Queen City would never have discussed the issue of wives working away from home—which was one of the reasons he'd decided to relocate to Morning Star. Bishop Jeremiah's leadership had breathed fresh life into Nelson's religious faith, and he felt brighter about his future than he had since he'd lost Verna.

Even though he had work to do, both in wooing Drusilla and starting up a whole new nursery operation, Nelson was filled with a heady, scintillating happiness. As he made his way outside, shaking hands with his new friends, he kept an eye on Jo so she wouldn't leave before he spoke with her. Rather than going to his buggy, he lingered on the bishop's lawn as the rest of the talkative crowd started home.

He wasn't surprised that Jo came directly toward him, as though she'd also been watching for an opportunity to talk privately.

"It's been quite a night," she remarked as they walked around to the front of the house, away from the others. "I want to thank you, Nelson, for volunteering to become The Marketplace's manager—"

"And I wouldn't dream of taking that on without asking you to advise me, dear," Nelson put in earnestly. "I hope you don't feel I swooped in and took over, without asking your opinion first."

Jo shook her head, chuckling. "If you hadn't introduced that idea—and the one about husbands having the final say—the older men would never have voted in favor of such a change," she pointed out. "I could've proposed the same concepts, but they wouldn't have listened to a woman."

Nelson nodded. When Jo sighed and got quiet, her sad brown eyes and doleful expression reminded him of a dog that had lost its best friend. He gently grasped her shoulder. "I'm sorry Michael didn't come tonight—"

"Oh, not *half* as sorry as I am," Jo interrupted earnestly. "Before the words had fully left my mouth on Sunday, I realized I'd said *exactly* the wrong thing. It's no wonder Michael thought I was betraying him. I—I was hoping for a chance to apologize to him tonight."

"But we Wengerds both appreciate the way you stood up to Saul, even if, in your enthusiasm, you wounded Michael's pride," he said softly. "I've suggested to my son that he jumped to the wrong conclusion, because you did *not* say you were breaking your engagement, Jo. Still, that's how he chose to hear it."

Jo blinked repeatedly, as though she might cry.

"As you said, you *are* still a single woman until the wedding, after all," Nelson pointed out. "And long before June, we shop owners would've banded together to reorganize anyway. We've all got too much invested to allow an uninvolved party to take over our stores' management."

When Jo looked away, Nelson gave her a moment to compose her emotions. It was apparent to him that she was sincerely sorry for the way she'd voiced her opinion on Sunday. He admired her courage—and once again, he wished Michael were here to witness Jo's abject desolation and her need to talk things out with him.

"You—you really think so?" she murmured. "You're not upset with me?"

"I think my son's lucky that such a dedicated, competent

young woman has agreed to marry him," Nelson replied firmly. "After all, had you not organized The Marketplace, we wouldn't have opened a store that's so successful we're willing to move to Morning Star. And Michael wouldn't have found the woman God intended for him to love."

He looked directly into her eyes, glad to see relief—and hope—shining there now. "You've changed our lives in a big way, Jo. I'm grateful for that—and Michael is, too," he added. "He just needs to rethink his reaction to what you said. Nadine and I are working on him."

Her broad shoulders relaxed. A smile came out to play on her face.

"Did Nadine come with you?" she asked. Her expression shifted as another idea occurred to her, as well. "Are you staying at Molly and Pete's tonight, or would you like to come to our *dawdi haus* to—"

"My sister and I are at the Shetler place. It's becoming a second home to us," he said lightly. "As a nonmember, she didn't feel it was appropriate to attend the meeting, but she would love to visit with your *mamm*, if Drusilla—"

"Oh, that's a fine idea! Mamm's a different person when Nadine's around—not that she doesn't enjoy your company," Jo assured him quickly. "Come this evening, if you want. I baked a new coffee cake recipe today, so you'll give us a *gut* excuse to sample some!"

"Fabulous! I'll swing by to pick her up and we'll be there in half an hour—if you're sure that'll be all right."

Looking behind them, to the line of buggies that was thinning out fast, Nelson spotted Drusilla chatting with Delores and Cora. Her smile brought back the memory

of their walk in the woods, which had encouraged him—
had made him feel that he might win her over, after all.

But that was before Michael had seemingly backed out
on Jo. Drusilla might see her relationship with Nelson in
a different light now, considering her feelings about men
who behaved one way while they were courting and a
completely different way after the wedding.

"We'll be happy to see you both," Jo assured him. "We
have a lot to talk about after tonight's meeting, ain't so?"

Chapter 25

As always, Nadine's presence brightened Mamm's outlook on life. Nelson's vivacious sister, wearing a magenta cape dress, climbed down from their rig and immediately asked to see how the early vegetables were doing while there was still enough daylight. Jo and Nelson followed as the two women headed toward the plots.

"I hope your *mamm* hasn't written Michael off—or suggested that she no longer wants you to have that parcel of land," Nelson said in a low voice.

Jo sighed. Seeing the pleasant mood her mother was currently in, she hated to elaborate on Mamm's comments concerning Michael. "Well, you know how moody she gets," Jo hedged. "She didn't like the way the preachers handled that meeting herself, so she was jumping to plenty of conclusions before Michael walked away from it."

As Nadine and Mamm approached the nearest garden plot, Jo slowed her pace to converse privately with Nelson—who had just as much at stake when it came to that land.

"Now that you'll be managing The Marketplace and

opening a branch of your nursery, we need to be sure you'll have that piece of property for your greenhouses, *jah*?" she asked quietly. "I have every intention of marrying Michael, but . . . but if he believes I won't consider our marriage a higher priority than running my bakery—"

"I think he'll come around, Jo," Nelson put in sympathetically. "But if worse comes to worst, I'll purchase that parcel of ground from your mother and build myself a small house on it, alongside the nursery facilities."

When Jo imagined Nelson's house on that road—rather than the one she and Michael had asked Pete to build for them—a fresh wave of regret washed over her. "Let's hope it doesn't come to that!" she whispered. "Shall I go back to Queen City with you tomorrow to talk to him? I really do want to apologize—"

Nelson hugged her. "I've never doubted your sincerity, Jo," he said firmly. "Let's see how it goes, shall we? And let's catch up to my sister and your *mamm* so they won't think we're plotting or keeping secrets back here," he added lightly.

Jo chuckled. Nelson's confidence made her feel better—and so did his smile as they approached the two women. Nadine and her mother were carefully walking between the rows of broccoli, cauliflower, and cabbage seedlings, chatting happily about how well the plants were growing.

Nadine turned, flashing Jo and her brother a grin. "Would you look at these baby veggies! Drusilla's plants are probably a week ahead of anything I've seen growing in our area."

Nodding, Nelson stopped a few steps away from the two of them. "They're doing really well," he agreed as he held Mamm's gaze. "Maybe you've gotten some rain that didn't fall in our area—but maybe you also have an exceptionally green thumb, Drusilla. I'm glad those seedlings are doing so well for you."

Mamm's smile faded suddenly and she looked away. "*Jah*, now that I've gone to all the work of planting and hoeing them, I suppose you'll expect to sell these vegetables in your Marketplace store because they were yours to begin with," she remarked brusquely. Without another word, she stepped over row after row of vegetables and stalked toward the house.

Jo blinked. Faster than she could snap her fingers, Mamm's mood had swung to the negative side—for no apparent reason, except that she'd jumped to a conclusion.

Nadine and Nelson exchanged a startled glance.

"I'm not going to let Drusilla think you'd ever do such a thing with her produce, Nelson," Nadine said as she followed in Mamm's footsteps. "Let's get to the bottom of this, shall we?"

Jo shook her head sadly. "I have no idea what brought that on, Nelson, but—"

"Let's venture inside," he put in as he, too, headed for the house. "I suspect Nadine will have better luck than I at coaxing Drusilla to talk, but I need to be in on the conversation. It's now or never."

As she followed the rest of them, Jo wondered if Nelson might soon reach a point of no return where her *mamm's* emotional outbursts were concerned. She couldn't blame him for walking away at this point, because he'd tried so many times, so patiently, to convince her mother that he wanted only the best for her—and for any relationship they might share in the future.

But why would *any* man stay with a woman whose moods were so volatile? And if Michael was convinced that Jo would rather manage The Marketplace than marry him, maybe the Wengerds would decide it wasn't worth the emotional or financial investment to establish a new branch of their nursery in Morning Star. And if they had no business to run here, why would Nelson take on the management of The Marketplace shops?

In her frightened heart, Jo could imagine all the positive mileposts of her future falling like a line of dominoes if they couldn't convince her mother to stop doubting Nelson . . . and maybe convince Mamm to get some help for her mood swings.

Bless her, Nadine walked right into the kitchen, refusing to be silenced by Mamm's glare. "Drusilla, can we please talk this out?" she asked gently. "After getting to know you these past weeks, I can't believe you really mean to inflict such pain with the things you say to my brother. We want to help you," she added pleadingly. "We want to *understand* why you don't trust Nelson's intentions— for your vegetables, or for your feelings, either."

Nelson slipped into a chair at the kitchen table, gazing steadfastly at Mamm. "When I gave you those seedlings, they were a gift, Drusilla—no strings attached," he reminded her gently. "I would *never* expect you to turn over the vegetables you're growing for your own stand—I'm not that kind of man. After all the months you've known me, I was hoping you'd realize that."

Jo gingerly sat down on the other side of Nelson, sensing she should be quiet and give him her emotional support. She'd considered serving some of the new coffee cake, allowing her mother time to pull herself together, but maybe Nadine's direct approach would be more effective.

Or maybe it would bring this difficult conversation to a head and the Wengerds would be on their way sooner rather than later.

Her mother remained by the sink, her arms crossed tightly over her chest to deflect Nelson and Nadine's remarks. For several moments she gazed toward the window, as though trying to decide how to handle the friends who were pressing her for an explanation.

Jo held her breath and her tongue, sensing the tense silence that filled the kitchen would eventually prompt her mother to respond.

"Intentions," Mamm finally muttered. "Men and their intentions. If you must know, I'll lay it all out for you. But it's not a happy story."

Jo braced herself for whatever her mother was about to reveal. After a moment, Nelson's sister took a seat at the table to give Mamm more space.

"I didn't marry until I was twenty-five, and Big Joe Fussner was thirty-eight," Jo's mother began in a faraway voice. "Both of us had pretty well written off marriage as an option, and I can tell you, we weren't exactly head over heels the way most couples are. But it seemed like the thing to do, considering how the church leaders and our parents had been prodding us."

She sighed, shaking her head. "Long story short, Joe jumped the gun one evening—as men often do. I knew it was a sin to have relations before we married, but I . . . I didn't know how to stop him."

Jo's eyes widened. Neither of her parents had ever hinted at such a thing. Jo didn't dare look at the Wengerds, wondering if they were as startled and embarrassed by this revelation as she was.

"A short while later, when I discovered I was in the family way," Mamm continued in a brittle voice, "we moved up our wedding date to avoid a scandal. Shortly after we were married, before I was even showing, I lost that baby. Joe accused me of trapping him—of *lying* about the baby to get him to the altar before he changed his mind."

Her expression soured. "After that, it seemed to me that Joe took his pleasure as a way to get back at me, to dominate me," she said, as though the words were as distasteful as the memory. "I—I lost three more babies before Jo was born."

Instinctively, Jo hugged herself, hoping to hold herself together. Her mother had just said more about her marriage to Dat in a few sentences than she had in all of Jo's lifetime—and what a bleak, unpleasant picture she'd painted. It was a comfort when Nelson laid his hand lightly on her shoulder, expressing his empathy.

Mamm drew in a shuddering breath and looked at the three of them before focusing on Nelson. "That's why I've hung all my hopes on Jo—and why I want no part of being married again," she continued, seeming determined— almost desperate—to have her story heard. "Despite the doctor's warning that I should not conceive again after Jo was born, Joe believed that his rights overrode the doctor's orders *or my health*. His sense of entitlement— of being the head of this family—cost me two more little souls before I finally got beyond my ability to conceive."

A small sob escaped Jo, and when Nadine turned to comfort her, there were tears shining in her eyes. How had Mamm endured such treatment and such heartache from one day to the next—from one miscarriage to the next? Her mother had apparently let on to *no one*—hadn't had emotional support from friends or family during all those years.

Why did I never sense this discord between my parents? How could I have remained totally unaware of my mother's emotional turmoil—and my father's lack of concern for her?

Jo sensed that long after the Wengerds went home, she would still be trying to understand her *mamm*'s stark, startling revelations.

"So Nelson, I'm telling you straight out that I won't marry you," Mamm said firmly. "It'll save us both a lot of heartache and misunderstanding."

Nelson exhaled painfully, clearly affected by her past—and by the finality of her rejection. "I'm sorry all this has happened to you, Drusilla," he whispered. "I can understand why you've hung your hopes on Jo, and I have no intention of coming between you. But at our stage of the game, marriage can be about *companionship* rather than—"

He stopped short of mentioning the topic that had so badly upset Mamm for her entire married life. "We can continue being friends, *jah*? Wouldn't sharing a home be better for both of us than growing old alone?" he asked plaintively. "That's why most folks our age remarry, after all."

Her mother shrugged. "If I want companionship, I'd rather have Jo—or Nadine—around than allow another man to take over my life. That's the way of it. End of discussion."

Mamm sagged against the counter. She seemed drained, yet in control of her emotions—as though she'd been discussing what to cook for supper rather than making hash of the future Nelson had been hoping for. After all the mental anguish her mother had exhibited over the past months, her final words—so cool and aloof—sounded downright eerie.

After a few moments, Nelson rose from the table. "All right. You've made your point, Drusilla. We'll be on our way," he murmured. He turned with a sad smile. "Michael or I will be in touch with you soon, Jo. Take care, dear."

Jo had the immediate urge to go with them—to distance herself from Mamm so she could sort out her feelings about what she'd just learned. She sensed that Nelson and his sister could give her much-needed perspective on some of the highly personal matters her mother had mentioned.

Were her mother's devastating marital experiences the rule rather than the exception? Did the majority of Amish wives sacrifice their personal happiness when they married?

Jo pressed her lips together tightly. She'd be too embarrassed to ask Nelson or Nadine about such intimate matters—especially when she wasn't sure Michael wanted her back. And once he'd learned what Mamm had said to his *dat*, he might not want to become involved with her family anyway.

"Drusilla, I'll call you later, after your feelings have settled," Nadine said softly. "I'm not telling you what to do, understand, but maybe you should see a doctor about your hormonal imbalances. And maybe he can recommend a mental health professional you can talk to about what you've shared with us. You're carrying a heavy load, dear."

When Mamm turned her head, like a little girl refusing to hear her parents' advice, Nadine looked at Jo. "We'll keep you both in our prayers. Don't give up, Jo," she murmured. "Every road has a few potholes."

As Jo watched the Wengerds hitch up their rig a few minutes later, she was filled with a deep, dark desperation. First she'd said, in front of Michael and the entire congregation, that she intended to keep managing The Marketplace because she was single—and now Mamm had just declared to Nelson that she would never marry again. Between the two of them, they'd sent a message that was pretty hard to misinterpret, hadn't they?

Jo was in such a funk that when Nelson slid a plastic sack onto the porch and clambered back into his buggy, she didn't have the heart to go out and fetch it.

"So now you know why I've warned you about the pitfalls of getting married," Mamm said behind her. "Do you understand why I'm trying to protect you from the heartache I went through with your *dat*? And why I told Nelson to stop wasting his time?"

Tears sprang to Jo's eyes as she slowly turned around. "No, I'll probably never understand what you went through. And I don't believe Michael or Nelson would subject us to the same sort of—*heartache*," she echoed when she didn't dare use stronger words. "But we can't unsay what we've said. I have a lot to think about."

Jo headed upstairs, wondering if the small bedroom down the hall would be where she slept forever.

She would never look at her mother—or her father's memory—the same way again. As a *maidel* who'd led a sheltered childhood, Jo had no idea what to think of Mamm's story, and she would forever wonder if Dat had seen their marriage in a similar, troubling light. The best she could do was pray long and hard for a depth of understanding that only God could grant her.

Early Thursday morning, as Jo fed and watered Nellie, Starla's empty stall served as another bleak reminder that Michael was gone. Why hadn't he called and left her a message? Or sent a note along with his *dat* or his aunt?

The answer's clear: I drove him away, and he has nothing more to say to me.

Suppressing a sob, Jo finished the horse chores as quickly as she could. As she emerged from the stable, the sun's first rays glimmered on shiny, bright green leaves and the pink and yellow tulip blooms still folded in their evening's repose, but the fresh beauty of the April morning was lost on her. The best way to deal with the pain of Michael's silence—and the dejection she'd seen on Nelson's face last night—was to bake and decorate Easter cookies all day.

If she was to be a *maidel* shopkeeper for the rest of her life, she might as well devote herself to making a huge success of Fussner Bakery. It would help her rise above whatever mood Mamm was in today, as well.

Jo was going up the front steps when she spotted the sack Nelson had tossed there before he and Nadine had left—she'd gone outside through the mudroom, so she'd missed it earlier. When she peered into the sack, she saw a large bundle of folded pink fabric—a shade of pink that glowed like tulips bathed in afternoon sunshine. And when she pulled out a white envelope in the center of the bundle, she saw that it was a pattern for making men's shirts.

Jo blinked. Why on earth would Nelson have tossed this parcel on the porch—or even purchased fabric and a pattern in the first place? She could not imagine Michael's *dat* wanting a shirt in any bright, snappy color, least of all pink. And he'd said nothing to her about sewing for him, so this little mystery surely had to involve her mother.

Buzzing with curiosity, Jo entered the kitchen, where Mamm was getting out a skillet to cook some eggs. She seemed subdued, as though she was still drained from telling her painful story to the Wengerds—and revealing such personal information to her daughter.

Jo hadn't spoken to Mamm since she'd gone to her room last night, but the pink fabric was too juicy a morsel to leave on the kitchen counter without asking about it.

"I, um, found this on the porch. I have no idea what it means, but *you* surely do."

Mamm frowned at the white plastic sack with no sign of recognition. When she peered inside, however, her eyes flashed with surprise—and then with irritation.

"Puh! Nadine and her pranks—but this time she took it too far," her mother muttered. She stuffed the entire sack into the wastebasket under the sink before returning to the stove. "I'm scrambling eggs. You can make the toast."

Jo's challenge was on the tip of her tongue, but she held it. Nadine might've chosen the fabric, but *Nelson* had placed it on the porch with a resigned expression Jo hadn't missed. It occurred to her that after years of practice at hiding her true feelings about Dat, her mother had just created another fib on the spur of the moment and then gone on as though nothing had happened.

It saddened Jo that Mamm had perfected such a habit, probably out of self-preservation.

After breakfast, when her mother had gone out to tend the garden plots, Jo fished Nelson's sack out of the trash. The color might be flashy, but the fabric was a high-quality cotton-polyester blend that would launder beautifully and require no ironing—and there was far too much of it for just a shirt. Even if neither she nor Mamm ever made a dress from it, surely they could use the fabric for a quilt back or something useful.

She carried the sack upstairs and placed it on the sewing machine cabinet—in case her mother had a change of heart. After all, Mamm had sent Nelson and Michael away in no uncertain terms at Christmas, too, and they'd come back. And wasn't Easter a time of renewal and rebirth—the season for Jesus rising from the dead? If the Lord had blessed His followers with everlasting life, maybe He could work a miracle for the Fussners and the Wengerds, too.

When Jo returned to the kitchen to begin her day's baking, her heart felt lighter. She didn't have Michael back—yet—but she certainly had an interesting little secret to think about while she worked.

Chapter 26

Morning Star was several miles behind them on Thursday morning before Nelson felt ready to discuss Drusilla. While they'd stayed the night at the young Shetlers' *dawdi haus*, Nadine had given him the gift of her silence concerning what they'd heard at the Fussner home. They'd gotten a very early start, while it was still dark, and he was grateful that little traffic was on the rural roads. He'd been so wrapped up in his woolgathering that he was startled when he stopped the rig at an intersection—and then realized it was their turnoff onto the county highway leading toward Queen City.

Nadine cleared her throat to disguise her laughter. She was fully aware that he'd nearly missed their turn but was gracious enough not to point it out.

"Seems to be no doubt about Drusilla's wishes," Nelson said with an exasperated sigh. "In the interest of damage control, I should stop trying to save this relationship. I need to take her at her word and walk away. For *gut* this time."

"But we both know you're nothing like Joe Fussner must've been," Nadine insisted. "And as I've thought about

Drusilla's situation, I have to wonder if her point of view has been skewed—first by the pain of Joe having his way with her before they married, and then by her resentment because he accused her of lying about her miscarriage."

Nelson considered her words, frowning. "Why do you say that?" he asked carefully. "I can't think you have any experience with such matters—"

"As I recall, Verna miscarried once," Nadine reminded him gently. "And how much did you know about it? How much did she share with you?"

He blinked. "I—I'd forgotten all about it," he admitted softly. "She wasn't even sure yet that she was carrying, so I had no idea that she'd lost the baby until she . . . her body resumed its monthly schedule. Men are mostly in the dark about such things."

"Exactly. And Verna didn't make a lot of fuss, because if a tiny bunch of cells detaches rather than growing into a child, it means something wasn't right with it anyway. And our lives go on. We hope for the next time."

Nadine gazed pensively at the road ahead of them. "So if Drusilla insisted that Joe move up their wedding date, and then she lost the baby shortly after they married, he could've been clueless about it, too," she reasoned aloud. "Depending on how Drusilla handled it, I can understand why he thought she'd manipulated him with a baby that was never really there."

"You're sticking up for *Joe*? He didn't sound like a very considerate—"

"We don't know that Drusilla went to a doctor to confirm her pregnancy—or following the miscarriage," she pointed out. "As newlyweds who were older than most, Joe and Drusilla probably had their own assumptions and expectations when they married. Neither of them apparently sought advice from friends or family—maybe out of embarrassment—so they got off to a bad start and they never got over it."

Nelson shook his head. "I don't know. If Joe turned their bedroom into a battleground to assert his control over her, what chance of happiness did she ever have?"

Nadine smiled sadly. "You're saying that from the perspective of a man looking back on many fulfilling years of marriage, *jah*? Unfortunately, we know about Drusilla's current habit of unhappiness—who says she didn't also see the glass as half empty when she was a younger woman?"

He let out a frustrated laugh. "That's my point! Why would any man choose to spend the rest of his life with such a negative woman?" he demanded. "Drusilla seems a bit calmer of late—she was stone-cold sober as she told us her story last night—but I've seen what she can be like, haven't I? She's an emotional shipwreck that never sinks."

Nelson stared at his perceptive twin until she met his gaze. "You're pointing out all the same things I am, Nadine, yet under the surface you're hinting that I shouldn't give up on her. Why?"

"Because I know how lonely you've been since Verna passed. And because there's no one for you to hitch up with in Queen City."

As always, Nadine had nailed it. He *had* been wandering like a lost soul, burying himself in nursery work to disguise his loneliness. And it wasn't as though he was being picky: Except for a couple of gals who'd been widowed in their late eighties, all the women in his district and the nearby Amish settlements were married.

"Living alone still seems wiser than marrying Drusilla," he countered. "Maybe this means Michael and Jo will build their new home and a new store in Morning Star while I remain at the current nursery. I'll see them weekends when I take plants and produce to The Marketplace."

"But you've told Bishop Jeremiah and the other leaders in Morning Star that you'll be taking over as the manager," Nadine reminded him. "How's that going to work if you live at such a distance?"

"I know, I know," Nelson replied with a heavy sigh. "But that was before Drusilla shot me down. Again. I have a lot of sorting out to do."

For the next few miles he focused on keeping the rig on the road's shoulder so pickups and cars could pass him. But on his mental back burner, the pot was still simmering: if he lived in a *dawdi haus* at the kids' new home, how would he feel—what would he say—whenever he saw Drusilla? He couldn't avoid her at Sunday services. And the situation would get awkward whenever they met at the kids' house for supper or other occasions . . . like visiting grandchildren.

It would be different if he couldn't recall moments when he'd truly enjoyed Drusilla's company—like when they'd walked in the woods after the timber cruiser had been there, and in the early days when she'd welcomed him and Michael to the table with wonderful, tasty meals. He could still hear Drusilla's laughter when he'd insisted he would wear a pink shirt made of the fabric he'd hastily dropped onto her porch.

Why keep it? And why imagine you'll ever see her wearing the dress you dared her to sew from it?

Nelson sighed glumly. He might never marry Jo's

mother, but she would still live on the fringes of his life—unless Michael decided that *he* didn't want to deal with Drusilla, either.

And that would present a whole new set of problems, wouldn't it?

At the sound of a horse's hooves, Michael looked up from the young perennial landscaping plants he'd been transferring to individual pots. His *dat* and aunt were arriving home quite a lot earlier on Thursday than he'd been expecting them, which made him wonder what had happened in Morning Star.

Was Dat so excited about the vote and other events that he couldn't wait to share them? Or had he left before dawn for reasons that weren't so pleasant? The pasted-on smile his father wore as he approached the potting bench a few minutes later warned Michael that the news might not be good.

"Hey there, Dat. You rose before the chickens *and* the rooster to get here this early," he remarked cautiously. He scooped more potting soil mixture into the three plastic planting pots lined up on his bench. "How did the Members' Meeting with Bishop Jeremiah go?"

Dat took a moment to see what Michael had been doing so he could assist with the repotting while they talked. "It was a momentous occasion—a progressive step most church districts in this area won't consider for years, if ever," he replied as he separated more plastic pots from the stack. "After a lengthy discussion, folks decided that married women may work away from home, though their husbands will have the final say about it.

Everyone except the two preachers and Saul voted yes, so it was a resounding victory for the young women who established The Marketplace."

Michael nodded. As Jo's face flashed in his mind, he heard her definitive words for at least the hundredth time: *I'm still single, and* I *will continue to manage The Marketplace!*

"I, um, suppose Jo was ecstatic about that," he murmured.

Dat's steely-gray eyebrows rose, suggesting otherwise. "When I watched her during the vote, I sensed Jo was having second thoughts," he said softly. "Afterward, she thanked me for offering to manage The Marketplace— which was the main reason the men agreed to make this change. Jo is anything but *ecstatic*, however."

His father's statement felt ripe with layers of hidden meaning Michael wasn't sure he wanted to explore. Jo's devotion to her bakery and The Marketplace's success still stung him to the core. Would she ever declare her dedication to *him*—to their marriage—with the same unwavering fervor?

"Jo also told me that she was hoping to apologize to you, son. She hasn't called or sent a letter because she'd planned to speak with you in person. But you stayed away from the meeting. She was very disappointed."

Michael sighed. It had been a cowardly move, remaining in Queen City. If Wengerd Nursery was to continue its lucrative operation in Morning Star—at least on Saturdays—he would have to face Jo sooner or later. And *she* wasn't one to hang back. Jo would face their situation head-on, even if it hurt.

"Michael, she was sincerely distressed," Dat murmured.

"She realized immediately that her words at Sunday's meeting probably wounded you, and that was never her intention. But she can't tell you that if you refuse to listen, or to consider the possibility that maybe you misconstrued her true meaning."

His father sighed as he scooped potting soil into a few more containers. "If you ask me, this situation begs for a little forgiveness and a chance to talk things over. But you didn't ask me," he added with a rueful smile.

Michael cleared his throat, ready to voice a protest that was beginning to sound weak and repetitious even to his own ears—but his father's expression gave him pause.

"What else happened?" he asked, separating a few of the small coneflowers he was potting. "You look as dejected as I've been feeling lately—and that wouldn't be because of anything *Jo* said to you."

"You're changing the subject," Dat pointed out. "But you're right. Jo invited Nadine and me to the house after the big meeting—and Drusilla was very much in favor of allowing married women to work, by the way. But we hadn't been there five minutes before things slid downhill."

"Drusilla was in one of her moods?"

"Oh, it went back much, much further—to the very personal, private reasons she's been warning Jo away from marriage," he replied in a faraway voice. "I'm not going to repeat everything she said—had you been there, you'd have heard it yourself," Dat added meaningfully. "But Drusilla's main point was that she never intends to marry again. Not me, or any other man.

"So Nadine and I left," Dat finished with a shake of his head. "There was no point in staying around to argue my case."

The rock-bottom sorrow in his father's voice touched Michael deeply. After witnessing the escalation of Drusilla's roller-coaster moods over the past months, he was aware that Jo's *mamm* often made negative statements she later took back. But this time he sensed that she'd delivered her final rejection.

His father had a lot of reasons to feel stung. Cast off like trash tossed in a can.

Michael realized his father's emotional wounds ran much deeper than his own, and they deserved acknowledgment. "I'm really sorry to hear that, Dat," he murmured. "You've had your ups and downs with Drusilla, but lately I've had the feeling you two were finally getting your act together."

"*Jah*, me too. But I was wrong."

I was wrong.

Many times Michael had heard his *dat* admit to mistakes, yet this time those three words rang with a sense of defeat and finality. This time Dat sounded ready to walk away and lick his wounds, never allowing Drusilla Fussner to hurt him again.

"I'm sorry, Dat," Michael repeated softly. "You were planning your future just like I was—and you seemed happier than you'd been since Mamm passed. I wish it could've worked out differently for you."

With a resigned shrug, his father placed soil mix in three more pots. "You and I had decided to let your cousin Mervin manage the Queen City nursery while we expanded the business at our new home, but now—assuming you and Jo make up—you'll be the man of the family there in Morning Star, Michael," he said in a flat voice. "Drusilla didn't withdraw her offer of that land for your new home, and she didn't say we couldn't build the greenhouses we've been planning—but you'll be on your own. I should probably remain here in Queen City."

As he centered a small, sturdy coneflower in a pot, Dat continued. "If *I* were to suggest expanding the nursery on her property someday, she'd probably dismiss the idea. She'd say we were taking over her land—and her life. If you and Jo suggest such improvements, she'll see it differently."

Michael placed a couple more coneflowers in the pots and carefully pressed soil mixture around them. Then he frowned. "But didn't you just tell me you'd be taking over the management of The Marketplace? If you won't be living in Morning Star, does that mean I'm supposed to fill that role? We both know I've never been as organized as you—and certainly not as *gut* at running the place as Jo—"

"Actually, I suggested that the management become a cooperative venture, with Glenn and Gabe and the other fellows who have shops helping out," Dat replied. "But *jah*, I said I'd be the lead dog. I should tell Bishop Jeremiah things have changed—"

"But why can't you come to Morning Star and live with Jo and me?" Michael put in quickly. "I thought we'd agreed that if things didn't pan out with Drusilla, you could have a *dawdi haus*—"

"Are you listening to yourself?" Dat challenged. "You're talking as though you and Jo will be getting married, even though you ducked out on her on Sunday."

You ducked out on her.

Michael went silent. In his sudden fear about taking on The Marketplace's management, he'd forgotten about the separation between him and his fiancée . . . a separation he'd caused himself. This revelation slapped him in the face, because he'd been so focused on Jo's hurtful words that he hadn't thought about how his reaction must've looked to *her*—and to everyone else in the congregation.

From all appearances, he had indeed walked away. Everyone, including Jo and her *mamm*—especially Jo and her *mamm*—had reason to believe he'd given up and gone home. Without so much as a word to Jo.

Michael sighed, lost in his dismal thoughts. Did Jo believe he'd called off their engagement without even having the courtesy to tell her? Was her mother now saying *I told you so*, expressing the doubts she'd had about Jo marrying him all along?

Did Jo believe once again that she was doomed to live with Drusilla for the rest of her life? Doomed to endure the mood swings and harsh words her mother had been dishing out lately, without anyone around to support her?

I left Jo in a dark place without many positive options. It's up to me to shed some light—to close the gap between us—because Jo won't make the three-hour drive to Queen City.

And why should she? This is my fault. All my fault.

Chapter 27

As Jo carried a large pan of decorated sugar cookies through the back entrance of The Marketplace on Saturday morning, she let the peaceful silence of the large, empty stable envelop her. She always savored the building's calm solitude when she came a couple of hours before anyone else arrived, because it helped her focus on the upcoming sales day. After she arranged her cakes and cookies in her glass display cases, she began baking brownies and cinnamon rolls so their enticing aromas would greet customers when they arrived.

When she reached the entry to Fussner Bakery, however, she nearly tripped on something she couldn't see because the pan of cookies blocked her vision. Hefting the pan to her left hip, Jo spotted a pot of exquisite pink calla lilies in a container wrapped in iridescent, pearl-colored foil.

"Michael!" she whispered, instinctively gazing across the large commons area toward the Wengerd Nursery shop.

But no one was there. Jo was the only one in the entire building—which meant Michael had placed the lilies at her doorway yesterday when he and his *dat* arrived in town. They usually unloaded their flowers and vegetable seedlings when they first got into Morning Star on Friday afternoon so it wouldn't take them as long to prepare for Saturday's business—and yesterday, Michael had been thinking about *her*.

Jo's heart hammered as she unlatched the gate to her bakery and pushed it back against the stall divider that separated her shop from the Flauds' furniture store. After she slid her flat metal pan of colorful eggs, ducks, bunnies, and flowers into her bakery case, she fetched the lilies from the doorway and carried them to her back counter to look at them.

From the dozens of potted lilies, hydrangeas, pansies, and other springtime plants the Wengerds had brought, Michael had selected these lilies because they had the largest, most perfect, most beautiful blooms—when he'd given her seasonal gifts before, he'd always saved back the very best for her.

It seemed only right to stash a plate of her prettiest cookies and a pan of chocolate date muffins on her back counter for him. The thrumming of her heart and soul told her that Michael intended to visit her today, so they could bridge the desperate emptiness that had stretched between them this past week.

Jo hummed as she baked, carefully composing the right words for her apology. She was glad she'd worn her new lavender cape dress today, so she'd look her best when she spent time with the man she still loved with all her heart.

Soon it was nine o'clock—time to open the double doors so eager customers could come inside. Several of

Jo's regulars immediately called out their greetings as they headed to her bakery first, before she ran out of breads and coffee cakes and cookies. Michael and Nelson would be busy first thing, as well, because the colorful display of blooming hyacinths, lilies, and hydrangeas arranged outside their corner nursery shop would attract folks when they drove in from the road.

Around ten, Jo stepped outside her shop for a moment—but she saw no sign of the tall, dark-haired man her heart longed for. At noon she slipped away from her nearly empty display cases to gather cups and plates from the tables where folks had been enjoying the coffee and goodies Alice and Adeline had been selling.

Considering the way Michael had offered the proverbial olive branch by giving her those beautiful calla lilies, Jo realized it was her move—especially because she was the one who needed to apologize. As she carried a tray of dirty cups and saucers back to the bakery, she planned out what she would say—

But customers in her shop were buying the last of her coffee cakes and cinnamon rolls.

"Something tells me *somebody* is champing at the bit to visit the nursery store," Alice teased when it was just the three of them in the shop.

Adeline put detergent in the dishwasher and closed its door. "*Jah*, we've seen the way you keep looking over there, Jo," she teased. "You might as well go visit Michael while we run the store for you. We were relieved to see his peace offering on the back counter this morning. You two are meant to be together—"

"And it'll take more than a silly misunderstanding to keep you apart," Alice put in confidently.

Jo studied her identical redheaded assistants, seeing only sincerity on their fresh, freckled faces. Did they really think the separation between her and Michael was a silly misunderstanding? To Jo, it had felt like the end of her world when her fiancé had walked away from last Sunday's meeting—and as each day had passed without word from him, she'd assumed the worst.

Had she blown Michael's reaction to her impassioned words out of proportion? Or had he decided her priorities were in the wrong place?

Or had the Shetler twins seen the situation from the outside looking in and, in their teenage naivete, assumed Jo's issues were simpler than the reality?

"All right, I'll walk over there," Jo murmured, heading for the doorway.

But Nelson was arranging a large selection of potted perennials outside the Wengerd Nursery shop, which attracted a whole new crowd. Michael was nowhere in sight, which meant he was probably running the cash register—so it wasn't an optimal time for the kiss-and-make-up scenario Jo had been praying for.

By the time the bakery was cleaned and left ready for next Saturday, it was nearly four thirty. Jo sent the twins out for a final busing of the commons tables and then shooed them off.

Her heart fluttered nervously. She'd run out of time and distractions. She really needed to make her way over to the shop at the far end of The Marketplace. Jo stood at the counter to collect her thoughts and bowed for a brief prayer, standing in front of the beautiful potted lilies.

Give me courage and the right words, Lord, because this apology is mine to make. And if these flowers were intended as a goodbye—or if it was actually Nelson's way to console me, and not from Michael at all—help me deal with the disappointment that comes next.

Michael paused in the bakery doorway, ready to blurt out his apology—but Jo stood with her back toward him and her head hanging low. Was she upset, or crying? Was she disappointed that he'd left the lilies at her doorway rather than giving them to her face-to-face? Maybe Jo thought he was a total coward, unable to man up and claim the blame that was totally on him.

In her fresh lavender dress and white *kapp*, with a few loose tendrils of dark hair escaping it in the back, Jo made a fetching picture. The pink lilies he'd chosen for her were exquisite, but they were nothing compared to her natural, radiant beauty. His heart yearned to be in her good graces again, and the longer she remained quiet and withdrawn, the more fearful Michael became about the outcome of this visit.

When she sighed deeply and lifted her head, the eloquent opening lines he'd carefully composed flew out of his head. "Jo, I've missed you so much that I just had to come over and—what I mean to say is—"

She turned suddenly, her dark eyes wide with an emotion he was too nervous to interpret. "Oh, Michael, I was just coming over to tell you—well, I've missed you, too, and I'm sorry for those stupid, thoughtless things I said—"

Michael hadn't realized his feet were moving, but suddenly he reached out and Jo grabbed his hand as though it were a lifeline.

"I'm sorry, Michael, and I—"

"Not half as sorry as I am, Josie-girl! I—"

Her warm, solid body was the blessing he sought as he took her in his arms. And Jo was hugging him back with the same desperation, the same love, overflowing his heart.

She still wanted him! She still needed him in her life to feel complete—and Michael's soul surged with relief and gratitude for her tolerance of his shortcomings. He held her close, rocking slightly, until his lips found hers, seeking the forgiveness he'd yearned for.

Jo's kiss centered him, halting the downward spiral of his worries. A sense of rightness and pure joy overtook him.

"Say there," came a stern male voice from the adjacent shop. "You two know better than to engage in such a display of affection in public."

Startled, Michael stepped away from Jo but kept hold of her hand. "Martin!" he rasped, knowing the owner of the furniture store was right. Old Order ways strictly forbade kissing and embracing where others might see. "I—I was apologizing to Jo and got carried away."

"We forgot ourselves," Jo put in as the color rose in her cheeks.

When Martin cleared his throat, Michael suspected he was covering a laugh while trying to maintain a proper sense of decorum. "I don't want to see that behavior again until your wedding day, understood? That's what courting buggies are for," he added under his breath.

Wide-eyed, pulse pounding from Martin's chastisement, Michael nodded penitently. He put about four feet between him and Jo, waiting for Gabe's *dat* to go on about his business.

"Anyway," he continued in a flustered voice, "I assumed the worst when you said you'd continue managing The Marketplace. I should've known you didn't mean you were giving *me* up to do that. And then I licked my wounds and hid behind my hurt feelings all week—until it struck me that you and everyone else might've figured I'd walked out for *gut*."

"And why *wouldn't* you think that?" Jo countered softly. "I sounded like a *maidel* who intended to keep going her own way no matter whose feelings I hurt. But I never intended to hurt *you*, Michael. I love you."

"And I love *you*, Josie-girl," he whispered. "One of the reasons I admire you is because you speak out for what you believe in—and you were telling Saul exactly what you thought of his takeover idea. Somebody needed to do that. And who better than *you*, the woman who made The Marketplace a reality in the first place?"

Jo swiped at her eyes with her fingers, smiling in tremulous relief. "I suppose your *dat* told you how the rest of the meeting worked out? Are you all right with the changes we voted on?" she asked almost shyly. "Had Nelson not offered to reorganize the management, the other men would never have gone along with letting married gals keep working in their shops, you know."

Michael smiled. Wasn't it just like his Jo to give credit to others while remaining modest about her own strengths and achievements?

"It came out just right," he said. "With Dat and Gabe and Glenn—and Bishop Jeremiah—all helping out in this new cooperative, you ladies can still run your shops without having to see to every last administrative detail.

Many hands—and minds—will make lighter work for you, Jo. So you'll have more time to be my wife, *jah*?"

She appeared ready to cry again, yet her face shone like the April sun. "That's the way I want it, Michael. I—I'm so glad you see it that way, too."

"*Gut*." He exhaled the remainder of his misgivings, feeling blessed. Dat had been right: He'd blown things way out of proportion last Sunday. He couldn't reclaim the week he'd lost to pouting and assuming all the wrong things, but he and Jo could move forward now, stronger because they understood each other better.

"I was hoping to return to Morning Star midweek so we can observe *Gut* Friday together and celebrate our first Easter," Michael suggested.

"And then we can have a fine, fun time on Easter Monday!" Jo agreed. "I want you to feel like a part of this community by the time you move here, Michael. Maybe if you and your *dat* and I—and Nadine—put our heads together, we can figure out a way to bring Mamm back into our circle of happiness, too."

Michael nodded cautiously. After his *dat*'s chat about damage control and leaving Jo's *mamm* to stew in her own juices, he wasn't sure how that idea would go over.

"I felt horrible when she sent them away so coldly," Jo continued with a sigh. "But I hate to give up on her. I hate to think about what her life—and ours—will be like if Mamm remains alone. You know how that'll likely be."

Michael nodded. As man of the family, he would take responsibility for Drusilla's welfare, but he couldn't imagine that it would be a happy situation for any of them. He and Jo would have their new home, but her mother's disposition would likely deteriorate if she was left to live in her farmhouse all by herself.

"I'm still working through the harsh things she said about Dat and their marriage," Jo continued in a whisper, "but we all know your father would treat her differently. Mamm knows that, too, if she'd only move forward instead of dwelling in her past."

Once again Michael wished he'd been present for the disheartening story Jo's *mamm* had shared, but he knew enough. "The only way to find out if Dat's willing to try again is to ask him. Shall we go? By now the customers should be cleared out of the shop."

As the two of them strolled across the commons area side by side, Michael felt ten feet tall. The power of Jo's instant forgiveness—her willingness to assume she was equally to blame for their separation—was all the proof he needed that God had intended for her to become his wife. There was no finer woman on the face of the earth, and he felt blessed to know that Jo would be his forever.

Chapter 28

As Nelson drove the loaded wagon down the Fussners' long lane on Thursday afternoon, he truly understood the old phrase *walking on eggshells*. Michael and Nadine had joined forces, insisting that Jo's *mamm* deserved one more chance. His twin sister had even suggested that she stay with the Fussners for the long holiday weekend, to help pave his way into Drusilla's good graces again.

Jo had initiated this invitation, bless her. She'd agreed that Nadine's presence could only help them in their mission to win over her mother.

Michael, ecstatic to be with Jo again, had driven his courting buggy to Morning Star earlier in the day. This gave Nelson and his sister more time to discuss their strategy before he dropped her off at Drusilla's and took his and Michael's luggage to the Shetlers' *dawdi haus*.

"It's all well and *gut* that you'll be speaking to Drusilla on my behalf," Nelson said. He was slowing the wagon, allowing himself longer with his twin before Jo's *mamm* might appear on the porch. "But if I'm to have any kind of relationship with her, I can't expect you to intercede at every little cross word."

Nadine nodded, focused on the Fussners' home. "I agree. And if we can't get Drusilla past her misgivings about marriage during this visit, I promise I'll not pester you about her again, Nelson."

"I'm mostly doing this for Michael and Jo, you know."

His sister held his gaze, her expression full of love and purpose. "No, Nelson, you need to pursue this relationship for *you*," she insisted softly. "You know exactly what it takes to nurture and maintain a marriage—to support a wife financially and emotionally. And you also know how empty your life feels when you live alone, *jah*?"

Nelson sighed. He couldn't stall any longer, because Jo had spotted the wagon through the window and was stepping out onto the porch.

"Give yourself the gift of a second chance at love, dear brother. Although you and I could live out our final days together quite comfortably, I don't think that's what would make you truly happy."

Nadine turned her attention to the young woman standing on the top step as Nelson drove the wagon closer. "So *gut* to see you, Jo!" she called out. "*Denki* for the invitation to stay at your place. It'll be like a sleepover for us girls, ain't so?"

Nelson chuckled. Leave it to his sister to put such a youthful, positive spin on a weekend that might become emotionally charged in all the wrong ways.

"Your room's ready, and we're excited to have you!" Jo put in. She looked much happier and more relaxed now that she and Michael had reconciled.

"And you should see what Jo and Drusilla are cooking up for the holiday meals!" Michael said as he, too, came outside.

Nelson was relieved to see that his son had arrived. It was also a good sign that he'd apparently been in the house chatting with Drusilla—who joined Michael and Jo on the porch a moment later.

Jo's mother, wearing an apron smudged with flour and whatever else she'd been cooking with, brightened the moment Nadine clambered down from the wagon seat. As the two women hugged like longtime friends, Nelson could only hope that someday Drusilla would welcome *him* that way—as though she'd missed him and was glad to be spending time with him.

He sat absolutely still when Drusilla looked over Nadine's shoulder to meet his gaze. For a moment, everything around them went still. She didn't appear overjoyed or especially eager to see him—but she didn't avert her eyes or frown at him, either.

"I can't wait to see—and taste—what you've been cooking up, Drusilla," Nelson said with his best smile. Part of him wanted to climb down and join the others, but he remained seated. He felt like a nervous teenager who wasn't sure what to say to his date. "I'd like to take our plants to The Marketplace to unload them, rather than drive any farther with them jostling in the wagon bed. What time would you like me to return?"

"I've planned our supper for six o'clock," Drusilla replied. "Any time before that."

"I'll go with you to unload," Michael said as he started down the porch steps. "We'll leave the hens to do some clucking while we get all those potted plants arranged at the store."

When his son had climbed up to sit beside him, Nelson

waved at the ladies and drove the wagon into a wide turn. "Everything going all right so far?" he asked softly.

"Jo's *mamm* seems a little subdued, but I think she's happy to have folks around for the holiday weekend," Michael replied. "She said she and Jo were making side dishes they hadn't eaten in a long time, because they hadn't felt like fussing over an Easter meal for just the two of them these past few years."

"Glad to hear it. I didn't expect Drusilla to go to a lot of trouble for us," Nelson said pensively, "but maybe focusing on food will keep her moods at bay—or keep her busy enough that she won't find things to be upset about. Like *me*."

Michael let out a laugh as the wagon reached the road. "And maybe our *Gut* Friday observance tomorrow and the Easter Sunday service will remind us about what's really important right now," he said in more somber tone. "If God loved the world enough to sacrifice His Son, and Jesus loved us enough to go through with dying on the cross, surely we Wengerds and Fussners can find a way to love one another and be happy together. It makes our end of the deal sound pretty simple, ain't so?"

Nelson gazed over at his son, deeply proud of the sermonette he'd just delivered in a couple of sentences. "When you put it that way, Michael," he remarked softly, "*jah*, we should at least give that love our best effort."

After checking for the umpteenth time that all the food was on the table and all the places were properly set, Drusilla smoothed her apron. She took the last unoccupied seat at the table, which was at Nelson's left.

Why did she feel so self-conscious, so aware that she was assuming the place where an Amish wife tradition-ally sat? It was the spot she'd occupied during all those Friday suppers she'd shared with the Wengerd men last fall, yet this evening she felt *different* about it.

Unspoken expectations filled the kitchen. With Nadine seated directly across from her, and Jo to her left facing Michael, Drusilla was surrounded by friendly, well-meaning people—no matter *how* she felt about Nelson being at the head of her table again. She was surprised that he'd returned, considering the intimate, unpleasant details she'd shared about her marriage last week.

She couldn't go on the way she'd been, riding such an emotional roller coaster. She just couldn't. It was time to either move forward into a future with Nelson, or to de-clare that the Wengerd family would remain good friends who deserved her honest answers and best, most emotion-ally stable behavior.

Nelson smiled at her, appearing as calm and collected—and as handsome—as ever. When he bowed for their silent grace, Drusilla joined everyone else in a few moments of prayer.

This is nerve-racking, Lord, and I need Your help to get through it. I've taken more of those supplements Margaret gave me. I've done my best to cook food I know these folks will enjoy for their holiday—but it has to be about more than the things we see on the table, doesn't it? Now that the Wengerds have heard about my past, I've got to open myself to accepting them on a deeper level . . . and I have to trust them.

"Amen," Nelson murmured. As he reached for the platter of pot roast smothered with fragrant baked onions, he inhaled deeply. "This is so much better than anything we'd be eating at home," he said with a gentle chuckle. "*Denki* for the time you've put into our supper, Drusilla, and for welcoming us again."

"And everything looks so special served on Jo's new sunflower plates and yellow tablecloth," Nadine put in brightly. "I can't wait to get the dishes I've ordered from that same gift shop in Willow Ridge."

Nelson's appreciative words had left her at a loss for a reply, so Drusilla was grateful for the thread of conversation his sister had tossed her like a lifeline. "What colors and pattern will your dishes be?" she asked. She almost dropped the meat platter when Nelson's fingers brushed hers as he passed it.

"Rainbows!" Nadine exclaimed. "Each piece will have the seven bright colors in stripes that go out from a center circle. The centers will be different colors, so no two pieces will be exactly alike."

Once again Drusilla was amazed that an Amish woman would select such a flashy pattern. But wasn't that one of the things she enjoyed most about Nadine?

Maybe if I could venture into a bolder, more colorful outlook on life, I'd have a lot more fun instead of remaining in the same old rut . . . alone.

"Rainbow stripes! What a great idea," Jo put in as she helped herself to the green beans. "And think of how many different tablecloths those dishes will go with."

As she finished filling her plate and began to eat, Drusilla drifted along on the waves of a perfectly ordinary, unemotional conversation about what flowers were in bloom around Queen City and how Nadine's garden was coming along. Nelson was focused on his food, but he followed their talk with an occasional nod or change of his facial expression.

When there was a moment's pause, however, Nelson laid aside his fork to look at Drusilla. His eyes were a warm brown, and although his voice had a hesitant edge, he spoke with an air of calm control.

"I really appreciate the way you shared your qualms about men and marriage the last time we were here, Drusilla," he began softly. "That was a very brave, difficult topic to talk about. Not everyone could've admitted the issues they'd had with their spouse of so many years."

Drusilla felt the blood drain from her face. How could she possibly respond to Nelson's heartfelt remarks?

Thank goodness he didn't seem to expect her to say anything. He continued as though he was warming to his subject, getting more comfortable with it—and with her, as well.

"I can't pretend to understand the burdens—and the losses—you bore all those years," Nelson said, his expression softening. "But I can see why you couldn't have discussed such matters with the church leaders because—as men—they probably would've taken Joe's side and put you in your place as his wife. And with Jo at home, too young to understand, you surely felt you had nowhere to turn."

A little gasp escaped her. Drusilla's fork dropped onto her plate with a clatter that filled the kitchen. Michael, his aunt, and Jo remained absolutely still, respecting the tone of Nelson's remarks—and probably wondering where he was going with them, just as she was.

Nelson smiled at Jo then, obviously very fond of her. "And Jo," he continued in his low, resonant voice, "I better understand now that you are your mother's miracle. I hope you both know that I wouldn't dream of coming between the two of you."

He paused to take a breath, as though he needed strength for what he was about to say next. "Even if your *mamm* decides she—she doesn't want to be more than my friend, I'll encourage you and Michael and help you as you need me, without competing against Drusilla for your affection."

Drusilla's mouth dropped open, but somehow she had the presence of mind to close it so she wouldn't appear addled. No one had ever suggested that her daughter was her *miracle*—probably because Big Joe had been the only one who was aware of how many other babies she'd lost over the years.

"I—*denki*, Nelson," Jo whispered. "I've had a lot to process since Mamm told us her story. After I got past the shock of it, I came to realize that God had a purpose for me when He allowed me to survive. Maybe I was born for such a time as this, when Mamm's on her own."

When her daughter reached for her hand under the table, Drusilla clasped it as though her life depended on it. After so many years of not expressing her emotions, it came as a jolt when suppertime conversation centered around the most private parts of her past.

And yet Drusilla followed Nelson's kind words in awe, grateful that he hadn't merely dismissed her years of lonely struggle, as many men would do. He'd made an effort to understand her plight without diminishing it by telling about his own tough times, as though they were more difficult or more important than hers.

Across the table, Michael and Nadine followed the

conversation closely without butting in. Drusilla was pretty sure neither of them had known beforehand that Nelson was going to go down this conversational road with her, yet their expressions remained kind and supportive. They seemed as surprised as she was that he'd broached the subject and spoken his truth without any preamble or fanfare.

That was the thing about Nelson. He was, very simply, a kind and generous man—considerate of other people's feelings. He gave without expecting anything in return.

And Lord knows I haven't given him much reason to stick around.

Once again Drusilla was at a loss for words when it was her turn to contribute to the conversation. Thankfully, Nelson didn't seem to expect a response.

"As I felt the weight of the burdens you've borne over the years, Drusilla," he continued, "I was reminded of the method I use to release my own struggles when I have a hard time forgiving someone I feel has done me wrong."

Drusilla blinked, taken aback.

Forgiveness. In all the years I was married to Big Joe Fussner, why did I endure what he dished out but never think about forgiving him?

Maybe she'd been so focused on making it from one day of her marriage to the next that the concept of forgiving Joe hadn't even occurred to her. Yet Nelson was discussing forgiveness as though it was as familiar to him as the socks he put on every morning.

"When I feel crosswise with somebody, I compose forgiveness statements," he explained further. "Sometimes I say them over and over—ten times—until I feel the resentment draining out of my soul. But most often I write the statement on paper ten times, until the repetition—and the act of writing—settles my confrontational thoughts."

A faraway look came over his face and the laugh lines that bracketed his eyes and mouth softened. "Oftentimes I come to realize that the person I'm upset with really hasn't done anything to offend me," he admitted. "It's my own attitude or expectations that need adjusting. The church leaders and the Bible tell us it's best to go directly to the offensive party to settle differences with him or her, but this forgiveness method often saves me from having to do that. It's even a way to forgive people who've passed on, when you don't feel at peace with their memory."

Drusilla was listening intently, not even trying to respond now. Nelson had been drawing her more deeply into a mysterious process she'd never heard of—yet it felt accessible. And maybe it would make her less vulnerable to her negative recollections and the resentment she'd harbored.

"To show you how it works, I myself will begin to forgive Joe," Nelson continued softly. "Depending on the seriousness of the offense, I might have to repeat this process several times, over several days, before I feel the relief I seek. But it's better to start somewhere than to let it keep festering."

He closed his eyes to gather his thoughts. When he placed his hand gently on Drusilla's wrist, she didn't draw away. She was too caught up in what Nelson might do or say next.

"I, Nelson Wengerd, forgive you, Joe Fussner, for doubting Drusilla after she married you, and for being unaware of her need for love and understanding," he said softly. His words resonated with a prayerful reverence, even though they dealt with a difficult situation. "I, Nelson Wengerd, forgive you, Joe Fussner, for doubting Drusilla after she married you, and for being unaware of her need for love and understanding."

Drusilla swallowed hard. She couldn't help following along, saying the phrases silently in her mind as Nelson spoke them aloud. Soon her eyes drifted shut and she felt lifted up by the simple repetition that seemed to write the words on her very soul. Although it was Nelson voicing his forgiveness for the way Joe had treated her all those years, Drusilla had put herself into the deceptively powerful statement.

I, Drusilla Fussner, forgive you, Joe Fussner, for doubting me after I married you, and for being unaware of my need for love and understanding.

Maybe it was Nelson's gentle, mesmerizing voice, or maybe it was the way he was opening a private part of himself to her, but as his forgiveness statement lingered in her mind after he'd finished speaking, the kitchen took on a sacred silence. When she opened her eyes, she saw that Michael and Nadine had just reopened theirs, as well.

Maybe I've been wrong to believe that Nelson Wengerd would treat me like Joe did. Maybe he's not like any other man I've ever met.

"That was incredible," Jo whispered, blinking away tears. "As a daughter, I saw my *dat* in a different light, of course. I had no idea what you were suffering all those years, Mamm," she added as she squeezed Drusilla's hand. "But saying and writing out statements like this one Nelson just gave us could help us deal with the upset we feel, ain't so?"

Jo leaned forward to smile directly at Nelson. "*Denki* for sharing your forgiveness method, Nelson. And Michael," she added as she gazed at the young man across from her, "I'm so grateful for your forgiveness, too. Forgiveness sets us free to move forward—"

"And that's what I want to do, Josie-girl," Michael assured her as he stretched his arm across the table to grasp her hand. "*Denki* for being patient with me even when I jumped to the wrong conclusion about your standing up to Saul last Sunday."

As Drusilla witnessed her daughter and future son-in-law revisiting their own forgiveness, part of her soul fluttered free, like a white dove sparkling in the sunrise. Surely she could learn from the simple wisdom of sharing her injured feelings rather than letting them fester, as she'd done with Joe. Indeed, as she found a smile for the man who sat at the head of her table this evening, he seemed so wise—so quietly wonderful—as he held her gaze.

"Nelson, you've given me a lot to consider as we observe *Gut* Friday tomorrow," Drusilla murmured. "You—and your sister—have been so patient with me, and I'm grateful that you've come here again despite my sending you away last week. I hope you can both forgive me."

Nadine nodded, visibly moved by the past few moments. "I can do that, Drusilla," she murmured.

Nelson's face eased into a serene smile Drusilla knew she'd never forget. "Consider it done, dear."

Chapter 29

"Gut morning," Jo said as she held the door open for the three Wengerds on Friday. "We're pleased to see you folks again today as we fast and pray."

"It's a blessed day we get to spend with you and your *mamm*, even if it's to be a solemn occasion," Nadine said as she preceded Michael and Nelson into the kitchen. She handed Jo a lidded metal casserole pan, and on top of it sat a small, plastic storage container.

"We're happy to share scalloped potato and ham casserole for whichever meal you'd like to serve it, and I brought along some of the chocolate-covered Easter eggs I like to make each year—although, compared to *your* goodies, they're pretty plain," she admitted.

Jo waved off her modest remark, carrying the food to the table. "I'm delighted you brought some sweets, Nadine. Truth be told, I'm always excited to eat food other people have made!"

Mamm turned around at the stove, where she'd removed the percolating coffeepot from the burner. "What with skipping breakfast for our *Gut* Friday fast, I could certainly light into a candy egg or two with this coffee," she said lightly. "But we'll save them for later. *Denki* so much for bringing them—although you certainly didn't have to. Seems Jo and I've been in the mood to cook like the old days again, so we've made a lot of favorites for the weekend."

"It'll be fun to compare notes on favorite holiday foods," Nelson remarked as he hung his hat on a peg near the mudroom. "You are what you eat, you know!"

Jo laughed along with everyone else, watching Michael hang his wraps, as well. With the warmer weather, he'd switched from his broad-brimmed felt hat to a black straw fedora. She liked the way its sleeker lines accentuated the angles of his handsome face and made his gray-blue eyes appear more prominent—even if she wasn't supposed to be focused on his physical attributes on the most solemn day of the church year.

"For my part, I brought along our family Bible," Nelson continued. "I figured we'd also be sharing holiday traditions this weekend. At our house on *Gut* Friday morning, we take turns reading passages aloud from Isaiah and the crucifixion accounts in the Gospels, and then spend time contemplating each one."

Jo glanced at Mamm to gauge her reaction, because Nelson's suggestion was quite different from the way Dat had always declared the morning was for silence and private prayer. She suspected he hadn't felt confident pronouncing some of the biblical names and places, so he'd rarely read from Scripture or led them in their praying.

"That sounds like a fine idea," her mother said after a moment. "It'll make the morning go faster, and it'll feel more meaningful than the complete silence we've usually observed. Big Joe didn't like to lead worship activities—

and he felt it wasn't appropriate for women to lead them—so that was the way of it for us."

"We Wengerds have always encouraged everyone to take a turn," Nadine explained. "It was a *gut* way to start Michael reading the Bible aloud when he was a boy—and nobody fell asleep, because sooner or later you had to be ready to read."

Jo chuckled. She'd often caught her *dat* nodding off during their silent Friday mornings—not that she'd been impertinent enough to point this out.

"Shall we take our coffee into the front room?" she suggested. "As overcast and rainy as it's looking, the atmosphere will be almost as gloomy as it must've been on the day Jesus died, ain't so?"

When Mamm had filled everyone's mug, they took seats. Nelson chose the upholstered platform rocker by the end table, and he took an appreciative sip of his coffee before removing a folded list from his large old Bible. Jo sat an appropriate distance from Michael on the smaller sofa, while Nadine and Mamm sat on the couch and put their mugs on the coffee table.

"Shall we begin with prayer?" Nelson asked.

Jo bowed her head along with the others, grateful that he was taking charge of their *Gut* Friday observance without an attitude of taking over—as though his way was the *only* way.

"God and Father of us all," Michael's *dat* began, "as we contemplate the unthinkable events leading up to Jesus' arrest and crucifixion, make us mindful once again that He endured such suffering on our behalf—that He went along with Your will, even though He met with a painful, humiliating death, to shatter the chains of sin that still bind us today.

"Please don't give up on us, Lord," he entreated softly. "Be with us as we attempt to make our paths straight, a highway for the King to reenter our lives and show us a renewed sense of Your purpose. Amen."

Jo opened her eyes, sensing that Nelson's low, resonant voice had cast a spell of solemn serenity. Their ordinary front room took on an air of supplication—a heightened sense that all things were possible because God was among them.

"Our first reading comes from the prophet Isaiah, who foretold so much of the Savior's life centuries before the Messiah appeared," Nelson continued as the thin pages of his Bible whispered beneath his fingertips. "I'll read from the fifty-third chapter, verses three through six. 'He is despised and rejected of men; a man of sorrows, and acquainted with grief . . .'"

Jo closed her eyes to let the ancient words wash over her. This was a far different experience of the Scriptures than she'd ever had at church—closer to home and more personal.

". . . 'But he was wounded for our transgressions, he was bruised for our iniquities,'" Nelson continued sadly. "'The chastisement of our peace was upon him; and with his stripes we are healed . . .'"

Across the room, Mamm sat with her head bowed, fully engrossed in this prophesy of Jesus' death. Beside her, Nadine sat with her hands clasped in her lap, nodding as her brother continued to read.

". . . 'All we like sheep have gone astray; we have turned every one to his own way; and the Lord hath laid on him the iniquity of us all.'" Nelson sighed softly as he closed the Bible with his list of readings between its pages. "Let's ponder these words that still hold true today—and Michael, I'll let you choose which gospel version to continue with, whenever you're ready."

Michael rose to accept the Bible from his father. For several minutes they sat in silence, yet the room felt alive with their yearning for a better comprehension of what Jesus' death meant. As the young man beside her quietly riffled through the New Testament, glancing at his *dat*'s list of suggested readings, Jo admired the way Michael had set aside his customary shyness. He was well prepared to read aloud because this practice had been instilled in him since he was a child.

"We'll continue now with how the religious leaders were plotting against Jesus—and how Judas Iscariot goes along with their plan," Michael said, pausing to look at each of them individually. "I'll be reading from the twenty-sixth chapter of Matthew, the verses that apply to these events. 'Then assembled together the chief priests, and the scribes, and the elders of the people . . . and consulted that they might take Jesus by subtlety and kill him.'"

Jo listened, drawn in by the sincerity of Michael's tone—his familiarity with the text, which allowed him to read with great expression. Even though he was dealing with passages describing a terrible time in the life of Christ and Christianity as a whole, his warmth made Jo glad once again that she'd soon be marrying a man so well acquainted with the words of their faith.

"'Then one of the twelve, called Judas Iscariot, went unto the chief priests. And said unto them, What will ye give me, and I will deliver him unto you?'" Michael continued, changing his voice to assume the furtive character of Judas. "'And they covenanted with him for thirty pieces of silver. And from that time he sought opportunity to betray him.'"

As Michael handed her the Bible, Jo's heart began to pound. The leaders of their church district had never encouraged members to study the scriptures on their own— and indeed, she'd rarely heard the Word read aloud by a woman. As though her fiancé realized this, he smiled warmly at her.

"The next verses on the list lead up to the Last Supper," he said softly. "When we've had some time to contemplate the deal Judas has made with the priests, you can start in at verse twenty. You'll do fine, Josie-girl."

The love light in Michael's gray-blue eyes made her forget all about Judas's betrayal. With the large Bible resting on her lap, Jo bowed her head and asked God to be with her as she took a more active part in this sacred observance. She had no idea how much time had passed, but when her nerves had settled, she opened the Bible to the list, which Michael had used to mark her place.

Jo prayed she wouldn't stumble over the words and ruin the mood the Wengerd men had established.

"Matthew twenty-six, verses twenty through twenty-five," she began, following the fine print with her finger. "'Now when the even was come, he sat down with the twelve. And as they did eat, he said, Verily I say unto you that one of you shall betray me. And they were exceeding sorrowful, and began every one of them to say unto him, Lord, is it I?'"

The words suddenly became much more powerful to her. Jo had to stop for a moment to consider that ancient question: *Is it I?* How many times a week—or in a day?—did she let Jesus down because she doubted His way and didn't seek out His will for her life?

Realizing that she'd stopped, and that the others in the room might think she'd faltered, Jo went on reading the verses about Jesus saying his betrayer was right there at the table, and that it would be better if he'd not even been born. "'Then Judas, which betrayed him, answered and said, Master, is it I? He said unto him, Thou hast said.'"

Jo swallowed hard. Judas seemed even more deceitful to her now because he'd *known* the answer to his question, yet he'd had the nerve to ask it as though he was innocent of any wrongdoing, like the other disciples gathered around the table.

Aware that Mamm and Nadine were waiting for the Bible, Jo glanced at the next passage on Nelson's list before deciding who should read next. She crossed the front room and gave the big book to her mother. "Next comes the supper part—the words we always hear at communion services," she remarked.

Mamm nodded, appearing grateful that she was to read a familiar passage that didn't involve the violence that would come in the garden of Gethsemane. After several minutes of contemplation had passed, her mother read the verses about breaking the bread and sharing the wine with quick efficiency, as though she didn't want to allow herself time to hesitate—or to lose her place on a large page filled with very small print.

Nadine then read about Jesus praying in the garden

while His followers nodded off, and about the appearance of Judas and the crowd who came to arrest Jesus.

Even with silent times to consider what they were reading, the morning passed quickly as Peter denied he knew Jesus, and Pilate condemned Jesus to death, and the crowd cried out for Barrabas to be freed while Jesus went on to face the grisly fate foretold by Isaiah.

By the time Christ had been spit upon, beaten, and hung on the cross to be further humiliated, the front room's atmosphere took on a sense of desperation. As they read about darkness covering the earth and Jesus crying out "My God, my God, why hast thou forsaken me?" before He breathed His last, Jo was blinking back tears.

How could Jesus' mother, Mary, Mary Magdalene, and the other women endure witnessing such a brutal death while an earthquake and other natural disasters were going on around them? What extraordinary faith had it required for those women to go to the tomb with Joseph of Arimathea to prepare Jesus' body for burial? They were surely afraid for their own lives, considering that the priests and the unruly mob might associate them with the King of the Jews they'd put to death that morning.

After Nelson had finished reading the final passage, ending when the tomb was sealed, he gently closed the Bible. "It's been a morning filled with deep meaning, and I'm grateful that you and Jo were willing to share it with us, Drusilla," he said softly. "We've observed our fast, and we've heard the ancient story so important to our faith. Whenever you ladies want to set out lunch, I think we're all ready to enjoy it."

"*Denki* for sharing your *Gut* Friday tradition with us," Jo whispered. "It's been an incredible experience. I'll never again see this day of fasting and prayer as something to be endured rather than as the saddest day we Christians observe. We—not just the folks of Jesus' day—are the reason for His suffering."

Chapter 30

Saturday morning's rain was a welcome gift, even if it diminished the usual crowd at The Marketplace. When Michael came back into the shop after checking the potted perennials in the outdoor display, Molly Shetler was waiting for him.

"Special delivery from Pete," she said, waving a thick white envelope at him. "And to go along with this, we'd like to propose a picnic this evening with you and Jo at your new homesite."

Michael's pulse sped up as he slipped a sheaf of folded pages from the envelope. "The house plans! Jo will be so excited to see these!"

"You look pretty excited yourself, Michael," she remarked. "Shall I let your dearly beloved know there's to be a picnic, or would you like to tell her?"

For a moment, he was too engrossed in scanning Pete's meticulous drawings and descriptions to answer. "Uh— why don't you girls arrange that?" he blurted out when he realized Molly was waiting for an answer. "She'll want to talk about the food, no doubt, and I have no idea about such things!"

"You men are all alike," Molly teased, waving him off. "See you later, Michael. I hope you like what Pete's sketched out for you. He's pleased that you asked him to build your new home—and he's *really* pleased that you Wengerds are moving to Morning Star."

As she turned to leave, it occurred to Michael that he already felt welcome here. Even though he'd begun to realize he'd be leaving a lot of longtime friends, cousins, and favorite places behind, his new life with Jo would fill in the blank spaces in his life. Until this past Christmas, he'd never dreamed he and Dat might pull up roots and head for a different Missouri community to start up a brand-new Wengerd Nursery store—and a whole new life.

What an adventure they'd taken on! And he'd be so busy overseeing the construction of the new house, the greenhouses, and the nursery plots that he'd have no time to miss his former life in Queen City.

"Looks like you must've gotten some *gut* news, son. That's quite a smile on your face," his *dat* said as he came in from outside.

"House plans! Want to see them?"

It was fun to study the various rooms and features Pete had added in, and to hear his father's comments about the quality and clarity of the plans. It was even more gratifying, however, to sense Dat's relaxed happiness.

"Jo and I are going to a picnic with Pete and Molly at the house site this evening," Michael said. "Maybe you'll want to mosey over to see what Aunt Nadine and Drusilla are up to. Just you adults without us pesky kids, you know."

Dat laughed out loud, a joyful noise Michael hadn't heard for a while. "You never know what we *mature adults* might cook up while you're gone," he teased. "It's a relief to feel that I can show up unannounced without Drusilla slamming the door on me. It'll be a chance to get better acquainted with her—maybe talk about what she'd like her future to include."

Michael couldn't miss the secretive smile his *dat* was trying to hide. "You gave her quite a blessing when you began forgiving Joe Fussner at the table Thursday night," he said softly. "And your forgiveness statements are a tool anybody can use—anywhere—to lift their spirits out of a dark place."

"Well, if anyone's spent a lot of time in a dark place, it's Drusilla." Dat refolded the drawings and handed them back to Michael. "I'm so pleased you and Jo will be starting out in your own home, son—and I'm confident that the new nursery here will provide us a *gut* income just like the one in Queen City has."

"*Denki* for starting a new store, Dat," Michael put in quickly. "And I hope that you and Drusilla will soon know, without a single doubt, that you're ready to move forward together. But there'll always be the *dawdi haus* at our place, if you need a home."

"Or if I'm ever in the doghouse," Dat teased. "At some time or another, every wife declares that her husband needs to clear out for a while. Or he just knows when it's best to make himself scarce."

As he and his father shared another good laugh, Michael's soul filled with hope. It seemed that this Easter season would be about rebirth for his family—and for that, Michael gave thanks.

* * *

Jo thrummed with excitement as Michael pulled the courting buggy onto the property where she would soon take up her new life as Mrs. Wengerd. Was it her imagination, or did this place look especially beautiful, with lush grass covering it and a liberal sprinkling of dogwood and redbud trees in the woods that grew along the creek?

"This will be such a pretty place to live," she said as Michael came around to help her down. "I can recall when Dat's Belgians grazed here. People came from miles around—even from other states—to buy dependable draft horses from Big Joe Fussner."

Michael smiled at her, still holding her at the waist. "I'm glad you have those positive memories of your father, Josie-girl," he murmured. "I wasn't here to listen to your *mamm*'s recollections of him, but I suspect some of them might've left a bad taste in your mouth. And that's a shame. I'm sorry."

She smiled wistfully, grateful for Michael's astute observation. "I can tell you without a doubt that he would've liked *you*, Michael—and that he'd have been tickled to know we're staying here on his homeplace rather than moving away."

Jo gazed out over their parcel of land, refusing to let Mamm's unfortunate past spoil this beautiful spring evening. "My mother's perceptions of Dat will always be different from mine—naturally," she mused aloud. "And you know, Michael, we all have beliefs that turn out not to be true. After all, I spent most of my life believing I'd never find a man who could love a tall, bulky girl who looked just like Big Joe Fussner.

"But here you are," she added softly. "And here we stand, ready to build a house and a life together."

Michael hugged her close. "I've never understood why you describe yourself that way," he murmured. "Why would I want a woman I'd have to lean over to kiss—not that I would've had the nerve to kiss one before you coaxed me out of my shell."

He eased away to gaze at her face. "To me, you're just perfect, Josephine Louise," he added in a reverent whisper. "Your complexion is flawless, and your beautiful brown eyes are the window to a soul that understands mine as no one else ever could. I feel blessed that you even noticed me last year when we set up shop at The Marketplace—when you invited Dat and me to stay in your *dawdi*—"

The *clip-clop* of hooves made them look toward the road. Molly and Pete waved at them, smiling as only happy newlyweds could.

"They look absolutely delighted with each other," Jo said as she returned the Shetlers' waves.

"We'll be grinning the same way when we marry on June fourth, Josie-girl."

After Pete parked the buggy, he got right down to business. "Let's figure out where you want your house—and probably a stable and a shed or two—and we can stake them out right now," he suggested. "That way, I can have our Mennonite construction friends dig your basement with their heavy equipment and pour your foundations so I can start *my* work."

A tremor of sheer joy shimmered up Jo's spine. "This is so exciting! It feels *real* now," she said as Molly came to stand beside her. They watched the men, who were already fetching the wooden stakes and spooled twine Pete had brought along.

"You can put the stable and sheds wherever they'll best fit your plans for your nursery buildings, Michael," Jo called out. "But I'd like the house to sit right there on that rise, where we'll see the sun come up each morning and watch it set when day's done."

Michael and Pete looked over to where she was pointing.

"*Gut* choice, Jo. Consider it done," her fiancé agreed with a nod.

Pete laughed. "*Gut* man, Wengerd," he teased. "Already letting your woman have things her way. Happy wife, happy life—right, Molly, my love?"

"You should know, Shetler," Molly replied lightly.

As the four of them chuckled together, Jo had a sense that she and Michael would soon become part of a new generation—a new little community within the Morning Star church district—along with Regina and Gabe Flaud, Molly and Marietta and their new husbands, and Lydianne and Bishop Jeremiah. And what better friends could they find to share the journey of early marriage, new parenthood, and the future of The Marketplace they'd all had a hand in establishing?

Chapter 31

"As we celebrate this blessed Easter morning together, friends, let us never forget that Christ's death on the cross was all about God's forgiveness of our sins," Bishop Jeremiah proclaimed to the folks gathered in his large front room. "And Christ rose from the grave as a sign that we are to move forward from our darkness to live in the light of new birth. Because He lives, we are a redeemed people!"

Drusilla sat up straighter on the pew bench as a jolt of excitement shot up her spine. The bishop was in fine form this morning, and the joy on his face as he preached the main sermon was contagious. As she glanced around the crowded room, it occurred to her that although folks were dressed in black church clothing, their faces radiated the blessing that Jeremiah Shetler shared with them.

Or was she seeing these friends through the lens of love—the new vision Nelson and Nadine had been encouraging during their weekend visit? Maybe these people were the same as they'd always been, but because the Wengerds accepted Drusilla for who she was—past damages, dashed hopes, and all—she was developing a whole new point of view.

She'd taken some time to start forgiving Joe, as well, by writing out statements similar to the one Nelson had spoken at the table. At first it had reminded her of writing sentences as punishment for talking too much in class as a young schoolgirl. But then, as she'd allowed the true spirit of the exercise to sink in, the words seemed to pry open her long-locked heart.

"Now is the ideal time to reach out to friends and family and share what we love about them," Bishop Jeremiah continued. "The brightness of Christ's love and mercy shines fresh light on our path. The old has passed away, and we must let it go. A new life in Christ awaits us if we will recognize it and accept it for the glorious gift it is. He is risen! Allelujah and amen!"

Seated beside Drusilla, Nadine let out a little gasp of happiness. "*Jah*," she whispered. "What a message. *That's* what Easter's all about."

The rest of the service passed quickly. After the bishop's ringing benediction had filled the front room, he smiled broadly.

"We'll have our annual egg hunt right after the common meal," he announced. "You kids know the drill—you're to stay in here helping your *mamms* set up for lunch without peeking outside! We'll meet on the front porch at one-thirty to hand out the baskets."

Folks sprang from their seats with unusual vigor, as though the adults were as eager to watch the egg hunt as their children were to scramble all over the Shetlers' large yard. Bishop Jeremiah and a few of the *dats* slipped out through the mudroom to begin hiding eggs—some were hard-boiled ones the kids had dyed at home, and the bright plastic ones contained candies and other little gifts from the bishop.

"My oh my, but your bishop can preach," Nadine remarked beneath the chatter of the other women heading for the kitchen. "Jeremiah's like a cheerleader for the Lord—so positive and upbeat. I imagine our friends back home are still enduring a sermon the bishop has lengthened because he feels Easter Sunday calls for an extra dose of admonition and chastisement."

She shook her head as she turned on the tap so she and Drusilla could fill water pitchers. "Our bishop seems to believe that because Christ had to suffer on the cross, we should bear the burden of guilt passed down through the ages—like original sin—without acknowledging His forgiveness," Nadine explained further. "And an egg hunt after church? Unheard of!"

Drusilla's eyebrows rose. "So come to Morning Star with Nelson and Michael!" she blurted out. "If you don't share the same beliefs as your bishop in Queen City, here's your chance to change the channel, *jah?*"

Nadine blinked. "Change the channel—like on a TV," she murmured. "I never thought of it that way."

"Maybe I spoke out of turn," Drusilla put in quickly. "I didn't mean to offend you, Nadine. Nelson says he's always depended on you to keep the books for the Queen City nursery, so—so maybe that's still your plan, and I should respect it."

What had gotten into her, presuming to tell Nelson's twin what to do and where to live? Nadine claimed she wasn't offended, and yet . . . wouldn't it be wonderful if she and Nadine could see each other every day?

As the two of them started for the front room with water pitchers, Margaret smiled brightly at Drusilla.

"You seem to be getting your bounce back," the bishop's mother murmured as she leaned close. "I hope you're feeling as perky as you look?"

Her hands were full, so Drusilla nodded sideways toward Nadine. "Having a new friend has been *gut* medicine for me—but I think those supplements you gave me are helping, too. *Denki* for your kindness and concern, Margaret."

She didn't want to go into the details about Nelson's forgiveness exercise—this wasn't the time or place to explain such a process. But wasn't it nice that the bishop's *mamm* had complimented her on how perky she seemed? Margaret's words made Drusilla feel even more upbeat, and she realized how very fortunate she was that the Wengerd family had given her another chance to spend time with them.

The Wengerds have given me something else, too—and if my outlook continues to improve from being around them, who knows? I might have to sew a pink dress and actually wear it!

The idea made Drusilla's eyes widen, and it was still simmering on the back burner of her mind as they all returned home after the egg hunt. She felt so carefree, she didn't blink an eye when Jo suggested that they get the lawn games out of the shed so they could spend Easter Monday playing outside and enjoying a picnic with the Wengerds.

"I can't recall the last time we played croquet or badminton," Drusilla said after Nelson and Michael had left for the young Shetlers' *dawdi haus* later in the day. "I think you were still a young girl, Jo. When it came time to hit wooden balls through wickets or swat the birdie across a net, your *dat* seemed to find other things that needed doing."

Nadine laughed out loud as the three of them gathered at the kitchen table for an evening cup of tea. "Truth be told, I can't recall the last time I held a croquet mallet, either," she admitted with a twinkle in her eyes. "I think we're all due for some playtime tomorrow, Drusilla!"

Monday morning, as Nelson wiped the dust from the diagram showing how the croquet wickets were to be arranged, he wondered what the day would bring. He and Michael were in charge of laying out the croquet field in the flat side yard, and then they were to put up the badminton net behind the house, where it would be shadier. Meanwhile, the women were figuring out how to serve the various foods they'd prepared in picnic fashion— which might involve carrying the kitchen table outside. The old wooden table Big Joe had built years ago was in a sad state of disrepair.

"Too bad we didn't know we'd be eating outdoors. We could've put together a new picnic table as a gift," Nelson remarked as he pressed metal wickets into the ground.

"Well, now you've got an idea for a future gift," Michael pointed out. "Who could've imagined Drusilla agreeing to an entire day of games? Even if it *is* Easter Monday."

"*Jah*, there's hope for her yet. Maybe it's another form

of resurrection we're seeing," Nelson said softly. The last thing he wanted was for Drusilla to overhear him and think he was making fun of her—which could trigger a mood swing that would send him packing for the very last time. "Maybe we'll see a side of Drusilla she's not shown to anyone for a long, long time."

"It'll probably help that none of us has played croquet for years," Michael put in as he wiped off the color-banded wooden mallets and balls. "It sort of levels the playing field—although if I don't win, there's something seriously wrong, ain't so?"

Behind them, Jo laughed loudly as she crossed the yard. "I heard that, Wengerd!" she called out. "And if you think I'm going to *let* you win, because I'm a nice, proper fiancée, you're in for a rude awakening. As a teenager, I could swing a pretty mean mallet when I played with my friends."

Nelson smiled, pacing off the proper distance between the next set of wickets. It did his heart good to watch Jo and Michael spar with each other. And if Jo was in high spirits, her *mamm* was more likely to have fun—the best possible situation for all of them.

"If you're interested, we have coffee, tea, and a pastry tray available before we start croquet," Jo announced. "It's my way of thanking you for going along with these games today. A lot of fellows would probably play under protest— or not at all."

Nelson straightened to his full height, surveying the wickets to be sure they were correctly aligned. "Easter Monday is supposed to be Easter fun day," he pointed out. "If nothing else, we'll have something to laugh about as we look back on our athletic ability—or lack of it—while we enjoy our picnic."

"And it gives us something to do besides sitting around visiting, like um, *older* folks tend to do," Michael teased. "Let's check out your goodies, Jo, before I get myself into more trouble with my smart remarks."

As Nelson slid into his seat at the kitchen table and snatched a large brownie with chocolate frosting and sprinkles from the tray, he flashed Drusilla his best smile. She and his sister had already been busy in the kitchen when he and Michael had arrived this morning, and the aromas of tangy beef and fresh bread filled the air.

"What smells so *gut*?" he asked. "You ladies are putting a lot of effort into our picnic—and I appreciate it! Once Michael and I go home, we'll be fending for ourselves again in the kitchen."

Drusilla raised a playful eyebrow as she took the seat to his left. "If you play your cards right, you might be taking home some sauced brisket, dinner rolls, and macaroni salad to get you through the week."

"What if I'd rather flirt with the cook than play cards?" Nelson shot back.

Where had *that* remark come from? Drusilla's expression told him he'd startled her as much as he'd surprised himself, because they were sitting with their children and his sister. Even when alone, they hadn't teased each other about affection or romance.

Drusilla's cheeks flushed a becoming shade of pink and she appeared downright shy—until she rallied.

"Careful there, Nelson. You're at the table with *three* cooks, you know," she reminded him. "You'll get your take-home food no matter what, but—well, maybe it wouldn't hurt to kiss up to me just a little. Who knows where it might lead?"

Nelson nearly choked on his bite of brownie. Had Drusilla really said the words *kiss up*? Was she throwing around some playful slang, or was she serious about the *kiss* part?

"We'll discuss what you mean by *kissing up* later," he murmured, holding her gaze. "We have young, impressionable ears at the table, after all."

After their coffee break they played a spirited practice round of croquet, followed by a game where they kept one another accountable for all the technicalities of properly hitting the wooden balls through the wickets and knocking an opponent's ball out of the way. It was a joy to see the sparkle in Drusilla's dark eyes as she engaged herself fully in play. The sound of her laughter bouncing off the side of the house kindled a new, brighter hope as Nelson played his best to keep up with her.

It was also fun to see Nadine playing with fervent concentration, laughing at every mallet stroke that went awry. "Loser has to fix lunch!" she teased when it appeared that she and Drusilla were going to come in last.

"I don't intend to eat a meal that a loser fixed, Nadine!" Drusilla retorted playfully. "I know who cooked all morning, and none of us have a thing to be ashamed of in that department."

"You've got that right, ladies." Nelson gave his blue ball a solid *whack*, driving it through the last wickets to strike the end post and win the game. "And I'm looking forward to our picnic so much, I don't even expect a prize for being the winner."

Nelson picked up his ball. As he walked over to the wooden croquet stand to hang up his mallet and drop his ball down the center slot, a hand grasped his elbow.

"You're a winner with me even when we're not playing a game, Nelson," Drusilla whispered. "So I know you'll figure out the best time to claim your prize."

With that, she returned to the playing field, aimed her red ball to hit Michael's orange one—and then placed her ball against his. With a solid *whack*, she sent his ball rolling halfway across the lawn to the tune of everyone's laughter and applause.

Nelson watched the remaining plays from the sideline. Jo came in second, followed by her mother, and Michael and Nadine finished last. As the game ended, Drusilla flashed Nelson a wink before she crossed the lawn to enter the house.

What was she up to? Instinct told him to mosey inside behind her, while his sister and the kids rehashed their final turns as they put away their equipment. Once inside the kitchen, he found Drusilla at the sink, where she could see the others through the window.

"Maybe you think I've been acting too forward," she murmured, "pushing you too far with such flirty talk and—"

"I think you're having a fine time today." Nelson walked over to stand beside her. "If you were serious about me kissing you, I'm serious about claiming my prize. Or if you'd rather wait until we could take a walk and be more private—"

With a final glance outside, Drusilla placed her hand timidly on his shoulder and gazed up at him. She looked as shy and frightened as a girl on her first date, yet longing was written all over her face.

Nelson also glanced outside, not wanting this long-awaited moment to be interrupted. When he saw that Michael and the others were bringing badminton equipment from the shed, he gently cupped Drusilla's face in his hand and kissed her. He eased away, giving her a chance to retreat—

But she rose on her tiptoes, her lashes fluttering against her cheeks as she claimed a second, longer kiss.

Drusilla's soft gasp told Nelson she'd enjoyed their moment of affection as much as he had. Heart pounding, determined not to overanalyze what they'd just shared, he stepped away. Hastily, he composed his expression before the cheerful voices on the porch came inside.

"What can I do to help, Drusilla?" Nelson asked in a voice that sounded strangely adolescent. "Shall we take the food from the fridge yet? Or shall I put water in this pitcher?"

Drusilla cleared her throat, regaining control of her emotions as Nadine bustled into the kitchen. "You and Michael can carry this table out into the shade," she replied a little more loudly than she needed to. "Put it wherever you can find a level spot, please."

"And I'll follow you boys with the place settings," Nadine put in. "We decided to use Jo's new cloth and the blue dishes today—perfect for a picnic, don't you agree, Nelson?"

Her tone told him that his sister might suspect what he and Drusilla had been doing. And why should he deny it? Nelson winked at her twice in rapid succession—the signal they'd shared as twins for most of their lives.

"Of course I agree," he teased, shifting the chairs away from the table. "In the presence of those who are handling my food, it's best if I go along with whatever I'm told, ain't so?"

Understanding sister that she was, Nadine congratulated him silently with her knowing smile. "It's *gut* for a man to know his place—right, Drusilla?"

"Absolutely," Drusilla replied without missing a beat. *Her* smile, along with the color in her cheeks, told Nelson that she was still feeling elated and pleased about their brief kisses.

And that made him happier than he'd been in a long, long time.

Chapter 32

As they lingered over their picnic lunch and played a few spirited games of badminton, Jo waited for the other shoe to drop. Her mother's buoyant mood seemed too good to be true. Even when Mamm had spilled her glass of lemonade and they'd scrambled to wipe it up—even when she'd batted crazily at the birdie and missed it several times—she laughed rather than becoming upset.

Whatever spell the Wengerds had cast was a balm to Jo's soul. Whatever Nelson had said or done when he'd been in the kitchen with Mamm had made her eyes sparkle as Jo hadn't seen, well—ever since she could remember. She recalled her mother's occasional moments of joy when Jo had blown out her birthday candles as a child, or had baked her first pie, but otherwise her parents had behaved like typical older people occupied with putting food on the table, keeping the house clean, and paying the bills.

Or maybe I just believed they were typical because they were the only parents I knew. Maybe in other families—the Wengerds, for instance—parents and children shared a lot more love and laughter as an everyday thing.

Jo blinked. Michael was trying for her attention. "*Jah*? You were saying—?"

His handsome face softened. "You seemed a million miles away, Josie-girl. Is everything all right?"

Jo noticed that Mamm, Nelson, and Nadine were carrying covered containers of food to the Wengerds' wagon. "Everything is *more* than all right," she replied. "Have you noticed that my mother didn't say one contrary word today?"

"Fingers crossed," he teased, holding both hands up with the digit and middle fingers entwined. "I wanted to be sure it's all right to leave the courting buggy and Starla here this week, as I did before."

"Absolutely. Nellie and I will take *gut* care of your little mare." Jo gazed at Michael, thrumming with the love she felt for him. "It's been such a fine Easter weekend—such a blessing to share the holiday with you and your family."

She took his hand as they walked toward the wagon. "Pete thinks his Mennonite friends will dig the basement of our house sometime this week," Michael said. "And after they pour the foundation, he'll ask the local fellows to join him for a work frolic or two—maybe as soon as next weekend!"

"That'll give us something exciting to watch," she remarked. "And it'll help the time pass faster as our wedding day approaches."

"Oh, I'll be doing more than watching," Michael put in with a chuckle. "Dat and I will be on the house construction crew—and Pete plans to have the concrete slabs poured for a couple of greenhouses and a shop after that."

"Mamm and I will organize the women to bring over some meals while you fellows are working," Jo said with a nod. She couldn't help smiling as they joined their parents and Nadine—because laughter went wherever Nadine did.

"We're in for some exciting times!" Nadine crowed as she hugged Jo. "I'll come along and assist with whatever needs doing while your new house is being built."

"*Denki* ahead of time for all the help you're giving us," Jo said.

Was it her imagination, or did her mother's eyes mist over as she, too, hugged Nelson's sister?

"Nadine, I hope you'll seriously consider moving to Morning Star with Nelson and Michael," Mamm said when she'd eased away. "I feel so *happy* when I'm with you Wengerds! I—I realize now that I've not gotten very close to other couples or made many *gut* friends over the years because I was hiding behind my unhappiness. And I don't want to do that anymore."

Everyone got quiet, pondering the major breakthrough Mamm's remark had just revealed. Nadine reached for her hand.

"For *you*, Drusilla, I'll consider it," she said quietly, glancing at her brother. "Nelson and I will discuss what it might mean for the nursery business in Queen City if I'm no longer keeping the books there—"

"We'll come up with something," Nelson put in firmly. He gazed at Mamm as though he saw her in a whole new light—and then, with an expectant smile, he opened his arms.

Jo swallowed hard. Her mother hesitated only a second before stepping into Nelson's embrace, resting her head on his broad shoulder as he held her close.

"I want you to be happy, Drusilla," he said softly. "No

matter what part I'll play in your life, I want you to keep feeling as bright and positive as you've been this weekend. If Nadine's company does that for you, so be it."

Mamm stepped back to gaze at him. "You know, Nelson, I'm starting to realize that emotionally, I've closed myself into a small, dark room for so long—and *you* have shown me that the key was in the lock all that time," she murmured. "It was my own doing that I stayed in that gloomy place. And I don't want to live there—I *refuse* to live there—anymore."

"Glad to hear it, dear," he said with a hitch in his voice.

When Nelson hugged her mother again, Jo had to blink back tears. It was a new thing entirely, to see her mother share affection with a man—but this wasn't the time to look back or to ponder what had gone wrong between her *mamm* and her *dat*.

It seemed that the miracle of resurrection they'd celebrated this Easter had taken place within her mother's heart and soul, as though a stone of discontentment had been rolled away and she'd come to life again, freed from her former unhappiness.

And for that, Jo was grateful to God.

"What would you think about me moving to Morning Star?" Nadine asked in a faraway voice. She'd been unusually quiet on the first leg of the journey home, and Nelson sensed she'd been processing all the matters that were on her mind.

"I wouldn't want to leave you shorthanded in the Queen City nursery," she continued. "I've always thought Mervin would do fine managing the place overall, but

I'm not too sure about him keeping the records organized for filing the taxes and such."

"I agree with your assessment," Nelson said with a nod. "Mervin's a go-getter, but a pencil pusher? Not so much. However," he added, slowing the horse for the upcoming intersection, "if we sell the business to him outright and concentrate our efforts on the new store in Morning Star—and the shop at The Marketplace—it'll be up to him to handle the business end of things or to hire somebody for that. It'll no longer be our concern."

"Do you want to be completely out of our nursery in Queen City?" Michael challenged from his seat behind the driver's bench. "I thought we were using some of the funds and nursery stock to establish the new place—"

"And we will," Nelson insisted. "If we sold the place, though, we'd have even more capital to invest in our new store—even if we gave Mervin a really *gut* deal."

"Do you think he can afford to buy it?" Nadine's frown expressed her doubts. "What if he doesn't want to invest a bunch of money—or get a business loan from the bank? He was figuring on our keeping it, after all."

Nelson had been pondering this aspect of his move to Morning Star over the past weekend. Drusilla's remarks about Nadine's presence had further cemented ideas that had previously only teased at him.

"The way I see it, a man does better with a business if he's fully invested in it—committed to it financially as well as emotionally. If Mervin doesn't buy it," Nelson continued with a shrug, "we can either keep the place and hire a different manager, or we can find a new buyer."

Nadine's smile suggested that she knew the answer to

the question she was about to ask. "And what, pray tell, has changed your mind about this situation, brother? If I'm hearing you correctly, you're saying you'd be fine with me moving to Morning Star—"

"Indeed I would."

"—because you're apparently ready to sever all ties with Queen City when you relocate."

Nelson smiled to himself, deciding he'd dance around his answer rather than giving his twin a direct response.

"We won't be severing *all* ties, because we'll still have our friends and family there," he pointed out. "But you heard Drusilla as we were leaving. Our presence makes her *happy*. I'd be a fool to make this major, once-in-a-lifetime move without fully considering her feelings, wouldn't I?"

Nadine slipped her hand beneath his elbow. "If I hadn't seen it for myself, I would've had a hard time believing the total turnaround in Drusilla's mindset," she admitted. "It was gratifying to hear that we've played a part in her coming out of her small dark room, ain't so?"

"It's been a labor of love from the beginning," Nelson replied softly. "I was flabbergasted when she made that remark about the key being in the door all along—but now I believe she and I can lead a fulfilling life together."

He shifted on the bench, checking the upcoming cross-road for traffic. "Drusilla will still have an occasional mood swing or hissy fit—like every one of us—but she claims she's finished having a constant negative frame of mind. And if she's giving *me* some of the credit for bringing her out of her darkness, who am I to question her?

"And truth be told," he added, focusing on the brown

eyes so like his own, "*I* would be happier if you came to Morning Star with us, sister. We've never lived apart—and I'm not sure I want us to. You've always been my personal ray of sunshine, you know."

"I was born to be a blessing," Nadine quipped, obviously pleased with his reply. "I wasn't looking forward to losing your company, either, Nelson. And what an adventure it'll be, to pack up and move to a totally different town at this stage of our lives!"

She smiled as she looked off into the distance, enjoying the lush, green countryside they were passing through. "I adore Bishop Jeremiah, too, so the prospect of hearing him preach on Sundays is even more of an incentive to make my home in Morning Star," she continued. "I'll need to figure out where to live, but we're *gut* at problem solving, ain't so?"

"Depending on how close you want to be to the rest of us," Michael put in from the back bench, "we could ask Lydianne if she's putting her house up for sale. She won't be living there once she and Bishop Jeremiah marry in May, after all."

"I'm sure Drusilla would put you up in her *dawdi haus* until you make a decision about where to live. I'm assuming you'll want your own house," Nelson said. He smiled, considering another possibility. "She'd probably even let you build a place on her farm, as she's allowing the kids to do. She seems inclined to bend over backward if it means you'll live nearby."

Nadine's face lit up as she laughed. "I have that effect on folks, don't I?" she teased. "You fellows have come up with some feasible ideas, so I'm not at all concerned about where I'll be hanging my hat in the future. I'm just really happy that I'll be spending my time with you and Drusilla, Nelson. And I'll be able to watch Michael and Jo start their family. It'll all work out."

"It will," Nelson agreed with a nod. "God always sees to that, doesn't He?"

Chapter 33

Over the next few weeks, as April gave way to May, Jo was caught up in a whirlwind of activity. She and Mamm were busy writing to faraway friends and family about coming to the wedding on June fourth. Although she'd assumed business at her Marketplace bakery would slow down after Easter, she kept busy baking all during the week and closed up her shop with empty shelves each Saturday.

The only disappointment was the weather: Several days of rain stalled work on the new house, so it was the last weekend in April before the Mennonite crew could dig the basement and pour the foundation.

Jo and her mother decided to sew their wedding clothes while it was too muddy for Mamm to work in her garden plots. It excited them both to see a finished wedding dress of vibrant sky blue hanging on a padded hanger, along with a beautiful white organza apron embellished with a row of white embroidered roses along the top. Mamm's dress for the wedding was black, as befitted a special church occasion, but it looked crisp and fresh compared to her other clothes.

The final Saturday of April also gave Jo something to speculate about. She'd loaded her wagon and said good-bye to Mamm early before her day at The Marketplace—but she returned to the house for the notebook in which she kept track of baking supplies she needed to buy. As she hurried past the upstairs room next to her bedroom, her mother looked up from the sewing machine with a startled expression.

Mamm's fabric was bright pink. And so was her face.

Her thoughts swirling, Jo continued into her room, but on the way out with her notebook she paused in the next doorway. "What's that you're making?" she asked lightly, recalling the shirt pattern that had been in the sack with that fabric.

Mamm appeared to be making up a quick story—but then she laughed as though she knew she'd been caught.

"As you know," she teased with a raised eyebrow, "the Wengerds left this fabric on the porch a while back, after Nelson dared me to sew a dress as bright as Nadine's. I might never get up the nerve to wear it," she admitted, "but working with this pretty pink makes me feel younger—and it gives me hope that maybe Nadine will move to Morning Star."

"I suspect she'll find a way to do that," Jo remarked. "The Wengerd twins like to make things happen, ain't so?"

"They do. And I'm glad Nadine can come this weekend—her phone message said she's found a new bookkeeper for their cousin, so their nursery business is all settled now."

Jo nodded. Even though she'd intended to arrive early at her bakery, she thought about what her mother had revealed a moment ago. This was the first she'd heard about

Nelson's dare, but his words had obviously had a positive effect on Mamm—and that deserved mention.

"Something tells me you're a lot happier about Nelson moving to Morning Star than you used to be, and I'm glad, Mamm. He's a dear man."

Mamm focused on positioning her fabric under the machine's needle, as though pondering her response. "He is," she finally agreed. She looked up from her sewing, wide-eyed, appearing hesitant to continue. "Michael's a fine young man, too, and I—well, I owe you a huge apology, Josephine."

Jo swallowed, gripping her notebook. Her mother had rarely shown her softer, more vulnerable side—nor had apologies ever been easy for her. But Jo sensed Mamm had come to a crossroad sometime after the Wengerds' Easter weekend visit. Her emotions were probably undergoing a radical change as she thought about what her future might look like if she opened herself to more of those embraces she and Nelson had shared.

"All those years I tried to talk you out of getting married?" Mamm whispered hoarsely. "All that time I insinuated that because you look so much like your *dat*, young men might not take to you? I was trying to protect you from being disappointed with a *maidel* lifestyle—even as I was saying you couldn't *trust* men, so you shouldn't marry one anyway.

"I was wrong, Jo," she said with a deep sigh. "I was so misguided, treating you that way, dear daughter. I'm sorry I said those hurtful things—repeated them so often over the years. I realize now that they're just not true."

The bottom dropped out of Jo's stomach. Her world began to tilt. Over the past few months, Michael's love had proven that Mamm's longtime objections to men and marriage didn't apply to him, so she'd stopped listening to her mother's rants on the subject. Mamm seemed to cave in on herself as she slumped at the sewing machine, so Jo decided not to affirm that yes, Mamm's remarks had indeed hurt her as she'd been growing up.

"Mamm, you—you don't have to explain or apologize or—"

"But I do!" Mamm blurted out. She gazed at Jo with a stricken, heartsick expression. "When I think about how *I* would've felt if my mother had constantly told me such painful—well, I don't know how you've managed to live under the same roof with me for all this time. Most girls would've left home, I think. Can you forgive me for treating you so poorly, Jo?"

The last words came out in a rush, stunning Jo with their intensity. There'd been a time, not so long ago, when Mamm would've been fussing and crying out as she'd held this conversation, but this morning her mother was calmly collected, in control of her thoughts and emotions.

"Please, Jo," Mamm whispered, rising from her chair. "You and I need to be right with each other. I know I've caught you at a bad time, when you're wanting to be at your shop—"

Suddenly, opening Fussner Bakery two hours early wasn't important. Letting her notebook drop to the floor, Jo rushed forward to give Mamm the reassurance that only she could provide. Her mother's head came to her shoulder—because, yes, Jo *was* made in Big Joe Fussner's image—but her words had opened an emotional floodgate.

"I do forgive you," Jo rasped as she held her trembling mother close. "I always knew you wanted the best for me,

Mamm—wanted me to choose a life that would sustain me as a *maidel* who could live independently. When Michael came along and convinced me that *his* vision of me was true, however, I went along with that instead."

"Bless his soul, Michael couldn't be a finer, more decent fellow, and I love him to pieces," Mamm murmured, blotting her tears against Jo's dress. "He's a saint for putting up with me, and for doing things that will be best for you as a couple."

Sniffling, Jo couldn't help but smile. "The apple didn't fall far from the tree, you know."

Her mother eased away to gaze at Jo. "*Jah*, Nelson's a saint as well, and I'm lucky he didn't give up on me long ago. But do *not* tell him I'm sewing a shirt with that pattern he brought!" she added emphatically. "It's a surprise. For one of these days when the time's right."

Jo sensed there was more to the story than her *mamm* was telling, but didn't she and Nelson deserve a few secrets? And if it meant Nelson would be seen in public wearing a bright pink shirt—possibly at the same time Mamm was wearing a dress that matched it—Jo didn't want to miss *that*! Just the picture in her mind, of the two parents greeting church friends in such apparel, would keep her entertained until she saw them actually carrying out the dare.

"I won't breathe a word. Some secrets are just too *gut* to reveal ahead of time, *jah*?"

"I thought you'd see it that way." Mamm smoothed the front of her apron and gazed lovingly at Jo. "I have Nelson to thank for teaching me how to release my old hurts by writing those forgiveness statements. I feel a lot better now that I've let go of those mean old feelings that dragged me down."

"That's usually the way it works," Jo observed.

"*Denki* for hearing me out. You go on to The Market-place and have yourself a *gut* day, all right?" her mother continued as she stooped to pick Jo's notebook up from the floor. "I suspect we'll be talking more about the Wengerds' future plans when the men come for supper tonight."

With a final hug, Jo took off for her Saturday at the bakery. Whenever she caught a glimpse of Nelson in the commons or chatting with customers outside, where he sold hanging plants and perennials, the thought of him wearing a bright pink shirt made her chuckle to herself.

It was the most fun she'd had since Easter weekend, sharing such a secret with her mother.

After Drusilla finished pressing Nelson's new shirt, she held it up on its hanger to admire it. *Years* it had been since she'd sewn a man's clothing, and with any luck— and some help from God—she'd take on that task again someday soon. It would feel a little odd and scary to have a man upstairs again, perhaps sharing her bedroom . . . and her bed.

Quickly, before the idea of resuming *relations* with a man could spin her into an anxious mood, she hung the shirt all the way in the back of the closet where she and Jo stored their fabric and sewing supplies—right along-side the dress that matched it. If Nadine spotted the color-ful garments during one of her weekend visits, Drusilla's proverbial cat would be out of its bag and she'd lose control over when Nelson saw his new shirt.

She went downstairs to the kitchen, happily lunching on cold, leftover casserole as she stood at the counter making two pies. For supper, she was going to roast a whole chicken with carrots, onions, celery, and potatoes—such a simple meal, yet simple things made her feel very contented these days. Drusilla could already imagine the grateful, delighted expression on Nelson's face as he took his first bite of the juicy chicken and slathered butter and jelly over fresh biscuits.

Making Nelson happy was starting to feel like a very worthwhile life mission—and if he invited her to do that over the long haul, Drusilla knew she wouldn't refuse.

Chapter 34

Late Friday afternoon, as Nelson began putting away his tools, he felt a deep sense of satisfaction. It was the eighth of May. After numerous rain-related delays, the men of Morning Star had finally held a work day to frame in Michael and Jo's new home. Thanks to Pete's organization, all the building materials had arrived. He'd already cut a lot of the lumber to size—and he and Glenn had even constructed some of the exterior walls and trusses—so the structure had gone up in the space of a day. The plywood roof was on it, too.

"Let's call it *gut* for now," the blond carpenter called out to the crowd of workers. "While you Wengerds and Flauds spend your Saturday at The Marketplace resting up, the rest of us will put on the shingles and get cooking on the interior walls. *Denki* for your *gut* help today, everyone!"

"No, *denki* for your *amazing* help," Michael chimed in over the men's low chatter. "I was getting concerned about the place being finished in time, but you fellows are the *best*! Jo will be flabbergasted when she sees today's progress."

"It's best to keep the women in a state of surprise and delight," Glenn remarked. "Happy wife, happy life—right, Gabe?"

"Don't I know it!" Gabe replied. "Especially because this is Mother's Day weekend."

Nelson couldn't miss the smile on Gabe's handsome face, which was now framed by a beard that was filling in nicely. His wife, Regina, was getting very round with their first child.

"Something tells me Jo's been watching us through her binoculars," Gabe continued lightly. "She was only here while she was serving lunch today, but I'm betting she knows exactly what we've accomplished—and who was working on which parts of the house, too!"

Michael laughed out loud. "You're right, Gabe. Jo doesn't miss much."

Nelson agreed with his son's assessment, and he suspected that Drusilla had been sharing Jo's binoculars. As the women had gathered up the lunch dishes, she'd remarked that she would wait until the house was completely framed in before she walked around inside it, so she wouldn't be in the carpenters' way.

That suited Nelson fine. He had a walk planned for later this evening—and he had a few other plans that included Drusilla, too.

When would be the best time to give her the quilt stashed in his buggy? He believed Drusilla would be delighted with its bright colors and the bold pattern Martha Maude and Anne had chosen—but she would also realize that such a gift represented a considerable cash investment on his part . . . which she would see as a sign of his commitment to their future together.

He couldn't just hand Drusilla the large, rolled bundle—which Nadine had helped him wrap in gift paper—without prefacing his presentation. He had to express what was in his heart and soul, not just say what had been on his mind for the past few weeks.

Easter weekend had given him an entirely new perspective on Jo's mother. Nelson sensed she was finally ready to accept him—to love him—as her husband, but he couldn't take her feelings for granted. Every woman wanted to be wooed.

Exchanging pleasantries with the other men as they left for home, Nelson took his time tucking his smaller tools back into his leather tool belt. The large metal box in the back of the rig held his power tools, which were adapted so they'd plug into the car battery he'd also brought along.

At last Pete gave him a wave, and Michael was the only other person who remained at the work site.

"We made a lot of progress today, son," Nelson remarked, clapping Michael's shoulder. "How about if you walk on back to the house and give Jo the lowdown—and tell Drusilla I'll be there for supper in a bit? Now that your house is in place, I want to visualize how the nursery buildings and greenhouses will fit on the rest of the property."

Michael's eyebrows rose, because *he* should probably participate in such a visualization—and after a tiring day, he'd probably rather ride in the rig than walk. But he seemed to sense another purpose behind Nelson's rather flimsy request.

"Will do," his son agreed. "But don't come crying to me if all those coconut brownies and cinnamon bars left from lunch have disappeared before you show up, Dat."

"If you eat them all, you deserve to be sick!" Nelson shot back. He waved as Michael started off through the woods at the back of the lot.

When he was finally alone, Nelson gazed at the house that hadn't existed when he'd arrived this morning. What a marvel, that because Pete and Glenn had worked ahead, their crew had raised entire walls into place with ropes and pulleys before securing everything together in a single day. The older fellows had installed the windows and doors while the younger ones had worked high off the ground, carefully attaching the heavy plywood roof panels to the trusses on the second-story rafters. It was another sign that the folks in Morning Star wanted the Wengerd family to feel welcome, and to belong in their community before they'd even pulled up stakes in Queen City.

Not wanting to be late for the evening meal—or to raise anyone's suspicions—Nelson took the wrapped bundle from the back of the rig. As he entered the house, he looked for a spot relatively free from the sawdust that had accumulated on the subflooring while the men worked. When he saw how the late-afternoon sun beamed through the window to brighten a corner of the kitchen, he gently placed his gift there.

Somehow—and sometime—before he brought Drusilla here after supper, he would think of the perfect words to express his love for her. As he drove to the Fussner home, Nelson recalled bungling his proposal as a young man head over heels in love with Verna. He hoped that his years as her husband—and the past few years without her—would help him express himself more eloquently this time around.

As he entered Drusilla's kitchen, the tantalizing aromas of chicken, baked onions, and especially celery made his stomach growl. He'd raved so much over her roasted chicken a couple of weeks ago that she'd prepared it again—but how could he do the wonderful meal justice when he was fiddling with phrases to find just the right ones?

Nelson sat down, determined to show his gratitude to Drusilla for her thoughtful efforts. After he'd led their silent grace, the platters and bowls were passed and everyone began to eat. Was it his imagination, or did Nadine and Michael seem intent on dragging out the meal with their talk of planting green beans and other garden crops? As their supper progressed, he felt as squirmy as a little boy who longed to run outside and play—and take Drusilla with him—until she rested her hand on his arm.

"You seem a million miles away," she said softly, beneath Michael's animated chat with Jo and his aunt. "Something on your mind, Nelson? Anything I should know about?"

He blinked. Did she suspect that he was composing the ultimate, foolproof proposal, guaranteed to elicit a *yes*?

"How about if you leave the kitchen cleanup to these other folks and take a walk with me?" he blurted out. "I think you'd enjoy seeing our progress on the house while there's still enough daylight."

Drusilla's smile seemed catlike, as though she suspected what he was up to. "Anything to get out of doing the dishes," she teased, looking across the table at their three companions. "After all, I know who did the cooking."

"You two run along," Nadine said a little too loudly.

"*Jah*, a nice long walk will keep your joints from stiffening up after all that carpentry work you did today," Michael teased.

Nelson refused to rise to his son's insinuation that he was *old*. When he saw that Drusilla's plate was scraped clean—and that, in spite of all his inward focus, his plate was clean, too—he stood up. "Shall we?"

"Let's go."

It was a relief to stroll across the yard and beyond the barn with Drusilla, just the two of them. Nelson suspected that his sister and the kids were already talking about his ulterior motive for this walk—just as Drusilla seemed aware of what he was leading up to. But a man had to jump through all the hoops. When it came to talk of their happily ever after, he knew better than to take any shortcuts.

"It was *gut* to have a sunny day to build the house, after all the rain we've had these past weeks," Nelson said. Then he sighed. Was there nothing more pertinent, more impressive, to talk about than the weather, when he was yearning to express his devotion to Drusilla?

"*Jah*, it was."

He reached for Drusilla's hand, aware that she wasn't going to give him one iota of conversational inspiration. It was a grand feeling when her smaller fingers twined between his as though she felt totally at ease walking with him. Touching him.

As they approached Michael and Jo's future home, Nelson paused to take it in from this angle. "The folks here amaze me," he murmured. "Pete and Glenn had put together entire walls in the Detweilers' barn, to make up for some of the time we'd lost to the weather. And not a one of those fellows left today until the whole house was up and enclosed."

"That's the beauty of longtime friendships and a close-knit community," Drusilla said softly. "These men were generous with their time because at some point, every one of them has received the same sort of help with a new home or some extensive remodeling—or they will in the future."

Nelson nodded. He sensed that his courtship of Drusilla was going more smoothly because *he* had been the one to relocate rather than expecting her to live wherever he did. When she'd been having problems holding her emotions together, she would've refused any sort of romance with him if she'd had to pack up and move out of the home where she'd spent her entire adult life—even though her memories of her first husband weren't all that happy.

As he started walking again, Nelson's heartbeat accelerated. Once they stepped inside the house—once she spotted the large, wrapped package—he'd need to state his case. If he offered Drusilla the quilt before he proposed, she might think he was buying her answer.

Even so, Nelson felt tongue-tied as they approached the back door. His nerves felt as exposed as the home's unpainted boards when he reached for the doorknob.

"Careful of this step up," he cautioned, holding Drusilla's hand more firmly. "They'll attach the stairs tomorrow, I think—"

"I'm not so old that I can't get my foot this high," she informed him playfully. And before he could say another word or give Drusilla a boost, she'd clambered into the house. "Oh! Someone must've left the kids a wedding present."

Nelson let her statement stand, desperately searching for the opening words to tell her how much he loved and admired her—

But the expression on Drusilla's face made him forget all about speaking. Bathed in the light of the setting sun, she looked younger and fresher, with a flawless complexion and expectant, wide eyes as she gazed around the room that would soon be Jo's kitchen. To Nelson's way of thinking, she could easily have been a first-time bride herself—

Make your point, man. Ask her now—strike while the iron's hot—

"What a lovely home this will be," Drusilla whispered. "I'm so glad I let the kids build here. Most young couples have to make do, living with one set of parents for a year or two, but our kids are off to a much better start, don't you think?"

Nelson nodded, sidetracked by her wistful tone and expression. "Would—would you like to update your place, Drusilla?" he asked, earnestly trying to please her. "Pete would do a fabulous job of remodeling. I can ask him to put your name on his job list."

Drusilla clasped her hands before her, calmly gazing into his eyes. "The best thing that could happen to my old house would be *you*, Nelson. Moving into it."

Nelson's mouth dropped open. Just that simply, she'd stolen his thunder. There was no mistaking her meaning, because a faithful Amish widow like Drusilla Fussner wouldn't *dream* of suggesting that he live with her before he'd married her.

"I—I'd be delighted to join you, dear, if—if you'll marry me?" he blurted out.

Even to his own ears he sounded juvenile and inexperienced, hardly worthy of the woman who stood before him . . . a woman who'd miraculously changed her entire world view and mindset, who'd retooled her emotional makeup to welcome him into her life after an unfortunate first marriage had soured her on men.

"I will, Nelson—if you'll wear a bright pink shirt to church tomorrow," she replied with a sparkle in her dark eyes. "It's waiting for you back at the house."

Suddenly he started laughing so loudly that the empty kitchen rang with his mirth—and then with hers, as well. When Nelson reached for Drusilla she stepped into his embrace, not hesitating for even a heartbeat as he silenced their laughter with a long, fervent kiss. He hoped his affection would express his feelings better than his ragtag proposal had.

When he finally eased his lips away from hers, Nelson kept an arm firmly around Drusilla's waist. "So you made the shirt and you expect me to wear it to a Sunday service—knowing that every other man will be wearing the proper white shirt with his black trousers?" he teased. "What ever happened to unconditional love? If I say *no*—"

"If you say *no*, Nelson Wengerd, then you'll be wearing the pink *dress* to church instead," she challenged. "And don't think Nadine and I won't make you!"

Once again he started laughing, amazed at Drusilla's presence of mind—her sense of humor at a moment when most women were nervous and distracted.

"No need for that," he assured her quickly. "But if I'm

to wear the pink shirt, I expect to see *you* in the dress. If we're making a statement, it's going to be so loud and clear that no one can possibly misconstrue its meaning, *jah*?"

Drusilla smiled primly. "Think how astounded everyone will be at our unique and colorful way of announcing our engagement," she said. When she smiled at him again, her face softened until her beautiful soul shimmered in her eyes. "You make me so happy, Nelson. Imagine *me* saying *that*."

"And nobody's happier than I am to hear you say it, Drusilla," he whispered. "I love you more than I've dared to say to this point, but I won't hold back anymore. You make me ecstatically happy, too, sweetheart."

Again he kissed her, overjoyed at the fact that they were finally engaged—and relieved that his less-than-eloquent proposal didn't seem to matter. When they finally drifted apart, Nelson nodded toward the big, wrapped bundle in the corner.

"That's for you, Drusilla. It's your engagement gift."

Her mouth formed an *O*. "At this stage of the game, we hardly need to exchange gifts like a first-time couple—"

"Oh yes, we do. We've been around the block before, but we're taking a whole new walk together, Drusilla," Nelson murmured. "A fresh start deserves to be celebrated—and we'll certainly have our party clothes on tomorrow, ain't so?"

She chuckled as she started for the bundle in the corner. "If you'd rather not wear pink to church, Nelson, I'll allow you to take a rain check—"

"Absolutely not. Truth be told, I want to see the looks on people's faces when they see us."

Drusilla turned to gaze at him. "That's what I love

about you—and your sister, too," she said softly. "You're not afraid to defy convention. After all, it's not as though God's going to deny us our eternal salvation because we've worn clothing some folks will consider inappropriate."

"I agree completely. Want me to pick that up and hold it while you rip off the wrapping?"

"*Jah.* Some things are easier with a team effort," she said, waiting for him to lift her big, bulky package. "And from here on out, we'll *be* a team. No more going it alone."

A few moments later, Nelson knew he would never forget the overjoyed expression on Drusilla's face when she first realized what he'd given her.

"Oh my word, this is—why, I bet the Hartzlers made this quilt!" she cried out as she tore away the paper. "Nobody else would choose such bright, bold colors. Except maybe Nadine."

"She had a hand in it," Nelson admitted. "We agreed that Martha Maude and Anne would make you a quilt, but my sister suggested the colors."

"Well, it's beautiful," Drusilla whispered as he helped her unroll it. They slowly walked away from each other, holding the quilt between them so she could see it better. "Absolutely gorgeous. I—I know you paid too much for it, Nelson, but I'll not fuss at you," she said. "You're a man who knows how to give *gut* and perfect gifts. *Denki* so much."

Nelson wasn't used to being compared to God, Who, according to the Bible, indeed gave good and perfect gifts. But the way Drusilla was gazing at the quilt paid him back for every dollar he'd spent.

"We—we'll put this on our bed to welcome us home from our wedding, all right?" she asked shyly.

His heart turned a flip-flop. For months he'd wondered if sharing a bed with his new bride would be a possibility, and Drusilla had just made one of his most cherished dreams come true.

"More than all right," he murmured. "I—I'm really looking forward to it."

Chapter 35

As she entered Martin and Delores Flaud's home for church on Mother's Day, Jo chuckled at people's reactions when they noticed Mamm's bright pink dress—but Nelson's matching shirt was causing even more of an uproar.

"Well, Wengerd, that's a really, um, *pretty* shirt you've got on!" Deacon Saul called out.

"My stars," Martin teased, squinting and holding his hands in front of his eyes. "I'm going to need my sunglasses to stay in the same room with you, Nelson."

"This is some sort of Mother's Day joke, right?" Preacher Clarence asked stiffly. "Someone surely must be paying you to show up on the Sabbath in a shirt most men wouldn't wear to the county fair."

Bishop Jeremiah, however, spent a moment pondering the pink shirt. When he peered into the kitchen, finding Jo's *mamm* in the crowd of women there, his handsome smile came out to play.

"God be praised," he said gently—and then he turned to Nelson again. "Do you have an announcement you'd like to make before we take our seats, my friend? It might help folks focus their thoughts rather than staring from you to Drusilla all during the service."

Nelson beamed. "I do indeed have an announcement," he replied in a voice that carried above the laughter around him. "As you can see, Drusilla took me up on the dare I made when I brought her this fabric," he continued, happily plucking the sleeve of his shirt. "Isn't she pretty in pink? The most beautiful girl in the world agreed to be my wife last night!"

"Oh, but that's *gut* news!" Martha Maude called out as applause filled the house.

Margaret Shetler made her way through the women around Mamm to grasp her shoulder, smiling brightly. "What a blessing to see you all decked out like a summer flower, Drusilla," she said. "Congratulations on your engagement to a fine man! When's the big day?"

Mamm appeared flustered by all the attention as she stood beside a beaming Nadine, yet Jo sensed she secretly relished it. It was a happy day, indeed, because in all her life Jo couldn't recall her mother wearing pink—much less such a bold, bright shade of pink.

"We haven't set a date," Mamm answered, returning the smiles of everyone around her. "We were talking about so many other things—"

"Why not get married on June the fourth, with Michael and me?" Jo blurted out.

She'd said the words before she'd had time to think about them, yet it seemed like a fine idea. And when she found Michael peering in at the kitchen door and met his gaze, he nodded his agreement.

Her mother turned, wide-eyed. "Oh, but that's *your*

big day, Jo," she protested. "You and Michael have been making your plans, and I wouldn't feel right about—"

"Why not?" Michael interrupted. "You've been inviting folks from all over to come for our wedding, so why wouldn't they want to attend a double wedding? It might save them from having to decide between our celebration and yours if they can't make two trips—"

"And think of the fuss it'll save as far as the food and all the lodging arrangements for the guests," Jo put in. The more she thought about it, the more she liked the idea of the two Fussner-Wengerd ceremonies being held on the same day. "After all, everyone really enjoyed the double ceremony when Molly and Marietta hitched up with Pete and Glenn. And how often do folks get to attend a ceremony for parents *and* their kids?"

Her mother appeared flummoxed yet excited—until another thought occurred to her. "But June the fourth is only three weeks away—"

"About three and a half," Michael corrected gently. He glanced back toward the front room and then gestured for his *dat* to stand beside him, so Nelson could share this conversation with Jo's *mamm.* "If you marry the same day as we do, you won't have a lot of time to stew over the details—or to get cold feet," he teased.

"And Bishop Jeremiah would only have to preach one wedding sermon instead of two!" Glenn piped up from the front room.

As folks chuckled, her mother met Nelson's steady gaze. After a moment she stood taller, as though she'd come to a decision. "I appreciate your idea, kids," Mamm said, "but there's no need to decide right this minute, ain't so? Nelson and I will discuss this and figure it out for ourselves."

"There you have it!" Martha Maude declared. "How about if we get seated for church and get on with our Sunday? This being Mother's Day, I can't wait to sit in the yard after church while the men carry out the common meal for us—and then clean up the kitchen afterward!"

"Amen to that!" Delores chimed in.

Jo had to smile as she slipped her arm around her mother's shoulders. "*Gut* for you, Mamm," she murmured. "You have a right to a special day for your wedding just like I do—"

"But I'm truly touched that you'd offer to share your wedding day with me, dear," Mamm said softly.

As Jo paused to meet her mother's gaze, the crowd around them temporarily disappeared. All she could see was a dear woman who looked as fresh and blooming as a rose on a trellis—and who appeared calmly in control of her thoughts despite the rapid-fire remarks that would've sent her careening into a tailspin not so very long ago.

And this was her own dear mother, the woman who'd lost so many babies and had somehow endured so many years when happiness had seemed like an impossible dream—something that came to other women, but not to her.

"Mamm, I can't think of another soul I'd rather share my wedding day with," Jo whispered quickly. She pulled Mamm close for a hug. "God gave me the best gift of all when He created me to be *your* daughter. *Denki* for all you've done for me, all through my life."

Arm in arm, they entered the Flauds' big front room,

where Mamm took her seat with Nadine and the other older women near the front of the women's side. Jo slid into the row of pew benches with Regina, Lydianne, Molly, and Marietta.

"I'm so happy for your *mamm* and Nelson," the bishop's fiancée murmured.

"*Jah*, me too," Molly chimed in with a grin. "And *gut* for them, defying convention by wearing a bright, happy color to church today! Truth be told, I think they should wear those clothes for their wedding."

Jo smiled to herself. The way things were going between her mother and Nelson, there was no telling what they might do as time went by.

On Tuesday of the following week, as Nelson sat on the front pew bench alongside Jeremiah, Michael, and Pete, he thrummed with joy. Never had he imagined the bishop would invite him to be a side-sitter at his wedding— but hadn't a whole new world of pleasant surprises opened up for him since he'd decided to move to Morning Star?

Although Jeremiah had admitted he'd made his invitation at the last minute, it had been earnest and sincere: he'd previously chosen his nephew, Pete—which meant Molly would serve as one of Lydianne's *newehockers*— and his bride had long ago asked Jo to serve, which meant Michael would, too.

But the bishop had been so delighted to learn that Nelson and Drusilla would soon marry, he'd insisted that they honor him at his very special ceremony. It wasn't every day that a bishop remarried—nor was it a common occurrence to have *two* bishops from other districts conducting the service—but Vernon Gingerich and Tom Hostetler had been Jeremiah's friends for so many years that Jeremiah hadn't wanted to exclude either of them from the festivities on his and Lydianne's special day.

That was one of Jeremiah Shetler's most notable talents: making everyone feel special and indispensable. Nelson felt he'd joined a very select group when the bishop invited him to serve as a side-sitter—

But the biggest thrill had come when Drusilla had also accepted the bishop's invitation. At first she'd balked, saying she didn't have a dress the same color as the other *newehockers'*, and that she was too old to be a side-sitter. But when Nelson had held her gaze, silently assuring her that she could handle such an unexpected honor, Drusilla had agreed. Lydianne had provided the fabric and Jo had made her mother a dress within days, and now here they were with front-row seats . . . gazing at each other as the regular church service ended and the wedding was about to begin.

Both of them had attended countless weddings in their lives, yet as their own ceremony drew closer, Nelson was more aware of the weight of the vows he and Drusilla would exchange—the responsibility that came with them. And now that Drusilla had dealt with her troubled attitude about the past, he was so ready to start a new life with her.

Bishop Vernon Gingerich from Cedar Creek rose from the preacher's bench. His snowy-white hair and beard set off a round face that radiated serenity and goodwill as he gazed over the large crowd gathered in the front room of the Shetlers' remodeled home. When he nodded at them,

Jeremiah and Lydianne rose to stand before him, sharing tight smiles that attested to their jitters. Nelson, Michael, and Pete stood up, too, and positioned themselves to the right of the groom, while Drusilla, Jo, and Molly took their places to Lydianne's left.

Bishop Vernon had the bluest eyes Nelson had ever seen, and they glimmered as he began to speak.

"Friends and neighbors, brothers and sisters in the family of God, we gather today for a much-anticipated celebration," he said in a clear, steady voice. "After the years following his beloved Priscilla's passing, our Jeremiah has found a fitting new mate in Lydianne Christner— and Lydianne has recognized Jeremiah Shetler as the fine, upstanding man the Lord has intended for her to spend her life with, as well.

"Make no mistake!" Bishop Vernon exhorted them. "God in His Heaven *delights* in our happiness and blesses us all with a glimpse of His paradise each time we follow His will for our lives! Therefore," he continued in a rolling, resonant voice, "if anyone present knows of *any* reason why this man and this woman should not be joined in Holy Matrimony, speak now. God's listening."

Nelson stood mesmerized, in awe of the command Gingerich had taken of the crowded room even as he appeared ready to burst forth in song or laughter at the slightest provocation. A wedding ceremony was a solemn occasion, yet Nelson sensed Bishop Vernon was one of the happiest men in the room because his good friend, Jeremiah, had found a new wife.

Same thing applies to us: Jeremiah was sharing his joy for Drusilla and me when he invited us to stand up with him. What wondrous love is this, that fills every moment I spend amongst these people of Morning Star?

When he glanced over at Drusilla, Nelson felt a shimmer of euphoria: She was already looking at him, hoping he would meet her gaze. She blessed him with the most beautiful, beatific smile he'd ever seen—which told him she was every bit as eager as he was to exchange the vows that would join them together. Forever.

Happy as I feel right now, Lord, forever won't be nearly long enough.

Chapter 36

Michael settled back in his lawn chair, immensely satisfied after sharing a potluck meal with the other Marketplace shopkeepers gathered in the yard behind the house he and Jo would soon occupy. On this final Thursday evening of May, the rays of the setting sun dappled the grass, and the maple trees provided welcome shade. So many of the folks who'd gathered for their organizational meeting were already good friends, and Michael anticipated becoming even closer to many of them as time went by.

Gabe Flaud gazed lovingly at his wife, Regina, who glowed as her first pregnancy advanced. Pete and Molly Shetler shared a quiet remark that made them both chuckle, as Riley snoozed in the cool grass under Pete's chair. Glenn and Marietta Detweiler were enjoying a rare evening without the boys, because Reuben had taken Levi and Billy Jay fishing. The Martin Flauds sat near Martha Maude, Anne, and Saul Hartzler, and newlyweds Bishop Jeremiah and Lydianne had joined them, as well.

Michael reached for Jo's hand, observing the way Drusilla—who was taking more of an interest in The

Marketplace lately—beamed as Dat called their business
meeting to order.

"I don't intend to belabor any organizational points or
suggest that we draw up legal papers," his father began
with a smile. "I'm glad you've all come this evening, and
I'm even more grateful to you—and for God's guidance—
as we decide on the guidelines for the wives amongst us
who've been the mainstay of The Marketplace since it
opened a year ago, on the first Saturday in June. I've offered to assume the leadership of the family co-op we
discussed earlier, but how do you envision that role?"

Dat paused. After a few moments when the others
thought about their responses, he continued. "Do you
want me to keep the books? Do you want me to step in
and decide when one of our wives should take her leave—
and then assist with bringing in the help to keep her shop
running?"

Lydianne smiled at her new husband and then spoke
up. "Jeremiah has suggested that Jo keep managing the
weekly records and scheduling the groups that rent our
commons space, while I continue keeping the ledger
updated and paying the bills from home—at least for
the foreseeable future," she added. "Is everyone all right
with that?"

Folks were nodding, because this arrangement had
served them well.

"You sure don't want *me* keeping the books," Pete
joked.

"Amen to that!" Molly put in with a laugh. "And truth
be told, I don't see Pete or Saul or other husbands assuming a role in running The Marketplace except for deciding

their wives should no longer work there—at least until we run into a situation that requires their assistance. Is that how the rest of you understand our new arrangement?"

"*Jah*, because why would we want Saul taking on our quilt shop?" Martha Maude chimed in without missing a beat. "For one thing, he's color-blind—"

"And he'd look pretty awkward sitting with needle and thread at our quilting frame outside the shop, the way we do," Anne remarked with a fond gaze at her husband.

Michael didn't miss Saul's slight frown of irritation as his mother and wife made a point of excluding him from their business—but the deacon held his tongue.

"I'm fine with keeping things the way they are, until one of the ladies needs to leave her shop," Martin said, nodding at the others. "With Nelson officially at the helm, I feel we've got a competent, committed male shopkeeper to make any important decisions that might arise—not that you haven't been a wonderful-*gut* organizer, Jo," he added with a smile.

A round of applause made Jo's cheeks bloom with modest pride—and awoke the golden retriever from his nap.

"I'm happy to let Nelson take the official lead," Jo remarked, squeezing Michael's hand. "And now that he and the rest of the Wengerd family will be settling in as Morning Star's newest residents and business owners, I anticipate a lot of other benefits from their presence, too."

"Hear, hear!" Bishop Jeremiah said. "And I have to congratulate you Wengerds on this fine new home we're sitting behind, as well as on the greenhouses and nursery shop taking shape here, too."

"And we're delighted that Nadine is buying my place," Lydianne put in happily. "Anyone who's interested is invited to our painting party on Monday. If we start around nine, I predict we'll have the interior brightened up for her by late afternoon—especially because a lot of us have warmed up our brushes by painting for Jo and Michael this past week."

"And we thank you for that!" Jo put in happily. "Our new home has gone together so fast—and so beautifully— because you've all been very generous with your help. And Pete, we're especially grateful for the way you did a lot of the work beforehand when the rain set in. Maybe bookkeeping's not your talent, but where would we be without your building and design expertise?"

"*Jah*, I think he's worked on most of our homes these past several months," Bishop Jeremiah said. "And come to find out, he's pretty darn *gut* at it!"

Pete's grin eased into a pensive expression Michael had rarely seen on the blond carpenter's face. "And where would *I* be if you folks hadn't given me a second—and third and fourth—chance to make something of myself?" he asked as he focused on Molly. "Last year at this time I was running the roads in my pickup and running up a tab at the pool hall after work, but you convinced me I was created for better—"

Riley let out an excited yip, making everyone in the yard laugh out loud.

Molly leaned down to stroke the big dog's head. "*Jah*, you miss those running-around days, ain't so?" she teased. "But you've settled into horse-and-buggy life now, and we're a happy family, Riley. It wouldn't be the same without you, boy."

As Riley barked again, adding a wistful yowl at the end of it, Michael realized that Pete's words applied to him, as well. For where would he be if Jo—and her mother—hadn't encouraged him out of his shyness and expected him to extend himself? His life in Queen City working alongside Dat had been comfortable, but if Jo hadn't opened his heart to bigger, better possibilities, he'd probably have become a fusty old bachelor . . . the sort of man mothers warned their sons against becoming because it was a lonely road to follow. And it wasn't the way God recommended living, either.

Soon folks were rising to gather up their picnic baskets, satisfied that The Marketplace was on a sustainable path that supported the basic tenets of the Old Order faith—even if in some Amish communities, their decisions about married women working away from home would be overruled as far too progressive. When the guests had all left in their buggies, waving and calling out their goodbyes as the sun set behind the distant trees, a peacefulness enveloped the yard.

"That went well, I thought," Dat remarked.

"*Jah*, even Saul knew to leave well enough alone," Drusilla said with a nod. "If your management system's not broke, why fix it? Before we head back, I want to look around this new house now that all the ladders and paint cans are cleared away."

"It's a fine home," Michael said as he and Jo followed their parents inside. "And we're grateful that you've let us build it here, Drusilla."

Jo's mother turned in the kitchen to gaze at him. "Let's call it a gift that'll keep on giving," she suggested gently. "A while back I wasn't ready to admit that my life was on a downhill slide, but with you kids and Nelson around, I'm the one who'll receive the biggest gift of all. The gift of *family*."

Michael's heart pounded steadily in his chest. He couldn't have said that better himself—and he could hardly wait until next Thursday, when taking Jo as his bride would change his life in the same wonderful way.

Jo's heart had been fluttering like a butterfly all morning, and she was floating on clouds of joy as the church service ended. She and Michael had decided to hold the wedding ceremony in their new home—because it had a far larger front room than Mamm's house—and then everyone would proceed to the commons area of The Marketplace to enjoy the wedding meal and the afternoon of visiting.

At last the moment had arrived. After Bishop Jeremiah pronounced the benediction, bringing church to a close, he smiled fondly at her and Michael. Jo rose from the front pew to stand where brides and grooms had exchanged their vows for centuries—before God, and before the leader of the earthly church He had chosen for them. They took their places slightly left of the center, because Mamm and Nelson were also rising to be married. It hadn't taken much convincing for them to share Jo and Michael's wedding date—which would make June fourth all the more special for years to come.

"It's my distinct privilege to officiate at yet another double wedding," the handsome bishop began, looking out over the friends and family members who'd come from near and far to attend. "I believe the Lord has blessed our church and the city of Morning Star with a wealth of youthful enthusiasm that will ensure our future—and with the steadfast wisdom only folks who've lost and learned to love again can share with us."

Bishop Jeremiah smiled at Jo, as though he could tell she might pass out from overexcitement. "I would urge all of us to take a *deep breath* and pause to savor this moment, for the vows we exchange at our weddings are second in holiness only to the promises we make when we join the Amish church."

The bishop gazed out over the crowd. "Those of you looking on, please recall when *you* were standing before the bishop with your beloved, for chances are *gut* you were too nervous to fully appreciate what was going on at that moment years ago."

The guests' gentle laughter eased Jo's tight stomach. As she gazed at Michael, she felt absolutely *right*, and she knew she'd found her true place in this life—at his side.

"As we follow along with the vows that haven't changed in centuries, may we also ponder the fact that God's love for us hasn't changed, either—and it never will."

Bishop Jeremiah stood taller, holding the gaze of several guests in the crowd. "We've come here to witness to the sanctity of marriage with Jo Fussner and Michael Wengerd, and with their parents, Drusilla Fussner and

Nelson Wengerd. If you know of a reason either couple shouldn't be married here today, say so now."

In the brief silence that rang in the large room, Jo heard her pulse pounding more loudly. She'd heard of rare occasions when someone in the crowd *had* objected, and thanked God that no one was going to disrupt their day— their lives—with a negative word.

"Very well, then. We gather here in the presence of God our Father to witness to the joining of the hearts and lives of Drusilla and Nelson first, and then Jo and Michael . . ."

From there, Jo clutched Michael's elbow for dear life, praying she wouldn't fall over while Bishop Jeremiah led Mamm and Nelson in their vows. She felt giddy and light-headed. She suddenly wished she'd had the sense to eat more than a piece of toast hours ago, as Mamm had encouraged her to do.

But the bedrock certainty of her mother's voice pulled Jo back to firmer emotional ground.

"I, Drusilla, take thee, Nelson . . ."

Who could've believed the day would come when Mamm was marrying again, and with such poise and confidence? Jo silently rejoiced that her mother had let go of the negative emotions that had held her captive during her marriage to Dat, freeing her to love Nelson with all the enthusiasm he deserved.

"I, Nelson, take thee, Drusilla . . ."

Jo inhaled deeply, calmed by the utter certainty in Nelson's sonorous voice. The light in his eyes as he gazed at Mamm took Jo's breath away. Would Michael look at her and speak to her with that same steadfast assurance when they were their parents' age?

She didn't have time to worry about it. Suddenly she and Michael were the center of the bishop's attention, and Jo focused on repeating the age-old words exactly as she heard them. "I, Josephine, take you, Michael, to be my lawfully wedded husband . . ."

And before she knew it, they'd made it to the end!

"I now pronounce you Mr. and Mrs. Michael Wengerd," Bishop Jeremiah proclaimed. "Michael, you'd better kiss your bride as though your life depends upon it—because it does!"

Laughter and applause erupted around them, filling the big room as Michael pulled her close for a kiss that stopped time and made their guests disappear—at least for a few sparkling moments.

"We did it!" Michael whispered.

"We did."

Jo gazed into his beautiful gray-blue eyes to center herself. At last, she could take a deep breath and relax, secure in the knowledge that she wouldn't bungle their vows in front of God and everyone they knew. "What a year it's been," she whispered. "I love you so much, Michael."

"And what a lifetime we have before us," he murmured, holding her hands in his. "It's all because I love *you*, Josie-girl, and—"

"Look at these beautiful, happy people!" Nadine crowed as she threw her arms around Jo and Michael and their parents to pull them into a group hug. "I can recall a time when this wedding was the furthest thing from any of your minds. But with God, all things are possible."

"With God and *Nadine* all things are possible," Mamm immediately shot back.

For the first time all day, Jo laughed out loud. As she took in the smiling faces around her, she knew that love and laughter would now be hers forever because these people believed in her—and they'd given her the grace to believe in herself, as well.

And for that, Jo knew she'd be eternally grateful.

Please read on for an excerpt
from Charlotte Hubbard's newest novel,
Family Gatherings at Promise Lodge.

**With two spring weddings to celebrate,
friends and family are reunited at the Amish
community of Promise Lodge, where nothing—
and no one—can derail an unexpected new love
when it's part of a glorious plan . . .**

In the year since he lost his wife in a tragic
accident, Lester Lehman has found healing
and purpose—helping construct Dale Kraybill's
new bulk store, enjoying the Kuhn sisters' hearty
meals, and settling into a tiny, built-for-one
lakeside house. Falling in love again is surely
not on Lester's mind. Yet despite his firm "no,"
two available ladies have set their *kapps*
on the handsome widower—in a boisterous rivalry that
weaves mayhem among the wedding festivities . . .

A welcome escape comes from a fresh-faced
newcomer. Marlene Fisher disarms Lester with her
witty quips on his romantic predicament,
while her sparkling eyes inspire surprising thoughts of
a shared future. But the heartbreak that brought
Marlene to Promise Lodge runs deep, and the pretty
maidel believes she's not meant to marry.
In a season of vows to love and honor, scripture holds
the key to building their happiness together:
love is kind, and above all . . . *patient.*

Family Gatherings
AT
Promise Lodge

Chapter 1

As he tilted his chaise lounge back to stretch out in the afternoon sunshine, Lester Lehman felt like a new man. It was unusually warm for a March day in Missouri, and after spending the winter in his tiny home on the shore of Rainbow Lake, he reveled in the chance to soak up some rays out on his dock. He'd worked hard all morning installing the aluminum siding on the new Dutch bulk store—a wonderful addition to the other businesses of Promise Lodge—and he'd enjoyed a nice lunch in the lodge's dining room with his friends. And now, nothing was going to stop him from doing absolutely *nothing*. It felt downright sinful, being this lazy on a Monday afternoon. The gentle lapping of the lake lulled Lester as he reclined full-length on the mesh chaise. He folded his arms beneath his head and let his mind go blissfully blank.

Out-of-town families would start arriving today to attend his niece Gloria's wedding on Wednesday as well as Laura Hershberger's wedding on Thursday, when they married the Helmuth brothers, Cyrus and Jonathan—but for now, Lester could revel in the hush of a solitary sunny afternoon. Living alone in his tidy house all winter had taught him a sense of self-reliance that had cleared his soul—had given him an unencumbered sense of freedom he'd never expected. His bobbing dock rocked him like a cradle. He felt far, far removed from the grief and despair that had followed the loss of his wife, his son, and his brother last spring, and as Lester eased into a state of semi-sleep, he knew the true meaning of inner peace.

At long last, all was well with his life. With the help of his family and friends here at Promise Lodge, he was moving forward . . . floating on the fluffy clouds of a nap . . .

"Yoo-hoo! Lester, honey! Thanks to Delores, I've found you!"

Lester jerked awake. Whose voice was that? And why had she implied that his dear, deceased wife had led her here?

When he opened one eye, he saw a pudgy little woman starting across the expanse of grass that surrounded Rainbow Lake. Her brown cape dress fluttered around her thick legs as she hurried toward him. Clutching her *kapp* with one hand to keep it from flying off her head, Lester's uninvited guest appeared so excited—and in such a state of overexertion—that he feared she might be bringing on a heart attack. He remained absolutely still, hoping she'd believe he was asleep.

"My stars, here you are at long last!" she blurted out, huffing between phrases. "I've ridden all the way from Sugarcreek—for Gloria's wedding—because with my Harvey gone—Delores has been telling me—for quite some time now—that she wants me to take care of you, Lester! So here I am! Because I know better than to—to ignore heavenly guidance."

Lester sighed. Agnes Plank, his wife's best friend, had never known the meaning of *silence*. She barely drew a breath at the end of one sentence before she shot headlong into her next burst of words. There would be no ignoring her now that she'd almost reached his dock, so Lester reluctantly raised the back of his chaise. All hope for a nap was gone. He felt a headache prickling around his temples.

"I've been *so* excited since our bus arrived about half an hour ago! I looked around, but I didn't see you anywhere," Agnes continued as she struggled to catch her breath. "It was such an adventure to come all the way from Ohio—I've never been to Missouri before—and our friends are so pleased that Gloria's found herself a young man to settle down with—and it's such a joy to attend not one but *two* weddings while I'm here. All that food and visiting time and—and doesn't the sense of springtime *romance* in the air make you feel like you could start all over again, Lester? Don't you just *love* weddings?"

I was indeed looking forward to these weddings—until a few moments ago.

"Of course, ever since you Lehmans moved here, I've been following Promise Lodge's weekly reports in the *Budget*," Agnes went on as she peered at the land and buildings around them. "I was so tickled when Gloria took over as your district's scribe and—well, she's so descriptive, but I had no idea what a *lovely* settlement you'd come to. And of course, you and your brother, Floyd—God rest his soul—installed the windows and siding on these new homes, and with everything except the lodge building being only a couple years old, it seems like the perfect place to start fresh!

"Before that terrible traffic accident took Delores away from us," Agnes continued with a brief frown, "all she talked about was coming here to live in the fine new home you'd built for her. Lately she's been telling me how lonely you've been, Lester, and—well, you know me, I just have to *help* people. The way I see it, Gloria's wedding is a heaven-sent opportunity."

Fully awake now, Lester swung his feet to the dock. When he could get a word in edgewise, he needed to deflate Agnes's high-flying hopes in a hurry, because in her vivid imagination, she was already standing before the bishop with him, repeating her wedding vows. As he opened his mouth to speak, however, another urgent female voice hailed him.

"Lester! Lester Lehman, it's me—your Elverta! I read about Gloria's wedding in the paper, so it seemed like the perfect reason to come and see *you!*"

Lester moaned. His sense of freedom, peace, and unencumbered living had just hit another serious snag.

As the national newspaper for Plain communities, the *Budget* was a wonderful way to keep track of far-flung friends and kin, but he suddenly wished that Gloria—and Rosetta Wickey, their community's original scribe—hadn't been quite so descriptive in detailing the Lehman family's relocation. The tiny town of Promise, Missouri was out in the middle of nowhere, yet Agnes and Elverta had apparently followed every line of the newspaper's weekly reports right to his doorstep.

As Elverta Horst, dressed in deep green, strode toward his dock, her tall, skinny, ramrod-straight body reminded Lester of a string bean. He knew better than to express that opinion, of course, because the woman he'd broken up with to begin courting his Delores had never been known for her sense of humor.

"Wh-who's this?" Agnes asked him under her breath.

Never one to beat around the bush, Elverta stopped a few yards from the dock. She glanced at Lester before focusing on the flustered woman beside him. "And who might *you* be?" she demanded with a raised eyebrow.

Lester answered as indirectly as possible, because he knew these women would soon find out every little thing about one another. "Elverta, this is Delores's best friend, Agnes Plank. She lives down the road from our former home in Sugarcreek," he explained hastily. "And Agnes, this is Elverta Horst—"

"And I was engaged to Lester before he took up with Delores," Elverta put in purposefully. "First loves are often the strongest, ain't so? The flame may flicker through the years, but it never really goes out."

Immediately Elverta turned to take in the house, pointing her finger. "And what's this? A storage shed for equipment you folks use on the lake?"

"It's a tiny house," Lester informed her. He was accustomed to folks joking about the size of his place, but he suddenly wished he could lock himself inside it until these women went away. "I live here. And I happen to like it just fine."

"My word, Lester, you might as well live in a blue boxcar," Elverta shot back.

"But what about the house you built for Delores?" Agnes asked with a puzzled frown. "She described it as having two stories—like a normal place—and said you and Floyd had installed the windows and siding—"

"You're being funny, right?" Elverta demanded. "Teasing

us while you figure out how to send Agnes away so you and I can take up where we left off."

Lester's headache was throbbing full throttle now. "*Jah*, I built a house just up the hill from here," he explained with a sigh, "and in November I sold it to a couple who needed a place before cold weather set in. The young man who lives just up the hill behind us earns his living building these tiny homes, so he's letting me stay in this one—"

"I'll be staying in the lodge," Agnes put in with an eager smile. "My rent's paid up for long enough that you could build us another home—"

"I've got an apartment, too," Elverta interrupted triumphantly. "But the lodge is just for unattached women, so I won't be living there very long. Lester and I go way back, Agnes. You might as well—"

"Puh!" Agnes spat. "I'll have you know that Delores has been guiding me here for quite some time now, assuring me that I'm destined to take her place. Why do I suspect you're a *maidel*, Elverta, without any experience at being a wife and—and a lover?"

Lester nearly choked as his cheeks went hot, but Elverta wasn't deterred for a second.

"Why would Lester want another man's leavings? Let alone a confused, befuddled woman who claims she's getting advice from his deceased wife?" she asked with a scowl. "If folks get wind that you're hearing voices from beyond the grave, they'll likely have you committed to the loony bin."

Agatha sucked in her breath, which puffed her up like a toad. "You have no right to say that about Delores—my very best friend! I bet she'll find ways to stall you and block your intentions—"

"Oh, if anybody's blocking me it'll be *you*," Elverta spouted. "But not for long!"

As they moved toward each other, Lester stepped between them with his arms extended. "Whoa! Hold it right there," he said, looking from one woman to the other. "I'm telling you both right now that I'm not hitching up with either one of you! So instead of having a cat fight you can just head on back to the lodge—and after the weddings, you might as well get back on your buses to Ohio. Save us all a lot of embarrassment and bad feelings, will you?"

"*I* have nothing to be embarrassed about!" Elverta declared. "And I'm not leaving until *she* does!"

"Well, *I'm* not going anywhere until Lester makes his choice, right here and now!" Agnes blurted out as she stomped her foot. "I was here first, after all."

"But *I've* known Lester since we were scholars back in the early grades of—"

"Start walking," Lester said, pointing toward the lodge. "And don't think you're going to pester me about this tomorrow, because I'll be at my job site working. Let's go."

As he strode toward the timbered structure across the road, Lester couldn't recall when he'd ever felt so flustered. Not five minutes after these two women had arrived, they'd gone for each other's throats—over *him*. All he wanted was to get Agnes and Elverta out of his sight so he could enlist help from his friends and send the two women packing as fast as possible.

Approaching the lodge's steps, Lester saw that a couple of big buses were parked over in the Helmuth Nursery's lot—and folks were still getting out of them, claiming their suitcases. Agnes and Elverta must've been in such a toot that they'd each rushed to the lodge and inquired about where he lived, and then hurried over before they'd even unpacked. When he glanced back at them, the rivals were a distance behind him, focused on him rather than looking at each other. Even so, they appeared ready to spit nails.

Lester entered the lodge and headed straight for the kitchen, hoping to explain his situation before Agnes or Elverta got the facts twisted. Aromas of sugar, cinnamon, and roasting chickens filled the air, and as he passed through the large dining room he saw that the tables were set to serve dinner to several wedding guests who'd be staying in the extra rooms upstairs as well as in the cabins behind the lodge. He was relieved to see Ruby and Beulah Kuhn, *maidel* sisters who lived at the lodge, as well as Rosetta Wickey, who owned the building.

"Ladies, I've got a real problem," Lester blurted when they looked up from the pies they were putting together. "The two gals who're following me have both come to Promise Lodge thinking I'm going to marry them—"

"At the same time?" Beulah teased. "Ooh, la la!"

"Why, Lester, you amaze me," Ruby put in with a catlike smile. "Maybe *I* should put my hat in the ring."

He shook his head. These good-natured Mennonite ladies had become his close friends over the past year— and his situation *did* sound too funny to be true. Almost.

"No matter what they tell you—or what information they try to pry out of you to gain the upper hand—I *do not* want to hitch up with either one of them."